War of Succession

A Novel of the Road of Legends

Robert B. Marks

Published by Legacy Books Press
RPO Princess, Box 21031
445 Princess Street
Kingston, Ontario, K7L 5P5
Canada

www.legacybookspress.com

This edition first published in 2023 by Legacy Books Press in association with Nuada Press.
1

Printed and bound in Canada, the United States of America and Great Britain.

This book is typeset in a Times New Roman 11-point font.

Print ISBN: 978-1-927537-45-9

E-book ISBN: 978-1-927537-46-6

Cover art: *The Spirit of War*, by Jasper Francis Cropsey.(1823-1900)

Library and Archives Canada Cataloguing in Publication

Title: War of succession / Robert B. Marks.
Names: Marks, Robert B., 1976- author.
Description: "A novel of the Road of Legends".
Identifiers: Canadiana (print) 20220492999 | Canadiana (ebook) 20220493014 | ISBN 9781927537459
  (softcover) | ISBN 9781927537466 (EPUB)
Classification: LCC PS8626.A75417 W37 2023 | DDC C813/.6—dc23

This book is printed on aged and responsibly sourced parchment. This parchment is provided in the form of paper.

To my daughter, Isabel Rose,
and my son, Isaac Albert Malcolm.
Once upon a time, Daddy wrote this.

Introduction

This book is the hill on which my fiction career died twenty years ago.

To explain: Once upon a time there was a trilogy of movies titled *The Lord of the Rings*. This was a massively successful series, and the traditional fantasy publishers took note. By the time the third movie was released, they had glutted themselves buying up manuscripts. If you were lucky enough to get in at the start of the glut, it became very easy to sell a fantasy novel. If you weren't, the response times for even agented submissions went from months to years.

I was not one of the lucky ones.

It wasn't that I was lacking a manuscript to sell. In fact, in the wake of my first (and for a very long time, only) published fantasy e-book, *Diablo: Demonsbane*, I had a novel finished and ready to go – it was titled *Magus Draconum*, and it was a biographical apocalyptic mythical fantasy. I had also started work on a second book in the same *Road of Legends* universe, the one you are holding right now. My plan was to use *Demonsbane* to get a contract for *Magus Draconum*, and then the next book published after that would be *War of Succession*.

That was the plan, anyway. But, I ran into agent problems, the first of which was that my agent at the time (who will go nameless) thought that *Magus Draconum* was too hard to pigeonhole to sell as a first full-length novel. *War of Succession* would be far more conventional, and theoretically easier to sell. So, I was instructed to finish *War of Succession* first. The draft was finished in early to mid-2001, just in time for my agent to tell me that I had problems with my writing style and drop me as a client.

In fairness, the current draft of the book did have problems, one of which was that it needed a restructuring into its current form to focus the narrative. Unfortunately, the feedback she had given me was vague enough that it caused a massive over-correction of my writing style into purple prose. It was only thanks to Ed Greenwood, who I had met at a convention and become friends with, that the book was salvaged – he gave me the mentoring I needed to fix my style and consulted with me on the restructuring of the narrative. By the end of the year, I had found a new agent – George Scithers of the Owlswick Literary Agency (God rest his soul), who stuck with me until the day he retired. He and his partner, Darrell Schweitzer, advised me that selling the book would be an uphill struggle – while it was far closer to the "Big Commercial Fantasy" that characterized the market, it also included enough well-used tropes to make it a harder sell. That said, they tried their best for years, and so did the agent they passed me off to when they retired.

(In retrospect, we should have pivoted back to *Magus Draconum*, which would have benefitted from being more unconventional, not that it likely would have mattered after the glut.)

By then, however, it was 2002 and it was too late – the window for selling fantasy novels in the *Lord of the Rings* glut had passed. I can count on one hand the number of rejections the book received in fifteen years. I finally lost any faith in the traditional fantasy publishers when I found myself asking my agent how many decades I should be expected to wait for a reply. As far as I know, a copy of the manuscript is still in the last publisher's pile of agented submissions, waiting to be looked at.

So, why not just self-publish years ago? While it's easy for an author to self-publish today and get their work out, the same could not be said back in the early 2000s. Self-publishing back then was characterized by shady and predatory print-on-demand publishers who made their money through charging the authors exorbitant fees for their services, and then left everything from marketing to distribution to the author. There was also a heavy stigma attached to self-publication (this still exists in some circles, but twenty years ago it was almost universal).

Either way, with *War of Succession* getting lost in black hole after black hole, and *Magus Draconum* waiting in the wings for a book sale that looked more and more like it would never happen, I stopped writing novels. There just didn't seem to be any point when nobody but me would ever get to read them. It would be twenty years before I finished writing another novel, and that was *Re:Apotheosis*.

So, where did the idea for this book come from? My recollection is that there were two concurrent ideas that popped into my head. The first was a "what if?": What if you had a *Highlander*-style battle royale between wizards, but the people involved went off-script and co-opted entire countries to do the fighting for them? The second was a battle scene with two lines of dialogue: "Who do you think you are, Garwulf the Slayer?" followed by, "Yes." From these two ideas, the story flowed.

I guess the next question would be: Will there be any more *Road of Legends* books? And, to be honest, I just don't know. When I stopped writing back in the mid-aughts there was at least one more novel outlined and in progress. However, these books were written over two decades ago when I was in my early to mid-twenties. I'm in my mid-forties now, and my sensibilities are very different today. I suppose if *Magus Draconum* and *War of Succession* sell lots of copies and people start asking me for more, it can't hurt to dust off my notes and manuscripts and see if I've still got these stories in me and waiting to be told. But, no promises.

In the end, I'm just happy that after over twenty years, people will finally get to read and enjoy this. So, thank you for picking up and reading my book!

Robert B. Marks
September 28, 2022

Prologue

As Darbon bore the oak staff into the circle, he knew six people would die. He had watched the Order of Archmagi for his entire career, carefully avoiding the politics of the Order while he pursued his arcane knowledge. But he knew from the beginning that this generation of Archmagi was an ambitious one. There would be all seven candidates for succession.

He looked up at the funeral pyre for a moment, watching the Grand Magus' body burn, the smoke rising high into the sky. Some folklore said it was a good sign, that the higher the pillar of smoke, the quicker the soul would reach the Eternal One. Those who believed such things were generally dismissed as superstitious; most Archmagi claimed to know the true sources of power, but Darbon was never too sure about that. To him it always seemed more like arrogance than wisdom. He wiped away a tear as he remembered his friend, who had asked him to take up the staff of the Arbiter in his last moments.

He stopped for a moment to look at the circle. The courtyard was filled with Archmagi, all waiting for his arrival. For a moment Darbon grimaced, wishing he could retreat back into the great tower, hiding behind the stone walls until all the nonsense about succession was finished with. The sickeningly sweet smell of burning flesh from the pyre in the courtyard of the Grand Magus made the butterflies in his stomach flutter faster. If only the Grand Magus hadn't selected him, he would be able to spend this time with his wife. She was expecting their first child, and he wanted to be there. He swallowed, remembering his cottage, Kara's mousy brown hair rustling in the breeze as she tended to the garden, a quick smile ready for her husband no matter what. Shaking his head, he brought himself back to the present; some duties were more important than family.

He scratched his greying beard and looked at the staff. The wood pulsed with power, magic greater than any Archmagus could imagine. The length was carved with runes of protection and binding, holding magic to it that could not be bound otherwise. The power had come once the Grand Magus had died, retreating to its home in the ancient wood. Nobody was quite sure how old it was; it had been in the order since the dawn of time, some legends said. None questioned those stories, at least to Darbon's knowledge.

Taking a deep breath, he stepped into the circle. The Archmagi gazed at him, waiting for the rites all of them knew but none had witnessed. He silently rehearsed what he was supposed to say, hoping that if he got a couple of words wrong, it wouldn't matter.

Clearing his throat, he began to speak, voice rasping. "The Grand Magus, the great spell-weaver, has gone to the next world. He sleeps with the Eternal One, waiting for the rebirth of the world when this cycle ends. He watches the

Great Road, seeing those beyond us."

Darbon swallowed and took a breath. Would he ever understand half of what he'd just said? Probably not – even the Grand Magus was said to know only after he crossed from life.

"As per the old ways, handed to us by the First One, we begin the rites of succession," he declared, holding the staff out. The runes began to glow, and the relic itself began to shake. "We begin the first rite: we select the chosen ones. Who here claims right of Succession?"

Ten Archmagi stepped forward, their robes flapping in the autumn breeze. For a moment Darbon lost his train of thought, the coming winter and the supplies Kara would have to purchase flooding his mind. Then he returned to the moment, and frowned. Six people would die by the end of the year.

He held out the relic. He knew all the Archmagi; most were decent people who tended to keep to themselves, others were ambitious, some positively fearsome. Most of the ten who stood forward were middle-aged, and while he feared none of them, there were one or two he wished the staff would not pick. But the choice was out of his hands now. He already felt the magic taking control.

There was a sudden flash, and one of the Archmagi reeled back, a charred smell in the air, as though lightning had struck. Darbon cursed inwardly: he didn't terribly like Gesanus.

"Gesanus, you are granted a power of succession," Darbon declared, holding the carved oak out towards the Archmagi again. There was an explosion of light, and another wizard staggered backwards, a burnt mark on his robes.

"Feladon, you are granted a power of succession," Darbon intoned, pivoting with the relic held before him. The bolt of energy leapt forth, leaving a smouldering smell, and a candidate fell to the ground, blinking smoke out of his eyes.

"Conadar, you are granted a power of succession."

The staff flashed again. Darbon breathed a sigh of relief, feeling the power flow from the wood. Finally, once seven Archmagi in total were granted a power from the relic, the magic was gone. Once again, for a hundred years, the staff was just a carved piece of oak. Despite the chill growing in the air, Darbon wiped some sweat from his forehead. There was only one last thing for him to do for now.

Darbon saw the three remaining Archmagi step back into the greater circle, discontent in their eyes. Darbon shook his head; if only they knew how lucky they were the relic had not selected them. He cleared his throat to speak. "Gesanus, Feladon, Conadar, Bervus, Malichus, Tergibar and Hargan, you have all been granted Power of Succession. He who unites the seven powers, he shall be the Grand Magus. You must be careful, for no innocents must be harmed in the second rite. Thus it has always been. Thus it shall always be. The second rite, the contest for succession, shall begin in two weeks. Let he who survives, who bears the power of the Grand Magus, rule with wisdom. Let the six who fall be remembered with grace. The first rite is concluded."

Darbon strode from the circle, winding his way back to his room in the tower. He stared for a moment at the stark stone wall, the simple bed and desk, his eyes filled with longing for the rolling fields of home. He took out a pen and parchment and began to write, explaining to Kara why he wouldn't be coming home this winter even as he cursed the fate that kept him from his beloved, preventing him from witnessing the birth of his own child. A tear rolled down his cheek, but this time he made no move to stop it.

He was in mid-paragraph when the knock sounded at his door. He stood up, blinking as he noticed for the first time how low the sun lay in the sky. "I'll be just a moment," he called, using a tinderbox to light the candle on his desk. Once the candle burned brightly, he opened the door.

Hargan stood before him, rubbing his tanned hands to keep warm in the drafty hallway. "I'm sorry to have kept you waiting," Darbon said. "I got caught up in my letter. Please come in."

Hargan stepped in and sat on the bed, his brown eyes glancing around the room. "So you will live here until the rites are over?" he asked.

Darbon nodded. "It is my duty to ensure that the rules of Succession are upheld. If an Archmagus should break the rules by enlisting help, or something similar, I must use the staff to regain the Power of Succession."

"And it must all be single contests?" Hargan said, plucking absently at his crimson Archmagus robe.

Darbon nodded, puzzled at the question. "Of course. Surely your master taught you this when you were an apprentice Magus?"

Hargan smiled kindly. "I fear that he was a bit unclear about one or two things."

Darbon sat down beside the young Archmagus. Hargan was so young, he reflected. There was not even a wisp of grey in his beard. He wouldn't stand a chance against one of the more experienced successors.

"Why don't you ask me about anything you're unclear on," Darbon suggested, giving Hargan a fatherly pat on the back.

"Is it true there can only be one Arbiter?"

Darbon nodded. "Just as there is only one staff, there is one Arbiter. It is a great challenge, and I hope I am worthy of it."

Hargan smiled. "I'm sure you will be." Then he reached into his robe.

By the time Darbon realized what was happening, it was too late. Hargan's dagger slid between his ribs. Darbon's chest felt as though it was on fire, every breath burning.

Hargan twisted the knife, and the pain exploded. Darbon screamed, but Hargan only smiled at him. "I cast an enchantment before I came here," he explained. "I didn't want us to be disturbed." Darbon fell to the ground, turning his head to watch the Archmagus standing over him, a bloody dagger in his hands.

Darbon felt the shadows reach out towards him, dulling his pain. "Why?" he rasped, struggling to stay alive, desperate to see his wife one last time.

"The rules of succession are changing," Hargan replied. "Unfortunately, you're in the way."

Darbon tried to reach out, to tell Hargan that what he was doing was wrong, but the darkness took him first.

Watching the water drip into the puddle, he listened as it echoed in the cave. The light from his staff left a green glow on the moss beside him. He turned and gazed at the creature of power before him.

The Dragon's coils wrapped around the cave walls, the black scales reflecting the light from his staff. The great wyrm's head rose above him, gazing into his eyes with immortal indifference.

"I have waited a long time," he said. "I have traveled the Road, returning every century to see if the time has come. I bid you to answer, by what we once shared. Has my time come?"

The great head retracted into the coils, and for a moment there was silence. Then the Dragon's answer echoed throughout the cavern, a great, thunderous voice that shook the very ground.

"Yes."

Part I:
The Fugitive and the Monk

Chapter I — Murder

The moment Haldur burst through the door, muttering curses against some strange Archmagus, Tamlin knew that there would be trouble. His mentor had always been a calm, collected man, but his return from the capital seemed to have flustered him to no end.

Haldur was a rotund man, with keen, piercing blue eyes. His long red robes swirled around him as he paced about the sitting room of his cabin, running his fingers along the oaken table and bookcase resting against the wall.

"Have you finished reading those spells I showed you?" Haldur snapped, scratching his bushy white beard. Tamlin swallowed; Haldur's whiskers never itched unless he was *very* upset.

"Yes sir," Tamlin said as submissively as possible. "I memorized the fetching spell, and I've practiced it a bit, but I still don't really have the control to get large objects yet."

Tamlin shifted nervously. Unlike his mentor, he was tall and gaunt, dressed in the grey robes of a wizard's apprentice. He brushed some of his long, brown hair out of his eyes and waited for what was coming next, hoping that it wasn't a week's worth of chores.

Haldur sat down in a leather-backed chair. "I'm sorry, boy. I don't mean to be so rough on you. I'm just expecting difficulties ahead."

"Is there anything I can do?" Tamlin offered.

Haldur shook his head, pointing his finger at a nearby candle. The wick exploded into flame, the scent of incense rising into the air. "This is a matter for the council of Archmagi, not for a simple apprentice."

Tamlin bristled. He'd been learning from Haldur for almost six years, ever since he was a child of twelve winters rescued from the streets of Laketown, the capital of Fenegar. While Haldur had been almost impossible to get extra information from, he had been an effective teacher, and Tamlin was able to weave several spells.

"Show me your fetching spell," Haldur ordered. "Fetch me that book from the shelf there, the one marked with 'Laws of Succession' on the spine."

"Yes sir," Tamlin said, scanning the shelves for the volume. Finally he found it, close to the top, the red-tinted spine topped with a thin layer of dust.

"I'm watching you, so don't try to get away without casting," Haldur cut in.

Tamlin stepped back and raised his arms. He wove a pattern in the air, using the motions to focus his energy. With great care, he wrapped the magic around the tome, and gently pulled it toward him. The large codex floated into his hands.

He turned to find Haldur clapping quietly. "Not bad. Your motions were too large, though, so you probably wasted some energy, but not bad at all."

"Thank you sir," Tamlin said, passing the book to Haldur.

Haldur opened the volume to a middle page and began to read. Suddenly, he looked up and pierced Tamlin with his eyes. "I want you to read Galen's dissertation on the body's magical energies today. You should find it on the fourth shelf to the right. A thin book, with a blue binding. Remember to use your spell to fetch it."

With smaller motions, Tamlin summoned the codex to him. For a moment, the volume shook in mid-air, but with an abrupt pull he brought it to him, the leather cover smacking into his hands.

He turned to see if Haldur had noticed the brief mistake, but the wizard was deep in his book, his mouth moving as he read. With a sigh of relief, Tamlin sat down at the table and began to pour over the text.

Tamlin blinked as a shadow passed over the page he was reading. He glanced up to find the sun dropping below the horizon. Taking out a tinderbox, he lit a couple of candles, and then glanced at Haldur. When the wizard remained buried in his tome, apparently unaware of the indiscretion of not using magic for such a simple task, Tamlin grinned in relief and returned to his studies. Although he hated to admit it, he found that after a few spells he had difficulty studying.

His stomach growled, but he kept reading, resisting the temptation to ask for food. Haldur was in a strange mood, and he didn't want to intrude on the Archmagus unless absolutely necessary.

He had just managed to pull his mind back to Galen's dissertation when Haldur slammed his large tome shut, causing Tamlin to jump in shock. "Damnation," the wizard cursed. "There's absolutely nothing helpful here."

Haldur stood and stepped over to Tamlin, placing a light hand on the apprentice's shoulder. "You keep reading, and I will get you some food. I could hear your stomach rumbling even from where I sat."

Tamlin shivered as Haldur strode from the room. When the Archmagus had spoken to him, he had heard something in the voice that filled him with terror.

Fear.

He glanced at the red volume lying on the floor beside Haldur's sitting chair, wondering what could possibly be so terrible that it would make one of the most powerful wizards in Fenegar afraid.

That night, Tamlin dreamed of war and death. He saw himself, standing tall in the crimson robes of an Archmagus, fighting against several other wizards. As he killed one, another would step forward, and there was no end to the slaughter. He tried to scream, to some how make it stop, but the line of Archmagi only became longer and longer, the wizards laughing at him as they rose to attack.

He startled awake, his nightshirt and sheets soaked in sweat. Haldur's baritone resounded through the cabin, muffled only slightly by Tamlin's closed door.

"I told you master back in the capital that I will have no part in it. Go away and trouble me no more!"

"You would deny your service to the glory of Fenegar?" a strange voice said, rough and threatening.

"If your master actually served Fenegar, you would get a different answer," Haldur's voice growled. "But if he wishes to continue this monstrosity, he will have to do it without me!"

"There will be consequences, old man," the stranger warned.

"I have survived far worse than you in my lifetime," he heard Haldur say, becoming quiet. "Now go, before you discover what happens when an Archmagus is enraged."

"My master will see to you personally. I look forward to it."

Swallowing, Tamlin pulled on his gray robes and burst from his room, only to see Haldur closing the door softly. The wizard spun to look at Tamlin, the apprentice staggering to a halt.

"I had hoped that the confrontation would not disturb you," Haldur said sadly. "I apologize for disrupting your sleep."

"Who was that?" Tamlin asked. "Why was he threatening you?"

"It is something that you need not concern yourself with," Haldur stated. "Your studies are far more pressing right now."

Tamlin blinked. "But he said that there would be consequences."

"That self-important messenger has little knowledge of what a true Archmagus is capable of," Haldur declared. "And, in another ten years, if you leave these petty concerns alone and actually concentrate on your schooling, you may find out yourself. Now, did you read Galen's dissertation?"

Tamlin nodded.

"Fine," the wizard said. "Galen also wrote a treatise on nature magic. It was right beside the dissertation on my shelf. Find it, read it, and understand it. That is your assignment for today."

"Will you need anything else of me?" Tamlin inquired.

Haldur shook his head. "I have to go into town today to buy some supplies. You will have to see to your own food, as I expect to be back rather late. There is some dried meat and bread in the kitchen."

"Thank you sir," Tamlin said, wringing his hands.

Haldur smiled, but to Tamlin it seemed half-hearted. "Do not worry about this little spat. There truly is nothing to be concerned about."

Tamlin nodded, but somehow he had trouble believing his mentor's words.

Tamlin waited until the moon was high in the sky, but still Haldur did not return. In most cases, Tamlin would assume that the wizard merely had a great deal to do; the town was almost three hours away, and Haldur had a habit of only going in when he needed several items at once.

But today, a lump of fear formed in his stomach. Something was horribly, dreadfully wrong, and no matter how much Haldur tried to hide it, he knew that the Archmagus was afraid of something.

He had tried to study the text Haldur had instructed, but after hours of rereading the same paragraph he had finally closed it and cast his mind back to the confrontation that morning. Who was this "master" the threatening stranger had mentioned? And what sort of consequences could he possibly have referred to?

But as the night pressed on, it brought no answers, and Tamlin found it harder and harder to keep his eyes open. Finally, he staggered off to bed, barely able to see straight. And still Haldur had not returned.

Tamlin woke up that morning and pulled on his gray robes, hoping that Haldur would be there. Taking a deep breath, he opened his door and stepped into the sitting room.

What he saw caused him to smile with joy. Haldur was there, filling a basket with clothes. The old light had returned to his eyes, and he glanced up at Tamlin and grinned.

"Good morning, my boy! The sun is up and high already. It is a pleasant day for traveling!"

"Traveling?" Tamlin asked, his smile turning to a frown.

"Yes, my apprentice, we're going on a journey," Haldur declared. "I've been considering this for some time, and I believe that my own collection of books is too limited for your needs. I am going to take you to the great library on the Isle of Magic."

The wizard patted Tamlin on the shoulder, leading him to his chambers. "We will break our fast on the road; it has been so long since we have had a picnic together. Just think of it: tomes and codices as far as the eyes can see. Every subject you could imagine, discussed and disserted to your heart's content!"

Tamlin smiled. "It would be exciting."

"That's my boy!" Haldur said, handing Tamlin a traveling sack. "Now pack some of your clothes for the journey, and I'll pull out some books for you to read. If possible, I would like to leave by noon."

Tamlin began to fill the bag, stuffing his robes in as quickly as he could. As he worked, he heard his door creak, and when he turned it was almost shut, only the barest of cracks revealing the sitting room.

"Running away?" an aristocratic voice said. Tamlin rushed to the door and peered through the crack. Haldur stiffened and spun, facing a tall man in flowing crimson robes. The newcomer stroked a midnight black goatee and smiled, an amused look in his eyes. "That's hardly sporting, after all the effort I've made to turn you to my side."

"I was an Archmagus when you were still being coddled by your mother, Feladon," Haldur declared. "You were pathetic then, and you have not changed. What you

17

want is a monstrosity, and I would see you destroyed if I could."

Feladon's grin became malignant. "I didn't break the rules; I merely took advantage of the situation. We are both children of Fenegar here. Please don't make me convince you with...other means."

"The rules of Succession are sacrosanct," Haldur stated. "Were the Arbiter alive today—"

"But he is not alive," Feladon pointed out. "The Great Staff has been shattered. Times are changing, old man. You can either change with them, or be pushed aside."

"I will not serve you," Haldur said, raising his arms to begin weaving a spell.

Feladon's smile widened, and Haldur gasped in shock. Frozen in place, the wizard grimaced in effort, as though he could not move a muscle.

"I am more powerful than you could ever imagine," Feladon said, leaning forward. A sharp crack sounded, and Haldur cried out in pain. Tamlin gasped as he saw a broken piece of bone jut out of his mentor's robe, right below his heart, a dark stain spreading on the fabric.

"You have one last chance, old one," Feladon said, a gloating smirk on his lips. "Serve me, or die."

"I would rather burn in the Damned One's lair," Haldur gritted.

Feladon nodded. "If that is your wish..."

Gasping, Haldur fell to the floor, his eyes wide and sightless. A sudden stench filled the air as his lower robes became soiled. Tamlin shook, fists clenched, a tear running down his cheek; whoever this enemy was, he hadn't even allowed Haldur any dignity in death.

Feladon smiled, and glanced at the bookcases. Tamlin smelled a whiff of incense, and the tomes exploded into flame. Then the wizard looked right at Tamlin's door, his grin widening.

"Come here, little apprentice," Feladon said. "Perhaps you will serve."

Tamlin bolted and threw himself out of his window, landing hard in a rosebush. He bit his tongue, holding back a yelp of pain. Unsteadily, he gained his feet, staggering toward the treeline surrounding the cottage.

He broke into a run, dashing past the old oaks and elms. Brambles caught at his ankles, cutting into his robes. Finally, he looked back to Haldur's small home.

The house was burning, fire belching from every opening. The choking stench of smoke filled the air, and Tamlin turned away, stepping between the trees, wiping away the flowing tears.

"Running won't help you, young one!" Feladon's voice called, echoing through the woods. "No matter what you do, I will find you! And you will serve me, or die!"

His eyesight blurry as he wept, Tamlin kept moving, sometimes walking, sometimes running. He had to get away – that was all he knew. But, with Haldur dead, he no longer knew where he could go.

Chapter II — Journey's Beginning

For Brother Caelyn, Chronicler of the Abbey of Southmarch, a monastery of the Eternal One located in the lush lands of Fenegar, it was not a day like any other. He acted as though it was, but deep down inside he knew it was a front. It was the last day before he began his pilgrimage.

He rose at his usual early hour, arriving in the great hall just in time for the morning prayers. As was his habit, he left trimming his grey beard until after the service had ended. After all, the Eternal One was interested in his soul, not his appearance.

The service was a simple one – the abbot led the congregation first in prayer, then song. The notes wafted up into the air, something heavenly on earth to Caelyn's ears. There was a simple beauty to the music. Caelyn had always believed that the greatest elegance lay in simplicity.

Once the service had finished, Caelyn retired to his

room. He took out a mirror and trimmed his beard, cutting each stray whisker down to an even size, and then double-checking it with his fingers. He heard a footfall behind him, but when he looked up, the doorway to his cell was empty, and he turned to regard his own deep blue eyes.

He blinked and turned back to his beard, trimming the last of the hairs he had missed. He heard footsteps, and spun to find the abbot standing in his doorway.

Abbot Artus smiled kindly. He was a tall, elderly man, face clean-shaven and skin clear of most of the marks of his age. Even when Caelyn had first joined the cloister, Artus had been abbot, although in those days his hair had been a steel gray.

Caelyn rose and bowed. "Father Abbot."

"Even after thirty years, you are a creature of habit," Artus remarked with a slight chuckle. "Please tell me that you will at least take some time from writing your chronicle to pack."

Caelyn looked down for a moment. "I had planned to spend most of my time working on the chronicle and then in the garden. I do not have a great deal to bring with me."

Abbot Artus shrugged. "To each his own. When I went on my pilgrimage, I took many things. Most of it came in handy. Mind you, I spent my life in the cloister. You, on the other hand, were a soldier. Sometimes I think you are one still."

"Is it that obvious?"

Artus nodded. "Your discipline remains, even after thirty years. I think the pilgrimage will help you with that."

"How so?"

"In the end, you must let go of your past," Artus said. "Everybody is trapped by their history, in some way or another. The widow longs for her lost husband, and sometimes dies from the loss. The former nobleman weeps, for he has no servants. Once we have left our past behind, and live fully in the now, that is when we are truly free."

"I thought discipline was a good thing," Caelyn said.

"It is, when it is present to enhance life," the abbot said. "You, however, seem to hide behind it. I can see it in your eyes. You carry it like a shield, fearful that if it ever slips, your past will return. I know you fought in the Kaegar Wars; what did you see that made you hide so?"

Caelyn was quiet for a moment. "Terrible things. Events I would forget for the rest of my life, if I could."

Abbot Artus smiled. "As did every soldier in that war. In this pilgrimage, you will let them go. You won't be able to come back until you have."

"How will I tell when I can come back?" Caelyn asked.

"You will know. Do you understand where the shrine is?"

Caelyn paused for a moment. "East of Beregar, in the mountains south of the Eastern Wastes."

Artus nodded, a smile on his face. "Excellent! You've done better than most. Even I was unsure of where when my abbot asked me the question. Have you given any consideration as to your route?"

"I have been thinking of the northern roads across Bandre," Caelyn replied. "However I am not yet certain."

"Well," Artus said, stepping to the door. "We'll go over a map after dinner, and help you choose your path. Until then, I have no doubt there is a chronicle that you feel needs you."

Caelyn nodded at the abbot as he left. There were several things that required his attention, and a chronicle wasn't the least of them.

Caelyn had always used the midday prayers to gather his

thoughts for the afternoon. On most days, this was a simple matter: his day would consist of working on one of his chronicles for a few hours, then retiring to the abbey garden. While some monks would work on the vegetables, Caelyn usually tended to the flowers. He had already spent so much time occupying his days with efficiency and violence in the outside world that it was a joy to help something beautiful grow for beauty's sake alone. His means of escape.

On this day, it brought him little peace. He had spent the morning putting the finishing touches on an illumination, and then ate a small meal before prayer, frowning as he chewed. No matter what he did or tried to think about, his mind was flooded by the outside world. He had fled it so long ago that it now seemed alien to him.

Abbot Artus raised his hands, signaling the beginning of the service. Caelyn quietly sang the benediction, his voice blending in with the others. As the benediction ended, the abbot read from the Book of the Eternal, telling of the glory of light and the endless struggle against darkness. Finally, the passage ended, and Artus began the mantra.

"Eternal One, our Lord," Caelyn followed, his voice echoing the congregation's. "Protect us from evil and darkness. May our lives be meaningful and our actions worthy. And, should the Great War come to us across the Road, grant us victory."

Caelyn added another prayer regarding that last point; the very thought of the Great War terrified him. He glanced around the church, the scent of incense filling his lungs, noting with envy the placid expression on his fellow monks.

What would he find when he was out there?

He snapped back to the present as he heard Abbot Artus begin the final prayer, but then his mind began to wander again. How much had the world changed since he had hid from it behind the monastery gate? Would he be welcomed by his fellow man, or an outsider?

The service ended, and Caelyn followed the brothers out of the chapel. He walked past the garden and the lavabo, stepping up the stairs of the stone wall surrounding the cloister, and gazed out over the green world before him.

His rigid stance relaxed as he looked out into the distance. Somehow, between the view and the warm breeze, he found some peace. He gazed out at the small village on the horizon, watching the tiny figures working in the fields, smiling as they went about their chores. He had been tempted once to become a farmer, but he had toiled too often for survival to want to do it again. The idea of constantly being a step away from starvation horrified him.

He nodded, content. There were no fires of war, no charred remains of villages put to the torch. The landscape was peaceful, just as he had hoped. If it all remained like this, he would have little difficulty in the outside world.

From the corner of his eye he noticed a mounted figure drawing close to the abbey. He turned, watching the figure ride closer and closer. After a few minutes, Caelyn could made out the blue livery of a herald. He looked on with interest as the messenger neared, wondering what news the man could possibly be carrying.

He shook his head. Messengers from the crown were rare, but not unknown. Generally, they came when there was to be a royal progress, warning all of the towns and villages on the way to stock up. It was a courtesy known to prevent full-scale revolts; whenever the court traveled, they used up almost all the food on their route.

Caelyn blinked. Not only had the herald approached quickly enough that he had to be running down his horse, but he had drawn close enough for the monk to see that the man was haggard, barely able to stay on his horse. Whatever it was, it was not news of a royal progress.

Caelyn swallowed nervously, forcing down the thought that arose with absolute certainty. The messenger could only be bearing word of two things: a disaster that required the abbey's resources, or, even worse, war.

Caelyn was working in the garden when the summons came. Taking a break from his chronicle, he trimmed the weeds away from a rosebush. It was long, careful work, which he performed with great relish.

"Brother Caelyn," Prior Cedric called, stepping out from the shadows of a large elm. Caelyn gazed up to the tall man, dreading what would come next.

"Abbot Artus wishes to speak to me," Caelyn stated.

Cedric just nodded. "There is a matter of grave importance to discuss. I believe it has to do with your pilgrimage."

Caelyn stood and dusted himself off, looking wistfully at the flowers. Somebody else would have to finish his task. "I will be along presently." As the prior stepped back into the chapel, Caelyn straightened out his robe and strode toward Artus' offices.

The abbot had established himself in a small quarters once reserved for the gardening staff. Caelyn had heard that Artus had commandeered the building several years after the monks took over the maintenance of the abbey grounds. This had all happened some time before Caelyn had joined the Order, however.

He entered to find the abbot and herald deep in conversation, Artus sitting behind a large oak table covered with paper. Artus gazed up at him and motioned to a chair. With a gentle bow, Caelyn took his seat.

"Gerrald has come with urgent news from his majesty's advisor, Archmagus Feladon," Artus began. "I believe you should hear this directly, Brother Caelyn."

Caelyn turned to look at the wiry man sitting opposite him. The herald stroked his moustache and pointed at a parchment lying on the table. "The army of Bandre has gathered at our borders," the herald reported, tugging at his blue tabard. "There is no question in his majesty's mind that this is the beginning of an invasion. The Abbey of Southmarch, and all of its brother houses, are commanded to render whatever aid is necessary."

Caelyn blinked. "I do not understand. Why would Bandre possibly want to invade Fenegar? Their lands are richer, and we have always been good neighbors."

Gerrald spoke, and for a moment Caelyn detected a slight tremble in the messenger's voice. "The crown believes that an evil Archmagus has taken control of the monarchy of Bandre. They have declared that they will overthrow the pretender and restore the rightful king."

Abbot Artus nodded to the herald. "Thank you, Gerrald. Find Prior Cedric; he will see to your needs. When he left me, he was headed towards the chapel."

After Gerrald had stood, bowed, and left, Caelyn gazed at Artus and said: "This is very bad news."

Abbot Artus shrugged his shoulders. "We are at war in the east, my friend, for good or ill. I shall pray that this conflict does not last long. However, I do believe this will adversely affect your pilgrimage."

"Do you wish me to stay until the war is over?" Caelyn asked.

Artus shook his head. "The will of the Eternal One must take precedence over secular concerns. However, I am concerned for your safety. Might I suggest you take a southern route, through Toregien?"

"I am protected by the Great Convention," Caelyn

pointed out. "All of our brethren are."

"In the heat of battle, there are those who would forget the Great Convention," Artus said. "I would prefer to rely on more than treaty to safeguard those under my care. The Eternal One only knows that I will have enough concerns in the days ahead. I do not wish your safety to be among them."

Caelyn nodded. "When I leave tomorrow morning, I will take the road to Toregien."

Artus smiled. "I am glad. I know that this is not usual for our order, but in exceptional circumstances the Rule does allow brethren to bear arms. Considering this war, you may need protection. We have some swords in the armory, if you would take one."

Caelyn shook his head. "I will not bear a blade. Perhaps I will carry a walking staff, but no steel."

"I understand," Artus said. "When you leave tomorrow, I will pray for your safe passage. May your pilgrimage not be touched by these dark times that have engulfed us."

Caelyn stood and bowed. "My good wishes will join yours, I think. If you will excuse me, I still have some work before I go."

"Of course."

Caelyn stood and stepped outside, looking up at the wispy clouds overhead. He mouthed a silent prayer, not only for himself, but for the souls of all who would be touched by the war.

The next morning, Caelyn rose with the dawn. He trimmed his beard, then checked his pack, ensuring that he had all he would need. A spare habit was folded in with several bags of herbs, some for healing, some for tea, and some for cleanliness. Wrapped in a cloth lay his razor, and beside it were several rations of dried meat and a full waterskin.

He closed up his pack and nodded. Everything was there, and he was ready. He attended the morning service, leaving the leather sack in his cell. The sermon passed quickly, and after another well-wishing from Abbot Artus and the gift of a large walking staff, he left the monastery.

The cobblestone highway stretched out before him, a millennia-old relic of the Arcalien Empire. As he walked, he passed several marker stones, carved with a script few could now read. The hoary stones jutted out of the earth, the text almost worn away by the wind and rain. It all passes away eventually, he realized. Perhaps one day even the common tongue would perish in the mists of time.

The slightest hint of a choking aroma caught in his lungs, and he started, spinning to the east. Far in the distance, almost beyond the horizon itself, a pillar of black smoke rose into the sky. Although the wind carried little of the stench to him, it was enough to bring back foul memories.

He turned and began to walk southwards, his stomach churning with dread at every step. It had begun: war had come to Fenegar.

Chapter III — A Meeting with a Fugitive

Brother Caelyn trod down the cobbled road, gazing at the vibrant colors of autumn and the warm breeze. At times, he felt that fall was a time when nature, knowing that it would have to sleep for a few months, put on a show so that it would not be forgotten.

He took a deep breath, filling his lungs with as much fresh air as possible. A smile crept over his face. Somehow, surrounded by the beauty of the season, he found himself at ease, regardless of the war in the north. Still, he kept a careful watch, every now and then grasping the star-shaped symbol of his order when things seemed too quiet.

Yet no enemies came, and the land was peaceful. Regardless of the conflict, the south seemed to have remained untouched. At least twice Caelyn had offered up a silent prayer that it would remain so, but in his heart he knew it wouldn't – not for long, at any rate.

Each night he camped to the side of the road, greeting the occasional traveler and asking for news. They were always polite but distant. After all, Caelyn reflected, there was war in the land, and there were more important concerns than the queries of a wandering monk.

Every morning, he rose with the dawn, stretched, brewed some of his herbs into a strong tea, extinguished what was left of his meager fire, washed himself if possible, and continued his journey towards Toregien. It was the simple, peaceful existence he had hoped for during his pilgrimage, and he thanked the Eternal One for it with every breath.

Nine days after leaving the abbey, close to the Baranar River marking the border between Fenegar and Toregien, Caelyn's life became interesting. He started his day with his usual routine, sipping on some herbal tea before he smothered his fire. Then he walked through the light forest, pausing every now and then to admire the bright hues of the leaves, until he came to a stream, where he cleaned himself with the herbs from one of the pouches in his bags.

When he finished and came back out of the woods, he found a boy being chased by soldiers.

The youth spotted him, rushing towards him with desperation in his eyes. Caelyn raised an eyebrow, taking in the odd sight. The boy looked as though he had been running for a long time, his clothes worn and tattered. Behind him stormed eight soldiers, swords unsheathed and pikes ready, clad in the red tabards of the army of Fenegar.

"Please help me," the youth stammered, glancing with terror at the oncoming warriors. "I didn't do anything! Please, I don't want to die!"

Caelyn pursed his lips and nodded. Then he turned to face the soldiers as they slowed to a confident stride before him.

"The boy is ours," a sergeant said, stepping forward. "We have orders from the high councillor of Fenegar to take him into custody."

"This young man is under my protection," Caelyn stated. "What crime has he committed?"

"His name is Tamlin, and he was called to serve his lordship Feladon," the sergeant replied. "As he did not answer the call to arms, he will be treated as a deserter."

Caelyn blinked, turning to gaze at the quaking youth for a moment. Then he turned back to the men-at-arms. "This child is not of age for service; anybody could see that. He barely has the beginnings of a man's beard."

"If you will not deliver him to us, we will take him by force," the sergeant declared, motioning to his men. Two of the soldiers broke rank and strode to either side of the monk. "I don't want to hurt you, brother. Just give us the boy, and we'll be on our way."

Caelyn shook his head. "Not possible, I'm afraid. I have accepted his offer of service as a novice in the order of the Eternal One." He raised the amulet with the emblem of his order. "This places us both under the protection of the Great Convention."

"Lord Feladon will not be pleased," the sergeant said. "Let us have him, and we can forget this ever happened. You don't want to anger the high councillor."

The monk brandished his walking staff. "You may not have this child, and we are both now under the protection of the Great Convention. I suggest all of you leave before you commit an unpardonable offense."

There was a moment of silence as Caelyn and the sergeant glared at each other, but finally the soldier backed off. "Very well, but I doubt you have heard the last of this, monk," the sergeant growled. With an angry motion, he ordered his men to march back north on the road.

"You may as well rest for a moment, Tamlin," Caelyn

said, sitting on a fallen tree. "We have many leagues still ahead of us."

"Thank you, sir," the boy panted. "I don't know what would have happened if you hadn't protected me. But what just happened? Do I have to become a monk now?"

"You were saved by the Great Convention," Caelyn explained. "After the horrors of the Kaegar wars, the Convention was signed by all of the nations bordering the Inner Sea to protect non-combatants such as neutrals and holy men. I have made you an impromptu novice in my order.

"Don't fear, though. You are not committed to becoming a monk now; a novice can leave the order at any time if he finds the monastic life is not his calling. Until we leave Fenegar, however, I would suggest that you wear my spare habit. It will be rather loose around you, but it will keep you protected."

Caelyn paused, regarding the young man. He appeared to be very malnourished, which would make sense if he had been on the run for several days. His hounded eyes still glanced rapidly around, as though the boy feared some trick that would place him in further danger.

"My name is Caelyn," the monk said. "I am the Chronicler of the abbey of Southmarch. Why don't you tell me who you are and why those men were chasing you?"

"My name is Tamlin," the boy said. "But you already know that, don't you?"

Caelyn smiled kindly. "Relax. No harm will come to you here."

In halting, tear-choked sentences, Tamlin told the monk about how his master Haldur was murdered by Feladon. "I kept running until I couldn't go anymore. By then I was completely lost. So I decided to look for a road, and hoped that it would take me to a village where I could find some refuge."

Caelyn nodded. "Go on."

"But when I found a road, it was days before I came to a village, and by then I was starving. I walked into an inn, hoping that I could work for some food, but there were posters on the wall with my picture on them! They said that I was a deserter and a criminal!"

"And the innkeeper called the soldiers," Caelyn filled in.

Tamlin nodded. "I thought I had lost them in the woods, but every time I rested they were right behind me. I don't think I've slept in days."

"You look it," Caelyn said, fishing around in his pack. Finally his hands closed on his spare habit, and he passed it over to the young man. "Don't worry; you'll rest well tonight. But we have some traveling to do yet. Put this on. It should be more comfortable than those rags you wear now."

"Thank you sir," Tamlin stammered, pulling on the wool robes. They fit loosely, but they were not so oversized as to draw curious glances. "I don't know how I can thank you."

"You can start by calling me 'Brother' or 'Caelyn,'" the monk stated. "'Sir' does not sit well with me. And for now you are a novice in our order, so you will have to show proper deference."

Tamlin nodded, and Caelyn passed him some food. As the boy wolfed the meal down, Caelyn shook his head. "We'll have to go into a town or village before long. Rations for one will not feed two terribly well, I fear."

Tamlin started, and for a moment Caelyn saw the hunted look return to his eyes in full force. "Do not worry," the monk said, "so long as you wear that habit and travel with me, you are safe from any secular law."

After the young man had finished his meal, they began

to stride down the road, Caelyn keeping a slower pace than usual so that Tamlin could keep up. By the end of the day, they had only covered around five leagues, and Caelyn was forced to stop when Tamlin was stumbling so frequently that the monk feared the boy would do himself an injury.

Caelyn chose a spot just off the main road, close enough to hear what little traffic passed, but far enough away that they were hidden by the sparse trees. He bid Tamlin to sit and rest while he collected firewood, and by the time he returned, the youth had fallen into a deep sleep.

Draping a blanket over the sleeping form, Caelyn smiled and built the fire. After a spark from the tinderbox, the gentle flames danced with unearthly beauty, illuminating Tamlin's face with a reddish glow. The young man's features contorted several times, and Caelyn wondered what nightmares troubled the boy. He shook his head and bedded down, and soon drifted into his own dreams.

Tamlin awoke slowly, pulling aside the blanked draped over him. For a moment he regarded his new companion, and it seemed, mentor. The monk busied himself with a small pot, two cups, and some dark green herbs. His face was kindly, but Tamlin sensed a hidden steel under Brother Caelyn's serene visage.

The monk noticed he was awake and smiled. "I am making some tea," he said, dropping a pinch of the herbs into the pot. "It should be ready in just a moment. I find it very restful in the morning."

Tamlin stomach grumbled loudly, and he placed both hands over his belly, an embarrassed look on his face. Caelyn only nodded, and handed him some dried mutton.

"After your ordeal, I have no doubt you must be hungry enough to eat an entire town out of house and home. However, you will have to make do with my meager rations for now."

Tamlin ate quickly, barely tasting the meat. As he finished, the monk passed him a cup of steaming liquid. "I trust you slept well last night."

"Fairly," Tamlin rasped, wincing as the hot tea scalded his tongue. "There were some nightmares, though."

Caelyn nodded. "I fear those will not go away too quickly. The mind needs time to heal, and sometimes I think ill dreams are a part of the process. They will fade, though; believe me."

Tamlin downed the rest of the tea and handed back the cup. As the monk had promised, the aromatic drink was soothing. "So now what will we do, Brother Caelyn?"

"There is a small village just across the border in Toregien, about two days away," the monk replied. "We shall stop there and buy some new supplies. And then you will have to decide if you wish to remain with me, or make a new life for yourself there."

"Do you think the soldiers will try to stop us?" Tamlin asked. Surely by now the sergeant would have reported to his superiors that their quarry was headed south.

"It is possible, but unlikely," Caelyn said. "Not only would it violate the Great Convention, but there are far greater concerns for the army right now – Fenegar has gone to war with Bandre. I would not concern myself with it, if I were you."

He stood and stretched. "For now, however, I think you should clean yourself in the stream just a couple of minutes that way." He pointed. "I will be there shortly."

Nodding, Tamlin stood and strode through the trees, following the sound of the babbling brook. The ground beneath his feet was covered with red, orange, and yellow leaves, and the sky above had only a couple of clouds in the sky, promising a pleasant day ahead.

Finally, he found the stream, a small rivlet that one could easily jump across. He removed the habit and travel-stained clothes underneath and washed himself until he felt clean at last. There was a rustling behind him, but when he spun, it was only Brother Caelyn. The monk removed his robes, took some herbs from his pack and rubbed them on skin that was firm for his age, then poured water over himself.

Once they were both finished and dressed, they returned to the road and continued their journey. The cobbled way was lightly traveled, causing Tamlin to frown; surely there would be far more traffic during the harvest season. But when he mentioned the concern to Caelyn the monk brushed it aside, pointing out that with the nation at war, people would only leave their homes if absolutely necessary.

"After all," Caelyn said, "brigands also profit during wartime."

"What is to stop them from waylaying us?" Tamlin wondered, shivering at the thought of highwaymen.

"Partly the great convention," the monk replied. "But I also know something of fighting, in case the Convention fails us."

They stopped that evening on a hillside, the great river Baranar between Fenegar and Toregien a long blue ribbon near the horizon. Across the river was a large stone bridge, and just beyond that lay a speck that Caelyn said was their destination.

"Tomorrow, we will eat in a proper inn," he promised. "And there will be no signs with your likeness, I assure you."

Tamlin nodded in relief and sat down by the fire Caelyn had built. There had to be something he could do to help the monk; after all, the man had saved his life.

"I am going into the woods for a moment," Caelyn stated, standing up and smoothing out his habit. "Personal business."

As Brother Caelyn strode away from the dancing flames, Tamlin was struck with inspiration. He would save the monk some time, and make some tea for him. Caelyn had left his pack, and he had seen the monk put the tea in a small pouch close to the top.

Quietly, Tamlin opened Caelyn's traveling pack and fished out the pot and bag of herbs. He filled the pot from his own canteen, and dropped a pinch of the herbs into the water once it had boiled. Then he waited, watching the liquid become dark.

The smell was wrong, though. The brew wasn't as fragrant as it had been in the morning. Tamlin shook his head; perhaps Caelyn had brewed it to be much stronger. Still, it would probably be a good idea to check and make certain he hadn't done something wrong.

He pulled a cup from the monk's pack and filled it with tea. Then, careful not to burn his tongue, he took a sip, and immediately spat it out.

Whatever he had brewed, it was the most rancid, nauseating thing he had ever tasted. He had to fight down the urge to wretch.

"Are you all right?" a Caelyn said, and Tamlin spun to find the monk watching him. Caelyn wrinkled his nose. "And what in the name of the Eternal One possessed you to brew tea from my cleaning herbs?"

"I wanted to help you out," Tamlin rasped. "I thought if I could have some tea ready..."

Caelyn nodded, emptying the horrific brew onto the ground beside the fire. "In future, let me make the tea." Drying the cauldron with a rag, the monk added, "At least you've managed to clean my pot."

Still barely able to speak, Tamlin agreed on both points.

The next day, they began their journey at the crack of dawn. They didn't wash themselves, as Caelyn felt they had ventured too far away from the stream to be practical.

The hours passed quickly, the darkening clouds scudding above them, promising rain or hail. A chill breeze rose, forcing them to wrap their habits more tightly around themselves. As they came closer to the river, Tamlin swallowed.

He could see a small detachment of men holding the bridge.

They finally arrived at the bank of the river in mid-afternoon, as far as Tamlin could tell. The sun was barely visible through the overcast sky, and it felt as though it could have been much later.

But when they came to the bridge, Brother Caelyn merely strode forward and asked to pass, saying that he and his novice were on a pilgrimage. Tamlin glanced around, looking for quick escape routes should the soldiers try to take him, and finding none.

A burly sergeant stepped up to regard the monk. "Please pass, brothers. Sorry about the delay, but with Bandre invading in the north, his Majesty wants to ensure the security of his southern borders."

"Completely understandable," Caelyn stated. "May the Eternal One grant that your lives remain as uneventful as possible."

"Thank you, brother," the sergeant said. "That's a prayer I think every soldier would like to hear."

And with that, they crossed the bridge into Toregien.

Chapter IV — Sagarum

Tamlin and Caelyn reached the walled town of Couer at noon, the day after they had crossed the bridge into Toregien. The town was sizeable enough, although tiny compared to the twisting streets of Laketown.

The guard let them pass without question, taking note of their habits and asking them for a blessing. Caelyn conceded, and wished the guard and the entire town well. With that, they walked through the high arch into the cobbled streets.

The gate was located next to the market, and Tamlin was bombarded with a menagerie of sights, sounds and smells. One tent specialized in exotic food, and the musky scent of strange spices wafted through the market. A juggler hocked at the passers-by, tossing and catching what appeared to be razor-sharp daggers, the blades glittering as they flipped through the air. The felt hat underneath his feet was half-filled with silver coins.

Tamlin took it all in stride, a slight grin on his face.

Had he grown up anywhere other than Laketown, he would have been completely overcome with awe. But, with his early childhood spent wandering among the Great Market, he had become accustomed to such sights. There was some sense of wonder, as he had spent half a decade sequestered away in a cabin filled with books, but he had seen much of it before.

But when he turned to Brother Caelyn, expecting to see the monk's jaw open in wonderment, he blinked in surprise. Caelyn barely seemed to notice the distractions around him, dismissing the street vendors and entertainers that sidled up to him with a casual wave. When they passed a bard singing an epic of the Kaegar Wars, Caelyn quickened his pace, and Tamlin found it difficult to keep up until the song had become lost in the chorus of voices and sounds.

Tamlin frowned as he regarded the monk. For what seemed the hundredth time, he wondered what Caelyn had seen that would make him treat these things as though they were so...*ordinary*. Surely he couldn't have seen too many wonders in his cloister, could he?

"We will need to find an inn," Caelyn said, his calm voice somehow overcoming the din of the crowd. "A quiet place where we can buy supplies."

Tamlin looked around. They had left the market, and entered the winding roads of the trade guild quarter. As they walked by a couple of smithies he smelled the choking soot and heard the ringing of hammers on steel and iron. Passing the forges, they came to a line of scriptoriums, the occasional clerk rushing past them, supplies or parchment in hand.

"Not many straight streets around here," Tamlin said. "It reminds me of Laketown."

"It's for defense," Caelyn stated. "The roads are thin and winding, so that should an enemy breach the walls, they cannot gain the streets in force, and the defenders can ambush them at every turn. Something learned from the Kaegar Wars."

"What were the Kaegar Wars?" Tamlin asked. "You've mentioned them a couple of times, but you still haven't told me what they are."

"Were," the monk corrected. "I'll tell you once we have a room at an inn."

They passed another crook in the road, coming to a large wooden building. Over the entrance was a sign reading "Peir's Inn." Some laughter carried out into the street from the common room.

"This will do," Caelyn said, opening the door and stepping in.

Tamlin paused for a moment, then took a deep breath and followed, reminding himself that not only was he no longer in Fenegar, but he was also protected by the Great Convention. He entered the common room to find the monk already in negotiation with the innkeeper. The two talked for a moment, and then he strode back to Tamlin.

"We have a room for the night, and provisions for tomorrow," Caelyn said. "I will go upstairs and see that the room is in good order. I suggest that you sit down and have a bite to eat. I've asked Peir to bring you something to ease your hunger."

Blinking, Tamlin realized just how famished he was. He pulled up a chair at an empty table and sat down, watching as his rotund host ambled over to the table.

"I'm always pleased to serve brothers of your order," Peir said, stroking his greying moustache. "Your kind are always gentle, and never skimp on the bill. How hungry are you, young novice?"

"Very," Tamlin said.

"I shall bring you some beef soup, then," Peir declared. "It is a very hearty soup, and I think you will like

41

it. It will keep your hunger at bay until dinner, when you will eat the meal of your lifetime. Nobody goes hungry at my inn!"

As Peir sped away from the table, Tamlin began to smile. Somehow, he just liked Peir; the innkeeper had something about him that made him seem completely trustworthy and harmless.

Peir returned, bearing a gigantic bowl of steaming soup that made Tamlin's mouth water. The innkeeper put the bowl on the table in front of Tamlin, grinning. He then spun on his heels to help a new customer as the door opened and closed.

Tamlin turned to gaze at the newcomer, and a chill ran down his spine. It was not the stranger's powerful bearing, or the long robes that marked him as a wizard, it was the eyes. The two deep orbs flickered around the room, and when they passed over Tamlin, they seemed to stare right through him.

At that moment, Brother Caelyn sat down across from Tamlin, obstructing his view of the newcomer.

"I see that Peir has brought you something," the monk said. "How is it?"

Tamlin picked up the wooden spoon and tasted the soup, smiling as the wonderful taste exploded in his mouth. His eyes must have been grim, though, as Caelyn leaned forward and quietly said, "What's wrong?"

"There's a wizard sitting behind you, and he looked at me," Tamlin muttered.

Caelyn turned back to regard the newcomer, who seemed to be gnawing on a loaf of bread. When he turned back, he shook his head. "I wouldn't think anything of it, if I were you. Peir tells me that there seem to be a large number of Magi on the road this year, the Eternal One only knows why. I doubt that they would be searching for a boy in monk's robes."

42

Tamlin nodded, resisting the urge to get as far away from the stranger as possible. Rather than debate the issue where the wizard might overhear, he forced himself to enjoy his soup. Somehow, he was certain that Caelyn would be an adequate protector, even against magic, though he didn't know how he knew.

"What were the Kaegar Wars?" Tamlin asked between mouthfuls of soup.

"Around thirty-five years ago, the free city state of Kaegar decided to build an empire," Caelyn replied. "They invaded their neighbors, and sacked any city that refused to yield. Once they had conquered the Free City States, they turned their eyes to the nations around the Inner Sea.

"Within a year, they had conquered Tarese and part of Toregien. Thousands were crucified along the roads, and no quarter was shown to captive soldiers. It was enough to unite the rest of the Western Lands against them.

"The war was terrible and brutal. Sometimes Kaegar would make peace with one of its neighbors, but only long enough to throw them off guard and invade them. Finally, after years of bloody battle, Kaegar was defeated."

"What happened to the city?" Tamlin wondered.

"It was destroyed," Caelyn replied. "The ground was sewn with salt, and every single one of its people was put to the sword. Kaegar's only legacy is the memory of bloodshed."

There was a long moment of silence, in which Caelyn watched Tamlin return to his soup. No doubt the young man was uncertain of what to say next, which was fine with Caelyn. As he watched Tamlin eat, the monk listened.

When he had been a soldier, Caelyn had learned one lesson above all others: always be aware. He had seen, time and time again, that most casualties in any battle occurred within the first quarter of an hour. Invariably, the ones struck down the most were the new recruits, who didn't know what to watch or listen for. The veterans had learned from long experience how to survive, to pay heed to that twitching feeling as an enemy snuck up behind you.

So, while his eyes remained trained on Tamlin, Caelyn turned the rest of his attention to the stranger seated behind him. The man was still there; the monk could hear him breathing. The gentle scent of the man's food had vanished, and he could not hear the newcomer drinking any ale.

Caelyn's hackles began to rise. If the wizard had finished his meal, why hadn't he left? It was possible that the stranger was simply resting, allowing his food to settle, but Caelyn's instincts spoke differently. He felt a familiar twitch, and realized the stranger's gaze rested on the back of his head.

He grimaced slightly, but Tamlin showed no sign of noticing; the young man was too busy finishing off the last of his soup. The monk considered his choices: he could let the wizard make the first move in his own good time, or he could take the initiative.

He turned to meet the stranger's eyes. "I know you've been watching us since we sat down," he said. "Now, would you like to join us, or is the back of my head truly that interesting?"

Caelyn was aware of Tamlin swallowing abruptly in alarm, but kept his gaze firmly on the wizard. The stranger smiled and stood, stepping over and pulling up a seat.

"Obviously, I was not as subtle as I had hoped," the wizard said. "I apologize if I've made you uncomfortable."

"You must have been the one who followed us into town," Caelyn stated.

The stranger nodded. "Farther than that, actually. I've been following that young man since he fled into the woods in Fenegar. Very noble of you, to protect him as you did."

"Sometimes the innocent need protection," Caelyn said, taking careful stock of the Magus. He was of a good height, but not so tall as to be intimidating. His hair and short-cropped goatee were a dark steel grey, and his brown eyes were so deep that they suggested an ancient soul. He bore a long, smooth staff of some strange wood, which he rested against the table. "May I ask your name?"

"I am Sagarum," the wizard replied. "I believe the boy is named Tamlin, from when I overheard a couple of rather loud guards speaking of him. I fear I do not know your name, though."

"Brother Caelyn, Chronicler of the Abbey of Southmarch."

"Why were you following me?" Tamlin demanded, a hunted look in his eyes.

"You have nothing to fear from me, young apprentice," Sagarum said. "I am a wandering wizard of sorts; I have no allegiance to any who would demand services of me. Had I wished you harm, you would not be here now."

"You haven't answered his question," Caelyn pointed out. "Why were you following him?"

"He is touched by Wyrd," Sagarum said. "I could sense it; most Archmagi can. I wanted to see what he would do."

"Why didn't you reveal yourself?" Caelyn demanded.

"I did not know him," Sagarum replied. "Aside from which, had I revealed myself to him in Fenegar, I would have attracted the attention of Feladon. Events have occurred that have made it very hazardous to be a wizard there. Now I have watched both of you, and I feel that you are worthy companions."

Caelyn raised an eyebrow. "You would join us?"

Sagarum nodded. "The roads are becoming dangerous, and there is greater safety in numbers. Besides, I can continue Tamlin's training. No offense, good Caelyn, but I do not believe that is something you can do."

Caelyn hesitated. The decision lay with him, as Tamlin still held the informal rank of novice. But his instincts still twitched: there were some unanswered questions he would have preferred to have answered. At the same time, he had a sense of the man, and something told him that while the wizard might have his own agenda, it would not be to Tamlin's detriment.

"Assuming that Tamlin has no strenuous objections, you may accompany us," Caelyn finally said. "Understand, though, that until he decides otherwise, he is still a novice of the Order of the Eternal One, and is thus protected by the Great Convention."

Sagarum turned to Tamlin. "Do you have any objections?"

Tamlin shook his head, but his eyes were cautious. "If Brother Caelyn thinks you're safe, then I can trust that."

"I would suggest that we head out at first light," Sagarum said. "I fear it will not be safe here soon."

"The war is in the north, between Fenegar and Bandre," Caelyn stated. "We should be safe from it here."

Sagarum shook his head. "This conflict is not what it seems. It will spread, until all the world is consumed."

The table's attention was caught as the door flew open. A herald of Toregien strode into the common room, a parchment rolled up in his hand. With a flourish, he unrolled the parchment and began to read.

"The threat of invasion from Fenegar will no longer be tolerated!" the herald declared. "By order of his Majesty, King Lewys the third, and his Chancellor, Archmagus Gesanus, a levy will be raised to combat the threat. Let it be known that all able-bodied young men will assemble in the market at noon tomorrow for selection."

With that, the herald spun on his heels and walked back through the door. Caelyn shook his head. As Sagarum had just predicted, the war had spread. And only the Eternal One knew how much farther it would go.

Chapter V — Journeys and Lessons

They were only a week out of Couer, but Tamlin was certain that Brother Caelyn had become nervous. The monk kept a wary eye on the horizon, as though he was looking for some invisible enemy just out of reach.

Perhaps it was the armies that made him cautious; since they had left the town, they had encountered no fewer than two legions of men traveling northwest. The commanding officers in both hosts gave the trio a curious look, but otherwise left them alone.

"We are lucky," Sagarum said one night, supping on some of Caelyn's tea. "Very soon they will start conscripting men on the road."

"That was the practice during the Kaegar wars," the monk mused. "At least the Great Convention protects us now."

"It is as though the entire world is at war," Tamlin said, gripping his habit in the chilly night air. "What is going on?"

"Something has changed," Sagarum said. "Perhaps the world has gone mad."

Tamlin saw Caelyn glare at the wizard, but neither spoke of it again that night. If Sagarum was hiding something, Tamlin could not even begin to fathom what it might be.

"I think we are far enough from civilization to drop the pretenses," Sagarum declared. "I do not believe we have any need for secrecy out here. Brother Caelyn, will you finally allow me to instruct Tamlin?"

Caelyn shrugged, turning to stare at Tamlin. "That is up to Tamlin. If he wishes training now, then we are safe enough here."

"Do you wish it?" Sagarum asked.

For a moment, Tamlin's heart leapt in his chest. To be an apprentice again, rather than a wandering monk – it felt like recovering a lost dream! He nodded.

"We should step into that copse over there," Sagarum said, motioning to a small grove of elms, most of their leaves fallen to cover the ground with a yellow blanket.

Tamlin stood and took his leave, following the strange Archmagus. Sagarum sat down on a stump in the center of the grove and placed his hands together. It was a motion that reminded Tamlin of Haldur for a moment, but the memory felt dull and faded, as though from some distant dream.

"What is magic?" Sagarum asked.

"The manipulation of supernatural forces," Tamlin replied.

To his shock, Sagarum shook his head. "That is not it at all. Completely wrong. Try again."

Blinking, Tamlin ventured another guess. "The learning of lost knowledge?"

"If it is lost knowledge, how can one possibly learn it? That is a task for historians! Again, you are mistaken."

Sagarum leaned forward, his eyes glittering in the crimson light of the setting sun. "The world, the Great Road, even the universe itself, has a balance that must be maintained at all times. Whenever something dies, something else is born. For every good, there is an evil.

"The order of Archmagi exists for the sole purpose of maintaining that balance. Some knowledge was passed to the druids in ancient times, but they forgot too much, and used what they knew to worship gods rather than for true magic. Ours, however, is a truly sacred order."

"So magic is maintaining the balance?"

"Exactly!" Sagarum said, shaking his fist in the air. "Why do you think there are so few battle-magi? We can manipulate life, and we can take it, but only one of us could ever give it. The power of life and death is sacred, beyond the wisdom of almost all of us. Those who attempt it often become corrupted wizards, and have lost their way."

Tamlin sat down, shaking off a chill. "Haldur never mentioned any of this. He just wanted me to learn how to cast spells."

"Then the Order has lost a great deal," Sagarum sighed. "No wonder there is some madness."

"What do you mean?" Tamlin asked.

Sagarum shook his head. "Nothing you need to know right now. Trust me, you will learn much in time."

Every night they traveled, Sagarum gave Tamlin another lesson. He began with talking about the history of the Archmagi, and how long before the Arcalien Empire they had rebelled against their first Grand Magus, but even Sagarum did not remember the name of that powerful wizard.

After three days of discussion, Tamlin began to

wonder if Sagarum would ever actually teach him any magic. The Archmagus seemed more content to sit down and talk than to actually do anything arcane. The wizard's language was filled with terms that Tamlin didn't understand, such as the "Great Road," but whenever Tamlin ventured to ask, Sagarum ended the lesson and returned to Brother Caelyn's fire.

Finally, as they camped further towards Tarese along Caelyn's pilgrimage route, surrounded by a light woodland, Sagarum sat Tamlin down in front of two large rocks, sunk in the earth just out of site of the camp.

"One of these rocks has to go," Sagarum said. "Move it with your magic."

Tamlin closed his eyes for a moment, visualizing the rock and his power. Then he opened his eyes and began to weave the spell, his hands forming his energy into a net around the larger stone. As sweat beaded on his forehead, he motioned at the rock, bidding it to move. The net pulled the stone into the air, the rock sailing about two feet before the weave gave way.

"Not bad," Sagarum judged. "Your motions are too uncontrolled, but you seem to know the basics. It took a lot out of you, though."

Tamlin nodded. "It was a heavy rock."

"You are lucky I did not select a boulder," Sagarum said. "Then you would have had a nasty lesson. You have the potential, but it is very far from realized."

"So now what?"

Sagarum pointed to the smaller rock. "Move that one. Don't use all your power, though, and keep the motions smaller. That alone could save your life one day."

Tamlin turned to the other stone, weaving a net around it, careful not to make any grand gestures as he shaped his power. The weave of energies was coarser, but it did the job. When Tamlin willed the rock to move, it sailed into the trees, bourne until he dispersed the net with a quick wave.

"That was easier," Tamlin gasped, steadying himself. The front of his habit was covered with sweat, and he found himself panting.

"The stone was smaller, and you worked more efficiently," Sagarum said. "When was the last time you cast a spell?"

"Weeks ago," Tamlin replied, wiping his brow. "I usually practiced on books. Haldur never had me lift anything heavy."

"Spellweaving is just like exercise," Sagarum stated. "The more you practice, the stronger you will become. From now on, you will cast a spell every night. It does not matter what, but it must be more powerful than the one you cast last. Do you understand me?"

Tamlin nodded. "How will I know that I'm keeping the balance?"

"So long as you don't kill something, you will be fine," Sagarum answered. "The stones you lifted this evening returned to the earth, as they should. However, if you ever do harm, you must endeavor to do an equal good. If you are not balanced, you can become corrupted."

"What if I only did good?" Tamlin wondered.

"It would lead you to evil," Sagarum said. "There is darkness in all of us; to deny it only gives it strength. The greatest wrongs in the world have always come from good intentions. Instead, just be balanced."

Tamlin did as he had been told, and each day he became stronger. They continued on their journey, venturing into a bright, lightly forested land of rolling hills and valleys. As they came over one of the hills, they passed another army. This time, the commander, a well-grown man with a greying moustache, stopped them and asked a boon.

"Brother, the war is not going well, and we are heading into battle," the man said. "Will you bless us, that we may return home safely?"

Caelyn nodded. "It is my sacred duty." He began to walk up and down the column, muttering a prayer.

As the monk worked, Tamlin turned to Sagarum and asked, "Why don't they ask for victory in battle?"

Sagarum stroked his beard. "The Order of the Eternal One will not sanction the taking of life unless it is in the Great Conflict."

"The Great Conflict?"

Sagarum nodded. "The Eternal One and the Damned One war on each other across the universe. When either side conquers on one world, the war continues on another. They only fight on one world at a time, and the war determines the fate of that world."

Tamlin shuddered. "Has the war ever been here?"

Sagarum nodded. "Once, a long time ago. The Eternal One was victorious, and we can only pray that the war will not come here again."

"Could it?"

"The Damned One's generals were banished from this place, so they could not come here of their own volition. They could, however, be summoned. But very few have the knowledge or insanity to do that. It would utterly destroy the balance here."

Clearing his throat, Caelyn returned from the soldiers. With a call from their commander, they began to march again. "My work here is done," the monk reported.

"I was just telling your novice here about the Great Conflict," Sagarum said.

"I wish you hadn't," Caelyn sighed. "Tamlin has enough concerns without thinking of great wars against evil."

Tamlin blinked, a frown on his face. He opened his mouth to tell the monk that he was no longer a child, but Sagarum spoke first.

"The Order doesn't tell many people about the Great Conflict, does it?"

Caelyn shook his head. "It is usually best not to worry them. Aside from which, very few truly understand the nature of the conflict. The fact that you do I find very interesting."

Sagarum shrugged. "I am well traveled."

With that, they continued on their journey. Two and a half weeks had passed since the three had left Couer.

They settled down in the wilderness that night, the forest thicker and more menacing than it had been earlier. Little of the dusk peered through the trees, and the long shadows were dark and clinging. Still, Sagarum insisted on taking Tamlin off to the side for his lesson.

"You have been growing in strength," Sagarum said.

"I've tried a lot of new things," Tamlin stated.

The Archmagus nodded. "As you should. Magic spells all began as improvisations. The most powerful wizards are the ones who do not allow themselves to be bound by what they read in their spellbooks."

"So what are you going to teach me today?"

Sagarum leaned back against a tree. "It is the most profound secret of wizardry. There are Archmagi who do not know it. But for you to be able to fulfill your potential, you must learn it."

"What is it?"

Sagarum spread his hands. "There is a greater balance than the one we maintain. A balance set and regulated only by natural laws." He paused, stroking his beard thoughtfully. "Where does your power come from?"

"From inside me," Tamlin replied.

"Does all of it come from there?"

"Yes."

"It doesn't have to," Sagarum said, leaning down to a sapling. "This is an ancient wood, almost as ancient as the Old Forest far to the north. But even in this place there is new life."

Tamlin knelt by the sapling, examining the bristling foliage. The pine tree barely poked out of the earth and sod of the forest, a tiny speck of life trying to survive at the feet of giants.

"Do you know how it survives here?" Sagarum asked.

Tamlin shook his head. "Great luck?"

"The trees around it are giving it some of their life," Sagarum stated. "Every time this little tree grows an inch, the trees around it die a bit. Sometimes, it can be controlled, if an Archmagus is powerful and knowledgeable enough."

"How do the trees know to do that?" Tamlin wondered.

Sagarum shrugged. "The truly ancient trees have souls, or at least they seem to. Perhaps it is the forest itself that is alive. We could cut wood here without fear, but if we attempted to in the Old Forest, we would be bringing our deaths down upon us."

"But an Archmagus could do it too," Tamlin asserted, frowning as he wrapped his mind around the concept. "Siphon power from one thing to another, I mean."

Sagarum nodded. "One who truly understands could. An Archmagus with the knowledge and strength could become a conduit for these forces, allowing them to pass through him without using any of his own power. But, the balance is eternal. It cannot be broken. For something to become strong, something else must become weak. Just as you tire for a while after casting spells."

"I think I understand."

Sagarum nodded. "Good. More understanding will

come with practice, but most of this you will have to discover for yourself."

"What about the greater spells?" Tamlin wondered. "Why haven't you taught me any of them?"

"Some of them would require vast power, which you do not possess yet. And others, well, magic that strong would bring some unwanted attention. Perhaps later, when we have left the places touched by war, I will teach you those."

The lesson ended with Tamlin practicing moving several rocks around at once, and then he and Sagarum retired to the campsite. Despite the cold, Caelyn had not lit a fire, and Tamlin used his power to heat the monk's pot so that they could have some tea. The monk was still worried about something, but he would not say what it was.

The next morning, they crossed into the land of Tarese.

Chapter VI — Interlude

Hargan rode at the head of his army. Well, he reflected, by name it was the Glorious Army of the Haneric Empire, and no doubt the Emperor wanted to believe that he owned the military, but it really belonged to Hargan now. For that matter, so did the Haneric Empire.

It had taken him almost a year, but he had managed to convince the Emperor to mobilize the army against Tarese. From Tarese, he could take one of the seaports of the Free City States, and strike out at all of the other Successors.

All save one. For some reason, he had no accurate knowledge of the location of Tergibar. It was as though the Archmagus had vanished from the face of the earth. It was possible that another had killed the little wizard, claimed the power of succession, but he had spies everywhere. If Tergibar had died, he would have heard about it.

"We camp there tonight," Hargan ordered, pointing out a ridge to his subordinates. The officers serving under him nodded and complimented his choice of the high ground, but Hargan ignored them. He had another reason for choosing it: it was a perfect place for a scrying spell. From the heights, he would be able to scry everywhere from Toregien to the Eastern Wastes.

A perfect spot.

"Where will we fight first?" a familiar voice inquired. Hargan turned to face Malichus, a tall, gaunt man with a thin, unpleasant face. Malichus had inherited telepathy as his power of Succession, and had skills that made him invaluable alive to Hargan. And, when the thin man had no more use, Hargan would be able to easily kill him and take his telepathy. It would be his last act before declaring himself Grand Magus.

Hargan smiled at the weave of magical energy surrounding Malichus. The wizard had obviously thought to cast personal wards around himself before meeting, which was a good thing – it meant Hargan had not allied himself with a moron. However, Hargan had Spellsight as his power, and could see through the defenses. Had he wished, he could have killed Malichus with the simplest spell.

"I don't know," he finally replied. "The Taresian army could strike at any time, but hopefully we will be able to find good ground."

"I still don't see why we didn't attack Gesanus in Toregien," Malichus said. "There's no Successor in Tarese."

Hargan smiled. "You may be able to read minds, but you have no understanding of strategy. If we take Tarese, we will have a firm power base to launch an assault on any Successor we wish. And Gesanus is too busy dealing with Feladon to expect us to attack him anywhere but in the south. So we'll allow ourselves the room to fight in the south or the east."

"A pincer."

Hargan nodded. "Exactly. But I don't think we'll have to worry about Gesanus yet. I think we will go across the sea, strike at Bervus in Bandre. I understand his invasion of Fenegar is not going very well at all; by the time we get there, we'll be able to completely crush him."

"Or we could split up," Malichus suggested.

Hargan grinned. "I have thought of that. We could catch all the lands around the Inner Sea in a great stranglehold. The options are limitless. But first we must take Tarese for ourselves."

Hargan probably would split them up then. He could give Malichus a good general and order the invasion of Toregien, and then himself attack Bandre. They would be an indestructible force, catching all of the civilized lands in their claws. In the end, all of the Successors would be dead except for them. And at that point, Malichus would have outlived his usefulness.

Hargan calmly watched the wizard return to his horse. It was always possible that Malichus might read his mind, finding these thoughts, but he had one or two other tricks up his sleeve that not even Malichus could guess. Victory was only a matter of time.

The sun had set by the time the army had encamped. Hargan sat alone in his tent, gazing for a moment out the flap at the stars. The Demon had risen to encompass the moon, a sign that he had heard some astrologers read as a sigil of great doom. For a moment, Hargan wondered who the doom was for, but then he turned his thoughts away; there were more important tasks at hand.

He took out a plain wooden box the size of a thick codex and placed it on the makeshift map table. With a quick but careful gesture, he dismissed the wards surrounding the contents. Had anybody tried to open the container, the blast would have destroyed them.

Muttering a mantra, Hargan reached into the box and removed a small bundle, wrapped in crimson silk. The folds fell away to reveal a translucent stone, barely the size of his fist. Inside the crystal, he could make out vague shapes, which could have been a fog for all he knew; he had seen broken scrying stones before, and they had been dark and empty. Dead.

"I am empty, and I will see," Hargan stated, continuing the chant, clearing his mind with every word. "I will gaze upon the world. I am empty, and I will see."

Finally, his mind was free of thought, and the stone begin to grow. Larger and larger it became, until it was all he knew. And then he could *see*.

The world stretched out before him. He saw the soldiers huddled around the fires, crouching together against the autumn chill. A bit farther away some of his men had gathered with the camp followers, and as he passed he heard their moans as they rutted.

Casting his mind farther afield, he passed the camp and gazed out towards the villages. Some of the peasants dashed along dirt roads, headed to secret assignations or home to their wives and families after some late-night errand. And still he gazed onwards.

A group of men was gathering, an army of considerable size. Hargan flew past their pickets, into the midst of the camp. The banners of Tarese flew in the breeze, the colors muted by the dark.

Hargan felt nothing. He had passed so far beyond his own ridge that he had left his body and all of its baggage behind. His spectral form noted the numbers, and then turned back. He sped across fields and woodlands, passing a river so quickly that it seemed to writhe like a snake. And then, suddenly, he stopped.

Something was wrong.

Out in the distance, close to his camp, there was a black spot. A place where no light could shine. He passed over it, but he could not see into it. It was a bubble of darkness, hiding something; the fact that it existed at all made it of great import.

He took note of where it was, and then returned to the camp. Hargan felt a cold shock as he returned to his body, the scrying stone setting him free. He grimaced as a flood of emotions washed over him – hate, anger, surprise and joy, captured for so long, battled for release. He pushed them all down, trying to concentrate on the task at hand.

The Taresian army was large, but it would be easily conquered. None of the order of Archmagi marched with it, which came as a surprise. It was a blessing, though; the conquest of Tarese would be an simple task.

And yet, the black spot remained. Only an Archmagus of incredible power could have created it. What was it? An army, led by one of the successors? Or was it one of his brethren, trying to retain some privacy despite the wars around him?

Hargan carefully wrapped the scrying stone in the silk and placed it back in the box. He closed the container quietly, then reset the wards with a quick gesture.

Throwing on his cloak, he called for his second. The officer snapped to attention, resting his fist on his breast in the salute of the Haneric Empire.

"I am leaving for the night," Hargan said, saddling his horse. "If I am not back by noon tomorrow, march to meet the Taresians in the north-east. Malichus will direct the Archmagi in the battle. He is *not*, however, to select the tactics. Understood?"

"Yes, my lord," the officer said.

Hargan didn't acknowledge him. Instead, he kicked the horse into a gallop, racing down the ridge and across the countryside.

Hargan cast his warding spell shortly before he came to the bubble. It would have been foolish to simply walk in unprotected, especially if there was an enemy army there to greet him. Now, any enemy who looked at him would think that he was gazing upon a shadow of some sort, nothing to be concerned about at all.

He rode at a canter to the edge of the bubble, gazing with his Spellsight. A weave of power surrounded a small stone cottage with a thatched roof. Each string in the weave held a deadly potency, as though an intruder would die upon touching it.

Hargan smiled, casting a tunnel between two of the threads. If he was careful, the other Archmagus would never know he was coming. With a bit of pressure, the web opened up, giving him a doorway.

Dismounting, he tied his horse to a nearby tree. Then he walked through his makeshift tunnel, into the bubble. As he strode forward, he had a sense of nearby power, not unlike the feeling he had whenever he was around one of the Successors.

"One creature of power can always sense another," he remembered his teacher Kelerin saying. He had scoffed at it then, but now he saw the truth in the words. With a quick look, he checked the cottage door for warding spells, and then cast it open. If he could sense the other Archmagus, any possibility of surprise was gone.

As he stepped into the cottage, two large creatures flanked him, one grasping his shoulder. The thing appeared to be a walking tree of some sort, and it screamed as its flesh burned from Hargan's ward. The second creature fell back, watching him carefully. As a silence fell over the room, Hargan took stock.

He was in a small chamber, the wooden paneling on the walls glossed and shining. Another oak door, free of any magic, stood before him. Light poured through the cracks.

Hargan shrugged; there was nothing else he could do now except see this through. Gathering his energies around him like a cloak, he pushed the door open.

A short and rotund man, his moustache an iron grey, gazed upon him with piercing eyes. Hargan could only smile, looking at this Archmagus in dark crimson robes. "Tergibar. I wondered where you had gone."

Tergibar gestured angrily. "As far away from you and your abomination as I could. Where is your army, Hargan? Or have you actually come to fight me properly?"

"My army is close," Hargan stated, gazing around the room. He appeared to be in some kind of ante room, but he could feel eyes gazing upon him from the walls. The chamber was so full of life that he felt as though he had entered a forest.

Well, there were things he could do about that. With a wave of his hand, he released the power he had gathered to himself. A blinding flash filled the room, and he heard several thumps, as though a multitude of creatures had fallen to the floor. He didn't need to gaze around to know that they were now alone.

"You shouldn't have been able to do that," Tergibar sputtered. "All of those creatures were protected by my most powerful spells!"

"You gained the gift of Creation, didn't you?" Hargan mused. "In the right hands, it could be powerful indeed. To be able to bring life, well, I think I will enjoy that."

"You'll have to kill me first," Tergibar snarled. "And I don't think you can."

Tergibar raised his hands, and Hargan felt the energy coalescing around the Archmagus. He smiled, preparing himself. "Before you try to slay me, why don't you tell me why you've been hiding? I am rather curious."

"You destroyed the Rites of Succession!" Tergibar gritted. "You plunged the world into war, and I believe you murdered the arbiter. You are a monster!" With that, Tergibar released his spell.

Hargan grinned, noting the weave of the spell and moving to absorb its power. He gestured, and the attack broke around him. He inhaled deeply, exulting in the rush of new energy. "This will be too easy."

Tergibar was silent. Hargan had hoped that the Archmagus would at least rise to the insult, make a mistake to quicken his own demise. Instead, Tergibar was cold and quiet, and Hargan sensed he was gathering his inner power for another assault.

Suddenly, that power vanished. Hargan tensed. He looked around, but the room was quiet and still. He would have laughed, but he didn't believe for a minute that Tergibar's spell had failed.

And then the table attacked him. The leg reached out and tripped him, the table screaming as the fire from Hargan's ward consumed it. A chair began to approach, clacking angrily as Hargan scrambled to his feet. With a quick motion of his fingers, Hargan put the table and chair to rest.

"How are you doing that?" Tergibar demanded, gazing at the lifeless furniture in disbelief.

Hargan stepped forward, and Tergibar shrank back at the sight of him. "I spent a lot of time looking into the veil in-between," he replied, grinning. "And I made some new friends. Very powerful allies."

Tergibar's face became ashen. "By the Eternal One, please don't say you allied with *Him*!"

Hargan nodded. "Powerful allies," he repeated, relishing the look of horror on the Archmagus' face.

"You've destroyed us all!" Tergibar lamented.

"Only you," Hargan said, driving a spear of energy

through Tergibar's chest. The Archmagus flew back, pinned to the wall by the force. A dark stain began to creep across his robes as the wall behind him smouldered.

Hargan reached out and placed a hand on Tergibar's chest. "I claim your Power of Succession," he stated, relishing the moment as Tergibar screamed, his eyes rolling back in his head, a stench filling the room as the wizard's body soiled itself in its last moments. A rush of power flowed into Hargan, his arm tingling as the energy became a part of his being.

Hargan stepped back and smiled, enjoying the sensation of the new power. Tergibar's lifeless eyes gazed at him, a silent accusation. Hargan only grinned.

Powerful allies.

As he left, he gave the cottage to them. Mounting his horse, he looked back once more. Strange, unholy fires filled the windows, and for a moment he wondered what was happening in there.

Powerful allies.

Finally, he kicked the horse into a run. His army was waiting, and he had a battle to plan.

Chapter VII — Sagas

Tamlin wrapped his habit around him like a blanket, trying to fend off the chill autumn wind. If there was an impression he had of Tarese, it was of empty space. While there was the occasional woodland, the country seemed to consist of rolling fields, most of which were vacant. Deep in the east, he made out the peaks of distant mountains, but how high or far away they were, he could not say.

"Almost perfect farming country," Sagarum commented. "Nice, flat, and mostly fertile. At least, now it is."

"What does that mean?" Tamlin asked, gazing up at the sky. The sun clung to the western horizon, a great crimson orb basking the world in an orangish light. He blinked. For some strange reason, Brother Caelyn hadn't called a halt; this late in the day, they should have started making camp.

"During the last years of the Kaegar Wars, Tarese was

the main battleground," Sagarum explained. "Rather than let their enemies take the land and use it, the army of Kaegar sewed much of it with salt. The soil is only now beginning to recover."

Caelyn suddenly stopped, shaking his head. "It's too far," he muttered. "We'll have to stop here."

Tamlin gazed at the monk in amazement. "What is wrong with this place?" He stepped forward, only to trip over something half buried in the ground.

Caelyn strode over and pulled at something by Tamlin's feet. With a great heave, the monk freed a long, rotting polearm from the earth.

Sagarum smiled sagely. "Now I understand the rush. We're on a battlefield. But how did you know?"

Caelyn ignored the question, instead scanning the horizon, a hand shading his eyes from the sun. He pointed at a rise to the northwest, bald save for a couple of fir trees. "We'll camp on that hill."

"You fought here, didn't you?" Sagarum continued. "I guess this place brings back memories."

Caelyn walked towards the small rise. "Are you coming or not?"

"What's wrong with him?" Tamlin wondered.

"Often, old soldiers don't like to remember their battles," Sagarum said. "I imagine Brother Caelyn's recollections are quite unpleasant. I'm certain he will be back to his usual talkative self once we pass to the next village."

The jest brought a grin to Tamlin's face, and he saw Sagarum smile. "That's better," the Archmagus said. "Somebody has to bring some joy to this depressing place."

They rejoined the monk as he was gathering deadwood into a small pyre. With a quick gesture, Sagarum set the wood alight. Caelyn just nodded and gave a quiet "Thank you."

As the sun set, Tamlin watched the two older men gaze at one another. "I'm sorry if I've stolen your novice from you," Sagarum said, smiling. "I can give him back once I'm done."

"Tamlin has to choose his own path," Caelyn said, looking right at the young man. "All I can do is protect him until he can practice in peace."

"You're not like most monks I know," Sagarum said. "You're much more...dour. This pilgrimage is very personal to you, isn't it?"

Caelyn nodded. "I have done many things I would forget, if I could."

"But all you can do is learn to live with them," Sagarum mused. "I understand what you are going through; I had to deal with similar things."

"Not like mine."

"Perhaps more similar than you would think. I too have fought in brutal wars."

The monk just grimaced and looked away. As he did, something caught Tamlin's eye. He turned to see a flash of faint light, and for a moment he thought it was merely a reflection from the newly-risen moon.

But then he saw the figures, and his heart leapt in his chest.

Pale and ghostly, they stood in formation. An entire army of spectral soldiers, ancient banners waving. If Tamlin stared hard enough, he could see the ground through their armored forms.

"We're not alone," he stammered, causing Caelyn and Sagarum to turn. Both monk and wizard stepped forward to stand beside him as another legion began to form across the field, as insubstantial as mist.

"The army of Kaegar," Caelyn said, shaking his head. Kneeling, the monk began to pray. "May the Eternal One protect their spirits, illuminate them with his eternal light, and give them peace."

"What if they see us?" Tamlin asked, trying to force down the rising panic. "What would they do to our souls?"

Sagarum shook his head. "There is nothing to fear. They aren't even aware of us."

"Then what..."

Silently, the army of Kaegar charged, banners flapping in a phantom wind. The other army formed a shield wall, waiting for the onslaught. Without a sound, the two forces clashed, the attackers breaking against the wall like a great wave.

"Look at how many of them there are," Sagarum mused. "What do you think happens when so much blood is spilled in one place at one time?"

"The earth remembers," Caelyn cut in, causing Tamlin to jump. "It brings them back, perhaps hoping that the next time the blood will not be spilled. Perhaps it just wants to remember, to cherish the life once more before it ceases."

Below them, the army of Kaegar began to fold, unable to take the shield wall. The corners of the defending army began to collapse, trapping the remaining attackers in a pincer. On the ground, hundreds of forms lay still, their ethereal bodies fading even as Tamlin watched.

Sagarum blinked. "Did you learn this in your abbey?"

Caelyn shook his head. "I've had other teachers in my life."

Finally, the last members of the attacking army fell, and the banners became still. As Tamlin gazed on, the victorious army vanished, leaving only an empty field.

"I wish men had the memory of the earth," Caelyn said. In the firelight, the monk's eyes glistened with emotion. "So much pain could have been avoided..."

"But the land is eternal," Sagarum said. "And mankind is mortal. Even so, what is life without struggle, if it is not death?"

"I do not know," Caelyn said. "The Eternal One help me, I just do not know. Perhaps some day I will."

The spectral armies did not return that night, at least not while Tamlin was awake. He actually managed to sleep, although when he woke up he couldn't remember any of his dreams.

They wandered across the empty field, carefully picking a path to avoid cutting themselves on old, rusted blades that might be poking through the earth. Of the ghostly soldiers from the night before, there was no trace. The brown grass merely rustled in the breeze.

People died here, Tamlin realized. *I saw them die. I watched their ghosts fight.*

Indeed, the ground seemed soiled somehow, a sense of death filling the air, even though the bodies had long since been disposed of, either by scavengers or on funeral pyres.

By midday they had crossed the old battlefield, and Tamlin breathed a sigh of relief. As they crossed the threshold, finding themselves on a cobbled Arcalien road, he felt his spirits rise. Far in the distance, he saw a small town, barely a speck on the horizon.

"Is that where we are going?" Tamlin asked.

Caelyn nodded. "I think the town is called Caer Danaan, if I remember correctly."

"That is an odd name," Tamlin mused.

"It is an ancient settlement," Sagarum said. "Older than the Arcalien Empire itself. Local legends says that it was founded by a group of powerful wizards named the Tuatha de Danaan."

Tamlin shook his head. "I've never heard of them."

Sagarum merely smiled. "There is truth to the folklore, I assure you. But the Tuatha de Danaan have long since departed the Western Lands."

"Where did they go?" Tamlin wondered.

Sagarum shrugged. "Who can say? All I know is that they are not here. Perhaps they left and traveled on the Great Road."

Tamlin turned to Caelyn, but the monk remained silent, his eyes fixed firmly on the road.

The sun had sunk down in the sky by the time they reached the walls of Caer Danaan. The ancient stone battlements reached into the sky, some of the stonework darker and newer than the rest.

"State your name and purpose," the guard at the great wooden gate demanded.

"I am Brother Caelyn, chronicler of the Abbey of Southmarch," the monk said. "This is Tamlin, my novice, and Sagarum, one of his tutors. I am on my pilgrimage, and we need a place to stop for the night."

The guard nodded. "Pass, friend. I apologize for the harsh reception, but only two days ago word came that we have lost a battle in the south against the Haneric Empire. We now fear we will have a problem with turncloaks."

Caelyn nodded kindly. "I understand. We shan't cause any trouble. May the Eternal One protect you."

"Same to you, brother," the guard said, stepping aside.

"He let us pass rather easily," Tamlin commented once they had stepped into the narrow streets.

"The Great Convention," Caelyn explained. "Not only is the Order of the Eternal One protected, but it is also sworn to neutrality. During wars, this means that the order can negotiate terms of peace, so nobody is willing to abuse the Convention."

"Almost sounds like an ideal life," Tamlin said.

Sagarum shook his head, his eyes playful. "Well, except for the issue of celibacy; I don't think I could ever manage that."

"It is not a life for everybody," Caelyn conceded.

They wandered through the old stone houses, looking for an inn. As the sun was setting they found one, named "Ye Olde Gathering Hole." They walked through the door into a full common room, finally finding a table in the corner farthest from the door. A serving maid sauntered up and took their orders, then left them to the entertainment.

"Can we get rooms here?" Tamlin asked, closing his eyes as a couple of musicians played a haunting melody on their pipes.

Caelyn nodded. "I've stayed here before. The old innkeeper passed on shortly before I joined the Order, but I imagine there are still lodgings to be had."

As the food arrived, two skalds stood up at the front of the room, one holding a fiddle and the other bearing a lyre. "It is a dark time," the bard with the lyre declared, "but we can all take heart! I will sing you a song of a darker day, when the evil armies of Kaegar roamed across the Western Lands, destroying all before them."

Tamlin noticed Caelyn stiffen. But before he could ask the monk what the matter was, the skald continued.

"A hero arose, a man who would stand against all the armies of Kaegar and free the world! I will sing of this man, of the battle at Godmarch field, and of the victory of Garwulf the Slayer!"

As the crowd erupted into cheers, Caelyn stood quietly and walked across the floor and out the door.

"What is wrong?" Tamlin asked Sagarum.

The wizard shrugged. "Old memories, I would say. Often the only ones singing of the battle afterwards are the skalds."

As the instruments played, the skald with the lyre began to sing:

The armies gathered at Godmarch field,

> *Dolgan of Kaegar directing troops,*
> *salting the field, killing the land.*
> *Bitter vengeance for battle-losses*
> *he would seek, striking with soldiers.*

Sagarum shook his head. "He sings as though it is all glory. The only ones who think that are the young warriors who have never been bloodied. They learn soon enough, though."

> *Dolgan turned, seeking Veltan,*
> *giving orders without mercy.*
> *"Kill them all, take no quarter,*
> *find Garwulf and take his head!"*

"But isn't there some glory?" Tamlin asked, scratching his chin.

"Glory doesn't matter to the dead," Sagarum stated. "The veteran soldiers, the true warriors, live for survival. If they can make it through the battle, they are lucky."

> *The battle began, armies marching,*
> *soldiers striking against the foe.*
> *Warriors fell, staining the soil,*
> *young blood dying as war raged.*
> *Garwulf came, bringing death,*
> *slaughtering foes with sword-swings.*
> *He spoke an ancient battle-cry:*
> *"Ic willan ofslean eow!"*

"The young blood, the 'warriors' out to make a name for themselves are dead within a quarter of an hour," Sagarum said.

"Only a quarter of an hour?"

"Just that," Sagarum confirmed. "Those who survive

73

that long at least stand a chance of living through the battle, assuming they've learned something. Otherwise, they'll feed the crows."

> *Veltan stood, ready for slaughter,*
> *thinking death to the death-bringer.*
> *In battle they met, swords swinging,*
> *neither meaning mercy to another.*
> *Garwulf's blade found Veltan's eye,*
> *pierced his brain, struck through bone,*
> *brought glory to Garwulf's name!*

"But surely there must be something good to come out of it all," Tamlin protested. "Otherwise, why would there be war?"

"Sometimes the bloodshed is necessary," Sagarum said. "The Kaegar Wars had to be fought – if they hadn't, the Western Lands would have suffered an inconceivable darkness. But nothing good comes from wars fought for glory."

> *Enraged to battle, Garwulf sought more,*
> *saw Dolgan directing soldiers.*
> *Garwulf charged, killing warriors,*
> *seeking the blood of the Kaegar leader.*
> *Dolgan turned, drew his steel,*
> *met Garwulf fighting in battle.*

"I wonder what he heard that disturbed him so much, though," Sagarum mused. "He didn't react this strongly to the spirit battle."

The skalds played more vigorously, bringing the music to a crescendo.

> *Long they fought, both meaning death,*

> *swords clashing in glorious battle.*
> *Bodies of the slain lay around them,*
> *alone they remained, struggling on the field,*
> *whoever won conquering Tarese.*

"I should go talk to him," Tamlin decided. With a start, he realized he had been tugging at his habit.

"Wait until the saga is over," Sagarum suggested, placing a hand on his shoulder. "It would be rude to leave in the middle."

> *Garwulf struck, sliced through muscle,*
> *severed Dolgan's head with swinging sword,*
> *the ancient blade spilling blood.*
> *Striking for freedom he slew Kaegar,*
> *ended the battle and restored the light!*

With a flourish, the bards set down their instruments and bowed. As the crowd gave a deafening cheer, Tamlin wove his way past the serving maids and a few patrons looking for facilities. Finally, walking through the door, he found Brother Caelyn sitting on a wooden bench just outside the inn.

"Is the song over?" the monk asked.

Tamlin nodded. "You walked out right after the skald mentioned Garwulf."

"Yes."

"You've fought against him, haven't you?"

Caelyn shook his head. "I fought beside Garwulf the Slayer in that very battle. I watched him slaughter enemies without mercy. The man was no hero; he was a soulless monster. Hearing him lauded like that made me feel sick."

"But he's long dead, isn't he?" Tamlin asked. "After all, nobody's seen him in decades. At least, that is what I've heard."

"Even if Garwulf is dead, his legacy remains," Caelyn said. "The butcher is remembered and praised for his violence. I don't know what is more horrifying: what Garwulf was, or what his legend has become."

Tamlin managed a faint smile as the strains of a bawdy song began to sound through the door. "I think they've finished singing about Garwulf. Do you want to come back in and join us?"

Caelyn shook his head. "I think I want to pray for a while."

Tamlin nodded. "We'll be waiting for you when you come in."

With that, the young man strode back into the inn, leaving Caelyn to his memories, demons, and prayers.

Caelyn returned to the common room a few minutes later, the horrific memories under control again. As he stepped into the crowd, he took a deep breath. Then with a steady, controlled gait, he strode to his companions and took a seat.

"Tamlin told me about your experience," Sagarum said. "I had no idea the song would cause you this much pain."

Caelyn nodded. "Even after three decades, they are still horrifying. If you will excuse me, I would prefer not to talk about it."

"Fair enough," Sagarum declared, and the monk relaxed in his chair. "The mead here is quite good, as is the wine."

Suddenly, a commotion sounded from the door. Caelyn turned to see a tall man in the livery of a herald call for attention.

"The city of Taree has been destroyed, and all who dwelled there have been slaughtered!" the herald declared.

Blinking, Caelyn leaned forward to regard the man. The messenger's eyes had a glazed look, as though he couldn't believe the news that he shared.

"An army, supported by vile magic, has annihilated our forces," the herald continued. "The royal house is in exile, trying to raise support. All those who would help drive out the invaders, and avenge our great capital, must meet in the hills to the west outside the city, just north of the old battlefield."

Caelyn digested the news quietly, his face impassive, and regarded his companions. While Tamlin looked around, disbelief in his eyes, Sagarum leaned back, lost in thought. Around them, the noise of the common room died down into an uncomfortable silence as the messenger stepped out.

"What does it mean?" Tamlin blurt out.

"It means that there is no longer a nation of Tarese," Caelyn said. "It means that our lives have just become interesting."

"The reports suggest that an Archmagus is leading the army," Sagarum noted. "He'll be able to sense us if he is close enough."

Tamlin blinked. "I don't understand."

"When one becomes an Archmagus, one comes into incredible power. You could say one becomes a creature of power. And one creature of power can always sense another."

"But we can trust the Great Convention to protect us, can't we?" Tamlin said. "Can't we?"

Caelyn leaned back, pursing his lips as he stroked his beard. "We shall have to, if we are to continue on our way. But the Haneric army has already broken one part of the Great Convention, so we cannot be certain."

"How can you be so calm about this?" Tamlin demanded. "Our lives could be in jeopardy!"

"Panicking will not make anything better," Caelyn said. "Perhaps if we can make our way quickly to the north, we can find a neutral trader to take us by ship to eastern Bandre. Hopefully the war won't have reached there yet."

"We're still vulnerable," Sagarum stated. "That will be a difficulty."

Caelyn nodded, noting the young man and two women who had just entered the common room. Although the man himself was little more than a peasant boy, tall, dark haired, and wearing plain-cut woolen clothes, and one of the women, a shorter, sandy haired slip of a girl, was similarly attired, the second woman was tall, powerful, and dressed for war. A coat of mail shone beneath her cloak, and a sword rested in a sheath on her hip. The three newcomers spoke amongst themselves for a moment, and then walked purposefully over to his table.

Caelyn turned to face her and politely asked: "Can I help you?"

The warrior woman nodded. "Brother, we need to talk."

Part II:
The Exiles

Chapter I — Exile

Brodin forced himself to sort the herbs with care, cold fear dogging his every breath. The High Druid had come to his village, and it was time for the fertility rites.

"Make certain they are properly dried," Mylla instructed. "Once they're wet, they can't be used again." The healer regarded him with old, sage eyes, but Brodin's mind was elsewhere. The Harvester only took young virgins, and that meant that Telena was in danger. He jumped as the candle sputtered beside him. If the Druid was here, then the assembly would have been called for that afternoon.

At least the Druid only came to this part of Beregar once every five years. In a year, he and Telena would be of marriageable age, and they would be able to consummate their love. Then she would be out of danger. But first they had to survive this year, and no matter what he tried to tell himself, the terror remained.

"If your mind is not on these herbs, then you should not be here," Mylla said.

"I'm sorry," Brodin stammered. "I'm just worried about Telena."

Mylla sighed, her eyes softening. "Yes, I remember young love. Go then. Spend time with her before the assembly. And once the Harvester has chosen his maiden, we can all get back to our lives."

"I'll be back tomorrow," Brodin called, already out the door into the late summer rain. Pulling on a cloak, he dashed past several cottages, the thatched roofs wet and smelling of manure. Heart pounding, he reached Telena's house, and knocked on the pine door.

The door opened, and Telena flew into his arms. He stroked her sandy hair, crushing her slim form against his breast.

Finally, she looked up and wiped a tear from his eye. "I do not know who is more afraid; you or I."

"I just wish the Druid had not come," Brodin said. "Why anybody follows him is beyond me. Wherever he goes, he brings death."

"He also brings life," Telena added, pushing herself closer to him. "Without him, the Harvester would let us starve."

"I want us to leave," Brodin declared. "Once we're married, I don't want our children to fear every time the Druid comes."

Telena nodded. "We'll wed, and then we'll go. Surely the Harvester doesn't hold power everywhere."

Somebody cleared their throat from inside. "Child," Telena's mother said, stepping out from the shadows to stand by the door. "You have to get ready. The Druid has called the assembly, and you must present yourself."

Telena kissed Brodin chastely. "I won't leave you," she promised. "After this, we'll be together always."

Brodin felt a tear roll down his cheek as he let her go and the door closed after her. Telena had always been truthful; it was one of the reasons he loved her. But, on this day her words seemed hollow. He swallowed. There were plenty of girls for the Harvester to take this year, and he was probably afraid for no reason. After all, where love was concerned, these things always worked out in the end.

Didn't they?

Brodin watched the Druid stand in the holy circle, facing the congregation of young girls. Around them stood a group of villagers, looking on anxiously, each parent no doubt praying that their daughter would not be the chosen one. The large monolithic rocks jutted out of the earth, and Brodin had once heard that the druids also used the holy circles to measure the sun. On this day, however, the old man had a more deadly purpose.

The Druid always surprised Brodin. The first time he had seen the holy man come, he had expected a young man, filled with life. Instead, the Druid appeared ancient, with kind, caring eyes. If he hadn't known better, he would never have thought the Druid capable of human sacrifice.

But five years ago, against his father's orders, he had snuck into the holy circle after the victim had been chosen. He had watched in horror as she was bound naked to a slab, and then slaughtered like an animal, the Druid chanting in an arcane tongue as he drew the knife across her throat. He had bolted in terror that day, and his parents had spent almost a week trying to console him. Very soon after, he had fallen for Telena, and the two had taken to each other as though they had always been right together, much to the amusement of the rest of the village.

The Druid cleared his throat, and turned to face the villagers. "We are gathered here this day to pay homage to the Harvester. The Harvester feeds us, for he is the earth. And the Harvester claims us in our twilight hours, for he is nature, and nature is both life and death."

He pointed his gnarled staff towards the young girls. "One of the pure must be chosen," he intoned. "A virgin will be given to him. Two days from now, in this place, we will send her to be his handmaiden. Let the Harvester choose his maiden now."

He closed his eyes and began to wave the staff before him. For Brodin, time slowed, every heartbeat thundering in his ears.

The Druid stayed his hand and opened his eyes. Brodin's heart leapt into his mouth, and he would have whispered a desperate prayer, if he knew of some other god that would listen. But he didn't.

The Druid's staff pointed directly at Telena.

Two of the village elders took Telena by the arms and led her away. The rest of the congregation sighed in relief, thanking the Harvester that it was not their daughter who would be sacrificed.

As Brodin struggled to remain standing, his legs shaking in fear, rage, and sorrow, an idea came full-formed into his mind. Perhaps there was a chance. But he would have to act quickly, before the Druid began the preliminary rites that would bind Telena to the Harvester before she was dragged to the altar.

He broke into a run as he started back towards the village.

Telena's house had been put under guard, and it was only thanks to her mother that Brodin was able to enter. Their families had been friends for years, and when Brodin had fallen in love with their daughter, they had welcomed him as though he was already a kinsman.

Telena's mother cast a wary glance at Brodin as she took him to Telena's room. Brodin could not be certain, but from the bloodshot eyes, it appeared she had been crying. "You should say goodbye as gently as possible," she said. "It will be hard enough for Telena as it is. I will be outside, to ensure that there are no indiscretions. The Druid will come for her tomorrow morning to begin the first rites and check her purity."

Brodin mumbled his thanks as she opened the door. Telena sat dejected on her bed, tears flowing down her cheeks. He sat down beside Telena and embraced her, but she seemed too frail to return the hug.

"I don't want to lose you," Telena sobbed. "I told them I don't want to go. But they told me I have to. They told me it would be a great honor. They didn't listen."

"I have an idea," Brodin whispered in her ear. "You won't have to go."

She looked up. "What do you mean?"

"The Harvester can't take you if you aren't pure."

Telena shook her head. "It would not be proper."

"Proper be damned!" Brodin whispered. "I love you more than my life. I would rather die than lose you. We have a chance to live together. If I take your maidenhood, the village elders have to marry us."

"And how could we possibly stay here?" Telena demanded, her voice low. "We would be a disgrace."

"We'll leave."

She paused for a moment, then nodded. "I would rather be living with you than dead without you. But how will we get past my mother?"

Brodin looked around the room, his gaze finally resting on the window pane. The shutters had been left open, the crimson glow of the setting sun wafting in, the Druid relying on fear and Telena's honor to keep her from escape. Brodin motioned to the opening, and Telena nodded. He climbed out first, giving her a hand down.

They glanced around, seeing that nobody was in sight,

and sprinted to the nearby treeline. Brodin had taken Telena to gather flowers several times in the small woodland during the summer, and it was familiar to both of them. They found a deep gully that they knew was hidden from the scrying eyes of the village, and rested until the sun had finished setting, keeping a careful watch for any pursuers.

Brodin felt as though they had waited for hours, but nobody came. If a search was in progress, it had not come into their part of the wood. The darkness itself was a godsend; many of the older villagers feared the spirits of the night, and would not set out until morning.

"I think we're safe," Telena said, kissing Brodin. He held her close, gently cupping one of her breasts, his manhood rising as her kisses became more passionate.

With tenderness and uncertainty, they undressed each other and made love. Telena grimaced slightly as Brodin entered her, but then moaned in pleasure as they climaxed together. Then they lay in the dark, spent, holding each other as though there would not be another morning.

Once he had drifted to sleep in her arms, Brodin dreamt of vast armies marching across an alien landscape. He saw unknown mountains rise above him, and sailed on strange seas. Then something was shaking him, and he started awake.

Telena was clutching at him in terror, but the morning sun was directly in his eyes, and his vision was blurred. Something cast a shadow over him, and his heart nearly stopped. They were surrounded by the villagers, the Ealdorman and Druid both present and glaring at them.

The hearth fire in the Ealdorman's house flared up for a moment, casting the room in a harsh light. Brodin and Telena, both fully dressed at the Druid's orders, stood before the council of Elders. Brodin swallowed nervously; he had seen this gathering before – it was a council of judgement.

"Does the chosen one retain her purity?" the Ealdorman demanded, turning to the Druid. The Druid rose from his seat and walked slowly to Telena. With a sudden motion, he thrust his hand between her legs, causing her to cry out in surprise and alarm.

Brodin forced down the urge to leap forward and push the Druid away from her. She was his now, in all but one sense of the word, and the last thing he wanted was to see the woman he loved hurt.

The Druid took his hand away, and turned to the council. "She carries no child," he reported, "but she is no longer pure."

The Ealdorman's face became stony. "I see. Can this be rectified?"

The Druid shook his head. "This is not an act that can be undone. She had known a man, and is not a suitable consort of the Harvester."

"Can another be chosen?"

"Not from this village," the Druid said, stepping towards the exit. "Your young man has disgraced you all in front of that which is most holy. Perhaps I can find something to placate the Harvester in another village, Ealdorman Seamys, but that is uncertain at best. I will do what I can and return. If I find that justice has not been done here, then this place will be cursed."

Ealdorman Seamys waited until the Druid had left, then turned to his council. "I will deal with this matter personally," he said. "We will reconvene tomorrow to discuss the harvest."

There was a murmur of assent, and the council filed out. Finally, the Ealdorman leaned forward to regard Brodin and Telena.

"By all rights, I should have you burned at the stake!" he roared, causing both of them to leap back in alarm. "You have shamed your families, disgraced the village, and perhaps cursed the land. Do you have anything to say for yourselves?"

Brodin swallowed and tried to think of something, but it was Telena who spoke. "We're in love, and we could not bear to be apart."

Seamys glared at them both with his implacable brown eyes, then sat back and scratched his greying beard.

"If it were any other reason," he said, "I would have you both executed immediately. However, I too was once young and in love, and while I cannot approve of what you have done, I can at least understand it."

"Then we won't be killed?" Brodin ventured nervously.

"I didn't say that," Seamys stated. "You have still done something unforgivable, and there will be harsh consequences. Know now that you are both dead in the eyes of this village, this region, and the whole of Beregar. You must be gone by dusk, you may find no help from those you once called friends or family, and if you are found in the realm after the end of this moon, you will be executed on sight. Am I clear?"

Brodin and Telena nodded.

"I would suggest you travel through the mountains to the north to the heathen lands," the Ealdorman said. "Perhaps there you can have something resembling a life. Assuming, of course, they don't decide to kill you themselves. Now get out of my sight!"

Brodin and Telena bolted from the room. As they took to the woodland, leaving the village behind, Brodin both blessed and cursed his luck. They were alive, but they were exiled and alone. All they could do now was hope that they would survive.

Chapter II — Survival

Brodin and Telena gazed up at the great mountains jutting out before them. The immense peaks towered over the forest, the treeline rising several thousand feet on the rockface before tapering off to naked stone. The late afternoon sun cast the mountains in a harsh light, giving the entire range a sinister appearance as the shadows deepened.

Telena's stomach grumbled, and she suddenly had to steady herself against a tree. With a pleading look, she glanced at her beloved, but he stood motionless, transfixed by the sight.

"We need to rest, Brodin," she said. "I can't go up there tonight. I'm too tired."

Brodin shook his head. "They're so big. How could anybody cross them?"

They had been traveling for just over a week, resting only when it was too dark to move on. They lived off the land, eating what little nourishment they could find. Four days ago, some of the berries had made Telena sick to her stomach, forcing them to mark the fruit as poisonous and move on. She had felt nauseous for almost two days.

But they were running out of time. The moon had begun to wane, and Telena knew that Ealdorman Seamys would have sent riders to all of the villages, warning them about the two fugitives that had been declared dead.

"We'll go between those two mountains," Brodin said, pointing at a gap. "That should take us out of Beregar."

Telena shook her head. "Rest first."

He reached out and held her close, her head resting on his chest. As she listened to the beating of his heart, her hunger became bearable, but still present.

"All right," he said. "We'll rest first."

They chose a large oak tree to camp under, and then began to forage for food. The trees were depressingly barren, and Telena's mind kept going back to the life she had left behind.

Her mother must have been in tears, she realized. She had not even been allowed to say farewell. It would have been crushing for her – Telena was her only child.

But no matter what, she would have been dead by now. Either cut open by the Druid's knife, or declared dead by the village. At least this way she had a chance to start over.

She looked over at Brodin, but his face was impassive. He seemed to be handling the exile well, but this was not his first loss. His mother had been slain by the plague last winter.

"Telena, look!" Brodin called, motioning to her from behind a tree. She stepped over, avoiding the brambles that snagged at her already ragged shoes and dress. Brodin hadn't fared much better; his jerkin and breeches were torn in a dozen places, and while Telena found the rugged look appealing, she had to fight down the urge to take his clothes and start mending.

I'm becoming a wife already, she thought, amused and startled. But taking care of Brodin was a far more attractive idea than the possibility of starvation.

She looked at the side of the tree, and her eyes widened. An enormous mushroom sprouted from a crack in the rough bark, right at the level of her nose. It had to be bigger than both of her fists put together. Inhaling slightly, she caught a musky scent on the breeze.

"Do you think it's safe?" she asked.

Brodin plucked it from the wood and tore a bit off. He popped the piece into his mouth, chewed, and swallowed. Then they waited, Telena hoping that it wouldn't cause him to collapse in agony.

"I feel fine," Brodin stated after a couple of moments.

They divided the mushroom in half and ate. It didn't fill her up, but it did stave off the pangs enough that she could rest.

Holding each other, they returned to the oak. As the sun began to set, basking the world in a gentle glow, they lay down and curled up beside each other. Telena took comfort in Brodin's warmth, wishing that she could hold him in her arms forever.

Finally, she drifted off to sleep, her dreams filled with warm thoughts.

They arose at the crack of dawn, Brodin leaving Telena briefly to find some food before they tackled the great mountains ahead. After they had eaten what little he could find, they began to walk, keeping the gap between the two towering peaks before them.

As they traveled, the trees became sparse, the ground steepening. With a start, Telena realized that they must have climbed several hundred feet already. Indeed, when

91

she looked back, she saw the green fields and woods of Beregar stretched out before her, the villages little more than tiny specks on the land. Turning back to the journey, she followed Brodin along the rocky earth, the brambles from the forest replaced by loose rocks that threatened to topple and send them sliding down the slope.

Still, they strode onwards. The path led them between giant cliffs, the towering stone crackling around them. Every now and then small rocks fell around them, Telena turning nervously to look behind them each time. They moved in silence, making each step as quiet as possible.

Telena started as a rock dropped beside her. When she looked back, all she could see was the path winding between the mountains. Of Beregar there was no sign; not even a single green field remained in sight. Spinning on her heels, she picked up the pace, surprising Brodin as she passed him.

The sun had nearly set by the time they made camp that night, placing themselves cautiously beneath an ancient outcropping. Telena wondered if there was an end to the pass. All she could see in the murky shadows was the sides of the two great peaks, stretching off into the distance. There wasn't a single sign of life; the mere glimpse of an eagle or owl gliding above them would have caused her heart to flutter in joy.

That night, surrounded only by the hoary stone, they made love in silence, hoping it would not be for the last time. Finally, they fell into each other's arms and slept.

Telena felt lightheaded in the morning, and several times she shivered against the chill. Even though much of the pass was cast in shadow, when she looked back she saw it twisting and turning for miles like a sinewy snake. With a start, she wondered how high they actually were. When she gazed forward, the rocky road continued to climb.

Brodin hugged her and she pulled him closer, not wanting to let go. "We should start walking," he whispered. "It can't be too much farther."

She nodded, her stomach growling. It had better not be more than a couple of days, she reflected, or they would die of thirst or starvation. When she gazed into his deep eyes, she realized that his thoughts matched her own.

They set out, wrapping their meager clothes around them, hoping to fend off the chill. They kept close to one another, frequently walking while embraced, using each other's body heat to keep warm.

And as the sun rose high into the sky, the path continued to climb.

Telena found her mind wandering, thinking of her family again, and what they must be doing right now. Probably preparing for the harvest, trying unsuccessfully to put their wayward daughter out of their minds. She couldn't believe that they would forget her, and she hoped they would not soon have cause to mourn her.

Brodin pulled her to the side, snapping her back to the present. Telena started, noticing for the first time the deep, wide chasm that opened up before them. She swallowed, her throat dry; if she had kept walking, she would have fallen in.

Brodin took the lead as they made their way along the increasingly narrow ledge. The crevice widened as they moved, pushing the side of the path farther and farther, until the cliff face lay off in the distance.

Telena shook her head, trying to clear it. It was becoming difficult to think, and even breathing was an effort. The pass, at least, had leveled off, running parallel to the distant rock face. Close to the horizon, she saw what appeared to be the soft waves of the sea.

Her heart leapt in her chest. There was an end to the

pass! There was a world outside of Beregar!

Something caught her eye, and she turned to gaze at the distant cliff. She stepped back in shock, pressing her back to the cold rock face. Brodin looked at her quizzically for a moment, but his attention was caught when he glanced where she was looking.

On the distant rock, ancient figures were carved, regal giants with long beards on decorated thrones bearing weapons of war. Several smaller pictures surrounded the old kings, the eroded stone depicting great battles against inhuman foes. Along both sides of the carving, there stood several symbols, but they were so worn that whatever they had once said was lost in eternity.

"The ancient gods?" Telena breathed, completely awestruck.

Brodin shook his head. "I don't know. It could be older than Beregar itself."

After a few moments, they turned and continued on their way, leaving the ancient and forgotten carving behind them.

After several hours, once the chasm had closed up, the mountain pass began to slope downwards, and Telena found herself stumbling several times as the incline became steeper. She found it easier to breathe the longer the descent continued, and by the time they stopped for the night, barely able to see the road ahead in the darkness, it had warmed considerably.

They slept in each other's arms, rising at dawn to find themselves facing a gentle slope twisting and turning until it terminated on a great blue sea. Already, Telena could smell the salty air, and her heart soared.

They still moved with caution – neither of them wanted to slip and cause an injury. But the end was in sight, and it gave them hope, their hunger becoming something small and insignificant.

Clouds formed on the horizon, and soon they were pelted with a soft rain. Telena wrapped herself in her dress and pushed up against Brodin, trying to keep warm. Still they strode onward, coming closer to a new life with every step.

Finally, the rocky pass opened out into a light forest, the gentle incline giving them a majestic vision of green fields and open water. At the shore lay a grand city surrounded by white walls, the spires and shingled roofs unlike anything they had ever seen before.

Telena leapt up and embraced Brodin, kissing him passionately. "We made it," she said, again and again. "We made it!"

Chapter III — New Friends

Jyhanna was sitting at a corner table of Balin's Tavern when the pair arrived. They staggered in, every step haggard and tired. She ran a measured gaze over each one.

They were both wearing ragged clothes that were once probably quite nice. The man was tall and dark haired, his face covered with dust and the downy growth of his first beard. The woman, barely more than a girl, was shorter and thin, with sandy hair. She clutched at the man as though she might lose him at any moment.

Jyhanna sipped her ale, shaking her head. She recognized the look in their eyes immediately. They were exiles. Just like her.

Unbidden, the memories returned. She had led her father's army once, been both a princess and shield maiden of great renown. Her people had cheered her in the streets.

And then, in what seemed less than a heartbeat, everything changed. Her father's new advisor, the thrice-damned wizard Gesanus, had slickly taken her place at court. Within days, he had captured the king's ear, and his "wayward daughter" found herself exiled and hunted in her own kingdom.

Even now, Jyhanna didn't know what spell had been cast over King Lewys, but somehow she would find out. Even if it took her an entire lifetime, she would free her father and reclaim her place at his side. She might not be Garwulf the Slayer, but once she had a way back into Toregien, she would see Gesanus' head upon a pike.

She smiled in spite of herself. Grand words, grand gestures. But in the end, she was still a powerless exile, with only some money, a battered coat of mail, and a sword to her name. If she actually returned to Toregien, she would face a death sentence. At least she could make a living for herself as a sellsword, which appeared to be more than the young exiles could.

Jyhanna turned back to the newcomers. The man had stepped up to the bar, looked around, and waited for the barkeep. Finally, the burly man turned and ambled over to greet him, cleaning a flagon with a stained rag.

"Can I buy some food here?" the young exile asked, speaking with a heavy brogue.

"Best food in Kaplan's Peak," the barkeep growled. "Best ale too." Jyhanna suppressed a grin and looked down at her drink. She had never tasted horse piss, but surely the ale had to be close.

"We've traveled a long way, and we need food," the young man said.

"Silver up front," the barkeep demanded.

"Sorry?"

"Are you deaf?" the man asked, placing the flagon carefully on the bar. "Show me some coin, or you'll have no food."

"Surely, there's some bread..."

"The bread takes time to make, and time is money.

You want to eat, you show me some silver." The bartender paused for a moment, eyeballing the girl. "Or, you could let me have a tumble with your woman there."

The young woman recoiled in horror.

Jyhanna stood up and strode to the bar. "I'll pay for their food," she declared, placing two gold crowns on the oaken table. "And make it the best you've got. Not the mule shit you tried to pass off on me."

The barkeep feigned offense, but placed a slab of bread on a plate and handed it to Jyhanna. "I'll bring the meat to your table," he growled.

Jyhanna nodded. "That will do."

She led the two exiles to her table and sat down. They stared at her for a moment, obviously uncertain of what to do next.

Jyhanna cut the loaf into two halves, and passed one to each. "My name is Jyhanna, most recently of Tarese. Who are you?"

"Brodin," the young man said, swallowing some bread. "And my love is named Telena."

"I don't recognize the accent," Jyhanna mused. "Where are you two from?"

"Beregar," Telena replied, her brogue just as strong as Brodin's. She stuffed the rest of the bread in her mouth.

"I can't say I've heard of that land," Jyhanna stated. "Where is it?"

"Southeast, through the mountains," Brodin said.

"Does this land worship the Harvester?" Telena cut in. Jyhanna blinked. The girl's voice had actually quaked with fear.

"No, we all worship the Eternal One. Who is the Harvester?"

"A horrible god that demands human sacrifices," Brodin said. "We were exiled when we opposed Him."

Jyhanna nodded. "I see. Hmm...I had no idea there was

anything beyond the mountains, much less a land worshiping a blood god. Everything I have heard has said that the Great Peaks are impassable." She leaned forward. "Do you know where you are?"

Brodin shook his head.

"You are in the city of Kaplan's Peak," Jyhanna explained as the barkeep finally came with a plate of steaming mutton. "It is one of the Free City States, a port on the Inner Sea. One of the few places that does not seem to be at war right now."

"War?" Telena mumbled, trying to talk while stuffing part of the tender cut of lamb into her mouth.

"Yes. For some strange reason, suddenly several nations have decided to invade each other. It means there is a lot of work for a sellsword like myself."

There was a moment of silence while Jyhanna sipped her ale, wincing at the foul taste, and Brodin and Telena eagerly demolished the mutton.

"So what are you going to do now?" Jyhanna asked, watching the two young lovers lean back, their hunger sated.

"We want to start a farm," Telena said. "Is there some land we can settle?"

Jyhanna shook her head. "Not around here. The free city states don't have any fertile land; they rely entirely on trade for survival. You might find some in Tarese. So far the war hasn't touched there."

"How far away is that?" Brodin asked.

"Not too far," Jyhanna replied. "Perhaps three or four days journey. You'll need some proper clothes and protection, though. These days, the roads are dangerous. Lots of brigands trying to earn a living off the war."

Brodin leaned forward. "Will you help us? Please?"

Jyhanna raised an eyebrow. "You have no money. For that matter, you don't really seem to have any workable clothes."

"We'll do something to earn our keep," Telena promised. "Anything!"

Jyhanna scratched her chin, wondering if she was going crazy as she came to her decision. "Ordinarily I'd refuse, but I too know what it is to be an exile. Very well. I will get you some new clothes and see you to Tarese. Once you have your farm, you can pay me whatever you wish."

She smiled as Brodin nodded eagerly, licking his lips. There was something refreshing about these two youngsters, something she had long forgotten could exist. For the first time in years, she saw the innocence of youth.

The clothes turned out to be a more difficult task than Jyhanna thought. Not only was Brodin too tall to fit into the woolen tunics most merchants sold, but Telena was still just a slip of a girl, and in that age where she was too developed for a girl's dress, but too small for an adult fit.

Finally, after an entire afternoon of searching in the local market, she was able to find some clothes for the two. Brodin ended up with a grey tunic, dark trousers, and a brown cloak, while Telena wore a warm shapeless blue dress, belted at the waist. Finding traveler's packs for each was much easier, and she showed them how to sling the bag over the shoulder to make it easier to bear.

The sun was low in the sky by the time they finished, and Jyhanna took a moment to gaze out from the market square and regard the docks, framed by the spires of government buildings. The harbor was overshadowed by the tall ships, sailors climbing rigging and battening down the decks, preparing either to sail or stay for the night.

Brodin breathed a sigh of wonderment. "I've never seen a seaport before."

"This is one of the largest," Jyhanna said. "There hasn't been anything this grand since Kaegar. There are ships here from every nation and city-state. Even during wars, Kaplan's Peak is neutral, though the harbor master makes a point of keeping the vessels of those involved far from each other."

"Then we could sail anywhere in the world from here?" Telena asked, her fingers pressed to her lips in awe.

Jyhanna nodded, shivering for a moment as the sea air brought a chill breeze. A distant crack sounded in the wind, and she turned her gaze to the horizon. Two ships had drawn together, one flying the blue and white standard of Bandre, the other carrying the red and green of Fenegar. Between the two vessels, several ropes had been thrown.

"What is happening?" Brodin asked, pointing at the ships.

"Unbelievable," Jyhanna breathed. "It's a battle, in Kaplani waters."

"Who are they?"

"The one on the left is from Bandre," she replied. "The vessel on the right is from Fenegar. I know the two are at war, but this is unheard of; Kaplan's Peak is neutral, and the Great Convention denies any the right to fight on neutral land or water."

From the Bandrian ship, she saw a glittering of metal, and several small forms fall into the water. Jyhanna swallowed. One or two of them had definitely been maimed bodies. What would happen when the sailors from the victorious ship came ashore? Would they be arrested, or cause a bloodbath in the city streets?

There was another crack, and the foremast of the Bandrian vessel crashed into the water, taking at least three archers with it. Still more people poured over the side from the Fenegarian caravel, weapons glinting in the late afternoon sun.

"Why do they fight like that?" Telena wondered.

"One ship probably failed a ramming attempt," Jyhanna explained, turning to regard the two. They were now joined as the entire marketplace stopped to watch the seaborne battle. "At sea, if you can't sink the enemy by ramming them, you pull up beside them, grapple your vessel to theirs, and kill every last one of them. *Then* you sink their ship."

She saw Telena shudder, and then returned to gaze out at the water. Thin wisps of smoke began to rise from the Bandrian caravel, an almost picturesque sight. The tiny forms scrambled back across, abandoning the ship. She pursed her lips. It would be the end soon; once the ship was alight and the fire had truly caught, there was little the survivors could do but jump overboard and hope that the current wouldn't sweep them off to a watery grave. This would be the critical moment in the battle; if the other vessel wasn't fast enough, it would also begin to burn.

As the Fenegarian caravel pulled out, the sailors unfurling the white linen sails and tacking them to catch the wind, the other ship became consumed by fire. The flames belched out from the deck, leaping up the masts and along the furled linen. One or two fiery figures leapt into the sea, but that was all. The caravel burned, the smoke rising upwards, a blotch against the blue sky.

Jyhanna suppressed a shudder. She had heard stories of the fates of those lost at sea, especially those taken in battle. They became bloated corpses, eaten by whatever sea creatures were nearby, or, even worse, were conscripted to sail for all eternity on the ghost ship of Sarn, unable to ever find peace. Better to perish in battle on land; that, at least, was a clean death.

"What did it all mean?" she heard Telena mutter, and when she turned the girl was shaking her head in bewilderment. Jyhanna grimaced. She still remembered the sight of her first battle when she had only just become a shield-maiden; how she'd walked amongst the corpses, barely able to contain her nausea as she was surrounded by the fecid stench of death, half expecting the fallen to get back up again and return to their comrades.

"It means that the world is going mad around us," Jyhanna said. "Come. You can share my room at the inn tonight, and tomorrow morning I'll try to take you somewhere away from all this where you can be safe."

With that, she led them from the city marketplace, where the passers-by still stood, watching a tall ship burn and sink.

Chapter IV — Legacies

Brodin could no longer deny it: he was in a different world. Gone were the certainties of Beregar; the realm he had once thought he knew had vanished like so much mist into a larger, grander land. It was awe-inspiring and terrifying at the same time.

Since he had left Kaplan's Peak, he had seen a number of new things, each more wondrous than the last. He walked along the road, winding his way over towering cliffs, looking on as the waves crashed below, the salty spray leaping so high he could almost taste it. Three days after setting out, they had entered Tarese, and he saw fertile fields, just now in the process of being harvested. Each village they passed was crowned by a tall stone castle, usually on a man-made hill and surrounded by a deep moat. But every time they came to request an audience with the local lord, they were told that the noble was busy or away on matters of state.

Despite the constant setbacks, he smiled, gazing at the

two people beside him. Telena, his love, walked with him arm-in-arm, and the strange warrior woman, Jyhanna, guided them down the road, occasionally noting objects of interest.

The path was long and winding, a cobblestone way that was laid down over a millennia ago by the Arcalien Empire. Jyhanna told them that it was maintained by Tarese, but it had been built so solidly that very little was actually required.

After a while, it became too much for Brodin. Telena had listened carefully as Jyhanna spoke of a multitude of strange names, but Brodin could not stand being in the dark any longer.

"But what was the Arcalien Empire?" he blurted.

He saw Jyhanna sigh.

"Around fifteen hundred years ago, the city of Arcalus began to expand," Jyhanna explained. "They conquered the lands around them, and rather than treating them like vassals, made them equals in their government. That was the founding of the Arcalien Empire. The Council of Archmagi crowned Hanarsus the Emperor, and our calender begins on that date."

Brodin scratched his head. "So this would be..."

"This year was the Common Year fifteen hundred and eighty four. It had been almost sixteen centuries since Hanarsus was crowned, and almost eight hundred years since the empire fell. At its peak, the empire contained all of the lands around the Inner Sea, and the Haneric Empire."

"But what happened?"

"The same thing that always happens when a nation becomes too large," Jyhanna said, wiping her brow as the first drops of a chill rain began to fall. "Each province had a different vision of what the empire should be, and the Emperor became too weak to control them all. Finally, the empire just collapsed. Every nation I have visited has shared its legacy, though. Even though we claim we are from different nations, we are all Arcalien in spirit. At least, that is what our leaders say."

Although Brodin wasn't certain, he detected both bitterness and sorrow in her last sentence. Frowning at Jyhanna's tone, he held Telena closer to himself for comfort. Around them, the rain became a downpour, forcing them into the shelter of a nearby copse of trees.

"Do you think we'll find somebody who will give us some land soon?" Telena asked, wrapping her cloak around herself and snuggling up to Brodin.

"They won't just 'give' you the land," Jyhanna said. "It isn't quite that simple. Any landowner in Tarese has a responsibility to the king for military service and support. Most people can't afford that, and don't want to be called away from their harvest to go fight in some country they've never heard of.

"What will happen is you will be asked to sign a contract with one of the local lords. In return for farming a portion of his property and giving him a certain share of the harvest, he will protect you from the levy and from any invaders that should arrive. Should you not be able to produce enough to live, he will feed you from his own coffers. It is called a 'feudal contract.'"

"Would we be able to travel, and see the world?" Brodin asked.

Jyhanna shook her head. "Probably not. The lord might allow you some time during the winter or summer, when another vassal can work your share of the land, but it is unlikely. However, you are allowed to buy your way out of a contract, if you have enough wealth."

"That doesn't sound terribly good," Brodin muttered.

"If the Arcalien Empire still stood, it would be better," Jyhanna conceded. "But for those who work the land, right now a feudal contract is the only means of assuring security and stability. It is better than it sounds, and Tarese is a good nation to live in. I have heard that peasants in Bandre have to give the right of first night to their lord." She shuddered. "Absolutely horrible."

"What is 'first night'?" Telena asked.

"The lord gets to bed a new wife before her husband does," Jyhanna answered.

"Oh."

"Is the world more complicated than you had thought it would be?" Jyhanna inquired, a mischievous smile on her face.

Brodin shook his head. "I had hoped for something better than we had left, but I never thought it would be any simpler."

"I only want to find a place and settle," Telena cut in. "Just Brodin and I, raising a family."

"Simple dreams," Jyhanna mused. "There's nobility in that. But what comes after you fulfill your dream? Do you sit, content, or do you keep dreaming?"

Brodin shrugged. "We haven't gotten that far. What about you?"

"I keep dreaming," Jyhanna replied. "The day I stop dreaming is the day I die."

The rain slacked off around sunset, and they made their camp in the middle of the copse. Jyhanna lit a small campfire and kept a careful watch, smiling slightly as she heard muffled moans of passion from behind a couple of trees. Although some priests would not say so, they were innocents; they hadn't been corrupted and made bitter by the world.

For a moment she wondered where her own innocence had fled. It hadn't been with that young noble who had courted her just after she had become an officer in the army, regardless of how good it had felt. No, she had lost her innocence long before, when she had learned that true love was a myth in the circles of the nobility, and that her family name was more important to a potential husband than any passion she could ever show.

She saw Brodin and Telena step out from the old elm, both looking disheveled and flushed.

"Finished your business?" Jyhanna asked, raising an eyebrow.

Brodin nodded and Telena smiled.

"Better get some sleep, then," she said, gazing up to the waning moon. "There are only a few more hours before dawn."

"Won't you need some rest as well?" Telena asked. "We'd be happy to keep watch for you."

Jyhanna shook her head. "What would you do if a brigand did come? You don't know how to fight, and you both need the protection more than I. We will be coming to a small village tomorrow, and we can stay at an inn that night. Tonight, though, don't worry about me."

They nodded and bedded down, curling up into each other's arms. Jyhanna smiled again as she watched them sleep. True love. True innocence. Something to protect at all costs.

They awoke with the dawn. Telena stretched, yawning as the last vestiges of sleep fled from her eyes. Beside her, Brodin smiled and snuggled close. When she finally broke away from his embrace and rose, her lover dashing off to take care fo some business, she saw Jyhanna sitting, her back to an old elm tree. The shield-maiden's eyes were closed, and she seemed to be breathing deeply.

But as Telena approached, Jyhanna opened her eyes

and gazed right at her. "Did you sleep well?" she asked.

Telena nodded. "Yourself?"

"It was an uneventful night," Jyhanna said, standing up and stretching. "The only thing that passed was a nobleman in a carriage. Nothing really worth telling."

Brodin emerged from behind a tree, appearing somewhat more relaxed than when he had ducked in the first time. "Well, I'm ready to set out!" he declared.

"That is good," Jyhanna said. "Just wait for a moment while the rest of us prepare."

Telena stepped behind an tree, hiked her skirt, and relieved herself. When she came out, she found Jyhanna and Brodin cleaning up the ashes from the fire pit, carefully smothering the few remaining embers. She strode forward to assist, but Jyhanna waved her off, telling her that there was barely enough work for two, much less three. Instead, Telena set to collecting what they needed in their traveling packs.

Finally, the firepit was smothered and buried, and they returned to the cobbled road. The sun had yet to rise high in the robin-blue sky, and the day had become quite warm. To the north, the glittering sea stretched placidly into the distance, framed by the red and orange leaves of the oaks and elms.

When Telena took a moment to look behind, she nearly gasped in awe. The Great Peaks rose in the east, grey and white, the sun glaring off the snow-capped mountains. Although they seemed to reach into the sky, they appeared distant, and Telena wondered how far away they really were.

"It will be some time before we reach a village," Jyhanna stated. "This land was heavily damaged during the Kaegar Wars, and it is still healing. Most of the nobles tend to place their estates in the more remote areas of Tarese; that land is more fertile."

Telena saw Brodin frown for a moment, and point to the south. "But isn't that a city there?"

Telena turned, finding herself on a large rise. Below them stretched a great expanse of buildings, the hoary stone old and worn. Great streets wound through the structures, leading off into the distance.

Jyhanna smiled slightly. "These are the ruins of Civilis, one of the last Arcalien cities to fall. The road leading in is just a bit ahead of us."

"I think we should explore it," Brodin said. "What an adventure it would be!"

Telena found herself nodding in happy agreement. "I've never seen an ancient city."

Jyhanna paused for a moment, and then said, "Why not? You'll probably have very few chances like this after you settle down."

Ahead they found a fork in the path, the cobbled way stretching on one side down into the ruins, and on the other side out into the countryside. They strode down the southern road, coming to a large decorated gate after a short walk. The arch was carved with lions, and the cyclopean blocks boggled Telena's mind; she could swear that some of them were as large as she was.

"This is the Lion Gate," Jyhanna said. "It is still remembered in the bard's tales. It is said that Garwulf the Slayer fought a battle here, in one of the more inventive yarns. Utter fiction, but it makes for a good story."

"Why do you say it is fiction?" Telena wondered.

"Garwulf the Slayer fought in the Kaegar Wars, around a generation ago," Jyhanna explained. "But in the saga, he is fighting alongside the last Arcalien army."

"Who was Garwulf, anyway?" Brodin asked.

"Garwulf the Slayer was the greatest warrior of our age," Telena stated. "It has been said that he could kill a dozen men single-handedly, in only a couple of seconds.

He disappeared after the last battle, and only the Eternal One knows what happened to him."

With that, they strode through the Lion Gate, onto the cobbled streets of Civilis. The columned buildings rose above them, and Telena nearly gasped as they passed a large structure, its side collapsed, that was larger than her entire village.

"That used to be the Temple of the Eternal One," Jyhanna said, pointing to the emblem of a star on a balcony over the entrance. "Now the Order of the Eternal One is monastic, but it wasn't always that way. When the Arcalien Empire fell, many things changed."

"Incredible," Brodin breathed, gazing around at the ancient ruins. "And what was that?"

Telena twirled to face an even bigger building, giant columns supporting an enormous arch outside. The roof was gone, however, and near the top the stone had crumbled, leaving large holes from which they could see floors and an inclined ceiling. To the side of the structure lay a vast park, overgrown with trees and weeds.

"That was the Arena," Jyhanna replied. "There was a time when entertainers would perform to tens of thousands of people. Imagine games, jugglers, animal tamers, all to a cheering crowd. But, like so many things, those days are long past."

"It's amazing," Telena said, eyes wide.

Jyhanna nodded. "For over a thousand years, the entire world has held this as their legacy. We all aspire to have this again one day, to live in a golden age. Perhaps someday we will have it, too. At least the dream lives on, even if the reality is gone to dust."

"You may be dust someday too," a harsh voice called. Telena spun to find herself facing a large man, clad in dirty and worn leathers. He held a long, naked sword in his hands, and his grizzled face made her recoil in fear. Brodin stood in front of her, his hands held out in front of him.

"What do you want?" the love of her life demanded.

The man stepped forward, bringing the blade to bear. "Your money, and if that doesn't suit me, your life."

"We don't have any money," Brodin said. "We're just a couple of travelers."

Telena glanced around, looking for Jyhanna, but the shield-maiden was nowhere to be found. Her stomach tightened with fear; surely their protector hadn't betrayed them?

"Well, then, I guess I'll just kill you, take your woman, and kill her too," the brigand said. Telena watched him approach, sword raised, and felt a cold sweat run down her back.

And then she saw Jyhanna rise up behind the bandit, blade unsheathed and ready. The brigand suddenly paused, as though he sensed something, and then turned, snarling. With a hoarse cry, Jyhanna struck, and the outlaw staggered back, dropping his sword to clutch at his gaping chest. Finally, the man fell to the ground, flinched once, and lay still.

"Sorry about that," Jyhanna said. "I was wondering how long he would follow us before he moved."

"Why didn't you tell us?" Brodin demanded, and Telena noticed he looked rather pale. She swallowed, forcing down a rising nausea.

The shield-maiden shrugged. "All it would have done was worry you needlessly. You're not equipped to fight against somebody like him, and it would take months to train you with a sword."

Telena saw Brodin step forward and pick up the brigand's blade. But as he did, Jyhanna shook her head. "Don't," she warned. "That is a very poor sword to begin with, and you don't know how to use it. Aside from which, weapons attract weapons. You're safer without it."

Brodin shuddered and dropped the blade. Telena leapt forward, cradling her beloved in her arms.

After they had both recovered their composure, Jyhanna led them back out of the city onto the open road. Telena looked back, remembering the vast buildings and wide parks. She grinned as the dream filled her mind. And as they walked, she left the nightmare behind.

Chapter V — Tides of War

Jyhanna led them down the road until they crested a hill to find a small village, nestled under a castle and surrounded by farmland. Telena was hopeful that this might be the end of their journey, but the shield-maiden denied it.

"So there won't be a local lord that can help us here," Telena said.

Jyhanna shook her head. "This is the summer residence of Lord Kennyth; right now there are only a few retainers to keep the castle in good repair."

"So what are we doing here?"

Jyhanna gestured around as they entered the village, passing several wooden houses with thatched roofs. "It is the harvest! When better to get supplies?"

Indeed, the hamlet was filled with merriment and rejoicing. The young men and women made eyes at each other as they went about their tasks, the boys threshing hay and bringing in the harvest while the womenfolk helped out, both in the fields and the kitchens.

Brodin began to smile as the aroma of freshly cooked corn filled the air. "Now I'm hungry," he said, rubbing his belly.

"I think we can manage to feed you two," Jyhanna declared. "There is a rather good inn here; it's called Gerry's Place. While you two are filling your stomachs, I'll go out and get us some supplies for the rest of our journey."

"Where are we going, anyway?" Brodin asked.

"We need to speak to some of the more influential nobles," Jyhanna said. "The best place to do that is in Taree, the capital. That is where the Council of Lords will be gathered right now. Perhaps there we can find you a noble who will sign you into a feudal contract."

"How far away is that?" Telena wondered.

"About two more weeks," Jyhanna stated. "Which is why we need to get provisions. At least right now it is the harvest; supplies will be easy to come by."

As she spoke, they came to the front of the inn. It was a small establishment, just large enough to house those in the area surrounding the village. As they entered, they were greeted by the smell of ale, but Telena was relieved to find both the common room and occupants far more wholesome and welcoming than the place where they had met Jyhanna.

"What can I do for ye, my ladies, gentlesir," a tall gaunt man asked, stepping out from the polished bar. His hair was cropped short, but his beard was long and curly.

"My friends need a good meal," Jyhanna said, passing him a couple of coins. "And I'll be looking for something to eat when I get back as well."

"Not a problem! We have the best corn and barley in the countryside," the man declared, turning to Brodin and Telena. "Gerry is my name, and please feel free to call on me for whatever you need."

"You two find a table," Jyhanna said. "I'll be back in about an hour."

As Gerry showed them to a long, lacquered table and bench, Telena glanced at her surroundings. Several young men and women graced the other seats, the boys tending to their ladies like bees with delicate flowers.

"It's always a bonnie time, the harvest," Gerry said, placing two bowls of steaming barley and vegetable soup before them. "A time for celebration, and a time for love. But ye both look like ye know it."

"Is it that obvious?" Brodin asked, sounding slightly abashed.

Gerry chuckled. "Aye. I know folk married for two score years who aren't as close as ye two. It's all in the eyes, ye know."

The innkeeper meandered away, tending to some of his other guests, and Telena began to drink her soup. As promised, it was absolutely succulent, and for a moment she was reminded of home. Perhaps it was the distance, but the thought of her family brought more of a smile to her face than tears.

Her thoughts were interrupted as two soldiers in green and red livery marched into the common room, one bearing a large scroll. They both had swords sheathed at their sides and painted shields slung over their backs. All eyes turned to the two shield-men as the one with the scroll began to speak.

"The Haneric Empire has begun an invasion of our ancient lands, ceded to us in the last acts of the Arcalien Emperor. All men of eligible age are to answer the call to arms. By order of his Majesty and Lord Kennyth, all men fit for service are to assemble immediately in the village square for selection in the royal levy. All feudal contracts of protection from service are hereby suspended."

There was a muted, collective gasp of shock. Then, slowly, the young men began to rise from their places and walk outside. As they passed, Telena could swear that each bore a look of despairing disbelief in their eyes.

"Him too," the soldier said, pointing the scroll at Brodin.

"I'm not a citizen of this country," Brodin protested.

The soldier put the scroll in his belt and placed his hand on his sword hilt. "Young man, if you do not report for the levy, I will kill you myself."

"He's telling the truth!" Telena exploded, leaping from her seat. "Can't you see that he's not a villager here?"

The soldier drew his sword. "I see somebody willing to do anything to get out of his duty! Now get into the square!" As Brodin rose and slumped out, the soldier turned a lustful eye on Telena. "You can follow him, if you want. I'm sure the army will have a place for you in with the camp followers and prostitutes."

Telena bolted tearfully out the door. Brodin was already caught in a group of men, shepherded along by a group of ten soldiers. She ran towards the shops, almost falling down in her desperation. All she could think about was finding Jyhanna and getting help.

"You're asking too much," Jyhanna said, glaring at the shopkeeper. "This is only worth two crowns at best."

The merchant placed the canteen on the table. "Two and a half crowns, and not a quarter crown less. You know as well as I that there isn't anywhere else to go around here for these."

"Fine," Jyhanna conceded, dropping fifteen coins in front of the man. "Three canteens for two and a half crowns apiece. And don't think I'll be coming back here in the future."

As she dropped the canteens into her sack, Telena burst into the store. "Jyhanna! I've been looking everywhere for you! They've taken Brodin!"

Jyhanna spun to face the young woman. "Calm down. Tell me what happened."

Telena related how Brodin had been conscripted in the inn. "And I've been looking for you ever since! I must have been running for a good ten minutes!"

Jyhanna nodded and strode out into the street, Telena close behind. "You did the right thing. I'll take care of this. You said they're fighting the Haneric Empire?"

Telena nodded breathlessly. "I think that is what it was."

"So long as it isn't Toregien," Jyhanna said, coming to the square. A group of thirty men had assembled, but six of them had been put into a separate group. The ranking officer, a housecarl if she read the rank emblazoned on his colors correctly, was pointing to a couple of young men, who dejectedly joined the smaller group. Brodin stood with them, close to tears.

"Excuse me," Jyhanna said, stepping forward and pulling a parchment from her tunic. "This is a royal levy?"

"Yes, my lady," the soldier said, uncertainty in his eyes. Jyhanna suppressed a smile; the man had obviously never seen a warrior-woman before.

She pointed at Brodin. "That man does not belong in your army."

"He is an able-bodied man, and thus subject to the levy."

Jyhanna shook her head. "Only citizens of Tarese are subject to the levy. That young man, and his wife here, are both citizens of Toregien."

The housecarl grinned. "And what proof do you have of this? No doubt this is just another trick from the young

118

one's wife. She has enough to make a very good whore."

Jyhanna frowned and unrolled her parchment, showing it to the man. "As a duly appointed representative of His Highness, Lewys the Third, I think I am quite capable of recognizing one of Toregien's citizenry."

"His accent isn't from Toregien," the soldier protested.

"Do you really think that there is only one accent in Toregien?" Jyhanna asked, doing her best impression of Telena's brogue and hoping it sounded right. "Pick somebody else: that man's name is Brodin, and he is a member of my party. We have business in Taree with His Majesty."

"Very well," the housecarl sighed, turning to his men. "Take that man out of the ranks and pick another." He regarded Jyhanna for a moment. "Do you require a military escort?"

Jyhanna shook her head. "We will be fine alone. And in future, try to be more polite to your betters."

"My apologies."

"Accepted, this time."

Re-rolling the scroll and placing it back in her tunic, Jyhanna led a very shaken Brodin out of the line, taking him and Telena toward the edge of town. She put Brodin in Telena's care, and smiled as the young woman clung to him.

Now why can't I find somebody like that? Jyhanna wondered. Maybe there had been people who could have been perfect lovers in her life, but she hadn't recognized love when it stood before her. No matter now.

"I fear our journey may be more difficult that first imagined," Jyhanna said. "If a levy has been called, then that means the local nobles will be heading to war with their knights. They also will not be on good terms with the monarchy."

119

"Why not?" Telena asked.

"How would you feel if suddenly you were required to break your feudal agreements and decimate your own peasants?" Jyhanna asked, looking back at the village. Even in the distance, she could see a group of soldiers leading the small line of serfs from the town, in an almost mockingly amateurish version of a military march.

"But you can help us!" Telena declared. "We could go to Toregien! You're a representative of their government, aren't you?"

Jyhanna shook her head sadly. "I wasn't going to say anything within earshot of those shield-men, but no, I'm not. I took that scroll just after I was exiled by the king. Stepping foot in Toregien could mean my death."

They camped that night by a small hill overlooking another group of farms. This time, there was no castle protecting the hamlet. Still, they had arrived just in time to see a small group of peasants led out by soldiers, another of the king's levies.

Jyhanna shook her head and, despite the cold, instructed Brodin and Telena not to light a fire this night. There were too many soldiers around, and she knew that armies in wartime had a habit of conscripting anybody they ran across. She had tried to curtail the practice whenever she was in command, but she had held no illusions about trying to stop it completely.

Shivering in the chill breeze, Telena asked, "What will we do now?"

Jyhanna just shrugged. "We'll go towards Toregien and talk to some of the lords along the way. With the war, many will be tending their lands and raising their knights rather than attending court in the capital. Maybe we'll find one who won't let the king take his peasantry away, but that is doubtful. At least in a couple of days the levies will have ended, and we can venture into the villages again."

"And if we can't do anything in Taree?"

"Then we keep trying. That is all we can do."

Chapter VI — Encounters

Jyhanna led her two wards across the plains of Tarese, through the sifting grasses and light woodlands filled with evergreens. They skirted along the Queen's Road, making their way towards the long cobbled path of the King's Road into Taree.

The wide fields of grain lay before them, mostly untouched. Jyhanna frowned. The people of Tarese would be close to starvation this winter - too many peasants had been taken in the levy, and there were not enough remaining for the harvest.

"We're running out of supplies," Telena pointed out, holding up a half-full pack of food. The bread had staled far more quickly than expected, and very few vegetables were available this early in the harvest season.

Jyhanna nodded. "There is an old town just ahead. We'll get supplies there."

"Do you think there'll be a local lord there that can help us?" Brodin asked.

Jyhanna shook her head. "Caer Danaan has no lord. The mayors have managed for centuries to remain outside of the feudal contracts. I think the crown allows it because of Caer Danaan's heritage."

"Something from the Arcalien Empire?" Brodin wondered.

Jyhanna chuckled. "Far older than the Arcalien Empire. It's said that Caer Danaan was here since before humankind first walked in the Western Lands."

Coming to a small rise, they found themselves overlooking the windy plains. Tall grasses waved in the breeze, a shifting sea of green. Blazoned across the fields like a long grey snake, the road led off to a speck on the horizon.

"Caer Danaan," Jyhanna declared, pointing at the distant town. "If we make good time, we will be there by nightfall tomorrow."

"And then south to Taree," Brodin said.

Jyhanna nodded. "Hopefully, your journey will end happily there."

They walked quietly throughout the day, Jyhanna keeping half an eye on the horizon, in case of some unpleasantness with the army of Tarese. It was an ancient custom for traveling units to conscript those they came across as they marched, and she didn't want to be caught unawares.

That night, they camped under the stars, Jyhanna smiling as the two innocents clung to each other in the chill. For a moment she envied them, wishing to recapture the spark that had made the world seem wondrous and magical. But she had done too many things, shed too much blood, seen too much of humanity's cruelty to ever again see the absolute beauty she had once found everywhere.

How long has it been since I died inside, Jyhanna wondered. *How long since I have had all my soul?*

But, for one shining moment, she could live through these two young lovers. And, perhaps, through them she might find something of what she lost.

With these thoughts, she allowed herself to drift into a dreamless sleep.

Caer Danaan looked ancient. From a distance, they saw the hoary stonework, worn down and bleached by the millennia. Some high towers remained, shadows of an earlier age, harkening back to something far greater that had been lost in the seas of time.

Instead, the darker stone towers and walls stood, constructed with neither the grace nor skill of the earlier builders. Guards paced on the walls, marking them from afar. Jyhanna shrugged. So, their arrival would not be a surprise; it would simply make matters easier.

"We will be there by nightfall," she declared. "Once we get there, do what I say. The last thing we need right now is to get ourselves conscripted or arrested."

"Is that really a danger?" Brodin asked. "We're just travelers; what threat could we be?"

"As far as they are concerned, we could be spies for the Haneric Empire," Jyhanna said. "Remember, we are in the middle of a war. They will constantly be wary for somebody who has come to open their gates during the night and let in raiders."

"What a horrible situation," Telena muttered.

Jyhanna shrugged. "Your timing for coming into the Western Lands could have been better. But we will make do with what we have."

They reached the eastern gates of the town as the sun began to set, joining a long column of refugees. Young and old, they crowded the gate, some bringing carts driven by oxen, others bearing their possessions on their backs.

"What has happened here?" Telena asked.

Jyhanna frowned. "The war has made its way into this part of Tarese. These people are seeking shelter from the violence. For all we know, the Haneric army could be a mere ten leagues away."

She saw Brodin looking from man to man, noting the long faces, the weeping children, the misery so strong that it was a tangible force, hovering in the air. At the front, the guards were questioning each person who was to enter, leaving the rest of the line to wait for passage.

Brodin shook his head. "Those poor people."

"We are those people," Telena said. "The only thing that makes us better is that we have a guide."

"You'll get through it," Jyhanna said. "I swear it by the Eternal One."

Finally, the line moved forward, bringing them to the gate as the sun was setting. "Where are you from, and where are you headed?" the guard demanded, yawning.

Jyhanna took out her scroll of office and held it up. "I am Jyhanna, and these are my charges, Telena and Brodin. I am taking them south to Taree on the morrow."

The guard shook his head. "That would be very difficult, my lady. Taree has been sacked, and his Majesty has fled. You can stay here tonight; there are several warehouses that have been set aside for refugees. But I suggest that you head further north tomorrow."

Jyhanna blinked. "Is it that bad?"

"They took no prisoners, and burnt the city to the ground. We think they might be going east to the ports on the River Cyrion, but we can't be certain. It is said that they are led by a demon, who can make trees and rocks fight for him."

Shaken, Jyhanna thanked the man and led her charges inside the gate. She tried to figure out something, to work out where they could go from there. But she could not take them into Toregien, nor could she now take them east; both options had become too dangerous.

"Where now?" Telena asked.

"An inn," Jyhanna said distractedly. "I need a drink, and we need a place to stay."

"Won't they all be full?" Brodin wondered.

Jyhanna shook her head. "I know a place that probably won't be. It is rather out of the way, but it is very good. And the name discourages casual visitors."

"What is it called?"

"'Ye Olde Gathering Hole,'" Jyhanna replied.

Telena shuddered. "It sounds like that place you found us in Kaplan's Peak."

Jyhanna smiled. "That's the point. But if anybody tries anything funny, the innkeeper will give them a few broken bones. There's a large group that gathers there, but they are all regulars from the town."

"You've been there," Telena said. A statement, not a question.

Jyhanna nodded. "You could say that while I am here, I am a regular."

The news had spread, Jyhanna realized, glancing around the common room. Where every other time she had been there, the place had been bustling with activity, now it was still, filled with the muted conversations of isolated tables. The barmaids and innkeeper moved lifelessly, as though they were in some nightmare they expected to wake up from. Her gaze finally rested upon a table in the corner, where a monk, a boy who appeared to be his novice, and a cloaked traveler of some sort sat, talking quietly.

She snapped her fingers, startling Brodin and Telena. "The Great Convention!"

"What is the Great Convention?" Brodin asked.

126

"It protects innocent parties during conflicts," Jyhanna answered. "Brothers of the Order of the Eternal One are given particular protection in the charter, and it extends to all who travel with them."

Telena's eyes lit up. "Do you think-"

Jyhanna nodded. "We should introduce ourselves."

As they walked over, the monk looked up. "Can I help you?"

Jyhanna nodded. "Brother, we need to talk. I am sorry to bother you, but we are in need. My name is Jyhanna, and I am a former shield-maiden of Toregien. My companions are named Brodin and Telena; they're farmers looking for some land."

"I am Brother Caelyn," the monk said, but there was a strange distance in his voice. "This is my novice, Tamlin, and his tutor, Sagarum. I don't understand how I can help."

"I am an accomplished warrior, but in these times even I have difficulty protecting my charges. You, however, are protected by the Great Convention, and-"

"You were wondering if you could travel with us," Caelyn interrupted, finishing the thought.

"Yes."

"You don't even know where we are going," Caelyn said. "Aside from which, the Great Convention does not seem to hold as well as it used to, if the sack of Taree is any sign."

"It is a better chance than we would have otherwise," Jyhanna said. "So long as you are not heading into Toregien, I can help protect you."

While Caelyn raised an eyebrow, Sagarum suddenly spoke. "A shield-maiden would be welcome company on the road. And, it would be nice for Tamlin to have some people his own age to talk to, rather than having to deal with us oldsters. Besides, we are not heading into

Toregien."

"We wouldn't be a problem," Telena piped up.

"I've been told that I am very good with my hands, and I have some training as a healer," Brodin added. "Surely that could help."

"Very well," Caelyn said. "We are still planning our course, and if you are to journey with us, it would only be fair for you to have some say in our destination. Please, join us."

Relieved beyond words, Jyhanna pulled up three chairs, and sat down. It was still a longshot, but at least now she had a chance of seeing her wards to safety. But, she couldn't shake a feeling that things would get much more interesting before the end.

Part III:
Seeking Fate

Chapter I — Portents and Ceremonies

Jyhanna sat on her horse, watching the army before her. They marched forward, their banners displaying her colors, driving across the field to meet a shadowy foe. A light dusting of snow was scattered across the ground, and more was falling, tiny flakes with an ethereal glitter in the light. Yet, she was not cold, nor did she feel the terror that always accompanied her battle-rage.

I'm dreaming, she realized, the lucid revelation itself strange and alien. *In reality, I'm sleeping in a room with a monk.*

With a great cry, the two forces met, and the air was filled with the ringing of steel. The stench of death rose from the field, maimed men crying out for mercy, vengeance, or both. On the other side, by a rise, she saw a great shadowy figure, his hands raised. Suddenly, she felt a chill of fear, the dreadful certainty that she was seeing something unnatural.

A creeping darkness began to crawl over the field,

clinging to the earth. Everything it touched turned to madness, as soldiers spun to attack their own comrades, the enemy forgotten even as he plunged a sword in their backs. From rank to rank it spread, first destroying any order remaining in the enemy, and then reaching over to her own men.

Her heart leapt in her chest as the darkness began to climb the hill, filling the valley with the dead and dying. She wanted to wake up, to leap out of the nightmare, but she was trapped; what had been a dream was suddenly very real. She cantered further up the hill, keeping as much distance as possible between the darkness and herself.

There was an eruption from the center of the darkness, amid a pile of decaying corpses. Dreadful creatures, beings that could only exist in the most fearful nightmares, began to climb onto the field, feeding off the bodies of the slain and killing those who still had life. And on the hill, the figure laughed.

Jyhanna sat bolt upright, her nightgown covered in a sheen of cold sweat. She was in the room she shared with Brother Caelyn, the monk regarding her with a dispassionate gaze. The moon seeped through the cracks in the window shutters, bathing the meager furniture in a warm, but dim, glow.

"How bad was the nightmare?" Caelyn asked.

"Very bad," Jyhanna replied. "I wish I knew some way of getting rid of them."

"They fade in time," the monk stated. "Everything does."

Jyhanna shook her head. "And I suppose you have lots of experience with nightmares?"

Considering the age of the monk, and the cold mystery he seemed to wrap around himself, she expected a boasting answer, about how somebody her age couldn't possibly know what horrors lay in life. Instead, he just quietly answered: "Yes."

Lying back in her cot and gazing at the window, she marveled at the monk and his entourage. It was obvious that he had been a soldier at one point; she had seen military discipline so often in her life that she could recognize it at once. But, like so many veterans of old wars, he refused to talk about his experiences.

She rolled over and closed her eyes, thinking of Sagarum. Sagarum, like Caelyn, was a man of mystery. She knew he was a wizard, and he certainly seemed more open than the monk, but he actually revealed less. It was as though his soul was opaque, and no matter what she did she could not see into it.

Tamlin, at least, was relatively easy to understand. Like her charges, he was young and only just learning about the world. He had an air of innocence, but without naivety; it was as though he was still discovering the wonders in the world, but was already aware of the horror.

"You should sleep," Caelyn mumbled. "It will be a long day ahead."

Jyhanna blinked. How could he have possibly known that she was still awake? She was covered in blankets, and turned away from him. Then it occurred to her – he must have been listening to her breathing. If nothing else, it meant he had very fine hearing.

She shook her head and yawned. There would be plenty of time to learn about her new companions in the days ahead; the road was long, and the end was far from sight.

They chose a northerly course, following the refugees along the King's Road up to the Prince's Road, which ran along the coastline. From there, they would head east, seeking the protection of the Great Convention should they encounter any Haneric forces. Once they reached a seaport, they would take a ship to eastern Bandre, where Caelyn planned to continue his pilgrimage and Jyhanna to settle her charges.

The first day was slow, as the King's Road was choked with refugees. For hours they traveled on the plains beside the road, passing large carts filled with belongings, pulled by the dour oxen of defeated men and women. Caelyn knew that they still held some hope, but he was also aware that they realized how slim that hope was. Tarese had died with the destruction of the capital; while some did not want to accept it, it could not be denied as the truth.

They camped that night off the side of the cobbled path, just within sight of a large group of men and women, also resting by the road. As Tamlin and Sagarum went to collect what little deadwood could be found on the plains, Caelyn sat on a rock and gazed up at the stars.

The pinpricks of light shone down, twinkling as though they knew some secret joke. For a moment he wondered if Wyrd really was written in the sky, as some astrologers believed. *If so, what will happen to me?*

"Er...Brother Caelyn," a nervous voice said. Caelyn turned to see Brodin and Telena standing together, holding hands uncertainly.

Caelyn smiled. "What can I do for you?"

"Well, we're lovers," Telena began, "and we love each other very much. We had planned to get married back in Beregar, but we had to flee before we could. So, we were wondering if you could..."

Caelyn nodded. "I think I understand. Yes, I am ordained for holy rituals, although usually Father Abbot sees to such things. However, since he isn't here, I will see to it."

As the two embraced in joy, Caelyn called Jyhanna

over. "They would like me to marry them," he said. "And I require a witness in order to do so."

"What will I have to do?" Jyhanna asked, raising an eyebrow.

"Just answer honestly when I ask you a question," Caelyn said, turning to Brodin and Telena. "I fear that I do not have a prayer book, so I will have to improvise somewhat. However, I think we can manage."

He drew himself up to his full height and drew back his cowl, his grey hair glinting in the moonlight. "We should wait until Tamlin and Sagarum return before beginning."

As if on cue, the two appeared in the darkness, Sagarum shaking his head. "I knew we should have brought some timber from Caer Danaan. We shall have to make do without a fire tonight."

"But can't we use magic?" Tamlin asked.

"Not while a powerful and probably hostile wizard is around. I would rather not give away our position with a display of power."

Caelyn cleared his throat. "Gentlemen, I have been asked to perform a holy service. Do you wish to attend?"

"Depends on the service," Sagarum stated, a grin on his face. "I take it that these two want you to marry them?"

"How did you know that?" Brodin demanded.

"Anyone could see that you and Telena are madly in love with each other," Sagarum chuckled. "And, since nobody has died and it is not the solstice or equinox, there aren't any other holy services to perform. Simple logic."

"Would you like to attend?"

Sagarum smiled. "Only if I can give away the bride."

Caelyn shrugged. "Up to the bride, I guess. Now, we should do this and get some rest; we have a long day ahead of us." He turned to Brodin and Telena, waiting for Sagarum to take his place at Telena's side before beginning.

"We are gathered here, in the sight of the Eternal One, to link these two, Brodin and Telena, in the bonds of holy matrimony. In the bonds of love, of friendship, and of family." He turned to Telena. "Do you take this man to be your husband, to love, honor, and cherish, through darkness and light, in the name of the Eternal One, from here unto eternity?"

"Yes," Telena replied, her voice nearly a whisper.

Caelyn turned to Brodin. "And do you take this woman to be your wife, to love, honor, and cherish, though darkness and light, in the name of the Eternal One, from here unto eternity?"

"Yes."

He looked to Jyhanna. "Do you, Jyhanna, testify as a friend of the engaged that there is no reason, in the realm of the Eternal One or on earth, why these two should not be wed?"

Jyhanna nodded. "I do."

Caelyn smiled. "Then by the power vested in me, by Abbot Artus of the Abbey of Southmarch, and by the Eternal One, I name you man and wife, from here unto eternity. May your lives be happy and peaceful. You may kiss the bride."

As the two newlyweds embraced and kissed passionately, Caelyn sat down on his rock and looked about. "Time to rest, everybody. We have a long day ahead of us, and we'll all need our sleep on the morrow."

For the next two days they traveled north, finally making a good pace once the traffic of refugees petered out. The voyage was uneventful, although during the evenings Brodin and Telena often snuck out of the camp and returned around an hour later, both disheveled.

On the fifth day after leaving Caer Danaan, Jyhanna noticed a new scent in the air, the clean, salty aroma of the sea. She looked back, suddenly wary of being followed now that they might be close to a harbor, but the only thing in sight behind them was an old couple with their wagon, carrying their belongings.

On the sixth day, they came to the crossroads and turned onto the Prince's Road. The sea stretched out to the north, a brilliant blue strip across the horizon. The farther they walked, the more Jyhanna had a sense of wrongness. No seagulls danced in the air, and no fish leaped from the sea, as they often did in mid-autumn. As well, while it should have become warmer the closer they got to the Inner Sea, it had instead become more chill, forcing them to wrap their cloaks around themselves.

That night, at least, they were able to gather some deadwood and light a fire. They huddled together, taking what they could from the meager warmth, until they had to set out again at dawn. This time, Sagarum made a point of gathering extra, so that they would have some for the future.

The next day, two things happened: around noon they crested a hill to find the walled port-town of Nautia within sight, only a few days away. Around the same time, even though it was still only mid-autumn, it started to snow.

Chapter II — Revelations

Tamlin stood at the gates of Nautia, his monastic habit wrapped around him to fend off the cold, wondering if they would ever actually enter the town. The doors were filled with refugees, and even though he wished that Caelyn would use his influence to get them in more quickly, the monk merely waited, turning every now and then to help somebody in the line.

Beside him Jyhanna, who had to be the most impressive and impassive woman he had ever seen, ate some jerky as she kept watch over her charges. The two young newlyweds seemed quite patient, as though they were certain that the warrior would get them through untouched.

Tamlin, on the other hand, was not nearly as confident. The snow seemed unnatural to him, as though something was destroying the balance in the world.

The hours passed, and the waiting became harder. At least the snow let up, Tamlin noted with relief, trudging through several inches of it on the ground. At the rate they were going, he was surprised that half the line hadn't frozen to death.

He watched two people walk away from the front of the line, their faces downcast. For a moment, his heart pounded in his chest. Had they been turned away at the gate? Everything would be lost if they couldn't get inside.

He shook his head, reviewing for the thousandth time the events that had brought him here, waiting in a long line for somebody to let him and his companions into a port so that they might possibly find a ship. For a moment he found himself cursing under his breath, wishing that there was something he could do, anything to alleviate the boredom.

"Are they all with you?" a voice said, snapping Tamlin back into the present.

Turning, he saw Caelyn nod and motion to the group. With a start, he realized that they were right at the giant doors. "We are all together. Would you be kind enough to direct us to the docks?"

As the guard began to spout off street names, giving vague directions towards the waterfront, Tamlin drifted off again, looking at the line behind him. It stretched out farther than he could see.

Will anybody survive this war untouched?

"Come along," the monk directed. "We have somewhere to get to, and we should make haste."

As they entered the town, the crowd became stifling, but then thinned once they had passed beyond the stone gatehouse. The stench of the city, something Tamlin had rarely been exposed to in his time as an apprentice and on the road, nauseated him. Gazing around, he saw that Brodin and Telena also looked pale.

"They were turning people away," Jyhanna pointed out as they turned down a cross-street. "How did you get us in?"

"I told him we were trying to hire a ship," Caelyn replied. "I assured him that we would be out of the city within a day. Most of the refugees do not have our strong sense of purpose; they just want a place to stay until the war blows over."

"This war isn't simply going to 'blow over,'" Sagarum said. "There is much more happening than meets the eye."

"You know what this conflict is about, don't you?" Jyhanna said.

Sagarum nodded. "I'll tell you all once we get onto the ship."

"This had better be for a good cause," she grumbled. "If this is just so that some king can conquer some more territory, the price is far too high."

The captain of the merchantman turned out to be a dour, gaunt man named Nolan with sandy hair and an unkempt beard. He eyed the monk and his companions with a wary gaze, and then accepted Caelyn's money.

"Aye, that will get you to Bandre," Captain Nolan said. "But not too far in. I'll only take you as far as the coastline, and once you're there, you're on your own. And, if we run into trouble, I won't be spending a great amount of time worrying about your hides."

Caelyn nodded. "That is acceptable."

Tamlin wanted to shake his head, to tell Caelyn that this was the wrong ship, but something kept him quiet. Perhaps it was that he didn't want to show weakness in front of somebody who obviously had little respect for life in general. The money changed hands, and he found himself climbing on board a ship with tall sails and creaking boards.

"You'll all be in our guest room," the first mate

declared, leading them into a dark and cramped quarters. "The captain will have meals served on deck at the dawn and the dusk; if you aren't on time, there might not be much left for you."

"Thank you for your kindness," Caelyn said graciously.

Smiling, the sailor left, leaving the companions to contemplate their new surroundings.

"I've been in better," Sagarum commented. "I've also been in far worse."

"There isn't much privacy," Brodin complained, and Telena embraced him, drawing him close.

"For what we need, this will do," Caelyn stated. "This is a minor merchant, carrying an unimportant cargo. The captain and crew know we are just travelers trying to make our way somewhere without a spending too many crowns. We're unlikely to be disturbed during the voyage."

There was a lurch, and the cabin rolled, first to the left, and then to the right. Tamlin had difficulty keeping his feet, but Caelyn, Sagarum, and Jyhanna appeared to have no trouble at all.

"We've set sail," Sagarum said. "I do so enjoy a good sea voyage."

"I feel a bit ill," Telena complained.

"It will pass," Jyhanna said, opening a porthole. The cool sea breeze wafted in, and Tamlin suddenly felt refreshed. "It may take a while to find your sea legs, but if you spend enough time on the water, you'll get them."

"It's the chamber pots that will be really fun," Sagarum chuckled. Sometimes, it seemed to Tamlin as though the old wizard enjoyed himself far too much.

Seating herself on a hammock, Jyhanna crossed her arms. "Now, you promised you'd tell us what this war is about. Speak."

"I *would* like to know why my master was murdered,"

Tamlin said, leaning against a wall to steady himself as the cabin rolled and creaked.

"Every century the Grand Magus dies," Sagarum explained. "The Grand Magus has seven powers of succession, and they are instilled on several candidates. These Archmagi, known as Successors, battle for the right to become Grand Magus."

"I'm a chronicler, and I've never heard of any of this before," Caelyn said.

Sagarum nodded. "I'm not surprised. The battle is limited to those who have a claim, and no others are permitted to become involved. An Arbiter of Succession is chosen to ensure that the rules are abided by. No innocents are allowed to be harmed, and the rest of the world barely notices that anything has happened. However, this time somebody has broken the rules."

"So that is what this is all about?" Jyhanna exclaimed, rising from her seat in anger. "Some thrice-damned wizards want to become the next Grand Magus, and they're using armies to do it?"

Sagarum nodded. "Somebody murdered the Arbiter, and the rest of the world is suffering from it, as I knew it would."

"How could you possibly know that?" Jyhanna demanded. "Are you a soothsayer as well?"

"Actually, it's written in Balthus' Prophecies," Caelyn said. "I've always wondered what the rhyme meant:

> *After an Arbiter dies,*
> *Death spreads across the land.*
> *The one who will follow comes,*
> *Traveling in an unknown band.*"

"It does refer to us," Sagarum stated. "When Balthus wrote that, he had just spoken to the Great Oracle.

Unfortunately, the Great Oracle doesn't tend to be very clear."

"I don't understand something," Tamlin cut in. "Why seven powers of succession? Seven is not an important magical number. Three is important, four is important, eight is important, but not seven. At least, that's what Haldur told me."

"Your master was absolutely correct," Sagarum sighed. "And I wish you hadn't brought that question up, because it does require an answer. You see, there are eight powers of succession. The eighth has been lost for millennia, but is still extant.

"Originally, the Order of Archmagi was led by a man who had the Great Powers, now known as the powers of succession. But then, long before the rise of the Arcalien Empire, and even before the forgotten Ceraphim Empire of the North, the Archmagi revolted against their leader. Using trickery, they bound him and stripped him of all but one of his Great Powers. He was able to escape before they could kill him and take the last power."

As he spoke, a long-hidden bitterness had crept into Sagarum's voice. Tamlin recoiled with shock, chills running down his spine, suddenly certain of what would come next.

"And how would you know all of this?" Jyhanna demanded.

Tamlin could have mouthed Sagarum's reply even as he spoke it, he was so certain of the truth. "Because I am the man who holds the last Great Power, the power of Immortality. I have waited for millennia to reclaim my proper place as the leader of the Order, and now that time has come. I am the first Grand Magus."

In the silence that followed, the cabin heaved violently.

But the shock of the moment had been so great that nobody even felt ill. Sagarum waited, solemn, hoping that his new-found companions would not abandon him because of his long-kept secret.

"Why did they rebel?" Caelyn asked. Sagarum waited for a moment before replying, running the question through his head, looking for any signs whatsoever of malice or contempt. But all he found was curiosity.

Sagarum shrugged. "Even now I still don't know. I tried to rule with wisdom and honor. I attempted to teach them that they should uphold the balance, not interfere with the affairs of the secular world, and to show them just how wonderful knowledge of the arcane actually was. Still they bound and betrayed me."

"And you want revenge?" Jyhanna demanded. Sagarum sighed – there had definitely been hostility in that voice.

"I want to set things right," he replied. "The men who betrayed and raped me have been dust for longer than mortal memory. Not even the most learned of the Order of Archmagi remembers them now. But until the last few weeks, the veil of secrecy of the succession was so tight that I could do nothing. Finally, the successors are in the open, and I can reclaim what is mine."

"What will you do once you have this power?" the warrior woman pressed. Sagarum gazed at the two young lovers, who seemed completely lost in the entire discussion.

"I will leave this world via the Great Road," Sagarum declared. "If nothing else, this war demonstrates that the Great Powers should never have fallen into mortal hands. I will leave this land, and find some solace elsewhere. The Order of Archmagi can govern itself by some other means."

"So what do you plan to do?" Tamlin asked.

"If you will still have me as a teacher, I will continue to train you," Sagarum replied. "You have great talent. And, when the time is right, I will strike."

Once again, there was silence, as the ship slid through the dark sea into a starry night.

Chapter III — Songs of the Sea

Tamlin actually was proud of it in the end. He managed to last almost a day before he became seasick.

He discovered that morning that the ship was named the Sea Cutter, and now he leaned over her side, spitting the last of the horrible taste of what had a few hours ago been his lunch from his mouth, wondering how long the voyage would take.

The sails were becalmed, and he found himself trying to wrap his habit around him for warmth. Although he had heard that sea air was supposed to be warm and refreshing on land, in the middle of the Inner Sea the wind was cold and biting.

Shivering and miserable, he gazed around. Caelyn and Sagarum stood on the deck behind him, looking out over the water, quietly talking. Leaning against the railing to regain his balance, he staggered over to the two.

"Will you have to use your powers?" the monk was saying. Tamlin blinked in bewilderment.

Sagarum shrugged. "I hope not. With luck, we won't run into any trouble. If I do have to weave a spell, it will attract the attention of every single wizard in the area."

"What's happening?" Tamlin asked, swallowing hard as his stomach heaved again. Above him, the sails were utterly limp.

"The wind is not on our side right now, although hopefully that will change," Caelyn replied. "The captain is trying to tack against it, but that will take a very long time if we don't get a good breeze. And, there is bad news."

"There was a battle in the harbor of Kaplan's Peak," Sagarum stated. "A Fenegarian warship attacked a Bandrian merchantman, and Kaplan's Peak has declared for Bandre. We only just heard about it from one of the sailors."

Tamlin blinked. "We're on a Kaplani ship?"

Caelyn nodded. "And therefore open to attack. If we had known, we would have chosen another vessel."

Tamlin shook his head. "I knew that something was wrong with this ship. I wanted to say something, but I couldn't get it out."

Sagarum raised an eyebrow. "Next time, please do keep us informed. You are touched by Wyrd, and sometimes these premonitions are to be paid heed."

Tamlin frowned and looked toward the foredeck. Brodin and Telena stood framed against the mid-afternoon sun, hand in hand.

"At least they're having a good time," Tamlin grumbled.

"I think I'm going to be sick again," Brodin complained.

Telena gazed at her husband with worried eyes. Brodin had turned a sickly shade of green, and this was the second time he had needed to throw up over the side.

"Jyhanna says you'll get your sea legs soon," she said, patting his arm in what she hoped was a comforting fashion.

"I just hope I'll have them by the time we reach land," Brodin moaned. "I never realized how wonderful the ground was until this voyage."

"Well I rather enjoy it," Telena declared. "The breeze is refreshing, the water is gentle, and the weather is pleasant."

Brodin had just enough time to give Telena a stare that could have melted lead before he leaned over the side again, stomach heaving.

As she held him, cooing to him that it would be all right, she saw a speck on the horizon. Wincing, she tried to make it out, but it was too far away. Finally, she shrugged; it was probably nothing.

"I wonder if we will hear the songs of the sea," Sagarum mused, causing Tamlin and Caelyn to raise an eyebrow.

"Do you mean that is real?" the monk asked. "I had always taken it for a myth."

Sagarum nodded. "Oh, it is real. Remember, I've been alive for several millennia now. When I traveled on the Great Road after the betrayal, I even had the pleasure of studying under Delgar Dragonmage, although that name might not mean anything to you."

"Who is Delgar Dragonmage?" Tamlin asked. "And what are you talking about?"

Sagarum paused and took a deep breath. "Delgar Dragonmage is a very powerful wizard. He is Magus Draconum, the protector of all Dragonkind, and a wanderer on the Great Road. I found him to be very kind, but very sad as well. I think he always felt his burden was too great.

"And as for the songs of the sea, that is a story from when I was young. Back then, the Inner sea surrounded a large island named Caenwynn. Caenwynn was the home of a wondrous civilization, with great learning and literature. But where they truly shone was their music."

Sagarum's eyes took on a wistful look. "Their bards have never been bested, even in the millennia that followed them. They could sing songs that would reach into your soul, make you fall in love, bring you to heights of joy or plunge you into the depths of despair. It is said that they could cast magic into their music, just as we now weave spells.

"But the other nations, all barbaric in comparison, were envious of Caenwynn. They built ships of war, and attacked. Caenwynn had never been a warlike land, and it fell all too easily."

A tear rolled down the old wizard's cheek, and he wiped it away.

With a quiet sniffle, Sagarum continued his story. "The Tuatha de Danaan returned from the Great Road and tried to help, but they were far too late. So that the wonders of Caenwynn would not be corrupted by the barbarians, they cast a great spell, sinking most of the island. All that remained was the Isle of Magic, left to forever serve as a reminder that no matter how long mortals lived in this world, the best of them would always be gone, destroyed by spite and envy. The music had such power, however, that it could not be destroyed, and if you listen carefully, you can hear it faintly, deep beneath the waves."

He wept for a moment, finally looking up and saying, "I'm sorry. I lost somebody very dear to my heart when Caenwynn sank."

"Is that what immortality is like?" Tamlin asked,

hoping that he wouldn't cause Sagarum more pain with his question. "Always seeing the things you love pass away while you remain?"

Sagarum nodded. "Sometimes. For those who are not born to it, like I am, the long years can drive them mad. But while there is great sadness, there is also great joy. Immortal love and hate is much deeper than you mortals could ever know – it can last millennia."

Tamlin blinked, one more question coming to mind. "Then what is the Great Road?"

Sagarum looked at him, and then turned away. Caelyn, however, shrugged and replied, "It is the Road of Legends, the pathway between worlds that some can travel."

Tamlin saw Sagarum start, turning to stare at the monk. "A very good answer, but how could you possibly know that? It seems just a bit arcane for a mere brother."

"Our teachings are a bit more encompassing than most realize," Caelyn replied, and turned to look out at the sea.

Tamlin shrugged and leaned over the side, his stomach thankfully not heaving, although whether it was from being completely empty or him having acquired his sea legs, he did not know. As he gazed at the water, he suddenly thought he heard a wistful note.

Startling, he listened more carefully, but he heard nothing more than the lapping of the waves against the hull. Then, as he turned away, wondering if he had imagined it all, another ethereal note reached his ears.

It was sad, longing, a note that spoke of centuries of love lost and unfulfilled dreams. As it faded, he wiped a tear from the corner of his eye.

And that night, as the Sea Cutter drifted over what had once been Caenwynn, Tamlin dreamed of ancient music and wondrous loss.

"It's getting closer," Telena said, pointing at the horizon.

The Sea Cutter had barely moved that night, the wind against it for the entire evening.

Brodin squinted towards the distance, finally turning away and blinking. "It's a ship. I think the flag is red and green."

Telena heard Jyhanna's voice behind her. "What are you two looking at?"

"A ship," Telena said. "Out there."

But when she looked at the shield-maiden, Jyhanna had grown pale. "Damnation!" the warrior woman cursed. "She's flying the colors of Fenegar!"

Brodin shook his head. "I don't understand."

"Get below decks, both of you," Jyhanna instructed, running off towards the two monks and wizard.

Telena stalked off after Jyhanna, determined not to be simply kept in the dark like that. After all, she was a full fledged woman, wedded and bedded, and for all she knew she could be carrying Brodin's child in her womb. She wasn't a little girl anymore.

"A ship from Fenegar," she heard Jyhanna reporting as she approached, Brodin right at her heels. "Definitely not a merchantman."

Caelyn pursed his lips. "We'll need wind to make our escape. The Sea Cutter couldn't possibly stand against a warship of Fenegar."

Jyhanna shuddered. "I do not wish to be conscripted by the Ghost Ship."

"I think that can be avoided," Sagarum declared. "Time to make some wind. Tamlin, pay close attention to what I do."

The wizard looked up at the sails and began to motion with his hands, as though he was trying to weave something from the air. As he moved, the sails billowed out, propelling the Sea Cutter away from the warship.

Jyhanna looked back towards the Fenegarian vessel.

"They're still gaining!" She turned and stared right at Telena and Brodin. "I thought I told you two to get below decks."

Telena swallowed, suddenly uncertain of the wisdom of her actions. "I wanted to know what was happening."

"We could be about to fight a battle," Jyhanna gritted, loosening her sword in its sheath. "Now get below!"

Grabbing Brodin's hand, Telena dashed into the cabin, watching from the doorway as the sailors scrambled across the rigging, trying to take advantage of the good wind and make clean their escape.

"They must have a wizard on board!" she heard Sagarum declare. "That's the only possible way they could be catching up."

"Can you do something about it?" Caelyn asked.

Sagarum furrowed his brow. "Yes, but I'll have to be careful. If I use too much of my power, it will attract the attention of every Archmagus within a thousand leagues."

As the wizard motioned towards the aft section of the ship, Telena rushed to the porthole at the back of the cabin. When she looked out, she gasped in shock. A giant whirlpool consumed the water, pulling the warship off of its course. Then, the Fenegarian ship rose into the air, gliding across the maelstrom until it sank back down into the sea, far enough away to be safe.

Brodin shook his head. "Incredible. I didn't know magic could do that."

Dashing back to the open door, she saw Sagarum wringing his hands. Jyhanna had her sword out, and was glaring out over the water. Caelyn and Tamlin stood still, the monk saying something too quietly for her to make out.

Sagarum snapped his fingers. "I have it! Let the Archmagus deal with this!" He gestured, a wicked grin on his face.

A snapping sounded behind her, and she and Brodin

looked back to see the Fenegarian warship fall apart, the planks and men falling into the water. They blinked and looked at each other, and then, stunned with shock, stepped back out onto the deck, where they found Sagarum grinning and rubbing his hands with glee.

"We saw the ship..." Brodin began, but then, lost for words, he pointed at the debris rapidly falling back into the distance.

"There are some things that elemental magic can do," Sagarum said, "such as change the nature of an object for a short time. I gave the water underneath the warship the nature of a lodestone." He chuckled. "A *very* large lodestone. The nails from the caravel were very attracted to it...

"We shouldn't have any difficulty getting to Bandre now. Even without my help, this wind will hold for a least three days." The wizard turned on Tamlin, his gaze intense. "You, my young friend, are touched by Wyrd. And you had a premonition about misfortune happening to this vessel that nearly became true. I think that before we go anywhere else, you need to see the Oracle."

Tamlin nodded, uncertainty in his eyes. "If that is what you think is best."

"It is."

"I will go too," Caelyn stated. "Tamlin may be your apprentice now, but I still have a responsibility for his safety."

"I want to see an oracle," Brodin said. "Maybe it can tell us where we can find some land."

Telena nodded. "That is a good idea."

Jyhanna shrugged. "I guess I've got to come as well. These two are my wards, after all."

Sagarum frowned. "I do not know how the Oracle will react to this many people approaching it at once, but there may be some safety in numbers. Very well – when we disembark, we will head north, to the sanctuary of the Great Oracle."

"Will it be an easy trip?" Telena asked hopefully.

Sagarum shook his head. "I'm afraid not. I guess I am very lucky – I have actually been to see the Oracle in the last millennia and lived. I don't know of anybody else who has done that." The wizard shrugged. "But there is always a first time..."

Chapter IV — Landfall

Although the wind held, it took them farther west than they had planned, and they missed their port. Instead, they found themselves off the coast of Bandre, close to the Fenegarian border.

Shaking his head, Captain Nolan pointed at the hoary bluffs of the shore, waves crashing against the cliffs. "There's a place you can land just beyond that rise. But this is as far as I will take you; we're too close to Fenegar for comfort."

A cold drizzle began to fall, dampening Caelyn's robes. Spinning on his heels, he stepped over to where Sagarum, Jyhanna, and Tamlin stood, all watching the coast.

"He's going to put us off," Caelyn reported, shaking his head. "I think I recognize the area, though. There should be a town where we can get supplies about a day from here."

"So we can land, then," Jyhanna said.

The monk nodded. "The water will be rough, however. A storm is coming, and the captain will no doubt wish to ride it back into safer waters."

"Is that possible?" Jyhanna asked, sudden fear in her eyes.

"If the crew has sufficient skill, yes," Caelyn replied. "But it is something that must be done with the greatest of care. The Sea Cutter will have to stay ahead of the storm, riding the winds so that it doesn't get caught by the worst of it. Dangerous, but certainly possible. No less hazardous than remaining in hostile waters."

"I wonder what kind of boat the captain will place us in," Sagarum mused. "He certainly won't ask us to swim there, particularly since we did save his ship."

"He doesn't seem like a gracious sort, but I don't imagine he would be that discourteous," Caelyn admitted. "So, we head to shore, and then buy supplies at the village."

"Do you remember the village's name?"

He shook his head. "I'm afraid it's been over thirty years, and I was only there once."

Sagarum grinned. "And I thought you were a chronicler."

Caelyn shrugged. "All that means is that I can copy facts from books and tell stories."

The wizard sighed. "Someday, friend monk, you *have* to develop a sense of humor. I just hope I'm alive to see it."

Jyhanna chuckled. "You might be wasting your time on this one."

Caelyn just shrugged and strode over to the captain to make arrangements. He had too much on his mind to give in to their chidings, no matter how good-natured they might be.

Within an hour he was sitting in a small rowboat, which happily only leaked a little, pulling on one of the oars and leading his companions towards the small beach that would permit them to land. The stormy sky flashed with lightning, and thunder crashed through the howling wind.

The captain had been a bit more gracious than Caelyn had expected; he had provided them with some blankets and supplies, but only enough food and water for a couple of days. Still, with the village nearby, it was enough.

"I don't feel well at all," Brodin complained, causing the monk to look back at where he and his wife huddled together. His heart went out to the pair, trying desperately to make a life for themselves while surrounded by what future chroniclers would no doubt call "great events."

"We aren't too far away," he said, trying to sound soothing, even though he knew he probably couldn't be heard over the wind. The seas heaved around them, and when he looked away from the landing, the Sea Cutter had disappeared into the distance.

"Can we use some magic to make the seas more gentle?" Tamlin asked. Caelyn smiled. The boy had managed to get his sea legs at last. If only Brodin could have been as lucky.

Sagarum shook his head. "This close to Fenegar, we would in severe danger if either of us wove any spells whatsoever."

Caelyn stared back towards the bluff, noting with satisfaction the small ribbon of sand that had finally appeared. "We'll have to take shelter under the cliffs during the storm!" he called. "There's no way we can get to the village before then!"

"We can use the boat to shield us from the wind," Jyhanna declared. "If only for a while."

"Storms like this tend to blow themselves past very quickly," the monk observed, grunting as he heaved the oar through the water, catching one of the waves. "A while will probably be all the time we need."

For a moment they were all quiet, everybody except for the young lovers concentrating on rowing. The beach elongated as they came closer, and soon they could make out the details of the water crashing into the sand.

"Slow down now," Caelyn directed. "If we don't bring it in gently, we could damage the boat."

"Are we going to have to find a new place to land?" Jyhanna wondered.

Leaping out of the boat to splash into the shallows, Caelyn shook his head. "I hope not, but I always prefer to keep my options open." He pulled the boat onto the shore, moving with difficulty as the water bogged down his robes.

As Jyhanna climbed out of the rowboat to help, thunder rolled towards them. Shaking her head, the shield maiden looked at Caelyn and declared: "We'll have to move quickly. The storm will be upon us soon."

Between the two of them, they pulled the little boat to shore, beaching it on the sand. As the rest of the companions stepped unsteadily out, Caelyn began to survey the bluffs, looking for a good place to hide from the coming onslaught. His wet habit clung to his legs, but he ignored the chill and paced along the sand.

Finally, he came to an outcropping of rocks, forming a partial shelter. He allowed himself a small smile. If they placed the boat overtop of it, it would provide a decent place to wait. His smile faded as he heard some footsteps behind him, soft on the sand.

"This looks good," Jyhanna commented, stepping up behind him. "We can wait it out here, and there's enough room for all of us."

Caelyn nodded. "Go get the others, and have them bring the boat. Hurry."

As she dashed off, the monk gazed out at the oncoming storm. The dark clouds filled the sky, blotting out the mid-afternoon sun. Lightning flashed in the distance, followed close by crashing thunder. And, coming closer with every second, a merciless wall of hail and rain approached.

"This is a nice place!" he heard Sagarum declare, the wizard surveying the site with a practiced eye. "Come along, everybody! We'll need to use the boat as a roof."

Caelyn stepped back and took hold of the rough, worn wood of the rowboat, helping to ease it up over the rocks. Once it was firmly settled, he ushered the others into the makeshift shelter.

"Do you think it will hold?" Telena asked, as the monk took a seat on the sand and closed his eyes. A shrill pattering sounded as the rain began to fall.

"Oh, it should," Sagarum replied. "It was sturdy enough to carry us here. My concern is what the ground will be like once the storm is over."

"Why?"

"In this chill, the water will freeze on the rocks," Sagarum stated. "The ground may be quite treacherous once all is said and done."

Caelyn leaned back, eyes still closed, listening to the wind and rain. Finally, he allowed himself to fall into a light slumber.

The raging storm only ceased with the coming of the dawn. When Caelyn stepped outside, barely able to avoid slipping on the slick rock, a shining wasteland stared back at him. The storm had left a coating of ice on everything, the sunlight reflecting off the almost glacial scene.

Turning carefully to look at the boat, Caelyn noted that it was covered with ice. He shook his head. No matter

159

what, they would have to make their way on land; there was no way they could carry the rowboat with them.

Sagarum stepped out and looked around. "That was quite the storm, wasn't it? Rather odd for this part of the world."

Caelyn shrugged. "I've seen worse."

"I think most of us have," the wizard said. "All but three. Still, this war has changed the balance of nature, and not for the better, I fear."

The monk girded himself against the chill morning. "We should get off this beach. The ground will be easier to manage once we get onto grass and roads."

Caelyn saw Jyhanna emerge from the shelter and blink in shock as she stared at the landscape. He walked slowly off towards the path leaded away from the beach, checking to make certain there were no obstructions along the way.

"I'll wake the others," he heard Jyhanna say as he turned back.

"The path is clear!" the monk called. "The ground is treacherous, though. Walk with care."

Picking his way back to gather his belongings, he found his younger companions gazing around, utterly shocked at their surroundings.

"We never had storms like this," Telena sputtered. "I don't think I've ever seen this much ice."

"You'll see more where we're going," Sagarum declared, throwing his satchel over his shoulder. "Come along, all. I believe Caelyn has been kind enough to find the way for us, and we should be off."

With the greatest of care, the company stepped over the slick rocks, all the while shivering in the cold as they found their way off the beach.

The land that opened up before them as they came onto the main road was colorful and vibrant, with a slight shine from the freezing rain that had fallen. The sparse trees had yet to lose most of their leaves, and tall mountains, their peaks covered with snow, rose in the distance.

"Where are we going?" Tamlin wondered.

"First, we must travel through the Young Forest," Sagarum replied, pointing to the north. "That is approximately two days' journey from here, and we should see it by the afternoon. Then we will venture over the Shroud Mountains, and finally we will go through the Old Forest on the other side."

"Which is the dangerous part?" Jyhanna asked, her voice calm and professional. "I've never been to this part of the world before."

"It will be the mountain passes, or so I believe," Sagarum said. "The forest might have its share of brigands, but with the war they may be engaged in other activities. The Shield Mountains, on the other hand, are wild and perilous; when the Arcalien Empire drove many of the more monstrous creatures out of the Western Lands, that is where they took refuge."

"And the Old Forest?" Jyhanna pressed.

Sagarum shrugged. "That has...other dangers. It is an ancient woodland, and it remembers things that even I am not old enough to have seen."

"Can you be any more specific?"

"Some things are not easy to explain," Sagarum sighed. "To understand them, you must see them first-hand. No doubt we all will."

Caelyn dropped back for a moment, where Tamlin, Brodin, and Telena walked. The two young lovers held each other, and Tamlin looked around nervously.

"How are you faring?" the monk inquired.

"I've been better," Tamlin replied. "The storm shook all of us up, but I just can't shake this feeling that something is wrong."

Caelyn nodded. "Your feeling is correct. Far too many things are wrong right now. All we can do is hope to see them through."

Tamlin shrugged. "I guess. I can't stop wishing that this war had never taken place."

"I think most people feel that way during wars," Caelyn said. "Even the soldiers."

"Brother Caelyn!" he heard Sagarum call. "We have a problem!"

Caelyn bustled up to where Jyhanna and Sagarum stood, nearly slipping on the cobblestones. Finally, he crested a hill, looking down into a small valley.

"By the Eternal One," Caelyn muttered, making the sign of the star.

"What is it?" Telena asked, breaking away from her husband's embrace and stepping forward. When she saw what lay ahead of them, her mouth hung open in shock, and then she fell to her knees and vomited.

"We'll need another source of supplies," Jyhanna muttered, but when Caelyn spun to face her, he found that her face was pale, as though she might be sick at any moment.

Looking down again, he could understand why all too well. The village had been razed to the ground; all that remained were the charred remains of wooden buildings. And, ringing the perimeter like some obscene fence was a line of the villagers, each impaled on a long pole. Not even the elderly or the children had been spared.

Chapter V — Daelyn

Although the road held the icy sheen right to the gates of what had once been a prosperous village, inside the ruins Tamlin discovered the ground to be dry and gravelly. Ashes kicked up at his feet as he walked, and once they had passed the ring of corpses, every step became an effort not to become ill.

"I think we can work out what happened here," Caelyn stated quietly, walking before the apprentice with a careful stride. "They must have come shortly before the storm. There's some fresh blood on the cobbles over there."

Jyhanna pointed to what had once been the village square, but now was nothing more than a ramshackle collection of broken stone and charred planks. "A lot of blood there. They didn't go easily."

"It was Fenegar," Caelyn growled. "In the days of my own service in the army, I saw this sort of thing. The army of Fenegar decided to make an example out of this village. I guess they wanted to keep the other settlements in line."

For a moment, Tamlin wondered what thoughts stirred under the monk's controlled visage. He had never heard Caelyn speak in anger about anything.

"What about supplies?" Telena asked, poking at a burnt board, and then turning to embrace her husband. Whether she wanted to hold or be held Tamlin didn't know.

"We'll have to forage," Sagarum said. "Even this late in the season, there will be some food in the fields that we can use."

Caelyn shook his head. "Not for this village. I saw the fields from the rise; what they didn't take, they burned."

"Then we'll go to the next hamlet," Sagarum insisted. "And then, once we're in the Young Forest, we'll be able to live off the land."

"Should we give them a proper burial?" Tamlin wondered, motioning to the horrifying circle surrounding them.

Jyhanna shook her head. "If we do, it might incite the Fenegarians to greater violence. I would not bring the sword to the other villages nearby if we can avoid it."

Caelyn straightened his robes. "I do have a duty to them, however." He strode over to the first corpse in the line and muttered a prayer, then stepped to the next one.

"What is he doing?" Brodin asked, sidling over to Jyhanna.

"He is praying for them," Jyhanna answered. "That way, they can go guiltless to the Eternal One's bosom."

"Shouldn't we be hurrying north?" Brodin said. "If we barely have any supplies..."

Jyhanna shook her head. "We can survive without food for one day. Right now, their souls are more important."

"Are wars always like this?" Telena asked, wiping a tear from her eye. "Do the innocent always suffer?"

"Not always," Jyhanna said sadly. "But most of the time. I think there was a time, long ago, when only the armies fought, and the people were left alone. But now, everybody is an enemy to be destroyed, regardless of their age or if they can even pick up a weapon."

Stepping forward, Tamlin managed to hear some of the monk's prayer. "May the Eternal One forgive your sins, my child. May he see you safely to his light, where the Damned One may not touch you. May you be free from violence and death for the rest of eternity, until the cycle begins again."

By the time Caelyn had finished performing the last rites, the afternoon sun hung low in the sky. It was Sagarum who broke the respectful silence, saying, "We have a long way to go, Brother Caelyn, and we should get started."

The monk nodded. "I have done what I needed to do. Their souls have been sent to the Eternal One. Their bodies are now empty shells; what happens to them no longer matters. May the Damned One take the souls of those who started this war."

With that, they began their trek out of the village, and into the fields of Bandre.

By mid-morning on the third day after leaving the village, the Young Forest was in sight, a long, colorful stretch of trees that filled the horizon. As they walked on through the afternoon, finally resting at night under a small copse, Tamlin began to realize that they had already entered the outskirts of the woodland. A small fire, started by Jyhanna, crackled in its pit, a small rabbit Caelyn had caught, killed, and skinned, roasting over it.

"We'll have to go through that?" Tamlin said, listening to his stomach growl. "It doesn't look difficult at

165

all."

"There is some danger," Sagarum declared. "Some creatures from elder days, and some of the trees themselves may not make us welcome. It will not be nearly as perilous as the Old Forest, however, which has no tolerance for our kind at all."

Tamlin heard a dry chuckle, and he saw Sagarum, Jyhanna, and Caelyn all leap up in shock. Somehow, a stranger had approached, catching them all completely unawares. The newcomer was a tall man, wearing a strange green coat with buttons on the front over a grey tunic and pants. At his side was sheathed a long, thin, curved sword with an ornamented ivory hilt, and in his hands he held a wide-brimmed felt hat.

"I suppose you could call me a creature from elder days, but I doubt I would be dangerous to you, my friend," the man said to Sagarum. "You yourself seem to be keeping strange company."

"Daelyn!" Sagarum exclaimed, leaping up to take the man's hand. "It's been centuries!"

Moving with an almost inhuman feline grace, Daelyn sat down on a log by the fire. As he made himself comfortable, Tamlin noted that he had long blond hair that tied back in a ponytail, and that his eyes seemed different somehow, an alien quality that he couldn't quite put his finger on.

"My friends, please allow me to introduce Daelyn, the grey wanderer," Sagarum said, sitting down as the other slowly returned to their seats. "Daelyn is one of the Tuatha de Danaan, and an immortal far older than myself. Daelyn, this is Brother Caelyn, Jyhanna, my apprentice Tamlin, Brodin, and his wife, Telena."

Daelyn nodded. "A pleasure to meet you all."

Jyhanna blinked. "The grey wanderer?"

"I used to wear a lot of grey," Daelyn said. "Besides,

166

I love this coat."

Sagarum chuckled. "So why are you here, Daelyn? This world is a bit off the beaten path for you."

"I am searching for my people," Daelyn replied. "There was a crisis, and they were forced from their homeland some five millennia ago. I was away when it happened. Ever since, I have been trying to find them." He leaned forward. "Have any of you seen anything that could be of the Tuatha de Danaan? Mounds that might seem unearthly? Islands where time does not run as it does elsewhere in the land?"

Sagarum shook his head sadly. "I'm sorry my friend, but it has been a very long time since any of the Sidhe ventured here. There was never enough natural magic for your kind to take a great liking to this world. Millennia ago, there was only a small settlement, but they left this world for greener pastures."

Daelyn sat back thoughtfully. "Then I will have to consult the Great Oracle, as I had originally planned."

Tamlin blinked. "We are going there too. Sagarum says that I am touched by Wyrd."

Daelyn suddenly gazed at him, and it was all Tamlin could do not to recoil. The stare was so intense that he felt as though his entire soul was exposed for the Tuatha de Danaan to see. And then, abruptly, Daelyn turned and looked deep into the fire.

"Sagarum is correct, my young friend," he said. "You are touched by a very powerful Wyrd. Happily, you have a good teacher."

"I will do my best to prepare him for whatever is to come," Sagarum stated. "But what of my mentor, Delgar Daegar's Son? How is he?"

Daelyn leaned back and stroked his hairless face. "You did not know, did you? Delgar passed beyond around three millennia ago. I think he finally found peace."

Sagarum blinked away a tear. "That is fell news. I will miss him."

"Three thousand years is a long time to be out of touch," Jyhanna said. "Surely you mis-spoke?"

Daelyn shook his head. "I fear not. It truly has been three millennia."

"For immortals such as ourselves, who wander the Great Road, this sort of delay is not unknown," Sagarum explained. "The Road of Legends is endless and there are infinite worlds to visit and explore. The odds of one traveler encountering another are extremely slim."

"Immortality does seem to boggle the mind," Caelyn commented.

Daelyn shrugged. "For those of us who are born to it, it is not too complicated. I have been alive for twelve thousand years, and I am young compared to others of my kind. There are those who have lived for eons, but they are few and far between now."

"I don't understand," Tamlin said. "If they are immortal, doesn't that mean they would survive?"

Daelyn raised an eyebrow. "I said 'immortal,' not 'invulnerable.' I may be able to live until the end of the cycle, but I can still be struck down. The same with Sagarum, or Delgar, or even Otar the Sage, who has lived even longer than I."

"I wonder if we will meet him," Tamlin mused. "Otar, I mean. It seems that we are surrounded by ageless beings recently."

Daelyn chuckled. "I have no doubt that Otar would be delighted to meet you, but he is far away on the Road now. He follows the great conflict between the Eternal One and the Damned One, and I do not believe you want that to come here once again."

The Tuatha de Danaan suddenly turned to Brodin and

Telena. "You two are awfully quiet. Don't you have any questions for me?"

Telena shrugged. "I think that I've learned enough just listening."

"Besides," Brodin added, "what could we possibly ask that wouldn't be a trivial matter?"

Daelyn smiled. "Those are a very wise things to say. You both have a great deal of self-knowledge. I will tell you this, however: so long as you pay heed to your heart and follow your dreams, even death will have no fear for you."

"Thank you, sir Tuatha de Danaan," Telena said, nodding her head.

"Just 'Daelyn' will be fine. I don't stand on ceremony."

"Will you help guide us?" Sagarum asked. "There is strength in numbers, and we could use your sword arm, if not your wisdom."

Daelyn leaned back. "What you suggest has merit. The Shroud Mountains will be perilous, and so will the Old Forest. Yes, I think I will join you."

"There is a larger issue at stake," Sagarum began. "There is a great war, and-"

Daelyn held up his hand. "I have walked this world long enough to know what this battle is, and it is not a fight I wish to join. I will see you to the Oracle and then back again, but then I must follow my own path."

Sagarum shrugged. "I wish you would choose differently, but I still thank you for accompanying us."

Daelyn stood up and bowed. "It would be my pleasure. I spend too little time with good companions, and too much time alone on my own journeys."

As Daelyn sat down, Jyhanna and Sagarum parceled out the roasted rabbit. For a short time, the company sat and ate, everybody but Sagarum sneaking looks at Daelyn.

"Well," Caelyn said, straightening his habit and beginning to fold out some blankets for sleeping, "I think we should all rest before morning. Otherwise, we may not have enough strength for the voyage ahead."

Sagarum nodded. "That would be wise. I will stand first watch."

Jyhanna loosened her sword and handed it to the wizard. "I'll take the second one. If we are attacked, feel free to use this."

As Tamlin lay down, wrapping himself in a bundle of blankets, he regarded the newcomer with wary eyes. Something fundamental and intangible had just changed – he could feel it – and he had a feeling that he would not remain untouched by the Tuatha de Danaan's presence.

Then Daelyn seemed to startle and notice that Tamlin was staring at him. Smiling, the Tuatha de Danaan looked directly at him and said something quietly in his musical voice, but Tamlin could not make it out. Suddenly, sleep claimed him, casting him into dreams of forests and mountain passes.

Chapter VI — The Young Forest

Daelyn stopped abruptly, holding up his hand. Behind him, the company halted, looking around at the dense foliage. Birds chirped nervously in the trees, but then their song took on a more joyous note. Jyhanna waited patiently, wondering what the Tuatha de Danaan would do.

She still wasn't certain of what to make of Daelyn. He had the discipline of a soldier, and she had yet to see a wasted movement. However, there were other aspects that reminded her of a Skald or monk.

But, her instincts told her to trust him, and she did. He had yet to lead them astray, and the company had not encountered a soul since they had set out that morning into the Young Forest.

"There was a disturbance," Daelyn finally said. "But I think it has passed us."

"I heard nothing," Jyhanna pointed out.

"It was the land that told me something was wrong,"

171

Daelyn said. "My people are very finely attuned to the natural world. And this forest is more...friendly to your people."

"I don't understand."

Daelyn pursed his lips, as though he was searching for a way to explain it. "For those who know how to listen, the forest is friendly. To all others, it is simply there. Do not worry; it would take you a lifetime to learn how to hear what the land has to say."

"What was the disturbance?" Sagarum asked, stepping up. The wizard held his staff in his hands, the bottom end blunted and dirty from being used as a walking stick.

Daelyn frowned, and Jyhanna found herself concerned by the expression. "I do not know," the Tuatha de Danaan finally replied. "It was something unnatural, as though some creature has been let loose in the world. The forest shielded us from it, and will continue to, so long as we do not offend."

"How do we not offend a forest?" Brodin blurted. "It's all trees..."

Daelyn smiled, a grin filled with wisdom and mischief. "Exactly. When you must make a fire this evening, take only deadwood. If there is no deadwood, take only a little from the living trees, and speak gently to them before you do. Never forget that the land is alive, and it remembers."

"Like the ghostly soldiers," Tamlin muttered.

"Sorry?" Jyhanna said. "I didn't hear that. Did you say 'ghostly soldiers?'"

Tamlin nodded. "As Sagarum, Caelyn, and I were traveling together, we passed through an old battlefield. At night, spectral armies refought the battle. Caelyn said that it was because the land remembers all the blood spilt."

"It is the same principle," Daelyn said. "But forests are special places, where the land bears the most life. Their memory is much greater than the rest of the earth.

Especially when the woodland has been standing for tens of thousands of years, like this one."

"I thought this was the 'Young Forest,'" Jyhanna said.

Once again, Daelyn smiled. "In comparison, it is but an infant. When we reach the Old Forest, you will see a woodland that has stood longer than your race."

Leading them forward again, Daelyn stepped carefully over the rough soil, taking them through a path that only he seemed to know. Yet, although there was no way that Jyhanna could ever call it a road, the way was easy to traverse, and by the time the sun began to set, they had journeyed several leagues.

As they made camp, Jyhanna singled out Brodin and Telena to gather wood for the fire. They jumped at the chance, and she smiled; they had been allowed almost no time to themselves since leaving the ship. "Take no living wood if you can help it," Daelyn reminded them. "It is the goodwill of the forest that will allow us to travel safely."

Agreeing vigorously, the two newlyweds set out, leaving the rest of the company to pitch their blankets under the tall trees. Daelyn walked with them shortly, then returned to the camp and began to pace the perimeter, chanting softly and occasionally plucking an apple from one of the nearby trees.

"How much farther do we have to go?" Jyhanna asked.

Caelyn shrugged, crossing his legs under his habit as he sat on his blankets. "A few days, I would imagine. It will be a long journey if we must pass through the Shroud Mountains; I doubt we will be back by the end of the season."

"You've been there before," Jyhanna said. A statement, not a question.

The monk nodded. "In my childhood, I traveled quite widely."

"Some day, I would like to hear of the places you have

been," Sagarum declared. "There is still something about you I do not understand."

"My past is my own affair," Caelyn said.

"At least we will not need to post a watch tonight," Sagarum said as Daelyn returned to the camp, placing his own blankets on the ground. He placed the apples on the blanket and invited the others to share.

"Why not?" Jyhanna demanded, biting into the juicy fruit. "Daelyn himself said that unnatural things walk in the forest, and we are still in a nation at war."

"I have set a Tuatha de Danaan ward," Daelyn answered. "Anybody who is not of our company will be able to walk right through our camp and still be unaware of us."

"What about wizards?" Tamlin asked nervously. "We couldn't cast any magic because of enemy Archmagi."

"This is a different kind of magic," Sagarum said. "You could say that his spell was more a matter of convincing the forest to hide us, rather than actually putting up an enchantment."

"There is much more to it," Daelyn said. "But that explanation is accurate enough."

"So what do you seek?" Jyhanna asked. "I know why the rest of us are going to the Oracle, but I don't understand why a magical being like yourself would."

"I'm a magical being too!" Sagarum sputtered, a grin on his face.

"Yes, but you're taking Tamlin to the Oracle," Jyhanna pointed out. "You're not actually asking any questions of your own, at least not that you've told us."

"I have one question, and I have thought about it for centuries," Daelyn said. "The Great Oracle is known for only allowing one answer to any soul in their lifetime. I had to consider my question carefully."

"You're going to ask where your people are," Jyhanna

said.

Daelyn shook his head. "Even were I to ask where they are right now, by the time I got there, they might have moved on. No, my question is much different. I will ask if I will ever find my people."

"That's not a terribly helpful question," Tamlin said. "I mean, it doesn't actually tell you where they are."

Daelyn smiled, but this time there was a great sadness in his eyes. "On the contrary, it is the most important question I could ever ask. It is the question that will give me hope."

Sagarum nodded, picking up an apple and taking a bite. "That makes sense."

Jyhanna glared at the Tuatha de Danaan and Sagarum, wondering with annoyance why the "wise" always seemed to be so obscure. "Not to me it doesn't. Tamlin's right; it is a useless query."

"No, it isn't," Daelyn stated. "I know where your understanding of the question comes from, though. You are a warrior; you concern yourself with how to win the battle, rather than whether it can be won.

"I, however, have been a soldier, a bard, and a druid, among many things. And I have long known that there are two things that any creature needs to succeed: love and hope. It is hope that gives one the will to go on, and love that makes the task worthy. I have searched for my people for millennia now, and even I need to know that my task will have an end."

Jyhanna was silent for a moment, struck into awe by Daelyn's statement. She had spent so much time worrying about tactics in her life that she had rarely thought about such things.

"Now I understand," she said.

At that moment, Brodin and Telena, looking slightly flushed, returned with a bundle of firewood. As Caelyn took the wood from them and began to build a fire, she saw Sagarum lean forward, a mischievous grin on his face.

"I noticed that you were rather silent, friend Caelyn," the wizard stated.

The monk shrugged. "Jyhanna didn't appear to require my help to embarrass herself in front of Daelyn."

As she opened her mouth to protest, Sagarum staggered back, awestruck. "By the Eternal One! Did you just make a *joke*?"

Caelyn just returned to the fire pit, stacking the wood and then lighting it with his tinderbox.

"What happened?" Telena asked, gazing at the shocked company.

Sagarum burst out laughing. "Our dear, humorless Brother Caelyn has just spoken a very fine joke. There may be hope for him yet!"

"We should rest," Daelyn chuckled. "We have a long day ahead of us tomorrow, and we will be walking into peril shortly."

In the following days, the foliage grew denser, but Daelyn seemed to always be able to find a way through the forest. Sometimes he would stand still and sing something incomprehensible under his breath, and then lead the company down a different path than the one he had originally chosen. By the time they camped on the third day, Jyhanna was hopelessly lost.

However, she had to admit that Daelyn was seeing them through the woodland. The Shroud Mountains filled the horizon, reaching into the sky like stone giants, majestically claiming the world as their own.

And then, slowly, the woodland began to thin, the giant oaks and elms becoming few and far between as the ground grew grey and rocky. A cold wind blew down on

176

them from above, and on the fourth day upon camping they all wrapped themselves up in their blankets, only Daelyn and Sagarum leaving briefly to gather firewood and some food.

"Tomorrow we will be there, I think," Jyhanna heard Caelyn telling the younger members of the company.

"Will it be this cold?" Telena asked, teeth chattering.

Caelyn nodded, and Jyhanna's heart went out to the young pair. "Probably colder."

"Use your blankets as an extra layer of clothing," she suggested. "That will keep out most of the chill."

The next day, a light snow began to fall, making the world somehow seem more magical than usual. But as they ventured forward, a biting wind rose out of the north, blasting into them and forcing them to wrap their cloaks tight around themselves.

They staggered forward, Daelyn leading the way, but the path had become jagged and difficult. Even the Tuatha de Danaan sometimes had difficulty, stopping more often to hum quietly as he tried to pick the best route.

At least, that was what Jyhanna had concluded he was doing. There was still so much about Daelyn that she didn't, or thought she would never, understand.

Finally, as the sun began to set, they stood at the foothills of the Shroud mountains, gazing up at what appeared to be a giant crevice in the hoary stone.

"That is our mountain pass?" Tamlin wondered, stamping his feet to keep warm.

Daelyn nodded. "Now it truly gets dangerous."

Chapter VII — Hazardous Journeys

High above them rose the relentless peaks, the snow-capped ridge menacing even in the soft light of the morning. Still they strode forward, carefully picking their path along the thin mountain pass.

As they walked, Brodin chewed on an apple that Daelyn had picked the night before. They had all been very busy foraging that night, barely getting any sleep at all. But it was necessary; according to both Daelyn and Sagarum, it was at least five days before they would reach the end of the pass, and then another two days to the Old Forest.

He offered Telena a bite of his apple, which she gladly accepted. He had to fight back the instinct to just embrace his wife and never let go, but he had to put on a strong front for her. He could see the uncertainty in her eyes, and no matter what, he didn't want her to know that he felt exactly the same way.

But they had little or no choice. They couldn't have

stayed in their homeland, and the rest of the world appeared to be at war. What had begun as a simple hunt for some land to settle had become an exercise in dodging battle, a game that they had so far played successfully, even if only by the skin of their teeth at times.

He stumbled over a rock, breaking his chain of thought. As he fell, both Jyhanna and Telena caught him, keeping him on his feet. He smiled. At least they had good companions, the sort of people you could trust your life to. He shuddered to think of what it would be like if they were alone.

A chill wind kicked up, forcing him to wrap his cloak closer around himself. The higher they got, the colder it became. It reminded him of their journey through the mountains ringing Beregar, but here there were no ancient carvings to instill awe and wonder. With every step, he was certain that any mistake would be his last.

Daelyn held up his hand, his head cocked as though he was listening intently to something. Brodin stopped and watched, gazing around tiredly to see where they were. The pass had widened, and it appeared that a fork in the road lay ahead. The towering mountains still reached up into the heavens, casting them in the shade regardless of the clear blue sky.

Head still cocked, the Tuatha de Danaan drew his sword, motioning to Jyhanna and Caelyn. Tamlin stepped back, raising his hands, only to be stopped by Sagarum shaking his head. Brodin shivered and wondered what was going to happen.

Jyhanna walked back and whispered to both Brodin and his wife. "There is an ambush ahead. Be very quiet, and be ready to run if things go poorly." With that, she unsheathed her sword, the steel dull in the shadows, and took position between Daelyn and Caelyn.

Brodin swallowed, icy fear unsettling his stomach.

179

Memories of the incident at Civilis, where he had nearly lost his life, flooded his mind. He held Telena close, hoping that his fear wouldn't show, and watched the front rank of his companions. Sagarum and Tamlin stayed a bit back, the ancient wizard waiting calmly. The Tuatha de Danaan made some gestures with his hands, pointing first to the earth and then to the fork. The fear turned to curiosity as Jyhanna, Daelyn, and Caelyn began to pick up small rocks from the path.

He blinked, shaking his head in bewilderment. First the monk tossed a couple of the rocks, the stones landing only a bit ahead of them. Then Jyhanna threw her rocks, the stones thumping to the ground a bit farther out. Finally the Tuatha de Danaan tossed his pebbles, the rocks landing almost at the fork.

There was a great crash, and Brodin jumped in shock. A giant boulder landed just where the last pebbles had fallen, and a deafening roar filled the air. Two large creatures, so huge that they blocked the path, leapt out, their faces simian and primal, glaring with hatred.

Lumbering forward, they held large axes at the ready, death in their eyes. "WE KILL YOU ALL!" one declared, running forward, charging straight towards the Tuatha de Danaan.

So quickly that Brodin couldn't see the movement, Daelyn sidestepped and slashed with his blade. The monster knelt down, screaming in pain, trying desperately to hold in its intestines. With another quick stroke, Daelyn ended its suffering.

Brodin turned to gaze at Jyhanna, who was dodging and weaving, easily keeping out of range of the giant axe. The second creature screamed in rage, and Jyhanna yelled a warcry. Yet the two opponents were too perfectly matched; no matter how she moved, the best she could do was inflict a minor cut on the monster's thick skin.

The creature suddenly screamed in pain and fell, Jyhanna's blade twisted in its gut. Just when Brodin thought he would retch, he heard a scream, and another monster leaped down from the rock face, landing right before him, axe raised and murder in its eyes.

Spinning Telena behind him, he waited in terror for the blow, but it never came. A crack resounded in the air, and the monster slumped down. Behind it stood Caelyn, bearing his oak walking staff like a club. With a quick blow, the monk brought the tip of the staff down on the creatures throat, causing its entire body to jerk as it struggled for air. Caelyn looked up, and for a moment Brodin thought he saw something flash in the monk's eyes.

For a moment he saw the eyes of a cold-blooded killer in Caelyn's gentle features.

More grunts and screams erupted from the front, where Daelyn and Jyhanna fought against three more of the creatures. Daelyn dispatched the first, taking its head off with a swing so fast that Brodin never even saw the flash of the blade. Blood spraying from the wound, the body fell to the ground.

With a sudden slash, Jyhanna gutted the second one, only to have the third attack. The shield-maiden was forced back, the giant creature rearing its head and roaring with every devastating blow. Unlike the others, it was ornamented with bandoliers of feathers slung around its hairy chest.

With inhuman speed, Daelyn swung into action, slicing into the back of the monster. Screaming in agony, it crumpled to the ground, only to have both Jyhanna and Daelyn transfix it on their blades. With a scream of rage, Jyhanna pulled out her sword and drove it through the monster's forehead, splattering brains and fragments of the creature's skull.

The fetid stench of death filled the air as Daelyn and

Jyhanna surveyed their work. When one of the creatures twitched, Jyhanna thrust her blade into its body, no doubt to make certain that it was dead. Brodin couldn't hold it in any longer. Falling to the earth, he threw up, vomiting for so long he thought it would last forever.

As he spat, trying to rid his mouth of the bitter taste, he felt concerned hands on his back, patting him gently. "Don't worry," Caelyn's voice said. "It's all over. We're safe now."

Weakly, Brodin rose, accepting Telena's offer of her canteen. While his wife hadn't thrown up, she looked very pale and ill, and he wondered how close she had come.

"We should be safe until we reach the end," Daelyn stated, pointing at the monster with the feathered bandoliers. "I believe this one was their leader."

"What were they?" Tamlin asked, his voice still quivering.

While the apprentice did approach one of the creatures to get a better look, Brodin stayed back. He alternated between wishing he had never left Beregar and just wanting to run back to a port city and wait until the war ended.

"These are Ogres," Sagarum stated. "Some of the monsters driven out of the Western Lands by the Arcalien Empire, and by some of the other Kingdoms that have flourished in this area. They prey on what travelers and animals they can find. No doubt this was what they considered a good ambush point."

Jyhanna nodded. "Catch them at the fork, while they're trying to decide where they will go. Makes sense."

"We'll want to take the path to the left," Sagarum stated. "That will lead us out of the mountains."

"Where does the other way go?" Tamlin asked.

Sagarum smiled, his eyes suddenly euphoric. "Once, a very long time ago, there was a city in the Shroud

182

Mountains. It was a hidden city, a place of great magic and learning. But now it has been long since abandoned, longer than I have been alive. Even the name has been lost in the mists of time."

The wizard shrugged, an impish smile on his face. "I would take all of us there, but we do have so many more important tasks to worry about. Needless to say, it is a wondrous place, assuming the dark things haven't managed to conquer its wards."

"We should go," Daelyn stated, cleaning and sheathing his sword. "We have managed to overcome this peril, but the longer we stay here, the more likely it is that the Ogres will recover from the loss of their leader and attack us. Better to be in the Old Forest before then."

With that, the company walked past the reeking bodies and further into the mountains.

If there was a word that Brodin would use to describe the trek through the pass, it was "long." The range seemed to go on forever, the path twisting and turning as though it was a long snake. At least the Shroud Mountains didn't have any crevices such as the peaks lining Beregar, but that didn't stop them from suffering.

The food began to run out, and they found themselves almost constantly hungry, never able to eat enough to nourish them in the cold. Even though Brodin and Telena snuggled up together beside the fire every night, still somebody would have to wake them at least once an hour, just to make certain that they weren't suffering from exposure.

By the fourth day in the pass, they were all staggering along, so hungry and tired that Brodin was certain he would sleep for a week once they had made it through the mountains. A vision of the company carrying him through the Old Forest on a litter gave him a brief chuckle, but then he had to wrap his cloak around tightly, guarding against the biting wind that never left them.

Brodin blinked, straightening and startling Telena, who held him as she walked. In the distance, he heard a dull roar.

"What is that?" he asked, causing Caelyn and Jyhanna to stop and gaze at him.

"That should be a river, if I'm not mistaken," the monk replied. "It doesn't sound like a landslide or a creature."

"It is one of the mountain rivers," Sagarum said. "It had a name once, but that was long past. It had been millennia since anybody actually cared about this region enough to give this river a name."

Turning the bend, they came to a steep downwards slope, the path rocky and rough, almost as though there had once been stairs carved into the rock, leading down.

"We are close to the end," Sagarum said. "Once we cross the river, we will be merely a couple of days away from the Old Forest, and less than a week from the Great Oracle."

Choosing their steps with care, the company climbed down the slope, Brodin nearly slipping once, but catching himself before he tumbled down the path. At the bottom they found a canyon with the raging river, a rickety wooden rope-bridge leading across it. From where they stood, he could see that some of the planks were missing, creating small gaps in the crossing.

"Step carefully," Sagarum warned. "This bridge has stood up for millennia, but I doubt it has much life left to it."

Daelyn crossed first, one hand on one of the ropes and the other on the hilt of his sword. With each step the Tuatha de Danaan took, the planks creaked in agony, as though they might snap at any moment.

Jyhanna crossed second, followed by Caelyn and Sagarum. All of them moved as quickly as they could, constantly holding onto the ropes, just in case. When Tamlin crossed, the bridge creaked and whined more than it had earlier, and when Telena stepped over Brodin's heart leapt into his mouth, visions of the wood giving way and sending her plummeting to her death flooding his mind.

Brodin was the last person to cross. He took hold of the two ropes on either side, and placed his foot on the first plank. The wood groaned, but held. Step by step, looking down as often as he looked to the other end, he made his way along the ancient bridge, heart pounding so hard that he could swear the others would be able to hear it.

Suddenly, the plank he stepped on gave way, along with the one he had been standing on. Gripping wildly on the ropes, he tried not to scream out with fear, even as the others cried out in alarm from the other side of the chasm. The sweat ran on his palms, and his right hand lost its grip, sending him crashing to the left-hand side. With all of his strength, he gripped the rope with both hands, legs flailing as they sought anything that could be a solid surface.

His mind began to take control, forcing him away from blind instinct. His first priority was to get to a solid plank, one that would hold his weight. So he had to shift forward.

Gritting his teeth and praying to whatever gods might be able to hear that he would survive, he inched along the rope, trying to get his legs onto one of the planks. Finally, his feet found purchase, but he couldn't regain his balance, and he hung there, certain that he would lose his grip and plummet to his death.

"Take my hand," a voice said, cutting through the terror. Brodin looked up to see Daelyn standing, perfectly balanced, beside him, arm outstretched.

With a grunt, he took the Tuatha de Danaan's hand, and Daelyn pulled him up, not even breaking a sweat. Then, Daelyn led him across, frequently looking back to see how he was doing.

When they got to the end of the bridge, Telena leapt into his arms, weeping on his shoulder, although he could not tell if they were tears of joy or terror. Slowly they slumped down, and his own tears came.

Finally, as they regained control and disengaged from each other, Sagarum smiled at him and said: "You'll be happy to know that this was the last danger we had to face in the pass. We'll be out of the mountains tomorrow afternoon."

That night, they camped a few hours away from the river, the dull roar still audible despite the howling wind. Brodin slept fitfully that night, his dreams filled with nightmares of falling.

In the end, the wizard was absolutely right. The next afternoon, after a long and tiring trek, they emerged from the Shroud Mountains into a dry grassland, the Old Forest distant yet filling the horizon.

Chapter VIII — The Old Forest

It took them two days to reach the Old Forest, but at least they were able to forage beforehand. It was a welcome change from the times when Tamlin had thought they would not make it through the Shroud Mountains.

At Sagarum's instruction, he had ceased to practice his spell weaving. "Especially around the Old Forest, it is too dangerous," the ancient wizard had said. "This woodland has little tolerance for mortal things, and our kind of magic is a mortal thing."

And so, during the night, he sat by the fire, waiting for his turn at watch, when Jyhanna would hand him her sword and tell him to wake her if anything broke through Daelyn's wards. The chill wind kept him alert, and sometimes he wished that he had brought warmer clothes.

But winter had come to the Western Lands, and Tamlin knew that within weeks there would be nowhere to hide from it's frigid hand. The fact that it had touched the northlands first was one that could only be accepted.

After a hard trek through the grasslands, the first pines of the Old Forest stood before them, the midday sun streaming through the trees to illuminate the ground ahead. Although it looked beautiful, Tamlin felt a sense of unbelonging whenever he looked at the trees, as though they were just waiting to harm him. Daelyn raised his hand, and they came to a halt.

"From this point, there will be no fires," the Tuatha de Danaan stated. "We are unwelcome guests in an ancient land, and we must be cautious. Do not harm a single tree or animal, no matter what happens."

"How far is it to the Oracle?" Tamlin wondered, staring into the woods. A shadow seemed to creep along the ground, almost as though the trees were moving to block the sunlight, but when he looked closely it appeared to be just his imagination. He bent down to pick up a long piece of deadwood, both for a walking stick and just in case there was some danger inside the depths of the forest.

"Less than a day," Sagarum replied. "But first we must survive the Old Forest. It will not allow us to cross easily."

"I believe that I can provide some aid," Daelyn said, leaning down and singing softly as he touched the ground. Although Tamlin couldn't understand the words, the melody coursed through his veins, as though he could feel as well as hear the music. It was soft and sad, and spoke of an eternity of pain.

Cocking his head, Daelyn listened to the breeze, finally shaking his head and standing. "I do not know if the forest heard me. However, I have told it that we are coming, and that we will conduct ourselves well. Anything further would be an offense."

"But aren't your people ancient and magical?" Tamlin wondered. "From what I've seen you do..."

Daelyn shook his head. "There are things in this world that are far older even than the Tuatha de Danaan. There are wonders that no mortal eye has ever seen, that passed away long before the memory of most creatures on the Road. Only the Dragons have seen all, and they are few now, except in one world."

"This is one of those 'older things,'" Sagarum added. "This forest has stood since the birth of this world. It remembers the Dragon Masters, the Great Revolt, and the many sunderings that followed. For most mortals, it is closed. Very few who attempt to walk in it ever return."

Tamlin shook his head. "I don't understand what these things are. Dragon Masters? Great Revolt?"

"They are stories that would take longer to tell than we have," Daelyn stated. "However, I have a feeling that you will learn them in time. Come, if there is any moment when we should be entering, it is now."

As soon as he stepped foot in the Old Forest, a sense of dread crept over him. The trees loomed tall and menacing overhead, and sometimes he could swear that he saw something large move deep in the shadows.

Hearing a yelp of shock from behind, Tamlin spun on his heels, makeshift staff at the ready. Telena was gripping her husband, staring at the ground with horrified eyes. A bleached and decayed human skull lay at her feet, empty eyes gazing upwards.

"I think we've just had our first warning," Sagarum mused. "I wonder what his crime was. Starting a fire, perhaps. The Forest doesn't like that sort of thing."

"We should go on," Daelyn said. "Sagarum, do you know the way?"

The wizard nodded. "This is not the first time I have been here, my friend."

Carefully they picked their way through the trees, the oppressive silence rendering the pounding of Tamlin's heart deafening to his ears. Before them lay what appeared to be a clear path, but when Tamlin looked behind them, he found that the trees had closed up, trapping them.

Shuddering, he offered a silent prayer to the Eternal One to allow him to see another day. Suffering an unknown fate in a forest would be too much for him. Nowhere else to go, he followed his companions, certain that with every step the path behind grew shorter.

Daelyn held up his hand. As Tamlin approached, he saw that the Tuatha de Danaan was standing stiffly as he stared into a large clearing. At the center stood a large mound, around eight feet tall and twenty feet long. The hill was covered in grass, but perfectly round, as though it had been placed there by design rather than accident.

"I will be right back," Daelyn said. "Wait here, and don't touch anything." With that, he strode into the clearing, circling around the mound and chanting. What little of his song that reached Tamlin's ears appeared to be cautious but inquisitive. Finally, he shook his head and walked back to the company.

"That was a Tuatha de Danaan place," Daelyn said sadly. "But it has been abandoned for some time. Tens of millennia, I would say. The hill does not even remember who dwelt in it, and the earth has a very long memory."

"I never knew that your people once dwelt in this part of the Western Lands," Sagarum said. "I wonder why they left this place, and why the Forest decided to show it to you. Another warning, perhaps?"

Daelyn shook his head. "I doubt it. This mound was not breached by violence, and there is no sign of battle. I would guess that the time came for my people to leave, and they all left."

The Tuatha de Danaan shook his head, and when he spoke, Tamlin detected an extra hint of sadness in his voice. "We should continue on to the Oracle. There is nothing for me here."

Deep into the forest they walked, each step echoing in the endless trees, the great pines closing their branches behind them. Tamlin's dread increased with every step, and if it wasn't for the presence of Daelyn and Sagarum, he would have bolted long ago, even though he knew it would mean his death.

"We are close," Sagarum declared. "I can sense the Great Oracle now."

"What does it look like?" Tamlin wondered. "I've never seen an oracle before."

Sagarum grinned. "You'll see when you get there. I think you'll be pleasantly surprised."

Jyhanna snorted. "No doubt it will be a buxom maiden, from the way you talk."

Tamlin saw the wizard's smile widen, and he wondered what Sagarum was hiding. No doubt he would be rolling in laughter soon.

"We will first have to pass its guardians," Daelyn stated, standing in a pool of sunlight. The mid-afternoon sun shone though the foliage, taking some of the edge off of the woods.

"So long as we can make it to the entrance, we will have passed the most difficult guardian," Sagarum said. "To pass the others, all we must do is show that our intent is pure."

"How will we do that?" Jyhanna asked.

Sagarum shrugged. "Be honest. And shed no blood. Otherwise you won't live to rue the mistake."

With that, he led them forward, climbing over the rough terrain as the path sloped upwards. To Tamlin's shock, the trees became less dense, and their omnipresent malice lightened, only to be replaced by another threat. With each step, Tamlin became certain that he was being watched, as though hidden eyes lay behind every tree.

Abruptly, the path turned, leading them to a great

gaping maw in the ground. The cave sunk deep into the earth, but Sagarum didn't even break his pace, leading the company into the depths.

To Tamlin's surprise, the darkness gave way to an eerie green glow, the walls of the cave covered by a phosphorescent moss. The tunnel narrowed, and strange shadows began to flutter before his eyes. For a moment, he thought that they were creatures, but whenever he turned to stare at one, it was only the play of the light.

"You are known to us, Sagarum," a voice hissed. Tamlin spun, but no matter where he looked, he couldn't determine the source of the words. "You have had your question answered. Why do you return?"

"To ask a question on another's behalf," Sagarum replied, addressing the path through the damp, glistening rock. Some of the shadows shifted, and a sense of menace filled the cavern.

"I would know if I will ever find my people," Daelyn declared. "I am Daelyn, of the Tuatha de Danaan."

"We too have a question to ask," Brodin ventured, and Tamlin saw Telena nod timidly.

"There are two among you who are touched by Wyrd," the voice said, each word a deafening whisper. "Do you have the wisdom to listen? To understand what is said?"

"I do not know," Daelyn replied. "But Wyrd will work as it will."

"That is true," the voice stated. "You may all pass. Do not waste the Oracle's time. If you do, you will die."

Sagarum nodded and turned to the company. "Come along, everybody. We should be brief, lest we outstay our welcome."

Sagarum led them deeper into the caves. The corridor widened, until they found themselves in a giant hallway. As Tamlin's eyes adjusted to the new illumination, they widened in wonder and terror.

192

Coiled around the walls, its serpentine head resting on a giant rock, a giant black Dragon filled the chamber. Its eyes opened and it turned to regard each of the travelers in turn. When its gaze fell upon Tamlin, he felt as though his soul had been rent asunder and examined.

The great head reared and approached, the rest of the coils shifting silently. "So you have returned, Sagarum," the Dragon boomed. "What do you seek from me now?"

Chapter IX — The Oracle

❝*That* is the Oracle?!" Jyhanna stammered. The more she looked at the giant wyrm, the more her heart sank. Glistening black coils filled the cavern, wrapped around the walls so that she could not tell how long the creature was. The great serpentine head rose high above her, big enough to easily bite her in half. One word of offense and they wouldn't stand a chance. She may as well try to kill an armored knight with a blade of grass.

Sagarum smiled at her, and for a bitter moment she was certain he was enjoying every minute of it. "It takes a creature of incredible power to see into the future. There are few creatures of greater power than Dragons."

"I have lived as long as the Road itself," the Oracle stated, its head snaking down to stare into Jyhanna's eyes. For a moment she stood, transfixed by its gaze, inwardly screaming as the Dragon tore open her soul to look at it. Then, the head rose up to stare at the entire company, leaving Jyhanna breathing a sigh of relief that it was over.

"You have still not told me why you have returned Sagarum. I have answered your question."

"I come here on behalf of another," Sagarum declared. "And there are others here who would ask you questions."

"Then be brief," the Oracle instructed, its voice echoing deeply throughout the cave. "I must return to staring into the ether, for great events are coming."

Sagarum pushed Tamlin forward, and the Dragon gazed at the young man. "This is my apprentice," Sagarum stated. "I know that he is touched by Wyrd. But is he to be powerful, or will his Wyrd be his downfall?"

The Dragon closed its eyes, and then the great orbs opened again and the head snaked up to rest among the many black coils of its body. "He will be the greatest wizard to rise on this world."

"Are we touched by Wyrd?" Brodin blurted, and Jyhanna swallowed nervously. No doubt the Dragon would answer, but that was one less question that the young couple could ask.

"Only two of you are now touched by Wyrd," the Oracle replied, a whiff of smoke rising from its nostril. "The boy wizard and the Tuatha de Danaan. Be thankful, for great events are coming."

"Why would it be so bad to be touched by Wyrd, Daelyn?" Jyhanna asked, careful to direct her question.

"Every now and then somebody is born who has a destiny," the Tuatha de Danaan replied. "Wyrd will literally guide their actions, driving them to their fate no matter what they wish. It can be a source of greatness, but it can also cause the downfall of one who is innocent. Also, those associated with one who has been touched by Wyrd tend to have their own fates entwined in his or her own."

"It would be better to make one's own life," Jyhanna agreed.

195

"Indeed."

"Where will we find a good place to live our lives," she heard Telena ask nervously. The serpentine head slithered down to stare at the young woman, causing her to tremble in fear. Beside her, Brodin took her hand, but he was shaking just as badly as she was.

"You will find a place so long as you stay with your companions," the Oracle predicted. The giant head pivoted to stare at her once more. "And do you have a question, Jyhanna of Toregien?"

Jyhanna pursed her lips, thinking frantically. She could ask this creature anything she wanted, discover something that could win a battle years into the future. But, if she did, would she be setting herself on a path she could not control? Would she be bringing Wyrd down upon herself, or find herself desperately trying to avoid something, only to have it come to pass due to her actions? Finally, she shook her head. "I prefer not to have foreknowledge of what will happen. I think it would be better just to live life as it comes."

Although the draconic head was hidden in the shadows, she could swear that she saw it smile. "There is great wisdom in those words, shield maiden. If one is not careful, knowledge of the future takes away the ability to live in the present. Very few understand that."

The head turned to stare at Caelyn for a moment. "What of you, monk. I see that you were once touched by Wyrd, but no more."

Caelyn shrugged. "I seek self-knowledge and redemption. I don't know if I will find it on my pilgrimage, but I do know that you cannot give it to me, no matter what your powers are."

The Dragon nodded. "That is true. You are also a man of wisdom." With that, the Oracle turned to Daelyn. "You have come a long way to ask me your question. What do you wish, grey wanderer?"

"I wish to know if I will ever find my people," Daelyn said. "I have searched long, and I would know if there is an end to my task."

"You have been touched by Wyrd, and it still has its hold on you," the Oracle stated. "You will be the destroyer and savior of the Road. I will give you this rede, so that you may prepare for what is to come:

> *The Wanderer will find his people,*
> *The Ancient Ones will return,*
> *And across the Great Road*
> *The Eternal and Damned will war.*
>
> *Three Glyphs will be spoken,*
> *Three Glyphs will be drawn,*
> *The gates of hell will open,*
> *And the cycle will end.*
>
> *When the Wanderer finds his people,*
> *When the dead one arises once more,*
> *The sword of destiny will strike,*
> *And the Road will be no more."*

Daelyn shook his head. "That was not news I had wished for."

"I cannot change the fate Wyrd has given you," the Oracle stated. "You are at the center of the great events to come. Take comfort that these events will arrive shortly for us, but in hundreds of lifetimes for the mortals. Pay heed, for you are not only the destroyer of the Road, but you will be the hope of us all.

"I have answered all of your questions. Go now and fulfill your destinies."

"We should leave now," Sagarum stated. "To stay any

longer would be an offense."

Jyhanna nodded, staring at Daelyn. "And what will the world hold for us, I wonder?"

Upon emerging from the cave, Jyhanna drew her sword and turned on Daelyn. The Tuatha de Danaan stared at her, hands at his side.

"Considering what you are going to do, perhaps it would be better to kill you now," she said, praying silently that he wouldn't erupt in a flurry of activity and slay her. She knew that if he reached for his sword, she wouldn't have a chance; he was just too fast.

"Perhaps it would," Daelyn said. "But the Oracle told us this for a reason. He could have just answered 'yes' to my question and let Wyrd work as it will."

"Put up your sword," she heard Sagarum urge. "We'll need his help to get out of the forest and back through the Shroud Mountains."

Shaking slightly, the possible destroyer of the world standing right before her, she steadied her hand on her sword. One thrust, and she could save the Western Lands.

She jumped as she felt a hand on her shoulder. Not moving her sword, she turned her head to see Caelyn staring at her evenly. "He is touched by Wyrd, and there is nothing we can do to stop it. If he dies, another will take his place. All the violence will do is bloody your hands."

"He said I was the destroyer and *savior* of the Road," Daelyn said. "He did not say that I would destroy the worlds on the Road. Perhaps by knowing this rede I can save them from destruction when the Road ends."

"At any rate, the Oracle also stated that it would be hundreds of lifetimes before Daelyn's Wyrd comes to pass," Sagarum said. "Do not judge him now for events that will come, and may yet be avoided."

"But Wyrd cannot be broken," Jyhanna gritted, her sword now shaking despite her grip.

"Just because it hasn't before doesn't mean it can't be," Sagarum said. "People have tried, and come close. Perhaps Daelyn will be the first."

Sobbing, she sheathed her sword and sat down on a rock. Daelyn sat down beside her and held her gently. "I know how you feel," he said. "Just think of what it would be like to learn that you are the one who is going to cause an apocalypse. I promise you, I will do everything in my power to stop it. If I am the one touched by Wyrd, perhaps I can influence the events."

"I'm so sorry, I didn't think..."

When she looked up, she saw the Tuatha de Danaan smiling. "I think I might have done the same in your place," he said. "No offense has been taken, and do not concern yourself with it any longer."

Glancing around, she took in the scene. Brodin and Telena stood as still as statues, holding hands while they waited to see what would happen, looks of consternation on their faces. Tamlin stood behind Sagarum, trying to look impassive but failing. She couldn't read the expressions of either Caelyn or Sagarum.

"Once you've composed yourself, we should be going," the wizard said. "We have a long journey ahead of us, and I fear it will have more than enough peril for your sword arm to handle."

Chapter X — Return to Danger

To Jyhanna's relief, it was far easier to get out of the Old Forest than it had been to get in. It was almost as though the woods knew that they were leaving, and did not wish to hinder them. The pines and oaks that once watched them with malignant life now stood back, and the path to the grasslands was level and quick, allowing them to reach it within half a day.

As they sat in their camp, using some deadwood from the Old Forest to fuel a fire, she leaned back and gazed up at the stars. The shining orbs winked back at her, as though they were privy to some cosmic secret. She shook her head. It was all too much, too fast.

"According to the Oracle, we will have to stay together," she heard Sagarum say. "I don't know if that includes you, Daelyn."

"I doubt it," the Tuatha de Danaan replied. "One of my skills is to see the bonds between people. You all have a bond that I do not share; aside from which, I need some time alone, to think on what the Oracle has said. I will see you to the Young Forest, but then I will depart."

"Do you really think you can break your Wyrd?" Sagarum wondered.

"Delgar Dragonmage at one time thought he could," Daelyn answered. "If nothing else, I must find my people and warn them of what is to come. A few millennia is to short a time to prepare, but we may be able to do it. Regardless, I do not think that Wyrd can fully control us. If it did, then we would have no free will, and I do not believe the Road is like that."

Jyhanna closed her eyes. Although Daelyn had forgiven her for the altercation outside the Oracle's cave, she still couldn't forgive herself. She had fought beside him and trusted her life to him. To then threaten him was a betrayal of the worst sort.

"Jyhanna," she heard Telena say, and felt a hand softly resting on her, as though its owner was fearful of waking her up.

"I am only resting," she said. "Not asleep."

"What will we do?" the young woman asked fearfully. "Will we really have to follow them on Sagarum's quest for revenge?"

Jyhanna opened her eyes and sat up. "I wish I knew. I will try to find you some suitable land before we continue on Sagarum's quest, but I cannot see into the future, and the Oracle's words were very vague." Taking Telena's hand in hers, she added, "You will be protected. We will all see to it."

Standing up and helping herself to some of the tea from Caelyn's cauldron, she wondered if their protection would help. This incredible war was so much larger than any of them, and for the first time she wondered if it was possible to shield anybody from it.

Once she had drunk the tea, she lay down to rest. The

next morning would be busy – they had to spend at least half of each day in the grasslands foraging for food, for they all knew that there was none to be found in the pass. And even in the inky cloak of night, the Shroud Mountains loomed on the horizon, as though the peaks knew the company's destinies lay within its folds.

The fourth day out of the Old Forest, they reached the beginning of the pass, their packs laden with roots and whatever berries they could find. The wind had become bitterly cold, and Jyhanna could see flakes of snow whipping through the narrow path leading to the bridge over the river.

"This will be fun," she commented dryly, receiving a chuckle from Sagarum and Daelyn. The Tuatha de Danaan took point, Jyhanna first looking back to see that her charges were in good order, and then following. Sagarum and Caelyn had taken the rear, and she was confident in their ability to shepherd the younger members of the company along.

The bridge was just as they had left it, only now it swayed in the wind, planks creaking and groaning. Jyhanna shook her head. "We can't cross like this."

She saw Daelyn cross his arms. "I think things can be made a bit better," he declared, and began to stride across the bridge, singing softly as he walked. As he stepped on each plank, the bridge calmed, as though the wind could no longer touch it. Finally, the Tuatha de Danaan reached the end, smiling and motioning for the rest to follow.

"I am very pleased we have him along," Sagarum muttered beside her. "I wonder what we would do without him."

"Fall to our deaths, no doubt," Jyhanna replied, stepping onto the first plank. There was a slight creaking, but nothing even close to when they had crossed the first time. She quickly made her way across the ravine, stopping to stand beside Daelyn once she had reached the other side.

Wrapping her cloak around her to keep out the chill, she turned to Daelyn and asked, "What did you do?"

"Even wood that old has some memory of what it once was," the Tuatha de Danaan replied. "I merely reminded it of its former glory, and that we are its friends. You could call it a kind of magic, but I do not think it is. It is more...knowing how to communicate."

Smiling widely, Sagarum reached them, jogging up to stand beside them. "That was a very easy crossing. Thank you, Daelyn!"

Daelyn bowed. "It was the least I could do."

"So everything is alive," Jyhanna mused, thinking still on Daelyn's words.

The Tuatha de Danaan nodded. "For those who cannot see the life around them, it is easy to forget. I think that is why mortals have such difficulty keeping in balance with the natural world. What they cannot see, they do not believe exists."

Turning back to gaze across the bridge, she saw Brodin and Telena making their way over the ravine, Brodin gripping the guide ropes so tightly that his knuckles had flushed white. Once the young man reached the end, he exhaled, and Jyhanna noticed that his face was pale with fear.

"Do not worry," she said. "I do not believe we will have to do something like this again."

Sagarum nodded. "Thanks to the Arcalien Empire, almost all of the bridges in the Western Lands are made of stone. Much more solid."

Brother Caelyn was the last to cross, and once he had, they set out along the pass, wrapping their cloaks around themselves to guard against the cold. It was more bitter than the first time they had passed through, causing Caelyn to comment, "Winter truly has arrived."

At least this time through, they had gathered enough berries and roots that they would not go hungry, a blessing that Jyhanna thanked the Eternal One for once they had camped down every night. They made a fire, hidden from unfriendly eyes by Daelyn's wards, and Caelyn helped Jyhanna to cook some of the food.

For the entire journey, they did not once see the sun, although some light shone from the clouds. A heavy snow began to fall on the second day, and by the third day it was difficult to trudge through the pass, the snow making every step a Herculean effort.

On the fourth night, as they camped under an overhanging cliff in the hopes of gaining some shelter, Sagarum was glum, a fact that worried Jyhanna. She had yet to see a situation where the wizard couldn't find an excuse to banter or smile, but now his spirits had sunk, just like the rest of the company.

"At least another five days at this rate," Sagarum sighed. "The snow is slowing us down too much."

"Maybe if we could sleep through the night, we could make better time," Tamlin suggested.

Sagarum shook his head. "Too much risk of freezing to death in this wind. We'll be able to sleep properly once we're out of the pass."

"Can you do something?" Jyhanna asked Daelyn.

The Tuatha de Danaan shook his head. "It would take a legion of my people's druids to change the weather in a place such as this. All I can do is influence the earth; what is above is beyond my power."

She turned to Sagarum, but the wizard also shook his head. "If I were to use my power for something that large, it would attract far too much unwanted attention. Better to suffer for a few days and remain stealthy than venture in comfort and find an army of Archmagi waiting for us to emerge from the mountains."

Disgruntled, she returned to her seat and tried to wrap her cloak around her as a blanket. The howling wind swept around her, and in that moment she wished nothing more than to be back home in her father's comfortable palace.

The wind and snow let up a bit during the fifth day, allowing them to make some better time, but then it became heavy again as they camped. The white blanket filled the pass, now high enough to be up to Jyhanna's knees. She shook her head sadly and wondered if they would be able to see the end of the pass within a week.

"Can it get much colder?" Tamlin shivered, crouching close to the fire. His breath came out in a white mist, ice coating the stubble that had begun to cover his chin.

Caelyn nodded. "We are lucky we are traversing this pass at the beginning of the winter. I do not think we would be able to survive in the middle of the season."

"At least there will be no Ogres to attack us," Brodin muttered.

"We can hope," Daelyn said, stoking the fire. "We can only hope."

That night was bitterly cold, and she got very little sleep. She cursed under her breath as the first light of dawn began to peer through the overcast sky, cloaking the world in a shadowy light. She watched Brother Caelyn wipe ice from his ragged beard and impassively begin to recover what coals might remain from the fire, so that Daelyn could try to preserve and re-use them.

But the Tuatha de Danaan stood still, eyes shut, motionless as a statue.

"What is it?" Sagarum asked.

"I smell something on the wind," Daelyn replied. "I fear that we may have enemies to fight after all."

"Ogres?" Tamlin wondered.

Daelyn nodded and took the coals from Caelyn's gloved hands, wrapping and stowing them in his pack as he mumbled a song. "We should go. Whatever lies ahead, it is better if we face it while we still have our strength."

After they packed up their camp, they trudged through the snow, moving through the pass at a crawl. Still more snow fell, and Jyhanna feared that the path would be blocked by the time they found the fork they had crossed on the way in.

The sky remained grey but lit, the falling flakes shortening the field of view so that she could only see a bit ahead. She prayed that the Tuatha de Danaan had better eyes, and could pierce the curtain of snow. Daelyn raised his right hand, calling a halt. With his left hand, he tapped the hilt of his sword.

Jyhanna nodded and loosened her sword in its scabbard, the blade sticking momentarily. She cursed under her breath; the blade was covered by frost thanks to the cold. She'd have to clean rust off it when they camped that night.

With a wave, Daelyn motioned them forward. They crept ahead, Jyhanna drawing her sword as Daelyn brought forth his own blade. Still the snow fell around them, dampening all sound except the crunching of their boots as they strode through the soft blanket.

A soft grunting sounded from ahead. Daelyn turned, raised his hand and signaled several times, repeating for Jyhanna's and Sagarum's benefit. There were ten Ogres camped before them, and they didn't know the company was there. Additionally, Daelyn signed, there were no ways around them.

Jyhanna frowned. A surprise attack was their best

option, but maintaining surprise in these conditions was almost impossible. At the very least, the snowfall would slow them down and hinder their movements.

Caelyn stepped forward, bearing his staff and signaling that he could help. Daelyn nodded, motioned for the younger members to remain where they were, and waved the rest forward. Jyhanna crept ahead, her eyes peeled for any sign of the enemy. Finally, as she came to a bend, she saw several outlines in the snowfall, all sitting around what appeared to be a fire.

Daelyn held up his hand, counting down with his fingers. At the count of one, Jyhanna attacked.

The first Ogre she managed to take while it was still sitting. Bringing her sword down on its head, she split its skull, sending brains and bone fragments flying. The other monsters roared in fury, grabbing their weapons and leaping into the fray.

She heard two screams beside her, and a monstrous severed head rolled through the snow, carving a bloody valley in the white blanket. Her small size served her well as another Ogre attacked, forcing her to leap out of the way. The monster was even more hindered by the snow than she was, and she took the opportunity to carve a giant gash in its back, cutting through its spine.

There was a roar behind her, and then one of the creatures fell to the ground, its caved-in head nearly landing on her foot. She spun to see Brother Caelyn staring coldly at the corpse, his staff covered with blood and brains.

Jumping back into the fray, she barely dodged a giant axe that would have taken her head off, instead spinning to slice open the Ogre's gut, spilling bowels onto the ground. As the monster screamed in agony, she drove her blade into its heart, silencing it forever.

And then she, Daelyn, and Brother Caelyn stood alone

in the camp, surrounded by bodies. Daelyn's sword was covered with gore, the once shiny blade now a dark crimson. As he knelt down to wipe his sword in the snow, he pointed at one of the corpses, a deep slash ripped across its feather-ornamented chest.

"Another Ogre leader," the Tuatha de Danaan declared. "I think this battle has been for the better."

Jyhanna merely stared, wondering why the fetid stench of death that had begun to rise from the bodies failed to move her. Had she become so cold and battle-hardened already? Turning to Brother Caelyn, she noticed that his eyes had become sad.

"Will we be attacked?" Caelyn asked.

Daelyn shook his head. "I do not believe so. This tribe has just lost two of its leaders. They will be in mourning for some time."

"What about revenge?" Jyhanna said. "They have much to avenge on us now."

"So long as we are careful about hiding our tracks, they will think it was another Ogre tribe," Daelyn stated. "I will see to that."

"I'll fetch the others," Caelyn declared. "It will be best if we leave as soon as possible."

Daelyn nodded. "Quite true. More of them could come upon us shortly." The Tuatha de Danaan began to make a circle around the ambushed camp, singing softly. As he did, a shimmer came over the ground, and the tracks made in the snow from the battle shifted, the human markings becoming larger and more primitive.

Once he completed the circle, Daelyn nodded. "It is time for us to go. So long as everybody walks around the perimeter of the camp, we will be fine."

Indeed, as Caelyn returned, the rest of the company in tow, they stepped around the circle and further into the pass, their tracks vanishing in the snow as they walked. As they did, as though by some miracle, the falling snow began to lighten.

Three days later, the company came out of the pass, stepping down into the foothills that marked the border between the Shroud Mountains and the Young Forest.

"We're back," Sagarum mused, gazing around at the snow-capped trees. "I just wonder what the world has become while we were away."

Chapter XI — The First Parting

Tamlin was grateful to finally be out of the Shroud Mountains. The Young Forest was free of the biting, howling wind that plagued them throughout the pass, even though a blanket of snow covered the ground. Without the wind, the young apprentice discovered that it actually wasn't as cold as he had thought.

"What does the forest tell you?" Sagarum asked, turning to Daelyn.

The Tuatha de Danaan shrugged and looked up for a moment. Then, looking at Sagarum, he said, "There are more unnatural things walking these woods. However, we will be protected."

Tamlin found himself impatient. It would be days before they saw the end of the forest, and only the Eternal One knew what had happened in the month they had been away.

He felt Sagarum's hand on his shoulder. "Never fear," the wizard said. "All will be well in the end. Besides, for the rest of this part of our journey, Daelyn will see us safely through."

As they walked each day after breaking camp, Tamlin's mind began to wander. He tried to imagine what it would be like to be the greatest wizard in the world, but the concept was simply too large for him. Whenever he thought of magic, images of Haldur's cottage or Sagarum's quiet practice sessions filled his mind.

It was disappointing, really. When he had started his apprenticeship with Haldur, he had visions of casting grand spells, visiting foreign lands, and meeting kings and beautiful princesses. Now he couldn't weave spells because they would attract unwanted attention, the visits to foreign lands had been accompanied by incredible danger and hunger, and the closest he had gotten to meeting royalty was a battle-hardened shield maiden with a regal bearing.

On the fourth day, a light snow began to fall, bringing a magic to the air. Tamlin's spirits soared, and he noticed that the trees had started to thin, making the path back to Bandre easier to manage.

The closer they got to the edge of the forest, however, the more grim and serious Brother Caelyn became. The flash of merriment that had so startled Sagarum as their journey to the Oracle began had faded to a distant memory, and Tamlin feared at times that he would never see the monk smile again.

It was probably the war, Tamlin reflected, nearly tripping over an exposed root. From the distaste that Caelyn expressed for any kind of conflict, Tamlin got the feeling that the monk would be happiest if he could cloister himself away once more and never have to see anything military again.

That night, Caelyn seemed grimmer than ever, and no effort of Sagarum's to bring even a bit of joy to his eyes bore with any success. The mood was catching. Jyhanna spent a good amount of the evening cleaning and oiling her sword, and Brodin and Telena held each other silently, as though they feared what the future had to offer.

All Tamlin could do was stare at the fire and hope that some day he would actually have some control over his life again. He had become a follower, trusting in his teacher to guide him true.

The fifth day was spent in complete silence, the company making their way through the trees and stopping whenever Daelyn held up his hand. An occasional rustling would sound from somewhere around them, and the Tuatha de Danaan would gaze there with concern, but no words were said.

On the sixth day, they reached the edge of the forest, the snow-capped plains of Bandre stretching out before them to the east, and the crashing waves of the Inner Sea rumbling from the south. Before them stood a large squat hill, blocking much of their view.

"What is that?" Tamlin wondered. "It seems out of place."

Sagarum pursed his lips. "I believe that once was a city. But it was abandoned long ago, for what reason I know not. I remember wandering through its ruins. Slowly the dust built up, over millennia, and the land reclaimed it. Now this mound is what remains."

"Is that the fate of all things?" Tamlin asked.

Sagarum nodded gravely. "Nothing lasts forever, my apprentice. Even the land changes over time. The work of mortal beings is a mere blink of the eye compared to greater things."

Tamlin grinned. "You know, you've started talking like Daelyn."

Tamlin heard Daelyn clear his throat, and turned to face the Tuatha de Danaan. Daelyn smiled and gazed at each one in turn. "It has been an honor to walk with you," he said. "But it is time for me to go. I have much to think about, and even more to do."

Sagarum shook Daelyn's hand. "It has been good to see you again, old friend. I hope we will meet again soon."

Daelyn nodded. "I have the feeling I will meet one or two of you again in the future. I do not know for certain, however. Wyrd will work as it will."

"Farewell," Jyhanna said, giving Daelyn a crisp salute. "It has been a pleasure fighting at your side."

Daelyn chuckled. "There is more to life than fighting, my young friend. However, at this point in time, there does seem to be an inordinate amount of it. Farewell. May you all find the peace you seek."

With that, the Tuatha de Danaan strode back into the forest. Tamlin suddenly realized that he had forgotten to thank Daelyn for what he had done, but when he turned, the woods appeared completely empty.

"He has returned to the Road of Legends," Sagarum said. "I will wish him well on his path in my prayers. We should begin our own journey, though."

"Where do you suggest we go?" Caelyn asked.

"It is time to stop this madness that has engulfed the Western Lands," Sagarum declared. "There is an Archmagus in Fenegar who has much to answer for. I think we can start by finding him." He turned to Brother Caelyn. "I am sorry if this takes you far out of your way for your pilgrimage."

The monk shrugged. "On a pilgrimage, it is the journey that is important. The destination is merely a place. And I would prefer to help stop this war before it goes too far."

"Then we will go to Fenegar," Sagarum said. "When we do find the Archmagus with the power of succession, I will fight him alone. It is better if you are not in the

213

way."

Caelyn nodded. "That makes sense."

"But you'll need the help!" Jyhanna protested. "Surely we can-"

"If we are there, Sagarum will have to worry about protecting us," Caelyn said. "If we stay out of the way, he can concentrate solely on the fight."

"I would prefer to find Brodin and Telena some farmland first," Jyhanna stated. "That way they can stay away from the conflict."

Sagarum shook his head. "Until we can stop this war, there will be no place that is safe. You saw the village we passed – there had been no mercy. Even if one Archmagus is merciful, the one he is fighting might not be." He stepped forward, staring into Jyhanna's eyes. "All we need to do to stop this war is kill seven men. And I can take care of all of them."

"We should be going," Caelyn cut in. "The longer we stay here, the more likely it is that we will be found by a patrol from Bandre or Fenegar."

"True," Sagarum said. He began to walk up the hill, the rest of the company following. As they crested the rise, Tamlin's jaw dropped in shock.

An army lay camped before them, flying the blue and white standards of Bandre. The collection of tents and fires stretched out towards the horizon in a great circle, a large tent lying at its center. Tamlin saw Sagarum make a quick motion with his hands, and then signal to everybody to drop to the ground.

Tamlin lay on the ground, the snow seeping through his cloak and borrowed habit. "One of the Successors is in that army," Sagarum hissed. "I could sense him. I cast a masking spell, but I don't know if I managed it in time to escape detection."

"What do we do?" Tamlin asked quietly, watching the

men below marching through the camp, performing various military tasks.

"Hide in the fringes of the Young Forest," Sagarum replied. "They don't look like they're getting ready to move out, so they should still be here this evening. That makes it perfect."

"Why is it perfect?" Jyhanna demanded, her voice a whisper. "Don't we *want* them to go away?"

Sagarum shook his head, a smile creeping across his face. "On the contrary, I would rather see them stay right there. Tonight, under cover of darkness, I am going to enter that camp, find the Successor, and kill him."

Chapter XII — Beginning's End

As soon as the sun had set, Sagarum began to wind his way through the pickets, into the Bandrian camp.

The moment they had gotten back into the forest that afternoon, he had cast a shielding spell. It was a risk he had to take in order to protect his companions, and he only hoped that he had woven it well enough to keep whatever Archmagus was leading the army from detecting it.

It seemed to have worked. The company had lingered at the edge of the woodland, Jyhanna and Caelyn watching warily, in case some soldiers came to collect or slay them. But none had come, and Sagarum had spent his time preparing for the battle to come. It was difficult – there was no way of telling which of the Great Powers the Archmagus had, and any one of them applied at the wrong time could force Sagarum into flight, or even kill him.

Finally, the sun set, bathing the world in a crimson light. Sagarum stood up and brushed the light snow from his robes. Looking on Tamlin, he smiled, hoping that it would encourage the young man.

"If I haven't returned by sunrise, go to Caelyn's abbey and seek refuge on holy ground," he instructed. "Wait this war out, and then find an Archmagus who will continue your apprenticeship."

"But you'll come back, right?" Tamlin asked. Sagarum winced at the trembling voice.

"There is always a chance that Wyrd will hand me a surprise or two," he stated. "However, I believe that I will be back. As I said, if I haven't returned by sunrise, I haven't succeeded."

Jyhanna gave him a quick smile. "Good luck, old wizard."

"Thank you. Hopefully I won't need it."

When he turned to Brother Caelyn, the monk only gave him a nod. From Caelyn, though, that spoke volumes.

With that, he strode from the forest, weaving a spell of concealment as he walked. He felt the familiar surge of energies as he wrapped them around himself. A quick bit of finesse finished the spell, bringing a smile to his face. Any picket would just ignore him; Sagarum's spell would alter the impressions of any who gazed upon him, making him unimportant in their eyes.

Still, he walked slowly, in case he brought some unwanted attention to himself. Almost any creature will chase after something that runs, if only to see what it is. With every step, the fires of the camp grew closer, smoke billowing into the night.

Past two pickets he strode, the guards only giving him the barest of glances before looking away in contempt. Sagarum allowed himself a bit of satisfaction; the key to stealth was not invisibility, but to simply blend in and be unremarkable.

He heard a commotion from the west, and drew aside as four soldiers and a woman staggered past, so drunk that he could smell the mead on their breaths. The one farthest on the left had his hands around the waist of the buxom girl, the wench wearing only a tight, revealing undergarment. He shook his head; no doubt the prostitute would do good business this night. Even surrounded by companions and strangers, mortals would always find some way to indulge their lusts.

He passed another fire, this one surrounded by warriors singing a horribly off-key battle song about Garwulf the Slayer. A sudden idea occurred to him, and he added a swagger to his walk. Perhaps he could increase the illusion, making any passers-by think that he was just another soldier cloaked in the darkness, who had drunk just a bit too much, like everybody else.

The next fire contained a group of brawling men, one of whom fell on the flames and leapt up, shaking to put out his smouldering clothes as his companions laughed uproariously.

Stepping past them, he found himself in a cluster of tents, the night silent. Reaching out with his mind, he heard officers talking about plans to march against Fenegar. He nearly shuddered in relief.

Officer's country. That's all it is.

The large tent with the Archmagus began to loom before him, and as he approached he cast a quick seeing spell. The canvas was surrounded with spellwork, the weave of energy covering the tent in a great, intricate net. Some gentle probing revealed the nature of the enchantment, and Sagarum wove a bit of his own magic in, carefully hiding the strands of energy so that they would blend in with the Archmagus's work.

Then, taking a deep breath, he opened the tent flap and stepped inside. The inside was dark, illuminated only by a candle that had burnt almost completely down.

"I'm impressed," a raspy voice commented from a

shadowy corner. "Most wizards would have been burnt to cinders by the wards."

"I am not most wizards," Sagarum stated.

"I was expecting you, you know," the Archmagus said, bringing his grey-whiskered face into the candlelight, the flickering flame reflecting in his eyes. "My name is Bervus, and I felt you coming from the moment you crossed over the hill."

"So why didn't you send soldiers after me?"

Bervus chuckled, wood creaking as he stood, pushing a little oak chair behind him. "I knew you were alone. I also knew you would come to me when you were ready. And now, I know where you have been, and who you have traveled with. In a moment, I'll know your name."

"You have the Power of Hindsight," Sagarum said, stepping around the room, taking careful note of the dimensions of the tent. "Tell me, can you see the lines of life, as I once could? Or does it come in flashes, images of the past burnt into your mind that you can barely understand?"

"A bit of both, Sagarum," Bervus declared, drawing a sword from its sheath. The blade had a blue sheen that flickered, almost as if it had a life of its own. "Just imagine what a ruler I will be, able to see what men have truly done and judge them! True justice for all! But, as my fellow Successors have demonstrated, in the beginning, I will need to be ruthless. I think I will torture your companions after I've slain you. The monk Caelyn will not be very amusing, but the warrior-woman Jyhanna will be quite fun. The others, well, I think I can let my soldiers work out what to do with them. Brodin and Tamlin they'll probably kill, but no doubt the young girl Telena will give them nights and nights of pleasure. Please don't take offense, but I require *some* examples for the future."

Sagarum smiled, his heart hard. "You have to slay me

first."

"As easily said as done!" Bervus declared, lunging forward with his sword. Sagarum easily sidestepped, weaving a magical net to entrap the blade.

With a grin, Bervus brought the sword to bear, shearing through Sagarum's enchantment. "Two wizards died making me this blade," the Archmagus boasted. "It lives off magic, consumes it, and gives its power to me."

He swung again, forcing Sagarum back, until the old wizard tripped over the chair and fell to the ground. As he fell, he began to weave some energies with his fingers, filling the walls of the tent with magical threads. Laughing, Bervus pointed his sword at Sagarum's heart, a malevolent glare in his eyes.

"Any last words, first spell-weaver? Please, say something before I kill you and use your power to help me conquer these lands."

"You're insane."

"Who could rule better than I?" Bervus asked with a flourish. "Certainly, there would be some injustice in the beginning, but only for a short while. Now, I will have the power to live forever, thanks to you. Thank you for coming back, and helping me to realize my dreams!"

"Do you know what the problem is with using a weapon like that?" Sagarum asked, swallowing and staggering to his feet. He had to time it just right. Drawing on what Delgar Dragonmage had once taught him, he cast a net around his hand.

Roaring in rage, Bervus attacked, only to have Sagarum catch the blade with his enchanted hand. Now it was Sagarum's turn to smile.

"How did you-" Bervus sputtered.

"The problem with weapons like this is that you can't weave spells while you wield them," Sagarum stated coldly, forcing the blade around. "Well, unless you are me, for I know one or two ways around it. Also, this kind of weapon will only stop a certain kind of magic. Do you really think that in several millennia of exile I haven't learned some new tricks?"

Sagarum grinned at the sudden panic in Bervus' eyes as he quickly reached down and held the wizard's hand to the hilt. Even as Bervus' arms shook in effort, Sagarum forced the tip of the blade around to point directly at the Archmagus's stomach.

"Don't bother calling for help," Sagarum said. "I altered your enchantment around the tent so that we wouldn't be disturbed."

"I'll give you money," Bervus pleaded. "Power. Anything you want!"

"I want what was taken from me!" Sagarum declared, driving the blade deep into Bervus' gut. Dark blood fountained from the wound as the Archmagus's eyes went wide in shock, and then the man began to scream in agony. With a great heave of the sword, Sagarum lifted Bervus off his feet, blood streaming down the blade. Even as he cried out, Bervus began to weave a spell with his fingers, something that Sagarum was certain would allow the Archmagus some final, devastating strike.

Waving his free hand, Sagarum finished the spell he had woven. The magical threads around the room snapped taut, shearing through the inside of the tent with the power of a razor edged whip. Bervus' severed head landed on the ground, Sagarum dropping the decapitated body with a glare of disgust. From the corner of his mind, he felt the magical weave around the tent collapse, all but his own little offering.

With a pull, he yanked the sword from Bervus' corpse and cast it to the ground. Then he leaned down and placed his hand on the former wizard's chest.

"I claim what is mine," Sagarum whispered, feeling

the electric tingling through his arm as the Power flowed into him. He grinned in glee; for the first time in millennia he felt as though he might fill the empty hollow in his soul. The Power surged through him, as gentle as the caresses of a returning lover.

Casting his enchantment of concealment around him once more, he put the sword under his cloak, stepped out of the tent, and headed off into the night.

He returned to the company before midnight, stepping between the trees with as much stealth as he could muster, just in case part of his wards had failed during the battle.

"You were successful," Jyhanna said, standing up as he entered the clearing they had camped in.

Sagarum nodded. "It was a difficult battle, but I was able to win it. Bandre is now free of its Archmagus tyrant."

He gazed at Caelyn, the monk's history unveiling before his eyes. Suddenly, he understood why the brother had been so secretive, and how terrible his history truly was.

Taking the monk aside, he whispered, "I now know what you have seen, and you do not have to fear. Your past is safe with me."

Caelyn's expression was unreadable, but Sagarum did not sense a threat from the man.

"What now?" Tamlin asked.

"Now I will continue to train you," Sagarum replied. "And we will continue our little quest for justice. The final War of Succession has begun, and I swear by the Eternal One that I will be the victor."

Part IV:
The War of Succession

Chapter I — Decisions

The night after Sagarum killed the Archmagus in the Bandrian army, Caelyn dreamt of home. He stood in the center of his garden, tending some vegetables. For some strange reason they were unaffected by the winter, and no snow had fallen to cover the ground.

Abbot Artus ambled up, offering a kind word, and then strolled on past, called to other duties by the prior. Caelyn finished weeding and stood up to begin his walk to the scriptorium. Although he wasn't certain how he knew, he was sure a chronicle was waiting for him, something very important that he had to look at.

He passed through the door of the scriptorium, careful to close it without breaking the silence once he was in. The giant oak door creaked a little, but not enough to disturb anybody. Stepping quietly, he made his way to his desk and chair, a giant tome sitting on the angled desktop.

He picked up a pen and sat down, gazing upon the leather cover of the book. "A History of the War of

Succession," was inscribed on the leather, and when he opened it up he found a strange runic inscription in his own penmanship. One word, easily translated, stood out in his mind.

Devastation.

Caelyn leaned back, knowing that he had just seen something extremely important, but not certain of what it was. A smokey odor wafted through the air, but when he turned to see what was burning, all went dark.

He woke up next to the smouldering fire, surrounded by ancient trees, suddenly stifling a tear. Although he hated to admit such a weakness, he missed the Abbey of Southmarch, and his prayers every night invariably contained a wish that he could return there soon.

Glancing around the camp, he took stock. It was still early enough that the sun had yet to rise, and a chill wind cut through the air. Caelyn wrapped his habit around him for warmth and cast his thoughts back on the previous day. They had managed to travel westwards without running into any Bandrian or Fenegarian scouts by skirting the Young Forest, part of some plan of Sagarum's to circle around the large army camped nearby.

"I've just killed their leader," Sagarum had stated as they walked. "Even if he was hated, some of them will be out for blood. It would not do well to be found."

"So we will be heading east?" Tamlin had wondered.

Sagarum had shaken his head. "Eventually, we will go south. Having seen what we are up against, I would rather deal with the Successors in Tarese and Toregien before we head into Fenegar. Better to become stronger before having to walk into a stronghold of co-opted Archmagi."

Caelyn turned his gaze onto Sagarum, the wizard curled on the ground on the opposite end of the camp, quietly snoring. Ever since he had won the battle with the wizard, a change had come over him. Sagarum seemed more sage, more regal, as though part of some natural royalty had been restored.

There was also something worrisome now. Despite Sagarum's assurances that the monk's past would not be drudged up for all to see, Caelyn did not relish the thought of even one person knowing what he had seen and done, much less somebody being able to look into anybody's past the way Sagarum now could.

Beside Sagarum lay Brodin and Telena, spooning as they slept, an idyllic expression on both of their faces. Caelyn allowed himself a smile. It was good to see such innocence again; it reminded him of why the human race was redeemable. If they were extremely lucky, they could know a peace, both outer and inner, that Caelyn had never experienced, nor felt he ever would.

Beside them, Jyhanna sat on a fallen log, watching. As his eyes alighted on her, she gave him a quick nod of acknowledgment, and then turned back to her duty. Every now and then her hand gripped her sword hilt, a habit Caelyn remembered from his own army days. The last thing a man standing guard wanted to do was get caught without his blade.

Caelyn feared for her. She was a warrior, just as he had once been, but at least she still had most of her heart left, even if she didn't seem to feel it. The monk wondered if she would know when to stop, when to put down her sword and return to less brutal things, before the violence inside claimed her soul as it once had his.

Finally, resting between himself and Sagarum, Caelyn looked at Tamlin. The apprentice slept restlessly, as though their proximity to Fenegar itself caused nightmares. Caelyn wouldn't be surprised; Tamlin's master had died in Fenegar, and from the young man's words, Tamlin himself would never be safe there.

Still, something clutched at Caelyn's mind. It was

almost as if he had something he had to do, but he had forgotten what it was. He closed his eyes, letting his mind wander, hoping that he would find some answers.

And, as the sun finally began to rise, he found what he sought.

Caelyn didn't know how his announcement would be taken, but he knew what he had to do.

"I'm not going south with the rest of you," he declared as he helped to smother the last remains of the fire. Usually they would have been less cautious with the smoke, but they could not afford detection. Even a day away by foot was too close to what was now a hostile army.

Tamlin was the first to speak. "I don't understand."

"I am returning to Fenegar," Caelyn said.

Sagarum crossed his arms. "That is a very dangerous thing to do. Are you certain you wish this?"

Caelyn nodded. "It is something I have to do."

"May we know the reason for this sudden change in plans?" Sagarum asked.

"I have seen enough to know that the Great Convention is no longer respected in the Western Lands," Caelyn replied. "I fear for my brethren in the Abbey of Southmarch. They are not warriors, and would fall easily to an invading army. I must return and warn them."

"Surely they would know by now," Jyhanna cut in.

Caelyn shrugged. "I can hope so, but sometimes faith undermines reason. We have been successfully protected for over a generation by the Great Convention, and many will not believe that it has failed, even if there is ample evidence. If they have the word of a fellow brother, perhaps they will listen if they have not already."

"What could your warning accomplish?" Jyhanna

demanded. "They will still be monks, and still be defenseless. Aside from which, the army of Fenegar is one of the armies violating the Great Convention; you would be walking right into danger."

"Perhaps I can convince them to hide," Caelyn said. "Or at least to take some precautions. As much as you are my companions, they are my family, and have been for decades; I have a duty to them that I cannot ignore. It is a risk I have to take."

Sagarum shook his head, frowning. "If that is what you must do, then that is what you must do. You go with all of our best wishes."

"What about us?" Telena piped up. "Don't you remember what the oracle said? If the company splits up, we won't find a home."

Caelyn sat down on a rock, cursing himself for forgetting the Dragon's words. "That is a problem. It seems that I must choose between the lives of my brethren and my companions."

"What if we all went with you?" Jyhanna suggested. "We could warn your abbey, and then continue on our mission."

"That would be exceedingly dangerous," Sagarum stated. "Not only has the Successor in Fenegar co-opted the army, but he has also conscripted all of the magi in the country."

"We survived the Old Forest and the Shroud Mountains," Jyhanna retorted. "I am not afraid of some wayward wizards."

"You should be," Caelyn said. "Sagarum is correct. It will be very perilous."

"We will not be able to use magic in our defense," the wizard added. "Any spell-weaving would bring a host of magic-wielding foes down upon us."

Tamlin stepped forward. "If Brother Caelyn needs to

do this, then let us come with him, and try to avoid any combat. It will be no riskier than if we split up and try to hunt down another Archmagus."

Caelyn sighed. "You have a point. Very well – let's set off for the abbey. There will be enough guest quarters for all of us, assuming Southmarch isn't flooded with refugees."

For the next week they skirted the border of the Young Forest, always heading westwards. The land rose as they walked, and by the third day the Inner Sea was in sight to the south, a bluish-white expanse stretching to the horizon, much of its surface surrounded by a ribbon of thick ice.

On the morning of the fourth day, the sky clouded over, and it began to snow heavily. The giant flakes fell all around them, sometimes so heavy that Caelyn could barely see ten feet in front of him. But still they pressed on, led by the determined monk, who set a pace that the others had difficulty keeping at times.

Caelyn felt for them, but he couldn't let up. Every day they took getting there was a day that could hasten an enemy army to the monastery gates.

On the sixth day, they came to a small village, a ramshackle collection of wooden houses with thatched roofs, rendered picturesque by the snowfall, so far untouched by the war. The villagers were ecstatic to see a man of the cloth, and provided the company with warmer boots and woolen clothes, in return for Caelyn's blessings, which he gave in a large, public ceremony in the village square.

They actually had roofs over their head that night; Caelyn, himself in need of a rest, allowed everybody to relax and join in a village celebration. The hamlet's hospitality was startling; not only did they provide music, but they also cooked a giant feast, the best food Caelyn or anybody in the company had eaten in months. Basking in the smiles of the villagers and the younger members of the company, he prayed that this place would remain undisturbed.

"How close do you think we are to the border?" Sagarum asked, leaning across the feast table.

Caelyn shrugged. "Perhaps a couple of days. I would be surprised if it was more than a week."

"And then?"

"Around three weeks' journey to the abbey," Caelyn said. "We will travel into the heartland of Fenegar."

"Once more into danger," the wizard mused.

"We never left it behind."

The villagers put them up in several houses. Caelyn was certain that Brodin and Telena were doubly happy for that, as they had not had any time alone together in weeks. From what he heard about newlyweds, they would make up for that lost time in spades that night.

As for Caelyn, he found himself in a room with Jyhanna in the mayor's house, Sagarum and Tamlin having taken separate lodgings from one of the more affluent farmers.

"They really are happy to see you," Jyhanna said.

Caelyn nodded. "They've been without hope for some time. They think my prayers will help."

"Will they?"

Caelyn paused for a moment. He hoped they would, but he couldn't be certain. So many had suffered needlessly already, and many more would starve in the winter, their crops not brought in because half the village had been conscripted or killed. There was too much misery to believe that his prayers could make any real difference.

But still...if the Eternal One could save one village from harm because of his prayers, then perhaps that would be enough. He had heard that salvation comes in small steps, and maybe that was what the expression meant. And even being able to give this hamlet hope could help them in the dark days ahead.

"Yes," he finally answered. "I think so."

They left in the morning, the village mayor bestowing more clothes and supplies on them. "Go out and spread hope," he said. "For what you have done for us, we cannot thank you enough. I only pray that you can do the same for others."

Caelyn nodded. "I shall try."

With that, they strode away, still skirting the border of the Young Forest, in case they had to hide from a hostile army. The blanket of snow was now deep enough that the walking was difficult, but they were still able to make a good eight leagues by sunset.

The next day the sky was clear, but the wind was cold, forcing them to wrap themselves deeper in their cloaks. The Shroud Mountains had receded to the point that they were no longer visible above the treetops, and the Inner Sea also appeared farther away, a strip of blue on the southern horizon. Caelyn pushed back a combination of relief and unease; they were now very close to the border.

The day after that, they crossed over into Fenegar.

Chapter II — Devastation

Caelyn was not the only one who felt some discomfort upon returning to Fenegar. Despite the reassuring presence of Sagarum, Tamlin was afraid. They were not too far away from where Haldur's cottage had once stood, and the voice of the murderous Archmagus who had killed his mentor still echoed in Tamlin's head.

No matter what you do, I will find you! And you will serve me, or die!

Tamlin shuddered. He still had nightmares about the frenzied flight through the forest, the looking back, somehow certain that the killer was still stalking him. If they did run into this wizard again, Tamlin was not quite certain that Sagarum would be able to handle him. To be able to weave spells without even moving one's hands seemed unnatural, as though it was some evil power.

For the first three days, as they trudged through the snow, the path was mercifully clear. The ground beneath the snowy blanket became even and smooth, convincing

Tamlin that they were actually walking on a cobbled road. The land appeared deserted; even the usual rustling of small animals foraging for food in the snow was absent from the countryside.

At night, Tamlin found himself talking with Brodin and Telena, the only other two in the company who were even close to his own age. While he didn't have a great deal in common with Brodin, who he found a bit too impetuous, he was able to spend hours talking to Telena, who listened with rapt attention as he described his years as a wizard's apprentice. In return, she described her homeland, but would not tell him why she and her husband had fled.

Tamlin didn't press the matter; the pain of Haldur's death still weighed on him, and he could understand if there was something similar that had happened to them.

On the fourth day, they came across a farmer's field. Something didn't look right, however. Burnt stalks poked out from the snow, as far as the eye could see, some still bearing their fruit.

"Is there a village nearby?" Brodin asked, his voice desperately hopeful. "If they have trouble harvesting, we might be able to join them..."

Jyhanna shook her head. "This field was not harvested because nobody remained alive to do it. Whatever village once stood near here, it must have been razed to the ground."

Stepping up to one of the charred stalks, Tamlin found a husk of corn, withered from neglect. "What of the fields?" he wondered.

"Whatever army passed through here took what they wanted and tried to burn the rest," Caelyn stated, his face downcast. "I've seen it before. They were in a hurry, though, and weren't very thorough."

"Why would anybody do such a thing?" Telena cried,

234

trying to hide her tears as she clung to her husband.

"It is known as 'total war,'" Caelyn said bitterly. "The idea is to make resistence so costly that no enemy is willing to do it. And for so little gain, the cost is overwhelming. *This* is why the Great Convention was written. May the Eternal One curse the ones who have broken it."

"Could Bandre have done this?" Jyhanna wondered.

This time, it was Sagarum who answered, shrugging his shoulders. "You know as well as I that this war is too widespread to be certain what army did this."

The village must have once been to the south, for the Young Forest stood close by to the north, and they did not find any signs of habitation traveling westwards for several more days.

As the time passed, Tamlin became depressed and worried. None of the Western Lands had a brisk trade during the winter, but there should have been *somebody* on the road. Instead, the path they walked was empty, as though the entire countryside was abandoned. He looked to Caelyn, the only other man in the company from Fenegar, but the monk's expression was completely impassive.

On the tenth day, they came to a crossroads. Tamlin heard Telena gasp in shock, but she was the only one. Right at the northern corner stood a large wooden gallows. Several desiccated corpses swung from the ropes, a frozen pile of feces and clear fluid under each body. Although the clothes were too torn and faded to tell exactly who had once worn them, they did not look like the garb of the nobility or the military.

Tamlin viewed his own lack of reaction with concern. Had he really become so cold? Had he really seen so much that he could no longer be moved by the horror of death? Or was it shock? Would he wake in the middle of the night, shaking as the faces of the dead stared at him from his dreams?

They all stood respectful and silent as Caelyn stepped onto the gallows and administered last rites to each corpse.

"What was their crime?" Brodin whispered once the monk had finished.

"They were in the wrong place at the wrong time," Caelyn replied, stepping down from the platform carefully. The steps were slick, and Tamlin thought he saw the monk teeter for the briefest moment before regaining his balance. "We will leave them here."

This time, none of the company objected. If nothing else, the gallows had reinforced in Tamlin's mind the need for stealth.

"Why did they hang them here?" Telena asked. Tamlin turned to regard her, seeing that she had become decidedly pale.

"To set an example," Jyhanna answered. "And for protection. It is said that the wrongfully slain will sometimes return to seek their killer. If they are buried or left at a crossroads or a fork, they can't find their way back."

Sagarum shook his head. "All this misery and death for power. I should have returned long before this could have happened."

"There is no point in worrying about what you could have done," Brother Caelyn stated. "All you can do is try to make things better in the here and now."

"I will," Sagarum vowed. "I swear it by the Eternal One himself."

"We should get on our way," Jyhanna suggested. "Night is coming, and I, at least, do not wish to be around when the angry ghosts return to seek their vengeance."

That night, Tamlin awoke from nightmares of the dead, shaking uncontrollably. In a way, he was grateful –

it meant he still had most of his humanity left. Gazing around the camp at the sleeping forms, he wondered how many of them had suffered the same reaction. As he regained control of himself, snow began to fall.

They had taken the southwestern fork on the road after encountering the gallows, and the flakes continued to sprinkle down the next day. At times, Tamlin marvelled at how Caelyn knew where the road was, as the monk moved forward with such certainty that there could be no doubt that he knew where his abbey lay.

For another five days, they encountered nobody, and the food started to run out. Tamlin began to hope that they would encounter a town or village somewhere, one that hadn't been touched by the war, or if it had, could at least offer some shelter. The wind became more biting every day, and the apprentice realized that the fullness of winter had truly arrived.

On the seventeenth day, they finally came to what had once been a prosperous village. At least, Tamlin was certain that it had been, before it was abandoned. While the buildings hadn't been burnt, some of them were collapsing, thatched roofs caving in under the weight of the snow, and it appeared nobody had lived there for months.

"Where did they go?" he wondered. There were no bodies hidden in the snow, no blood on the building walls, no sign of violence whatsoever.

"They probably fled to Southmarch or one of the larger towns," Caelyn mused. "There might not have been an army here recently, but they fled from one."

"Wouldn't the army of Fenegar protect them?" Jyhanna asked, shaking her head. "That's what a country has an army for!"

"You're assuming the army of Fenegar wasn't the one they were fleeing from," Caelyn said. "Or it could have been elsewhere. Regardless, this settlement has no walls. They couldn't have put up anything even resembling a defense; it must have been a matter of flight or death to them."

"We should see if we can find some provisions," Jyhanna suggested. "Perhaps they left something that might be useful."

Although Tamlin thought her idea was a good one, he didn't hold out much hope. If they had fled from an army, they would have taken everything helpful and destroyed what they couldn't carry. In the end, his suspicions proved correct; while they were able to find some ragged blankets, there was no food left in the village whatsoever.

They took shelter that night in one of the few intact buildings, and set out at daybreak. Once again, the countryside seemed empty, and the road was absolutely deserted. The land became a bit hilly for a couple of days, but then it evened out. They passed another neglected field on the twentieth day, and Tamlin saw Brother Caelyn's mouth tighten at the sight.

"What's wrong?" Tamlin asked.

"These fields belong to the abbey," Caelyn said, pushing on ahead.

The next morning, they passed a faded wooden sign marking the Abbey of Southmarch. But as they crested the hill overlooking the monastery, Tamlin's heart leapt into his chest, and he saw Caelyn fall to his knees, weeping.

All that remained of the abbey was a burnt-out ruin.

Tamlin helped Caelyn pick through the remains of the monastery. The other members of the company simply stood by, uncertain of what to do. Tamlin couldn't blame them. It was a devastating loss for Caelyn, so much so that it had broken through his usual dispassionate guise.

Whoever had destroyed the abbey had been thorough. The upper floors had collapsed, as had most of the walls, so that nothing stood higher than Tamlin's waist. In some places Tamlin found cracked stone balls that appeared to have been fired from catapults, suggesting that there had been a siege, and the enemy had not wanted to leave anything standing. As it was, a rat couldn't hide in the remains.

Finally, the rest of the company descended into the ruins, Telena biting back a scream as she tripped over the corpse of one of the monks. The bodies lay everywhere, preserved in the cold. Many of them were horribly maimed, as though they had tortured before dying.

Tamlin began to speak, but fell silent when Caelyn stared at him. The apprentice looked down – suddenly, he could not meet that pained gaze. There was something else in it, though, something disturbing. It was as if the monk was now trying to hold something in, some rage the likes of which Tamlin had never seen.

"We'll give them a decent burial," Jyhanna suggested, striding forward. "It's the least they deserve."

Caelyn spun on her. "In what?" the monk demanded, his voice almost a shout. "The ground has hardened with the frost, and we can't use magic to thaw it. If we burn them, we'll send a beacon to whatever armies are around that we are here." He paused, taking a deep breath and regaining his composure. "There is nothing more that can be done than counting the dead and seeing to it that they have last rites."

With that, Tamlin stepped back, watching Caelyn work. Even with all the pain, Caelyn still moved methodically, making certain that none were left unshriven.

Once he was finished, Caelyn sat down on what had been an outer wall. "There were some survivors," he said.

"At least twenty of them. It appears that Abbot Artus and the prior both escaped. They must have fled just as the enemy breached the walls."

Caelyn looked up, and Jyhanna drew her sword. "Riders!" she shouted. "Many of them! Looks like a vanguard!"

Tamlin felt a cold sweat drip down his back. Had they come so far only to be captured after all?

"You there! Hold!" a voice ordered. "What are you doing here?"

Tamlin turned, watching with horror as Caelyn placidly stepped up to meet the rider, a large man in a strange black livery, bearing a long, naked sword.

"I am Brother Caelyn," the monk stated. "Formerly of the Abbey of Southmarch. These are my companions."

"They look harmless," a second rider said. "Only one of them is armed."

"If you sheath your sword, no harm will come to any of you," the first rider declared.

Caelyn looked at Jyhanna and nodded. Frowning, the shield-maiden slid her blade back into its scabbard.

The first rider dismounted and strode up to Sagarum, sword still in hand. "You are an Archmagus," he said.

"Some have called me that," Sagarum replied. "It is not quite true, but I have been given that title."

"It looks like our Lord Archmagus was correct," the second rider said. "There is a spell-weaver among them."

Tamlin thought he would collapse. It was only the presence of his companions that prevented him from fleeing. As soon as the wizard had been mentioned, Tamlin had no doubts that they had fallen into hostile hands.

"Our leader will want to talk with all of you," the first rider declared, remounting his horse. "Gelron, Davin, ride behind and inform his Lordship that we have found the people he told us about. Also inform him that tonight's campground is secured. Haldac, set up the perimeter; I don't want anything getting in or out without my authorization."

The rider turned back to the company, and his words sent chills down Tamlin's spine. "Don't worry," he said. "You'll all be dealt with soon."

Chapter III — Conadar

Had he been perhaps thirty years younger, Jyhanna would have found the Archmagus attractive. Even now, the man stood tall and fit, exuding an air of power that filled the tent. But there were wrinkles around his eyes, and his grey beard had become flecked with white.

The company had been forced to wait for nightfall before their audience with the wizard. The army slowly arrived and camped, first the vanguard making camp, and then the main force. Jyhanna was puzzled, though; many of the uniforms were ragged, some did not even match, and several of the troops were slow setting their tents, as though it was the first time they had ever done such a thing. None of it made sense for an army in the field in the middle of a war.

Finally, once the sun had set and the company sat around a fire, one of the guards stepped up and declared that the Archmagus would see them.

Jyhanna had glanced at each of her companions as

they stood up. Tamlin was pale, as though he was convinced he was going to die. Sagarum's visage was impassive, as was Brother Caelyn's. Brodin and Telena simply looked confused; no doubt it was their first time in the middle of an military camp.

Relieving her of her sword, the guards led them to a large tent, where a crimson-robed Archmagus poured over some maps on an oak table by candlelight, flanked by two men wearing dull coats of mail.

Looking up at the company, the wizard said, "We'll examine this later. Give me a moment alone."

The two mail-clad men nodded and stepped outside, leaving the Archmagus with the company and its guards.

"My name is Conadar," the wizard declared. "I would know who you are, and what you know of the Abbey of Southmarch."

Jyhanna shrugged. Even if she was able to slay the wizard, the guards would kill her before she could escape. "I am Jyhanna, Princess in exile of Toregien. My companions are Brother Caelyn of Southmarch, Tamlin of Fenegar, Brodin and Telena of Beregar, and Sagarum."

Conadar nodded and sat on a creaking wooden chair. "You speak true." He turned to Caelyn. "Did you see what happened to the abbey?"

The monk shook his head. "I was on my pilgrimage when I saw signs that the Great Convention was being violated. By the time I returned to warn my brethren, it was too late."

"Damnation," Conadar said. "Please accept my condolences for the loss of your home. I have my suspicions as to who was responsible, but I have yet to find an eyewitness account."

"So it wasn't you," Jyhanna broke in.

Conadar shook his head. "I would never attack an innocent, no matter what my fellows are doing." He turned

243

to face Sagarum. "You are a Successor; I felt it as soon as I laid eyes on you from my scrying glass. However, I have never seen you before. How can this be?"

Sagarum shrugged. "I got lucky in a battle."

Conadar frowned. "Please don't lie to me like that; I can sense all falsehoods."

"You have Truesight."

The Archmagus nodded. "It has served me well in choosing my companions. What I need to know now is whether you are trustworthy, or if I should have you all killed."

"I am the first Grand Magus, and I still hold the eighth Great Power," Sagarum stated. "I am here to reclaim what is mine. I have waited several millennia for this."

"Ah," Conadar said, leaning back. "If it were up to me, I would simply give my Power back to you. This Succession has brought out the worst in everybody, and I wish now that I had no part in it. I take it that you are the one who killed Bervus in Bandre."

Sagarum nodded. "It was a hard fight. The next one will be easier."

Conadar smiled. "No doubt you wish to kill me now."

"The thought has crossed my mind."

"I am sick of the entire affair," Conadar declared. "I do not wish your blood, nor do I want to die. I merely desire to re-establish the natural order. I wish a truce with you. If you swear by the Eternal One that you will not seek me out for combat, I swear that once this war is over and my work is done, I will find a way to restore Truesight to you. I will give it willingly. Is that acceptable?"

There was a moment of silence. Jyhanna's heart leapt into her throat. If Sagarum didn't agree, they might all be dead. Her hand crept down to where her sword would be, but all it found was the empty sheath.

She cursed under her breath. If a battle did begin, she

would have to disarm one of the guards and use his blade. How they could possibly fight their way out of the camp, though, was beyond her.

Sagarum nodded. "If you will swear it by the Eternal One, so will I. I will not shed blood over something that will be freely given."

Conadar motioned to the guards. "You may leave us. Wait outside."

As the guards shuffled out of the tent, Conadar leaned forward and stared at Sagarum. "Tell me what you know of this war."

The wizard shrugged and began to speak. He related how he had come to this world across the Great Road, sought the advice of the Oracle, and then found Tamlin and Caelyn in an inn. Then he talked about how they met the rest of the company, the journey across the Inner Sea, the trek through the Young Forest and the Shroud Mountains, and then the meeting of the Oracle. Finally, he told Conadar of the fight with Bervus and the journey to the remains of the monastery.

The Archmagus leaned back. "Then there is much that all of you still need to know."

"I am curious as to why you have led an army into Fenegar, when you fly none of the colors of Toregien or Bandre," Caelyn said.

"As a matter of fact, I am chasing the army of Toregien," Conadar explained. "Two months ago, Gesanus solidified his power in Toregien and murdered King Lewys. I am truly sorry, your highness. He had split the army in two; one portion was defending against attack from the east and south, and the second he was using to invade Fenegar."

Jyhanna choked back a sob. A tear flowed down her cheek. She would never see her father again, never be able to reclaim her place at his side. The grief welled up inside her, threatening to overcome her, but she pushed it down, trying desperately to concentrate on what was at hand.

"What of my brother?" she asked haltingly. "Does he still live."

"I believe he fled a month before the regicide," Conadar replied. "If you need some time, we can always continue this later."

Jyhanna shook her head. "I will be fine. I can mourn later."

Conadar nodded. "Very well. Once he had complete control, he took command of the army in Fenegar, hoping to strike against Feladon, the Successor here. Both sides have battle-magi, and there has been a standstill for the most part. However, Gesanus has of late managed to drive Feladon back, I know not where."

"So where do you fit into all of this?" Sagarum wondered.

"Since the war began, I have been traveling, hiding myself from the others," Conadar said. "I saw devastation, horror, and darkness, and finally I could tolerate it no more. So, in Toregien and Tarese I began to gather an army of my own. I did it slowly, so that the others would not notice. A group of deserters here, some displaced townspeople there, and happily I had enough sergeants to train everybody. Weapons were in easy supply, for we often passed the sites of recent battles, and bows and arrows we were able to make ourselves. Finally, about a month ago, we attacked Gesanus' rearguard in Fenegar, and were able to rout it. Several of them came over to our side – apparently Gesanus holds his power in Toregien by fear, rather than love. However, it did alert Gesanus to our presence."

"And he's been running away," Sagarum said.

The Archmagus nodded. "I think he fears us. We have held our own in battle, and he does not know how many battle-magi we have; I have cast a ward around my army that blocks his scrying. We have forced him to fight a war on two fronts. So, the tail end of his army has been running from us, burning and razing everything in their path so that we cannot provision. If we do not catch up with them soon, we may very well starve."

"What of the other Successors?" Sagarum asked.

"Two of them, Hargan and Malichus, are in Tarese, consolidating their power and beginning an invasion of Toregien," Conadar replied. "They march at the head of an army from the Haneric Empire. One of them, I do not know which, has killed Tergibar, who was in hiding. From what I have scryed, they are running into heavy opposition, both from rogue Taresian soldiers, and from the army of Toregien." He leaned forward. "Thanks to your actions, Bervus is now dead, leaving only Gesanus and Feladon in the north."

"So are your plans?" Jyhanna said.

"First, I will kill Gesanus, and then I will hunt down and destroy Feladon," Conadar answered. "From there, I will turn south into Toregien, where I should be able to engage and destroy the final two successors."

"Are you not afraid of being flanked?"

Conadar shook his head. "The only ones who could attack me from the rear do not know where I am, and would have to fight their way through Toregien first."

"So what would you have of us?" Caelyn asked. "I doubt you are telling us this because of the goodness in your heart."

Conadar nodded. "That is true. I would have you all join me and my army."

"I am the only warrior in the company," Jyhanna pointed out. "Brodin and Telena, who I am sworn to protect, are only farmers, and have never held weapons in their life, nor will they ever have to so long as they are my

247

wards. Tamlin is Sagarum's apprentice, and Caelyn has such a distaste for battle that I doubt I will ever see him on the field."

"I need people to tend to the wounded," Conadar said. "And right now, I have nobody to give spiritual aid to my men. If there are battle-magi to fight, I can use another wizard at my side, particularly one as experienced as Sagarum. Even an apprentice can be helpful."

Sagarum leaned forward. "How many wizards do you have right now?"

Conadar frowned. "Just myself. I am very powerful, though. I would be happier, however, if I had some help to fend off enemy magic." He turned to Jyhanna. "You I need most of all."

Jyhanna blinked. "Why is that?"

"Few of us are experienced battle commanders," Conadar replied. "Oh, I have some sergeants, and some minor officers from Toregien, Tarese, and Fenegar with me, but none who truly know what it is to command an army." He stood up and looked Jyhanna in the eye. "And if you, a princess of Toregien, were to fight at the head of my army, it would take the spirit out of our enemies."

Jyhanna took a deep breath. "We would all have to think deeply about this."

"I will have some tents issued to you while you consider," Conadar said. "But do not take too long. My scouts have informed me that Gesanus has turned with his army to engage me, and will be here within three days."

Chapter IV — Preparations

Jyhanna stood on a rise, watching the preparations around her. Conadar's army had chosen their ground, a large hill overlooking the site of the abbey, and were building their defenses. While Jyhanna felt that with experience they could move faster, she had to admit that their strategic reasoning was sound.

As she looked upon several soldiers pounding giant stakes into the earth, she heard Brother Caelyn step up beside her. Turning, she stared at the monk, who gazed back at her with placid eyes.

"How do you feel?" Caelyn asked.

Jyhanna shook her head. "Much as you do, I suppose. The pain is still overwhelming."

The monk nodded. "Losing family will do that. The trick is to mourn and heal, rather than grow angry and let the wound fester."

"I have an opportunity for revenge," Jyhanna said. "Do you think I should take it?"

Caelyn shrugged. "You must do as your conscience dictates. However, if you do fight for vengeance, you will find that the victory is an empty one at best."

"And you know from experience," Jyhanna said. Caelyn said nothing, however. Finally, the shield maiden added, "You know, Sagarum thinks we should stay and help."

"It would be easier to attack the next Successor if we had an army to help," Caelyn admitted. "But there are others to consider."

"Brodin and Telena."

The monk nodded. "Up to now, they have seen minor fights. Do you really want to expose them to a full-scale battle?"

"They would be in the rear, with you," Jyhanna stated. "They would be safe, and wouldn't see the fighting except from afar."

"No, but they would see the wounded," Caelyn said calmly. "How much misery could they handle, before it scars them forever? And what happens if Conadar loses this battle, leaving us all unprotected?"

Jyhanna sat on a large rock, the hoary stone rough under her wool trousers. "But how much more protected would we be without the army? It seems to me that we are now trapped between a rock and a hard place."

"I now have no abbey to return to," Caelyn said. "All I have left are my companions. Whatever is decided, I will support it."

"We may need your prayers," Jyhanna sighed. "I do not think we can win this with skill alone."

"Then I will try to be heard by the Eternal One," Caelyn said. "I will leave you to your army."

As the monk made his way down towards the camp, Jyhanna looked to the horizon. The army of Toregien was out there, somewhere to the north, but all she could see was the snowy landscape, a white collection of hills and trees cast into shadow by the cloudy sky. Shivering, she wrapped her cloak around her, covering the mail shirt she wore this day, just in case she had to fight.

The upcoming battle weighed on her mind, however. It would not be a skirmish against some invading foe, but instead she would be shedding the blood of her own countrymen. The people she had been brought up to lead one day, should her brother decide not to take the throne.

But now her brother was in exile, as she was, and her father was dead, murdered by the Archmagus who had turned him against her in the first place. How many of her people had he corrupted, forced to commit acts of horror? Her gaze wandered over to the ruins of the monastery. It had once been a house of the Eternal One, but Gesanus had ordered it reduced to rubble just to spite Conadar.

She gritted her teeth. Even if her countrymen were held in thrall by Gesanus, the only way to free them was to fight. Finally, she had a moment where she could hold the life of the Archmagus in her hands, and end it.

Standing up, she straightened her tunic and coat of mail. With long, purposeful strides, she walked down to Conadar's tent, where she found the Archmagus pouring over more maps, Gesanus' position marked by small colored pieces of wood.

"I will lead your fight," Jyhanna said as Conadar looked up at her. "Tell me what you know of Gesanus' army, and I'll help you draw up your battle plan."

It was midday when Brodin and Telena found themselves taken under Brother Caelyn's wing. The monk found them in their tent, holding each other gently as they wondered what the future would hold.

"Jyhanna has decided to stay and fight," the monk

said. Telena's heart leapt into her throat, and she glanced to Brodin, praying that he would not be asked to enlist.

"What will we do?" Brodin asked. "Will I need to join the army?"

Caelyn shook his head. "You are untrained, and would be no use to them whatsoever. No, we will be tending the wounded in the rear as the battle progresses. I will show you where we will be working, and what we must do."

Caelyn took them to a large tent on the southern side of the hill, far away from the fortifications being raised to the north. The canvas sheltered a number of small cots, all of which were empty.

"Most of the wounded will arrive within the first half hour of the battle," Caelyn stated. "After that, it will be a slow trickle, followed by a large flood once the battle has ended. Some wounds will be mortal, some will not. You will have to learn how to tell the difference."

"What do we do if a wound is mortal?" Brodin asked. Telena thought he looked a bit pale, although it could have been the poor lighting in the tent. She swallowed uncomfortably, already feeling nauseated even though the enemy had yet to arrive. It was so big and horrifying.

"Call me over, and I will provide them with some comfort," the monk replied. "There will be nothing else you can do for them. Of the others, some wounds will be serious, others will be minor. The serious injuries must be seen to first, and then the lighter wounds can be dealt with.

"The healers will be responsible for taking care of the serious wounds. Your task will be separate the wounded, and then bandage some of the lighter injuries. Feldon, the leader of the healers here, has asked me to show you how it is done."

Over the next hour, Telena found herself learning how to bandage, and listening in horror as Caelyn described the variety of wounds that were possible. The monk spoke as

252

though he had seen all of them personally, and she found his matter-of-fact manner disturbing.

But, by the end, both she and Brodin knew their tasks for the upcoming battle. She learned that black blood from the belly represented a mortal wound, while an arrow in the shoulder was serious but not fatal. She discovered that through repetition practicing on Caelyn, she was able to tie a tourniquet with a respectable speed.

Finally, as the sun began to set, Caelyn stood up and sent them to their tent. "You must be up and ready for daybreak," he said as he saw them off. "The battle will likely start shortly after then. Eat something light when you break your fast, as you will have to carry heavy loads, and may find yourselves sick for the first hour of the carnage."

Telena was not encouraged by the thought, and that night she spent curled up beside Brodin, clutching him as he held her, praying that the dawn would not come.

Conadar was exhausted by the time the sun set. After a few hours of consultation, they had their battle plan set. Jyhanna would lead the troops into the battle as Sagarum provided magical protection. Conadar, on the other hand, would lead a small party that would sneak into Gesanus' camp, capture the Archmagus, and deliver him to Sagarum.

It was not elegant, but it was simple enough that relatively little could go irreparably wrong during the course of the battle. Still, he was ill at ease. He had never fought a battle against a Successor before, and there was still too much he didn't know. Additionally, several of his scouts had been forced away from Gesanus' army before they could take an accurate count, despite Conadar's spells to shield them. It was as though Gesanus knew what was going to happen before it happened.

He paced through the camp for a while, talking to some of the soldiers sitting around the fires, giving an occasional encouraging word while hoping that his own anxieties would not show. He tried to remind himself that he did have around six thousand men, and Gesanus would have been worn down by his war with Feladon, but that did not give him great comfort.

Finally, he turned into Sagarum's tent, finding the Archmagus, like himself, still awake. Sagarum's apprentice, on the other hand, slept restlessly on one of the beds that had been provided.

"Amazing that he can sleep," Conadar whispered.

Sagarum nodded. "If we are going to talk, we should do it outside."

Stepping outside, Conadar turned as Sagarum followed, the old wizard taking a deep breath of the night air. Sagarum waved his hands for a moment, and Conadar felt the tingling of energies in the air.

"What ward did you raise?" he wondered.

"A guard against scrying eyes," Sagarum replied. "It is better that no battle-magus can hear us from afar."

Conadar nodded. "I see."

"Everything is set?" Sagarum asked.

"Yes," Conadar replied. "Jyhanna is staying with her troops tonight; she's spent the last few hours talking to their officers and going over plans."

"You shielded them, I trust."

"Of course," Conadar chuckled, smiling wearily. "As you say, we must protect against scrying magi. And what of yourself?"

Sagarum sighed. "I have waited a very long time for this. For millennia I made plans, waiting for the moment when I could interfere with the Succession and regain the Great Powers. And now that the time has come, I find that it is not what I thought it would be."

"And what did you think it would be?"

"Sneaking into wizard's towers," Sagarum replied. "Moving stealthily in the night. Taking the Successors by surprise."

"Not much honor or glory in that."

Sagarum shrugged. "It is not a situation that requires honor or glory. It is a mean, nasty business, and the sooner it is over the better. But now...now I find myself waiting in an army, hoping that the battle will turn to our side, certain that the other Archmagus knows that I am coming."

"Life is rarely what we think it will be," Conadar mused. "I had thought that I would be struggling in a secret war, testing strength against strength, and no innocents being hurt along the way. Instead, this Succession has brought the whole of the Western Lands to ruin."

Sagarum nodded. "All we can do is stop it quickly. And even that we must do in small steps."

Conadar scratched his beard. "And it all begins upon the morrow." With that, Conadar took his leave, retiring to his tent to get the rest he would need for the ordeal ahead.

The next morning, two armies confronted each other over the snowy field.

Chapter V — Opening Moves

Jyhanna stood on the hill, gazing to the north at the army of Gesanus. Beside her stood Conadar and Sagarum. The enemy had encamped just outside the range of her catapults and ballistae, and formed up in the frigid morning in orderly ranks several rows deep.

Beside the infantry, she made out two lines of cavalry, all bearing heavy lances. She smiled. Not only was their infantry evenly matched, but so was their cavalry. It would be tactics rather than brute force that would carry the day. The thing that concerned her was Gesanus' catapults. If she couldn't destroy them, they could pummel her men until they broke from sheer fear.

"Do we know their range?" she asked, motioning to the distant artillery.

"On even ground, the same as ours," Conadar replied. "And we now have the high ground."

"They'll want us to parley first, and no doubt there will be treachery," Jyhanna predicted. "If they can, they'll kill you two before the battle even begins, and save themselves the bloodshed."

"That would be in character for Gesanus, as I remember him," Conadar stated.

"Incoming barrage!" came a shout from the front, as several of the enemy catapults fired.

"Load artillery!" Jyhanna barked, startled by the sudden action. Behind her, there was a flurry of activity as men began to load rocks, vases of oil, and giant arrows into the siege engines. And then the enemy missiles landed, scattering among the front ranks.

She saw a messenger running up from the front of the line, three round objects in his arms. Strangely, the enemy artillery went silent; she had expected to see men loading the catapults for another barrage.

Then she saw what the soldier bore in his arms. Horror and anger overtook her, and for a moment she had to force herself not to scream in fury. The messenger carried three severed heads, the tonsures still visible despite the clotted blood in the hair.

When she turned, Conadar had blanched, and Sagarum stood dispassionately by. "So they want to dishearten us," Sagarum said. "No doubt they think the parley will be easy now."

"It has had the opposite effect," Jyhanna gritted, turning to her lieutenants. "Raise the black flag and my colors. Begin the barrage. One half of the artillery to concentrate on their catapults, the other half on their soldiers."

"But what about the parley?" Conadar protested.

"These are not men, but animals," Jyhanna stated, her eyes cold and angry. "We will show them no mercy. Begin the plan as soon as I lead the charge."

With that, she strode over to her horse and mounted it, pulling a long steel-tipped lance from the ground. With a kick, she sent it into a gallop. As she rode to the front, she heard the twanging of the catapults as they sent their deadly loads into the air.

"Incoming barrage!" somebody shouted, but she ignored it. As she joined her lines of knights, she gave them a salute. Beside her, the first of Gesanus' missiles landed, crushing infantry. Screams of pain erupted from the ranks, and she heard the front-line healers barking orders.

Raising her lance in the air, she addressed her men. "The black flag has been raised. These are not men, but animals. Treat them as such, and show no mercy!"

"NO MERCY!" came a cry around her. Jyhanna smiled, the battle madness already beginning to take her.

"Charge on my signal," she declared, staring down at the foe. Some of the fire-bombs had landed, the oil smearing the ground and sending men scrambling, their clothes and skin alight. In other places, the catapults were making large holes in the line.

The chaos was shared by both sides, she realized, gazing at her own ranks for a moment. A ballista bolt ran through one of the soldiers to her left, pinning him to the ground as he screamed in anguish, his blood and guts staining the snow. Another took a pikeman through the face, exploding his head in a pink mist as it went on to take another's arm off.

"They're moving," a knight stated, pointing at the foe. Indeed, both the infantry and cavalry had begun their advance, and a steady rain of arrows had begun to fall, the deadly shafts launched from both sides.

One her knights fell from his horse, an arrow in his shoulder. Turning, she ordered the man to the healers. Then she gripped her lance. The enemy was already halfway into the field; it was time.

"ADVANCE!" she barked, kicking her stallion into a trot. "Attack their cavalry first!" As her knights began to follow, she heard the sergeants behind her giving the order to march. The hill caused her mount to speed up, and as it did, the rest of the knights formed into their line.

"LANCES!" she cried, lowering her lance to point at the foe. The enemy knights had turned away from the infantry and were coming directly towards her, lances ready.

"CHARGE!" she screamed, kicking her horse into a run. As it advanced, she took aim at the leading enemy knight, her lance pointed squarely at his chest. The foe raised his own lance slightly, so that it was aimed at her head.

At the very last minute, Jyhanna went into a crouch, head lowered, body braced against her horse's neck. Her enemy's lance passed over her head by a hair, but the other man was not nearly as lucky. Jyhanna's weapon caught him directly in the center of his chest, punching through him, the sound lost in the sudden din of battle. The shock caused her to drop the shaft, and as quickly as she could she drew her sword, ready to strike a finishing blow.

It wasn't necessary; the knight fell from his horse, the lance running straight through him, part of his spine split and protruding from his body.

As soon as she turned back to the fray, she was beset upon. Parrying with her sword, she made a deep cut, punching through another knight's mail-coat and spilling his intestines. The third attacker she blocked with her shield, bringing her horse around to clash blades. As they did, another of her men rode up behind him and speared him on a lance, sending blood and bone flying.

She spun, just in time to take off the head of a dismounted enemy who was attacking one of her men. And then, she found herself in a field of friends, her sword heavy with blood and gore.

"Is that it?" she wondered, glancing around. Her

knights were the only ones left standing.

"We've killed them all," her lieutenant declared, a tall man named Gallant, wearing a once shining coat of mail.

"This doesn't feel right," she muttered. "There should have been more of them."

The first arrows began to land at her mount's feet, and she cursed herself for stalling. "On to the infantry! CHARGE!"

As the two armies clashed, deafening war-cries filling the air, she led her knights back into the fray.

As soon as the battle started, Caelyn had his hands full. The first victims of the barrage began to arrive, and he had to help men whose limbs had been crushed, many of whom would have to have them amputated.

Every now and then he would glance at Brodin and Telena, just to make certain they were handling things properly. He noted that Telena had dashed to a corner to retch when the first ballista casualties arrived, one man with a leg torn off, and another with a large sucking hole through his gut. Caelyn did what he could for that one, but it was only a matter of time, and soon the soldier exhaled for the last time.

And then he heard that the black flag had been raised, and his heart skipped a beat. Where before it would just be a bloody battle, now it would be a massacre.

"What does a black flag mean?" Telena asked, her blue dress already smeared with the blood of the wounded and dying.

"It means that this army will show no mercy," Caelyn stated. "They will take no prisoners, and they will expect no quarter from the foe."

He saw her swallow nervously, and then return to her duties, helping hold down a screaming man as one of the healers applied a bandage to a spurting leg wound.

"A thrice-damned arrow!" he heard a knight complaining as a healer pulled a shaft from his shoulder. "Cut down before I could even strike a blow! The Eternal One must have it in for me."

At any other time, Caelyn would have chastised the man, but instead he walked away to see if there was anybody else in need of last rites. He found two soldiers, one with a crushed chest, the other with a gurgling throat wound, both of whom he was able to give some comfort to before the end.

You should be out there, helping win the battle, an inner voice said, the voice of the past. He shoved it down mercilessly, as he would have done to his memories if it was possible.

The thudding of catapult missiles filled the air, and Caelyn prayed for a moment that none would find their way into the healers' tent.

The flow of casualties slowed down to a trickle, and Caelyn sat on one of the cots, resting. He heard Brodin step up quietly beside him, and looked up to see uncertainty on the young man's face.

"What now, Brother Caelyn?" Brodin asked.

Caelyn sighed. "Now almost all of the wounded are caught in the middle of the melee. The few who manage to make it here are those who can be pulled out. For the most part, we won't see many more until the end of the battle, when we'll be flooded."

Caelyn blinked. The pattering of horse hooves sounded from outside. Puzzled, he stood up and made his way out of the tent, until he gazed down the hill at five approaching men on horseback.

He frowned as he saw that the riders were in the livery of Gesanus' army. He stepped forward and let his arms fall to his side. As he watched, the first three men of the five drew their swords, the bright blades shining in what little sunlight managed to break through the clouds.

"There are no fighting men here," Caelyn stated calmly. "Only wounded."

The first man removed his great helm and threw it to the ground. "The black flag has been raised," he declared. "No mercy to anybody!"

"These men are out of the battle," Caelyn said. "I will not allow you to harm them."

The leader of the knights brandished his sword. "And what are you going to do about it, old monk?" he mocked.

A violent inner darkness surged upwards, forcing Caelyn to push it down. But still it lingered, waiting at the edge of his consciousness, inviting him to set it free.

Caelyn swallowed with the effort, seeing the commander's face break into a wide grin as he misinterpreted the action as one of fear. "If I have to kill you all, then I will do so," the monk said. "I do not wish that, however."

The knight pointed with his sword, and Caelyn turned to see that Brodin and Telena both stood outside, regarding him. "I think I'll kill that young man after you. The woman I'll take my pleasure with. After all, she has to die, but not immediately."

The darkness surged up, Caelyn barely able to keep it down. "Please turn back," he said. "None of you will pass me alive."

The enemy leader chortled. "Who do you think you are? Garwulf the Slayer?"

Caelyn gazed back at Brodin and Telena, and his heart sank. They needed to be protected, and there was nobody else nearby who could do it. As the knights laughed at their commander's joke, he let the darkness take hold. Brother Caelyn faded away.

"Yes," replied Garwulf the Slayer.

Chapter VI — Garwulf the Slayer

Jyhanna and her men crashed through the enemy infantry, bringing death to all before them. Those of her knights who still had lances took the first rank, cleaving a wide path for those without.

She found herself in the middle of the fray, Lieutenant Gallant at her side, swinging her sword as she ploughed through the enemy ranks. One strike split a soldier's helmet, spilling his brains to the earth. The next second she was thrusting, taking another infantryman in the face and driving her blade through the back of his skull.

She felt a sudden shock, and then she was falling, her horse screaming in agony. She tucked into a roll, feeling more than hearing the polearm blade that missed her head by inches. As she gained her feet, she swung, shearing an enemy's legs off at the knees. As the man went down screaming, she spun, shield raised, looking for some friendly faces in the crowd of enemies.

"Jyhanna!" cried Gallant, also unhorsed. He beckoned

to her from a group of knights who had formed a rudimentary shield circle, holding back a mass of infantry.

Stepping towards them, she found herself confronted by two soldiers, both bearing large axes. She dodged the first one, her counter-attack ripping through his leather armor and spilling his bowels, but she was only barely able to block the second one. The axe blade drove into her shield, her arm numb from the blow. She brought her sword down, severing his arm at the elbow. The man bellowed in pain, only to have her swing again, striking his head off.

Something blurred past her, and she ducked into a crouch, preparing to dash to meet her comrades. Glancing around, she spotted a man with a knife in hand, taking aim from behind several other enemy soldiers. In a smooth motion, she dropped her shield and took up the fallen axe, throwing it so that it took the assassin in the forehead, splitting his skull. As quickly as she could, she picked up her shield and pounded to her fellow knights.

"Where is the rest of our infantry?" she hollered, her voice only barely louder than the sounds of ringing metal and screaming pervading the air. She joined the shield wall just in time to see one of her men cut down. Revenge was swift, though, as the knight beside him sliced the assailant's throat with a swift stroke.

"Somewhere behind us, I think!" Gallant declared. She allowed herself the briefest of glances. Indeed, behind the circle there was the din of combat, as men on both sides fell. Neither side seemed to be able to gain a clear advantage.

"We struck too far forwards!" she cursed. "Damnation! We're cut off!"

Striking out, she took one of the foes in the throat, the man falling back and gurgling as blood bubbled at his mouth. She raised her shield to block another heavy blow, swinging below the shield to cut the man down from below the waist.

"We're beset on all sides!" Gallant reported, swinging desperately.

Jyhanna gritted her teeth and continued to fight. If they had been able, they would have taken the foe from the rear, rejoining the line and then pushing forward. But for every enemy she killed, another two seemed to take his place, and it looked as though no help was coming. As the press of battle and dying men became heavier, a bit of desperation crept into her strokes.

Sagarum and Tamlin watched from the hill, no longer flinching as the arrows and catapult missiles flew overhead. The sun was high in the sky, and the light glittered off the weapons as the mass of both armies clashed.

"It looks as though we're winning against their archers," Sagarum mused. "Same with the catapults."

"I don't understand," Tamlin said. "Why don't we just shoot into the battle? It would make more sense."

The wizard shook his head. "We would kill as many of our own men as we did theirs. No, right now our bowmen are shooting at their archers, and similarly with the artillery. The mainstay of the conflict will be determined by the men on the field, and Jyhanna has arrayed them well."

He looked off in the distance. Far to the west, his magesight could make out Conadar and his small escort, riding around the battle to take the other Successor by surprise. When he looked into the press of men, he saw the cavalry push into the enemy ranks, but then the foe swept around them, cutting them off from the rest of the line.

Something twinged at the back of his mind, but

Sagarum couldn't put his finger on it. It was as though there was something wrong about the battle, something he had overlooked.

Then it hit him. "By the Eternal One!" Sagarum cursed. "There's been no battle magic!"

Tamlin blinked. "Sorry?"

"We're here to counter the enemy's battle-magi, correct?" Sagarum began. "The battle has now gone on for half a day, and been stalemated for at least an hour. And not a single spell has been cast, not even by Gesanus!"

"Maybe all of the battle-magi have been killed," Tamlin suggested. "We are not fighting a fresh army."

Sagarum shook his head. "We wouldn't be that lucky. Either he's keeping them in reserve, or he needs them for something else..." Even as he trailed off, he began to walk to the rear, picking up a fallen crossbow and some bolts from one of the lines of bowmen.

"Do you remember what I taught you about counterspells?" the wizard asked.

Tamlin nodded. "Feel the weave of energies, and unravel it. Where are you going?"

"Conadar is walking into a trap," Sagarum declared, mounting a horse. "I have to save him, or all is lost. You stay here and watch for counterspells, just in case I'm wrong."

"But I'm just an apprentice!" Tamlin protested.

Sagarum stared at him. "You knew much when I started teaching you, and you now understand more than most journeymen Magi, even if you have had less time to practice than is desirable. If you are my apprentice now, it is only in name. Have confidence in yourself, do not initiate spells for it will give away your position, and be careful, *Magus* Tamlin."

With that, Sagarum kicked his mount into a gallop, racing down the hill.

Telena clutched at Brodin, not believing what she was seeing. Brother Caelyn was confronting five armed men, all of whom had drawn their weapons, when he did not even hold a staff.

"Please turn back," she heard the monk tell them. "None of you will pass me alive."

At that, the enemy leader chortled. "Who do you think you are? Garwulf the Slayer?"

She saw Caelyn turn to look at her and her husband, his eyes sad. And then, the monk's gaze became so cold and emotionless that it sent chills of horror down her spine. He turned back to the riders and calmly replied, "Yes."

"Come on, Halban," the lead rider laughed, kicking his horse into a gallop. "Let's kill this heroic monk!"

As the first two knights came forward, swords raised, the second horseman slightly staggered behind the first, Telena could already imagine Caelyn ridden down, the poor monk dying to protect them, and then her husband slain.

What happened next occurred so fast that she couldn't make all of it out. Caelyn stepped between the horses and spun, his arms a blur. When he stopped, he still faced the other riders, but now he had a bloody sword in his hand. Both of the leading horsemen fell from their mounts and lay still. When she blinked in shock, she saw that the first knight had been disarmed, a gaping wound in his back. Brother Caelyn strode forward with blade in hand to face the other three enemies.

The third foe spurred his horse onwards, sword pointed forward, as though it was a lance. The monk sidestepped and swung, the blade so fast it was a blur, and continued to walk forward, never breaking stride. Behind him, the rider clutched at the hole in his gut, struggling to

267

hold in his intestines, before falling off his mount in a gory pile of dying flesh.

Caelyn...she shook her head – the monk had already killed three men. She could no longer think of him as Brother Caelyn. Garwulf still advanced, the fourth man leaping from his saddle to hold his hands up in a supplication for mercy. The monk never stopped walking forward. With a quick stroke, he put his blade through the man's forehead, brains spraying out of the back of the head like a fine mist. Just as fast, he withdrew the sword and continued to advance.

The fifth rider gave a cry of horror and kicked his horse into a gallop that took him far around Garwulf and back down the hill. The monk threw his sword, the blade spinning in the air until it struck the horsemen in the head, cleaving the man's skull on the diagonal. There was a spray of gore from the wound, and then the rider slumped down and fell.

Garwulf stepped over to the corpse of the fourth rider and picked up his sword. Walking a bit farther, he also took up the third horseman's sword, testing the balance on each before he stepped up towards the tent.

As he approached, Telena gasped. Garwulf's eyes were emotionless, as though the monk had been fishing or writing instead of slaughtering people. She couldn't take it any longer. Falling to the earth, she vomited, losing what little was left in her stomach. Even as she spat to clear the last of the horrible taste from her mouth, she shuddered uncontrollably.

She had known men who wanted to sacrifice her because of their beliefs, witnessed people kill in anger or in the heat of battle, but she had never seen anyone slaughter people as though they were some kind of object.

She had just enough time to wonder if she could ever trust the monk again before the shakes returned, even worse than before.

Garwulf strode up the hillside, a sword in each hand. The balances were not perfect, but they would do. His body had also become a bit less fit than it had been at his prime, but it would accomplish what needed to be done.

Cresting the rise, he surveyed the battle. Most of the line was in a stalemate, neither side able to overcome the other. The lines fluctuated back and forth, but neither Conadar's forces nor the enemy's were able to advance before it was driven back.

Behind the enemy lines stood a small circle of knights, all dismounted, fighting against the overwhelming foe. In an instant, Garwulf knew what he had to do to win the battle.

The part of him that was Caelyn, the half of his spirit that had allowed him to regain his humanity, wept in dismay. Garwulf pushed it down, along with his distaste of this soulless slaughter.

Striding down the hill into the fray, he bellowed an ancient battle-cry, a call that had not been heard in three decades, and had soldiers gazing up in wonder to see from whence it came.

"IC WILLAN OFSLEAN EOW!"

And then he began to cleave through the enemy ranks, bringing death with both hands.

Jyhanna startled when the shout sounded. Blinking, she shook her head. The fatigue must be getting to her – after all, Garwulf the Slayer was a myth from the Kaegar Wars. Even if he had been real, he would be far too old to fight now.

But then she saw something coming through the field,

a spinning, whirling form that dealt death to whatever it touched. There was a strange precision as it burst through the line, not touching a single one of her men, but slew every foe nearby.

As it sliced through the lines towards her, she managed to make out some brown monastic robes flapping as they moved. Her jaw dropped in shock. It was Brother Caelyn, a sword in each hand, wielding them with a deadliness that no mortal man could ever match.

A sudden crush of enemies blocked him from her view, and then two of the foes went down, clutching at their vitals, the others swiftly following. Caelyn looked at her, his eyes so cold that they seemed inhuman, and then threw one of his swords.

The blade flew past her, and she spun just in time to see it slam into the chest of an enemy soldier who had been creeping up behind her. She turned back to see the monk casually pick up another sword and start to move again, killing all enemies who came before him.

Finally, he reached her small circle of knights. Jyhanna swallowed as she gazed upon him. Not a single drop of blood stained his robes, but his blades were covered in gore. His eyes were so cold that she felt an involuntary chill of horror. She pushed it down.

"You are Garwulf the Slayer," she said, trying to keep her voice steady.

The monk nodded and pointed. "If we strike that way, we can rejoin the line and win the battle."

She gave her assent and motioned to her knights. As a group they began to move, the rear of the circle fighting to keep them from being flanked. As she battled her way forward, she caught the blurred motion of Garwulf ahead of her, cleaving an easier path for them.

The monk was not as fast as Daelyn had been, but he was far faster than any mortal man she had ever seen. As

270

he moved, he spun and whirled, dodging one blade even as he struck out, each time landing a fatal blow. It was almost as though he knew where every single soldier stood and what they were doing at once.

And then they were behind friendly lines, turning around to face the foe. She turned to Garwulf, trying not to gaze at him with awe. "You should let them know that you are here," she said. "Tell the enemy that you are fighting against them."

Garwulf nodded. Once again, he bellowed his war-cry. In front of the lines, Gesanus' troops glanced around nervously, their line buckling slightly.

"Take heart, soldiers of Conadar!" Jyhanna roared. "Garwulf the Slayer fights with us! STRIKE NOW, AND BE VICTORIOUS!"

With that, she plunged back into the fray, Garwulf and Gallant at her side. There was a look of horror on the first foe's face as she cut deeply into his side, punching her blade through his mail and into his lung. Withdrawing the sword, she struck again, cleaving another enemy's head and splattering brains on his fellows.

The battle rage took her. Part of her heard herself screaming, "FOR LEWYS! REVENGE FOR LEWYS!" But she was spinning, killing, every stroke laying open an enemy's body to deal death. She felt something tear at her mail, but then she turned, slaying her assailant with a blow that tore his throat out. She felt a breeze as Garwulf tore past her, cutting a swath of death and destruction wherever he stepped.

And then, suddenly, there were no more foes before her. Exultation took her. They had buckled and broken the enemy lines! Already she could see some of the soldiers fleeing before the might of her army. A glee filled her heart as he turned to pursue them, now slaying her enemies as they tried desperately to retreat. "NO MERCY!" she

271

bellowed as she cut one young man down. She had just enough time to see the fear in his face before she took his head off.

Her smile widened. The battle was won! It had taken hours, but the enemy was broken, running, and soon dead. She turned around, surveying the field of maimed corpses and fallen weapons. And then she saw the monk.

Garwulf the Slayer was gone. Instead, Brother Caelyn knelt in the middle of a pile of bodies, each bearing the livery of Gesanus' army. Tears flowed down the monk's cheeks as he tried in vain to give last rights to each man he had killed. And in his eyes she saw a torment so great that she wondered how any mortal man could ever bear it.

Chapter VII — Plans Gone Awry

It was hard not to get up and pace around the tent. Gesanus waited in his chair, his last two battle-magi at his side. For a moment, he stared up at the ceiling. What in the name of the Eternal One was keeping Conadar?

He already knew exactly what would happen. The Archmagus would come with a small group of soldiers, all of whom would be paralyzed by the battle-magi the moment they entered the tent. He had seen Conadar's shocked expression as he took his last remaining embers of life in his visions, the Archmagus helpless against his power.

Gesanus smiled. Like so many things, it would come to pass as he had foreseen. Truly, the power of Foresight was a wondrous thing.

It appeared to have its limitations, though, much to Gesanus' surprise. He couldn't see into a person's future until he had actually touched the man. He had made some physical contact with as many of the other Successors as possible, missing only Hargan and Feladon.

He frowned at the thought of Feladon; the man had harried his men until all but two of his battle-magi were dead and most of his army was destroyed. It had not been without cost to the Archmagus, however; the army of Fenegar was finally defeated, the last remaining resistence trapped in the capital of Laketown.

For a moment, regardless of his impending victory, Gesanus cursed Conadar. The Archmagus's timing was simply atrocious; the battle would whittle away even more of his army, and the period after his vision of victory was clouded, as though a veil had been passed over his eyes.

"News of the battle, my Lord," one of his knights declared, bursting into the room and startling both battle-magi and Gesanus.

"If you had any idea of how close you just came to being killed," Gesanus growled, leaving off the threat in mid-sentence.

"My apologies, Lord," the knight said, bowing deeply. With some satisfaction, Gesanus noted the fear in the man's eyes. He had worked hard to prove to his army that he was a great man when pleased, and a terrifying enemy who would not tolerate defeat. Five high-ranking officers dangling from a tree had managed to impress that message upon them exceedingly well.

"Well, don't just stand there!" Gesanus said. "Speak!"

"The front line is a stalemate," the knight offered. "The commanding officer, who appears to be Princess Jyhanna, and her knights are trapped behind our lines and besieged."

Gesanus clapped in pleasure. "Excellent! Keep her from rejoining her line, and the enemy infantry will fall shortly after she does. The battle is ours, sir knight. The only thing that could stop us now is if Garwulf the Slayer himself appeared on the field."

"Thank you, Lord," the knight said. "Do you have any other instructions?"

Gesanus nodded. "Go back to the battle. When you return, bring Jyhanna's head. I want that upstart out of my way for eternity. Dismissed."

As the knight saluted and left, Gesanus regarded his battle-magi. Both wizards stood still, their expressions impassive. "A total victory, my friends," Gesanus declared. "Just think of it. If only Conadar would finally arrive; that would make my success truly great."

"He is coming," the wizard on the left reported, beginning to weave a spell. The second battle-magus followed suit, his motions slightly different. Gesanus wasn't quite certain what enchantments they were casting; he had told them that while they had to immobilize and kill Conadar's escort, he did not care how. He had a sudden vision, seeing the inside of the tent so bright that he had to shield his gaze. He smiled – so that was what they were going to do.

The ringing of steel upon steel sounded from outside the tent; Gesanus knew that Conadar's escort was fighting through his own guards, deliberately meager in number. He looked up for a moment and prepared himself, drawing and focusing his power. He stretched his fingers, for the more limber he was, the faster he could weave spells.

Conadar and four guardsmen burst through the door to the tent, and there was a blinding flash of light. Gesanus closed his eyes just in time. As he opened them, he found that both the men-at-arms and the battle-magi had been reduced to piles of ash, burned so quickly that they had not even had time to scream. Conadar stood before him, untouched, his hands held before him and already beginning to move.

With a nonchalant wave, he dispelled the magic Conadar had been attempting, adding a bit of extra force that pushed the wizard back. Conadar began to form magic around him, but once again Gesanus' Foresight warned him of what the wizard was attempting. With a small spell of his own, he turned the energies back onto Conadar, pushing him onto the floor in a magical net so tight that the Successor could not move any of his limbs.

"Your counterspell was quite impressive," Gesanus said, walking around the trapped wizard. "I don't think I've ever seen anybody kill a battle-magus that quickly before, much less two. However, the moment you had set out on your foolish quest to capture me, you were lost."

Conadar shook his head, tears beginning to flow down his cheeks. "Foresight."

Gesanus nodded. "I knew every spell you were going to cast before you even started. You didn't have a prayer. I do not understand why you would want to capture me, however. It would make more sense just to try and kill me. Perhaps you would like to explain that before I end your insignificant life."

Conadar smiled. "You're going to slay me anyway; why should I make it easier for you?"

With a gesture, Gesanus tightened the net, forcing Conadar to grunt in pain. "Because you can die slowly or quickly. Speak, and I'll show you mercy and give you a painless death. Otherwise, it could take you hours to die."

"Like the monks?" Conadar gritted. "What did they do to you?"

"They wouldn't serve!" Gesanus declared. "I, who am so much greater than them, was truly deserving of their worship, and they wouldn't serve me! When I have killed you and the others, when I have all of the Great Powers, I will be a god!"

"The Damned One will feast on your bones," Conadar grunted. "Torture me if you will, but you shall get nothing more from me."

Snarling in anger, Gesanus drove a spike of energy through Conadar's gut, the wizard writhing in the net and screaming in agony. Black blood spread across the floor as Conadar's vitals began to burn. With all of his rage, Gesanus cast spell after spell, wracking the Archmagus's body with torments. But each time Conadar looked at him there was no begging in his eyes, no silent plea for mercy. Only hatred and defiance.

Weaving with all his might, he sent one final energy spike into the wizard's chin, driving it through the skull and into the brain. With a wave, he dispelled the net, and then placed his hand on Conadar's lifeless chest.

"I claim your Power of Succession, foolish one," he said. "Perhaps the next Successor will prove to be more of a challenge." The energy tingled as it traveled up his arm, filling him with power. He took a deep breath, reveling in his newfound strength.

A jolt passed through his body, and a numbness crept over him. Looking down, he found a crossbow bolt deep in his gut, staining his crimson robe black with blood. A dull pain began to creep over him.

"The battle is lost," a new voice said as a black-robed wizard stepped into the tent. "And now, so are you."

Sagarum stood at the door to Gesanus' tent, watching the Archmagus slowly crumple, his hands clutching at the crossbow bolt through his gut. He had found it ridiculously easy to penetrate the camp, as no battle-magi remained to guard it from magical intruders.

"Who are you?" Gesanus sputtered, his eyes already growing glassy.

"I am Sagarum," he replied. "The first Grand Magus. And you have two things that belong to me." He stepped around to look at Conadar's body, the corpse still warm.

Whatever Gesanus had done to him, it had been a torture; Sagarum could see it in the body's face.

"Don't bother trying to cast anything," Sagarum said. "I enchanted the quarrel to drain you of energy. The only things it will leave untouched are the two great powers you currently hold. Do not fear, though – I will show far more mercy than you did."

Turning back to Gesanus, who wheezed and groaned in pain as his blood spread across the floor, Sagarum wove some magic around the crossbow bolt. With a clench of his fist, he stopped the wizard's heart. Gesanus flopped down on the ground, lifeless eyes staring into the ether.

Without a word, Sagarum knelt down and took what was his. Once he had finished, he strode out of the tent, mounted a horse, and rode out of the camp. What few survivors there were fled past him, hoping to escape destruction now that the battle was lost.

Standing on a hill, he surveyed the field. The snow was now covered in crimson, the landscape a sea of bodies. Soldiers from Jyhanna's army picked through them, slaying any enemy survivors, while the healers bore off the wounded. And in the middle stood Brother Caelyn. Even from such a distance, Sagarum could tell the monk was sobbing.

He shook his head. He had hoped that Caelyn would have been able to finally escape his past as Garwulf the Slayer, but it just hadn't been possible. For a moment, he wondered just what it had been that had set the monk off. Surely it couldn't have been anything small; from what Sagarum had seen using his Hindsight, Caelyn had such a distaste of violence that he would rather die himself than harm another human being. Unfortunately, that was not always an option.

With a swift kick, he sent his mount into a gallop. The battle was over, but he still didn't want to be caught by a stray arrow fired by an overenthusiastic archer.

He reached the camp. A long line of wounded stretched out into the battlefield, and the air was filled with the stench of death and the dying. Men without limbs screamed for mercy or their loved ones, barely aware that the enemy was already defeated.

To take his mind off the carnage, he tried to look into his future. He saw himself in battle with another wizard, but everything after that was shadowed, as though part of the future was closed to him.

Dismounting his horse, he tried again, but to no avail. He shook his head. It would be a while before he was able to use all of his powers again to their fullest; no doubt this was merely a symptom. It case it wasn't, however, he had some plans to make.

Tapping into his Hindsight, he cast his mind into Gesanus' past. With a shudder, he watched the Archmagus destroy the monastery, laughing in glee as the monks cried out in agony from their tortures. Tracing the line of the man's life forward a bit, he found himself at the gates of Laketown as Gesanus, taunting Feladon, challenged the wizard to single combat.

Sagarum smiled. Straining the Power he was once so used to using, he leapt from one lifeline to another. He saw Feladon retreating from Gesanus' superior numbers, losing vast numbers of battle-magi, but decimating his enemy's army at the same time. With a terrible patience, Feladon hid himself behind Laketown's walls, wearing down Gesanus' army, and then waiting from his position of strength to see whether Conadar or Gesanus won the day on the field of Southmarch.

Sagarum found himself nodding. The Battle of Southmarch was over, and he had no doubt that none of his companions had survived unscathed by its brutality. However, now he knew where the next battle would be.

Chapter VIII — The Man Behind the Legend

Jyhanna sat in Conadar's tent, regarding Brother Cealyn. The monk slumped, dejected, on a wooden chair, as though he was awaiting some kind of vile sentencing.

For what she thought had to have been the thousandth time, she ran her gaze across his features. All traces of Garwulf the Slayer were gone; his eyes were compassionate but sad, and his stature was humble. Once again, she found herself unwilling to believe that the man was capable of taking life like that, even for a moment.

But she could not ignore the evidence of her own eyes. She had seen him on the battlefield, mercilessly slaying all enemies who came before him. The strange dualism baffled her; the two personalities were so opposed that for them to be contained in the same body was almost inconceivable.

Tearing her gaze away, she glanced around the room. Brodin and Telena sat on the floor, both as far away from

Caelyn as possible, their eyes holding something akin to terror. Tamlin stood in a corner, shaking his head. No doubt he was trying to make sense of it all.

Grimly, Sagarum entered through the flap. "Conadar is dead," he reported. "Gesanus had the power of Foresight, and laid a trap for him. I tried my best, but I arrived too late to save him." He glanced around, a confused expression coming over his face. "Did I miss something?"

"Brother Caelyn is Garwulf the Slayer," Jyhanna answered. "He revealed himself in the middle of the battle."

"I knew that," Sagarum said, pulling up a chair. "I had hoped that he would have been able to escape that part of his past."

Jyhanna blinked, gazing at the wizard in a new light. "How did you know, and why didn't you tell us?"

"I have the power of Hindsight," Sagarum said. "I have had it since I killed Bervus. I can look down anybody's life-line, and see what they have done. And as for keeping it a secret, I did not feel it was my place to reveal it."

She turned to Caelyn. "We are all here, Brother Caelyn, or Garwulf, or whatever your name is. Considering what we've seen, I think we all deserve an explanation."

She saw Caelyn swallow, although his face was too impassive to tell if it was from discomfort. "My birth name is Garwulf, and I was born and raised in the northern-most reaches of Fenegar," he began. "My village was close to both the Northlands and the Northern Peaks. My mother and father were not rich, but they were respectable.

"It was the custom of my people to send children on their thirteenth birthday to be fostered for five years. We had some trade with a small colony of Dwarves, one of

281

whom thought he saw something special in me. Although it was completely against their traditions, the Dwarves offered to foster me, and my parents accepted."

"I thought Dwarves were a myth," Jyhanna commented.

Sagarum shook his head. "They're quite real. However, they are a dying people, split from their comrades long ago. Now they only exist as scattered groups, thinly spread across the Great Road."

Caelyn nodded. "That is indeed the case. They are also the keepers of much arcane art and knowledge, some of which they shared. Do not bother asking me what it was; I cannot tell you, for I have been bound by the strongest oaths. Regardless, for five years I learned from them, and finally they returned me to my village."

Caelyn wiped a tear from his eye. "When we came to my home, however, we found that it had been burned. The Kaegar wars had reached my village, and the armies of Kaegar had found my people wanting. Full of the passion of youth, I vowed revenge.

"In the north I fought several battles, sometimes aided by forces that even now I cannot speak of. For my valor, I became known as Garwulf the Slayer, and was soon brought into the army of Fenegar, already a hero and a leader.

"My revenge was total. I had become a cold-blooded killer, and I took vengeance for my family a thousand times over by the time Kaegar was sacked and razed.

"But every time I took a life, I died a bit inside. The fury that had driven me was gone within a year, and any feelings of love passed shortly afterwards. Soon I was fighting not for vengeance, not for justice, but because it was something I did. I had become a machine, without pity or remorse. I had lost my soul. When I stood in the ashes of Kaegar, my comrades celebrating around me, I felt nothing.

"And then, suddenly, I felt something. A sorrow for what I had become, a last flicker of emotion from my soul as it struggled one last time for survival. For a brief moment, I was alive again."

Caelyn choked back a sob, and Jyhanna found her heart reaching out for the poor man. Suddenly, she realized just how wretched he truly was, and how meaningless he found his great deeds.

Taking control of himself, the monk continued his story. "I held onto that spark with every bit of my being. That night, casting away my sword and armor, I snuck out of the camp, making my way back to my homeland. Every night I slept alone, without comrades-at-arms, lamenting what I had become. I tried so hard to keep that spark, that last bit of emotion alive, but even it began to fade. I had killed too much, taken too much beauty from the world. And then, just as the last of it died, I reached the Abbey of Southmarch.

"The abbot took me in, seeing only a weather-beaten traveler in need of food and rest, just like so many other refugees. I slept in a common hall that night, fearful that I would be recognized, returned to the nightmare I had fled, knowing that if I did, I would never find my soul."

Caelyn sighed, a sad sound that nearly broke Jyhanna's heart. "But nobody did recognize me, for I was without my armor and weapons, and I had never really been seen off of the battlefield. Abbot Artus must have noticed my distress, for he offered me some kindnesses that the other weary travelers were without. And then I realized that this was a place where I could begin anew, finding my soul, if any of it still lived.

"So, that windy, rainy night, Garwulf the Slayer disappeared into the sagas, and Caelyn the novice was born. I studied diligently, feeling pride as I perfected each challenging lesson in the practices of the Eternal One. As I learned to tend my garden, I discovered beauty once more. And, as I was brought closer and closer into the bonds of brotherhood with the monks, and made a full Brother of the Order of the Eternal One, I found that I could feel love again. My soul blossomed to life once more, and I thought that perhaps, just perhaps, given enough time, I could find absolution for the horrible things I did on the field.

"But the part of me that was Garwulf still lingered, a sickness in my soul from my days on the battlefield. I have long sought to destroy it, to kill Garwulf the Slayer forever, but no matter what I do, how much I pray, the shadow of Garwulf remains. And now, on this bloody field, I have brought him back to life."

"You won the battle for us," Jyhanna argued. "We would not be here now to discuss this if you hadn't been out there."

Caelyn shook his head. "How many wives have been widowed this day because of me? How many young lives have I snuffed out? How many more deaths must I now atone for? I cannot count them all; the blood on my hands is too deep and fresh. I may have won the battle, but I should never have fought."

"So what now?" Tamlin wondered. "Word is already spreading through the camp that Garwulf the Slayer was on the field. They may not know it was you, but they know Garwulf was there."

"History will record that the spirit of Garwulf fought on the battlefield this day," Caelyn stated, wiping away a tear. "Hopefully future generations will discount it as a myth."

"How can you be so certain of that?" Jyhanna demanded.

"I am the Chronicler of Southmarch," Caelyn replied.

"I am the one who writes the history books."

"What of the Abbey?" Tamlin asked.

Caelyn shrugged sadly. "My brothers are dead, and for all I know Abbot Artus is as well. Perhaps one of the other monasteries will send a mission to rebuild Southmarch, and I will join in that. Until then, I suppose I can offer spiritual support to those who fight here. Perhaps that will help me begin to atone for what I have done today."

"So what do we do now?" Jyhanna asked, turning to Sagarum. "You said that Conadar is slain?"

Sagarum nodded. "I wish it were not so, but I came too late. I managed to avenge his death, however."

"Then I am in command of the army," Jyhanna said. "Unless you would like to lead them."

The wizard shook his head. "I am no military leader, and Archmagi at the head of armies is what started this war in the first place. No, I will come with the army, offering what support I can, and try to take the next successor's life on my own. Besides, considering the suffering they have received at the hands of wizards, I doubt that they would willingly follow me."

Jyhanna cursed under her breath. She had hoped that somebody would take the mantle of authority from her, allow her to continue on her quest to protect Brodin and Telena. But she also knew where she was needed.

Resigned, she nodded. "If I must lead, then I must lead. But I do not know where we should go next. Should I return and liberate my homeland, or campaign elsewhere?"

Sagarum leaned forward. "The next successor, Feladon, is hiding behind the walls of Laketown. His forces are battered and few."

"And so long as he lives, I can't turn south without exposing my flank," Jyhanna muttered, running the possible courses of action through her head. Even though she did ride at the head of an army, it had been reduced considerably in size, and only consisted of around four thousand able-bodied men.

She knew that Toregien was being invaded by two Successors, but if she defeated them without destroying Feladon, she would be opening Toregien to just one more invasion. No, she had to deal with the threat in the north before she could take care of the one in the south.

"We will march north," she decided. "Once there, we will besiege Feladon and destroy him. Now, if you will all excuse me, I need some time alone."

Once her companions had stepped out of the tent, she let down her guard and began to weep. The battle had been truly draining, but combined with the death of her father, it was staggering. And now she was responsible for the fates of not just her four thousand men, but her entire country, and possible the whole of the Western Lands as well.

She wanted to take the mantle of leadership and just cast it aside, to run away and keep running, to mourn her father in peace. But, deep down in her heart, she knew that it could never be. She was needed, not only by her companions, but by her army as well. She had seen the world reduced to chaos, and she was tired of the carnage and the suffering, but she was needed. Once her task was done, then she could disappear, perhaps becoming a wanderer like Daelyn.

Her resolve quickening, she stood and glared at the map. She would march north. She only prayed that she had made the correct decision, and was not sending them all to their deaths.

Chapter IX — Last Rites

History recorded that the Battle of Southmarch lasted for an entire day, and cost almost seven thousand lives. At one point, the chronicles reported, the ghost of Garwulf the Slayer himself rose to fight against the foe, helping to utterly destroy the army of Toregien led by the usurper. The ground was so soaked with blood and covered with the arms and armor of the fallen that it would be another twenty years before anything grew there again.

But Princess Jyhanna's army could not break camp immediately after the battle. The great general knew that they were desperately low on supplies, and still had a long march ahead of them if they were to reach Laketown before Feladon quit the city. Aside from which, seven thousand mangled corpses littered the ground, staining the snow crimson, and they had to be seen to. With only one monk to provide last rites, it could take a while.

This did not bother Caelyn, however. He would wait until a large pile of corpses had been laid in the pit that was dug for them, and then give the entire group the last rites before they were buried in the hard earth. It was a long process, but he had much to redeem himself for, and tending to those he had slain was a good start.

He had not seen either Brodin or Telena for some time. Caelyn could only assume that they were busy with the wounded, who had been counted at a thousand souls. He knew it was possible that after they had witnessed his transformation they simply didn't want to be near him, but there was nothing he could do about that. Their trust was just one more loss in a sea of sorrows.

"Brother," one of the soldiers on grave detail said, gesturing at the pit. "We're ready for you."

Caelyn nodded. Making the sign of the star, he prayed for the souls of the dead, hoping that his words would give them a quick journey into the bosom of the Eternal One. Once he had finished, he stepped back, allowing the men to do their work as they filled in the grave.

He had offered to help dig, but they would have nothing of it. As far as they were concerned, he was a holy man, and above such things. He had let it pass; to tell them who he truly was would have only disillusioned them, and brought more misery to everybody involved.

Stepping back, he surveyed the ground. The battlefield was still littered with corpses, the stench of death kept at bay only by the intense cold that froze the limbs of the fallen. As a light snow began to fall, he heard one of the soldiers utter a curse, and then cut it off with: "I'm sorry, Father."

Caelyn shook his head. "'Brother.' I'm a Brother. 'Father' is reserved for an abbot." Wrapping his robes tighter around him, he turned away, a frigid blast of air ripping into his face. He took the chill pain without complaint; for all he knew, it was a punishment from the Eternal One for what he had done.

From the corner of his eye, he noticed some movement. He turned, seeing a small group of men standing at the top of a hill, regarding him. His heart pounded in his chest.

They were all wearing monastic robes.

It was all he could do not to break into a run. He made his way up the hill, nearly slipping once or twice on the slick snow. The figures stood still, their visages impassive as he scrambled up the slope. Finally, Caelyn reached the top, the cold wind howling around him, his eyes tearing up with relief as his gaze fell upon the tall, elderly man standing before him.

"Father Abbot," he sobbed. "I thought you were dead."

Abbot Artus clasped him in an embrace, holding Caelyn's head to his breast. "I nearly was. I very nearly was. But I survived, as did ten of our order. Brother Prior, however, was among several who were captured. I know not what happened to them after that."

"They were all butchered," Caelyn answered. "Their bodies flung at us at the very beginning of the battle."

A tear rolled down Artus' cheek, staining the ragged white beard the abbot had grown. Behind him, his fellow monks fell to their knees in prayer.

"I trust you gave them last rites and a decent burial," Artus said.

Caelyn nodded. "It was the least I could do, Father Abbot."

Abbot Artus shook his head. "These are dark days, and I fear they will only get worse. I will tell you all of it once we get into camp and find ourselves some shelter. Before then, however, I believe you may need some help."

Caelyn shook his head. "I have done something that requires penance, Father Abbot. I should be left to this task alone."

Artus shook his head. "Nonsense! These are good

souls who have perished here, and one man cannot see to them all. Once we have finished, and are all resting in a nice warm place, you may tell me what you have done."

Caelyn nodded, relieved to no longer be alone and without guidance. Wrapping his habit around him to keep out the cold, he followed Abbot Artus and his brethren as they descended from the hill to save lost souls.

Caelyn, Artus, and Jyhanna stood in her tent, the map table filled with papers as she decided how they would get to Laketown and re-provision.

"Abbot Artus," Jyhanna said, bowing and kissing the man's hand. "It is an honor and a relief to see that you are alive."

Artus chuckled, but to Caelyn it sounded a bit more hollow than the abbot's usual good nature. "Nobody is more relieved than myself, I assure you, Your Highness."

"Please, just call me Jyhanna," she said, sitting down. "Would you like a chair?"

"That would be lovely," Artus replied, pulling up a seat and motioning for Caelyn to do the same. "I have been walking in the woods for so long that at times I cannot remember the comforts of the abbey."

"What happened?" Jyhanna asked, leaning forward. "We thought everybody had been killed."

"When the war began," Artus said, "we did what the Eternal One always bids us to do in times of need. To those who came to us requiring shelter, we provided it, at least for a while. But the refugees kept coming, and more arrived every day, until we could hold no more, and had to pitch tents outside. I began to send messages to Laketown, hoping to find out how long the conflict would last, but no reply ever arrived.

"We had stored more than enough food for the winter,

but we had not planned on such a flood of needy souls. If we did not reach out for help to some of the nearby villages, we would soon starve, along with all those who had taken shelter behind and in front of our walls. So, I sent several of the brethren to the nearby hamlets, hoping that they would bring back wagons of food, or wood for some fires, so that some of the needy would not freeze to death."

The abbot shook his head sadly. "All they returned with was news of devastation. Toregien had invaded, and so many of the villages had been burnt. One or two still survived, but they were flooded with refugees as well, and could do nothing more than ask us for help that we could not provide. So, we gathered what we could, and set in to wait for the winter to end, praying to the Eternal One to see us through.

"It was shortly after that the first army appeared at our gates. It was led by a man named Feladon, and they conscripted many of the needy outside to fight. Any who resisted were killed. I sent a messenger to complain, to state that the refugees were under our protection, but his life was threatened and he was sent back to me with a message that if we tried to stop him, he would burn our abbey to the ground."

"And you didn't resist," Jyhanna cut in.

"Of course not," Artus said sadly. "How could we? We are not warriors; we only pray for the souls of others. Curse my actions, I let them take everybody outside the gates. I tried to find a way to stop them, I really did. But there were too many of them, and they had a great number of wizards. We would not allow them inside, however, and they did not know that there were refugees inside the walls. So, once they had taken what they pleased, they left us in peace.

"Almost a week later, as the snow fell heavily around

us, they returned, in some disarray. Even I, who had never been on a battlefield, could see that they were in retreat. The Eternal One bids that we must be compassionate, even to our enemies, so we gave them what supplies we could. One of the generals, a kind man named Veltan, warned us that another army was approaching, and destroying everything in its path. I told him that we were protected by the Great Convention, but he bid us to leave anyway."

A tear rolled down Abbot Artus' cheek. "I should have listened. I had even cautioned Brother Caelyn on the same perils before his pilgrimage. But I had such faith in the Eternal One and the Convention, it was inconceivable to me that anybody would actually break it. Thus, my pride led many to their deaths.

"As Veltan had predicted, the army of Toregien arrived at my gates less than three days later. Their leader was a wizard named Gesanus, and he told us to vacate the abbey and allow him to occupy it. I could not allow that; it would condemn so many refugees to hunt for shelter, and it was so cold that most of them would freeze to death before they found it. So, I refused, telling him that this was a peaceful order, and that we had a sacred duty to protect the innocent.

"I remember his reply; it is burned into my memory. 'There are no innocent,' he declared. 'You have given aid to the enemy, and you will be destroyed!' And then, suddenly, we were under siege."

The abbot shook his head, as though the memories were too painful for him. Caelyn wanted to reach out, to let him know that it would be all right, but he held back. It was not his place, and he had his own demons to deal with.

"It's okay," he heard Jyhanna say. "Gesanus is dead, and your losses have been avenged. Please, continue."

"Our monastery was originally a fortress of some sort," Artus said. "So our walls are very thick, and can

292

withstand even the most persistent of attackers. As I said, we are monks, not warriors; we tried to maintain the walls and get the refugees to safety, but that was all we could do. We hoped that the army of Fenegar would return, and lift the siege. We even sent some messengers to Laketown, but they never returned, and for all I know, they never even made it past the besiegers.

"We were able to hold out for a week, but then our walls fell. So many died; the rocks constantly rained down upon us, crushing the buildings and gardens, and a magical fire spread across the upper floors of the abbey, forcing us underground. Through that week, however, we had been digging a tunnel. The monastery had many underground corridors; all we had to do was extend one, and we could escape. The walls fell just as we were beginning our evacuation. Brother Prior insisted that I went first, along with the refugees, and, since the enemy had not breached our gates yet, I agreed."

His voice broke, and for a moment he sobbed. Neither Jyhanna nor Caelyn made a move; they had become completely transfixed by the story. Finally, Artus regained his composure and continued his tale.

"So few of us made it out. I heard some crashing as I accompanied the largest group of refugees, along with ten of our brethren. I realized that they had sealed the tunnel so that nobody else could follow us. When we came out of the earth, on a nearby hillside, I found the abbey burning, the walls crushed, and the monks being slain.

"Nearby there is a light forest. We hid there, sending the refugees to some of the port towns to the west. Hopefully, they will find some shelter there. But we could not leave; we had to give our brethren the last rites, see to it that their souls could rest.

"The army of Toregien departed, and we waited, just in case there were some scouts remaining to see if there were any survivors, so that they might be killed. Only a few days after the army of Toregien left, a small group of wanderers arrived, poking around the ruins."

"That was us," Caelyn interjected. "I gave our brethren the last rites."

Artus nodded. "I see. We were about to show ourselves, to warn you that there might be danger, when we saw you captured by another army, this one flying colors we had never seen. Then, once we had seen them fight the army of Toregien and win, we decided to make contact."

Jyhanna stood. "I only wish that we had arrived in time; we had a wizard among us, and we might have made a difference."

Abbot Artus merely shook his head. "There is no point in considering what might have been. We must face the horrors ahead. I take it you know what is happening?"

Jyhanna nodded. As concisely as she could, she told the abbot everything she had learned about the war, finally telling him where they would go next.

Artus leaned back. "I see. If you truly are that close to restoring peace to this land, then we should come with you. We cannot offer force of arms, but we can give spiritual comfort to those you lead."

"I would be delighted to have you with us," Jyhanna stated. "It would be a great help."

Gathering his robes, the abbot stood up, Caelyn following him. "In this time of darkness, I fear you will need all the help you can get," he said. "Let us hope that things will get better now, rather than worse."

Chapter X — Marching to Destiny

"So, what is this thing that you have done?" Abbot Artus asked, scratching his beard.

Caelyn blinked, trying to compose himself. He stood off to the side of the army, sequestered by a small copse of trees. The tents had already been stowed, and the various lieutenants were giving their men marching orders.

"I am Garwulf the Slayer," Caelyn admitted. "During the battle, I fought and spilled blood."

Artus paled, blinking in disbelief. Finally, he inquired: "How many did you send to their deaths?"

Caelyn looked down, suddenly unable to meet his abbot's gaze. "More than I can count, during this battle alone."

"Now that is something to consider," Artus breathed, leaning against a tree. "Why did you not tell me this before? You knew I was trustworthy."

The monk shook his head. "I have tried to escape the legacy of Garwulf for most of my life. I took a new name, began a new life, and I thought I had finally put him behind me. For all intents and purposes, I *am* Brother Caelyn. Or, so I thought until recently."

Artus began to pace, his hands clasped behind his back. For a moment, Caelyn felt fear tingle down his back; he still had a responsibility towards Tamlin, whom he had taken as his ward. If Abbot Artus sent him back on his pilgrimage, alone, he did not know what he would do.

"This is not a crime I can punish," Artus said. "You have shed blood, but from what I have seen and heard, those you slew were not innocents. And, you probably saved many lives. The fact that you have killed is not one to be proud of, but at least you did not do it without just cause. I think that the penance you have chosen for yourself is enough, so long as you do not take it to excess; that would be pride rather than humility."

Caelyn breathed a sigh of relief. "Thank you, Father Abbot."

Artus raised a finger. "However, in future, when something troubles you, you must tell me what it is! You are a member of my flock, and a good man. I cannot help heal spiritual wounds that I do not know about."

"Excuse me," Caelyn heard Sagarum say. Spinning, he found the wizard gazing on both of them patiently. "The assembly has been called. Unless you wish to be in the rear-guard, I would suggest that you join us." Sagarum smiled. "I even saved a place for you. I hope your friends are not nearly as dour as you are, friend Caelyn."

"We shall be along presently," Abbot Artus stated. He turned to Caelyn. "Dour?"

"Don't ask," Caelyn grumbled, stepping out of the copse to take his place in the line.

The rhythm of the march came back remarkably quickly. Caelyn walked now in the middle of the army with Tamlin and Sagarum, followed closely by Abbot

Artus and the monks. He found the military routine a comfort to return to. Every day, they would pack up their tents and begin the trek north, and every evening they would make camp. He assumed that pickets would always be set, but that was not his concern.

Usually, Jyhanna, Brodin, and Telena would join them at their fire at night. It was a comfort, as at times Caelyn became a bit overwhelmed by it all again. When he began to feel that way, he frowned – he had grown used to a small band of friends and the gentle companionship of the cloister. No doubt it had made him soft.

Brodin and Telena still kept their distance, sitting as far away from him as possible while still resting by the fire. But, as time went on, their eyes held less confusion and fear when they beheld him. Perhaps time would heal all wounds after all.

Sagarum rested in his tent, the canvas hastily raised for the evening. They had been marching for two weeks, and there had been no resistance whatsoever. This worried the wizard; from what he knew of Feladon, it was not like him to allow a threat to approach unhindered.

Pulling his scrying stone from his back, he drew back the velvet cloth to reveal its translucent blue surface, vague shapes flickering underneath. It was an ancient stone, and he had used it since he began learning how to nurture the Great Powers inside him, so long ago. He smiled as he regarded its smooth form; even though it had seen civilizations rise and fall, it still bore no marks of its age.

He took a deep breath, drawing on the four Great Powers he now held to calm and prepare him. Then he gazed deep into the stone, losing himself in its infinite depth. A soft glow permeated the crystal, drawing him into its warm light.

Suddenly, he was free of his body, flying over the landscape. With a push, he glided over Jyhanna's army, noting briefly that the company sat together at a fire, Jyhanna quietly talking to Caelyn while Abbot Artus approached from behind.

The lightly forested land stretched out before him, the snow wet with the first signs of the coming spring. One or two small animals scurried below, a squirrel leaping from tree to tree, its mate giving chase. Sagarum smiled as he stopped for a moment to watch; even in the midst of all the devastation of the war, some rhythms of life still continued, untouched by human hands.

He sped on to the north, a vast lake opening up as he glided toward it. Ice ringed the water, except for the area around a sprawling city. The settlement covered an outjutting into the lake, and was surrounded by high stone walls. There was no doubt in his mind; he had arrived at Laketown.

Sagarum frowned. Still, he could see no sign of any soldiers, or anything that could present any resistence to the army. He sped back for a moment, watching with a wizard's eye for any signs of magic. Yet not even a single weave touched the ground; it was almost as if the land had been scoured of all spellcasters.

Shaking his head, he sailed back towards Laketown. As he floated around the city, watching and counting the soldiers march along the walls, he sensed another creature of power, floating somewhere nearby. The essence was tainted, however, as though it was something dark and oily.

Sagarum swallowed and spun around, searching for some sign of the scrying eye.

I don't know who you are, a voice thundered in his mind, *but I am waiting!*

298

And then the presence faded, leaving Sagarum's solitary spirit floating above the city. Determined not to let this mystery lie, he flew towards the large palace in the center of town, carefully marking a route he could take on foot.

The palace walls towered above him as he passed through the stone into a maze of corridors. Once again he felt a creature of power, although the taint was not present. Following his instincts, he flew down a corridor, past two guards and into a room filled with magical tomes and equipment. There, for the first time, he came face-to-face with Feladon.

Whatever the wizard had been doing, he was finished now. As Sagarum looked on, he saw Feladon place a green scrying stone into a small wooden box. Carefully, Sagarum marked the man's features, burning the cold eyes and midnight-black goatee into his mind.

But there was something else; he could feel it in his very bones. As Feladon cast a ward around himself, Sagarum drove himself deep into the earth, below the great castle, where the dungeons lay. Deeper and deeper his instincts dragged him, curiosity alone keeping him from returning to his body.

Finally, at the lowest level of the prison, he found a thin, starving man. His clothes had once been regal, and the hair on his brow was matted down, as though it had once supported a crown.

Satisfied at last, Sagarum sped back towards his own body, his thoughts racing. Even though he could see that the enemy was undermanned, instead of confidence for impending victory, he felt a great disquiet. It was only as he returned to his body and put the scrying stone away that he realized why.

Feladon wants us to come to him unhindered. He wants me to know that he's here.

Suddenly, it made sense. The lack of opposition from the countryside, the complete absence of wards until after Sagarum had seen him. From his brief time there, Sagarum had sensed that Feladon had the single most powerful Great Power: the ability to Mindcast. The Archmagus was waiting for them, waiting for *him*, drawing them into his trap just as a spider stalks a fly. Not only did Feladon know they were coming, he had seen to it that they would fight on ground of his choosing.

For all intents and purposes, they were walking into a trap. Sagarum hoped to the Eternal One that knowing that fact would be enough to save them.

As he bolted from his chair to tell Jyhanna what he had learned, another question popped into his mind. If he hadn't felt the taint on Feladon while he was scrying, than what was the other power that he had encountered?

Brother Caelyn idly poked at the fire with a branch. He had spent some time at prayer with Abbot Artus, but had received no great insight into his soul. Now he found himself, like on so many other nights, killing time with his companions as they all waited for the next battle to arrive.

"We are about a week away," Jyhanna predicted, sitting down beside him. "Sagarum will be joining us soon."

"He's scrying," Tamlin added. "I've tried that once or twice, under his supervision. It takes a lot out of you."

Caelyn murmured something under his breath.

Jyhanna blinked. "What troubles you?"

"The spring is coming," Caelyn said. "But it's at least two weeks too early."

"It could be a false summer," Jyhanna suggested. "We sometimes have that in Toregien. It's when the winter warms up, and then becomes cold again."

Caelyn shook his head. "No, this is a true spring. But it shouldn't be here yet. It is almost as though the seasons have been thrown out of alignment."

"Whatever it is, it is beyond our control," Jyhanna stated. "Right now, we should see to the march. We have been very lucky so far; no resistence from skirmishers."

"There won't be any," Sagarum declared. Caelyn turned to see the wizard emerge from the shadows. As he stepped forward, Sagarum waved his arms, and Caelyn felt a tingling of power, almost as if an invisible net had suddenly surrounded them.

"Why the wards?" Tamlin inquired, raising an eyebrow.

"I don't want anybody to scrye us out," Sagarum replied. "I have urgent news. Feladon knows we are coming."

Jyhanna snorted. "That's not a great shock! There's no way he could miss us!"

"He's picked his ground, and is waiting for us," Sagarum said patiently. "No doubt he knows exactly how many we are, and has one or two surprises ready for us."

Caelyn turned to see Jyhanna frowning, her gaze suddenly intent and calculating. "So we're walking into a trap."

"There's more," Sagarum stated. As the others listened, he reported what he had learned, and related his discovery of the regal but pathetic figure in the dungeon.

Caelyn leaned back. "Feladon must have co-opted the entire government, then. That's the only conceivable way he could have imprisoned King Caelgar without causing a revolt."

"For all we know, there might have been one," Sagarum mused. "Feladon has the power of Mindcasting, which is easily the greatest of the Powers of Succession. He can weave spells at the speed of thought. It will take all of our efforts to hold him at bay, if we can even do that."

"So how do we stop him?" Tamlin wondered. "With that Power, he could be a god."

"He has not lived as long as I," Sagarum replied. "That means that I can last longer before my reserves of energy run out. We will wear him down, and then go for the kill."

Although Caelyn was silent, his mind began to spin. The battle would be even bloodier than Southmarch; that was easy enough to predict. They would be laying siege to a walled city, while an opponent of great magical strength waited within. If Jyhanna was lucky, one in ten of her men would survive. It was all Caelyn could do to stop from shuddering. In that moment, he wanted to just return to his abbey and his chronicle, and forget that the rest of the world existed.

But he couldn't do that. His monastery was gone, razed to the ground at the orders of a man who lived no more. Whether he liked it or not, the world had come to him.

Caelyn heard a shuffle behind him. When he turned to look, he found Artus had stood up and begun to pace by the fire. "This is an abomination before the Eternal One!" the abbot declared.

"Anger will not solve anything, Father Abbot," Caelyn said.

Artus shook his head. "It does not matter. I have seen my abbey reduced to ruins by men who cared nothing for life and everything for power. And now they have completely usurped the natural order, and society itself in their bloodthirsty quest."

Caelyn swallowed. "Father Abbot, if we take a definite side, the Order will never be able to claim the protection of the Great Convention again. We will become as political as the ones who fight."

"The prophet Balthus once wrote that evil will triumph

if good men do nothing," Artus stated. "I remember that passage well. And now, the world is being destroyed by the actions of evil men. How can we call ourselves holy when we simply sit back and allow this to occur?" The abbot spun to face Jyhanna. "Princess Jyhanna, as the former Abbot of Southmarch, and the Prior of the Order of the Eternal One, I declare that your cause will be taken up by our order. We will do whatever we can, for we now consider your campaign to be a holy war. Should your men need shelter, it will be granted to you and denied to your enemies. Should your weapons need strength, we will bless them."

Caelyn could only stare at Artus in shock. In one moment, any hope he had ever held of returning to a quiet life in the Order had been shattered.

Chapter XI — Before the Walls of Laketown

Jyhanna's army stood before the hoary walls of Laketown, banners fluttering in the light breeze. A new standard had been added, a silver star that all knew had once flown on the walls of Southmarch. And, across the ground that would soon be filled with the screams of the dying, all was silent.

The army had arrived a week before, carefully camping outside of the range of any catapults in the city, only to discover that Feladon had burned down all of the trees within five miles. Only one small forest remained within reach, and the details that had been dispatched to fetch some wood soon discovered the way there was littered with traps.

Some of the snares had been magical, blinding and burning the eyes out of any soldiers who came across them. Others had been physical; blades that swung out of bushes to disembowel anybody unlucky enough to be leading, and deep pits dug into the earth filled with sharp spikes. And every day, there seemed to be more of them, as though the enemy was sneaking out of his fortress under cover of darkness to make mischief.

"They have us pinned here," Jyhanna gritted one night, pacing in her tent as Sagarum looked on. "My men are dying by the score, just to get supplies!"

"That is exactly what Feladon wants," Sagarum stated. "He will wear us down by pieces, until in desperation I come to him. And then, only when he is ready and certain of victory, will he attack."

Jyhanna shook her head. "The tactic seems to be working; I have a trickle of provisions, and nothing more. It could be a month before I can raise a full siege."

Sagarum leaned on the table, and with a flick of his finger cast a ward of silence around them. He had done it often enough in their conferences that Jyhanna had come to recognize the motion on sight. "Then don't raise a full siege. Strike as soon as you have enough for an attack."

Jyhanna suddenly stood still and blinked. It could work; if Feladon was holding back while he had the appearance of strength, it could very well mean that he was as unprepared as she was.

"We force his hand," she muttered.

She saw Sagarum smile, his usually friendly grin now predatory. "Ignore the ladders, and smash the walls down with catapults. Tamlin and I will do what we can to protect you against his magic. And then, once he is so worn down that he is just trying to keep us in check, we will sneak in and kill him."

"I will need to have a detachment of scouts scouring the area," Jyhanna mused. "There might be another army lying in wait for us."

Sagarum shrugged. "I have scryed nothing of the sort, but I will check every night. Do not tell any of our plans unless Tamlin or I am there to ward away any scrying eyes, and see to it that your subordinates know to do the same."

Jyhanna nodded, plans for the battle taking shape in her head as she stepped outside to gaze upon the high stone walls in the distance. They might look impressive, but there were weak points. All she had to do was find them.

Two days later, her army gathered at the walls of Laketown, armed and ready for war.

Silence cloaked the field. In the back of the army, Jyhanna waited impatiently. The catapults were all loaded, the ballistae ready, the archers prepared to pick off anybody who showed their heads over the wall.

She turned to Gallant. "Are their lines of communication cut?"

The knight nodded. "Scouts are lying hidden on all of the roads out; any messenger that breaks through our lines will run into them."

"Good," Jyhanna said. "That makes it easier." She looked over to Sagarum and Tamlin. "What is taking them so long?"

The two wizards were pacing and motioning with their hands, although to what effect Jyhanna could not tell. Through the intricate ritual they stepped, sometimes walking towards her, other times away from her, and sometimes standing still. Occasionally one would say something to the other, eliciting a nod or shake of the head, and then they would continue.

Gallant stared at them and then shrugged. "Who can tell when dealing with Magi? Sometimes I think they are in their own world."

"To a degree, I think you're right," Jyhanna said. "I

just wish they would hurry up with it, whatever they are doing. We are losing daylight hours."

"Do you have a family?" Gallant asked.

Jyhanna blinked, startled by the question. "Just a brother, now. Why do you ask."

"I have been thinking of my own family," the knight replied. "My daughter Emilye is almost four years old now. I haven't seen her or my wife, Alyson, since she was two. Now, with the horrors I have seen in this war, I fear for her safety."

"Where are they now?"

"Last I knew, in the capital," Gallant said. "I told them to go there, because it was the best fortified. But this war has been so unnatural, I wonder if the walls will protect her."

"We must have faith," Jyhanna said, surprised at her own words. Was she trying to convince Gallant, or herself? "Faith in ourselves to be able to make a difference, and faith in the world to come out right in the end. Without that, what are we?"

She truly hoped that Gallant would answer that question; her faith had vanished long ago, and now she was trying to fan the brief flicker that had arisen over the past few weeks.

"We're finished!" Sagarum called. "Your army is now protected from any spells Feladon might cast. You need only fear the usual means of battle."

Jyhanna spun to face him. "Will you be able to help us with some battle-magic of your own?"

Sagarum grimaced. "It will be very difficult. This shield will take a great deal out of both Tamlin and I. However, we shall see what we can do."

Jyhanna nodded. "Then we should begin." She turned to Gallant. "Call the commanders."

Within moments, she stood before a line of officers

and knights, all wearing ragged armor, and gazing at the walls with the calculating stare of the experienced veteran.

"In a few moments, we will begin our siege," Jyhanna declared. "You all have your orders. By the time we have finished, we will have rid the world of one more Successor, and brought the war one step closer to its end."

She clasped her hands behind her back. "A wise and holy man once told me that for darkness to triumph, good men and women must do nothing. We have seen our homes destroyed at the orders of men who wanted nothing more than to dominate, men who did not care for us a single whit. Four of these wizards are dead, and there are only three more to go, all of them evil men. At the beginning, we may have thought the war was about countries and land, but it is not.

"This is a war that is being fought not for any nation, or ideology, but for peace. We now fight a holy war against those who would destroy everything. Go now and take up your arms, not for Toregien, or for Fenegar, but for all of the Western Lands! Let's end this, and restore peace!"

A great roar erupted from the assembled men, and they raced back to their units. Jyhanna turned to the commander of the catapults. "Begin your barrage," she ordered. "Fire-pots first."

The officer ran off to the rear. Suddenly, the twanging of the artillery filled the air. Flaming missiles, fired from catapults and ballistae, flew through the sky, impacting on the wall. With a great crash, an explosion of fire erupted from the parapets, soldiers screaming and falling to their death as they burned.

"Incoming barrage!" she heard a lookout shout. She gritted herself for what was coming. Throughout the line, great rocks landed, crushing flesh and bone. One landed close by her, forcing her to shy away as fragments of stone

308

were flung into the air, cutting and maiming. As she watched, a ballista bolt took out two men, reducing the first one's head to a pinkish mist and pinning the second to the ground.

There was another twang of the catapults, and her own missiles flew towards the fortifications, this time only half of them fire-pots. Great shards of rock were chipped from the towering walls, some of the crenelations crushed to dust where the missiles fell. The torso of what had once been an enemy soldier fell to the ground, the man still wailing from the agony of his lost legs. Burning arrows filled the air, knocking people down from the battlements.

"Incoming barrage!" the lookout cried. Where they could, the soldiers on Jyhanna's line scattered to avoid the falling missiles, but many of them were too late. The screams of the dying once again filled the air.

Jyhanna pulled Gallant aside. "If I were Feladon, any minute now I would send a company of knights out from the gate to break our lines. Get the cavalry ready; we need to fight them back, and take the gate."

"Yes, my lady," Gallant said, bowing and racing to the line. Jyhanna stood at her command post, ready at any moment to give new orders in case the situation changed. She noticed a strange, dangerous beauty about the scene, as flaming arrows soared through the air like little comets, and fire wracked the battlements.

"Get the battering ram ready," she ordered, pulling a subordinate aside. "Start using it if the knights fail to take the gate."

"Incoming barrage!" a lookout called.

With a clinical eye, she surveyed the scene, even as rocks fell on her men. Her own catapults and ballistae were concentrating on an old patch of wall, trying to make a hole. With every firing, the enemy barrages had become lighter, as though they were running out. For all Jyhanna knew, though, that was only to lull her into a false sense of security; she would not allow herself to be fooled. After all, it was better to overestimate an opponent than to underestimate him.

With a great creaking groan, the high wooden gates opened, knights pouring out with their lances lowered. They were met by Gallant's men, and where they fought, all she could make out was confusion. Some men had been knocked off their horses, and she saw blood on the ground, but both sides seemed evenly matched for the moment.

She forced down an urge to leave her post and join them. Unlike a field battle, this was a siege, which required careful planning and minute-to-minute commands. She was needed in the rear, no matter how badly she wished to be in the front.

With another groan, the gates closed, and Jyhanna cursed under her breath. Feladon wasn't going to let her enter the city that easily.

As she gazed on, her knights took the field, felling the last of Feladon's cavalry and parting to make way for the battering ram. The ram was a giant log, the end sharpened to a point that could easily skewer a man. Overtop was a tough leather awning, something that would protect her men from arrows and flaming oil, or so she hoped. It had taken days to build, and she had only one of them.

"Incoming barrage!" the lookout screamed. More missiles fell on her men, crushing bones and flesh. A deafening twang resounded as her own artillery answered them.

"Something is wrong, Jyhanna," she heard Sagarum say, and spun to find Tamlin and the wizard regarding her. How he had managed to approach without her knowing was beyond her.

"Go on," she said impatiently.

"There's no battle magic being cast from there at all,"

Sagarum stated. "No shield around the walls to stop your artillery, nothing."

"He's planning something," Jyhanna said.

Sagarum nodded. "And he has King Caelgar as a hostage. Feladon could be planning to burn the city to the ground before we can take it, or allow us to do it for him."

She frowned. "Then we're out of time. Sagarum, I need a hole in that wall, and I need it now. We have to take the city before sundown."

The wizard nodded. "Consider it done. Tamlin, will you please see to the shield while I weave?"

As Tamlin nodded, she watched Sagarum close his eyes for a moment, no doubt working out what spell to use. With a wave of his hand, the wizard sent a white hot ball of fire hurtling towards the wall. The fire hissed through the air, melting the stone as soon as it impacted, the massive explosion sending bricks and fragments flying.

"Your hole," Sagarum said. "A bit spectacular, but it got the job done, and you'll have a moment before they can react."

Drawing her sword, Jyhanna bellowed, "Into the breach! Attack!" As she rushed forward, leading her men into the gap, she heard a brief exchange between Tamlin and Sagarum.

"Come Tamlin," Sagarum said. "It is time to begin hunting."

Chapter XII — Endings

Caelyn performed the last rites on the screaming man, hopefully giving the soldier's soul some rest before his journey to the Eternal One. The wounded man had been struck in the gut by an arrow, the shaft piercing his vitals. Perhaps, in another age, there might be a cure for it, but here it was just a matter of time.

At least there had been relatively few wounded by arrows; crushed limbs were easy to deal with, as were most sword gashes. But an arrow could strike deceptively deep, sometimes even delivering poison into the wound.

The cries of agony dulled to a low murmur. It wouldn't be long now. Caelyn gave his hand a comforting squeeze and moved onto the next man. From outside the tent he heard a dull thudding; the catapults, no doubt. At least this time they were far enough away that they weren't in danger of being attacked.

"Telena," Caelyn called, motioning her over. "This man needs some bandaging. Will you please see to it?"

She nodded and began to minister to the man. Caelyn stepped back to find Brodin staring at him.

"Why?" the youth asked.

"Because he doesn't need a full-fledged healer," Caelyn replied, bustling off to see if Abbot Artus had any instructions for him.

"Wait!" Brodin cried, rushing to catch up with him. "That's not what I meant. Why are we here, instead of fighting in the battle."

Caelyn stopped walking and turned to face him. It took him a moment to decide how to word it, but finally he spoke. "You have an innocence about you that we would all protect. That is why you have not been trained with weapons or been allowed close to any combat."

Brodin waved at the scores of wounded littering the dankly lit tent. "I've seen more horror here than I had ever imagined possible. I doubt I shall ever forget what I have witnessed here over the past few weeks. How could I possibly be innocent now?"

Caelyn pursed his lips. "There is a difference between seeing something that cannot be unseen and doing something that cannot be undone. When you look back on these days, you will remember the horror, true, but you will also remember that you were helping to alleviate it, and giving comfort to its victims. You will have no blood on your hands, and, believe me, when you are older, it will matter a great deal to you." The monk paused. "The moment you take a life, you are changed forever, and not for the better."

Brodin nodded. "I see."

Caelyn smiled. It was so refreshing when somebody actually appreciated being protected. He had known so many soldiers in his day who had thrown their lives away for nothing more than a brief moment of glory.

Suddenly, Caelyn blinked. Something had changed. It

313

took him a moment to put his finger on it: there had been a loud thud, and then the thumping of the artillery had ceased.

The monk frowned. "You'd better get ready for more wounded," he told Brodin. "They've either just been forced back, or have breached the walls. Either way, many more men will die before the night falls."

Tamlin walked beside Sagarum, trying to make his steps as quiet as possible. Under his monastic habit he found himself sweating in fear. He had wanted to change into something more befitting a Magus, but Sagarum would have nothing to do with it.

"We will need every element of surprise we can muster," the wizard had said as they prepared the night before. "So long as Feladon doesn't know you're a wizard we have an added advantage."

Considering what they were actually up against, Sagarum's words did not cheer him. He knew that they were walking right into a trap, and that their only hope was to catch Feladon unawares while he was concentrating on the siege.

"Does your Farsight tell you anything?" Tamlin wondered, gazing around at the buildings. In the distance, he could hear the ringing of steel on steel; the fighting was progressing slowly through the streets, Sagarum's ward the only thing that allowed them to break off and journey along their own route.

Two enemy soldiers ran past them, not even glancing in his direction. Tamlin breathed a sigh of relief. Sagarum had told him that the ward would make them appear completely inconsequential, and it appeared to be working. Once again, he found his mind casting itself back to the previous night.

314

"Why not invisibility?" Tamlin had asked.

"If we were to become invisible, then a soldier could detect us by bumping into us," Sagarum had replied. "The moment he would be knocked over by nothing, he would know that there was magic afoot. Instead, we make ourselves seem unimportant, so that they avoid us on their own."

"Nothing," Sagarum said, bringing Tamlin back to the present. "My vision of the future is completely clouded. This does not bode well."

"What could it mean?" Tamlin wondered.

Sagarum hesitated a bit too long for Tamlin's liking before he answered. "It could mean that the Great Powers are no longer at home within me. If that is the case, then we might not have the strength we though we had."

Silently, they picked their way through the streets, Sagarum leading him down a path he had selected when he had been scrying. The streets were almost completely empty, the people probably fled indoors to avoid the fighting. As Tamlin watched, a small boy dashed across the street, his gaze desperate and terrified.

"This way," Sagarum whispered, pointing down a cobbled road. "This will take us to the palace."

As they strode down the path, a large building rose before them, spires reaching high into the sky. For a moment, Tamlin was overcome by the grandeur of it, before his mind returned to the deadly earnestness of the task ahead.

They stood at the door, Sagarum gazing up at the battlements. "Get a spell ready," the wizard instructed. "Weave almost all of it now, and then just release it when we get inside. Something that will damage several at once, but make certain you can choose your targets."

Tamlin blinked. "Why?"

"All of the battle-magi are still in there," Sagarum

replied. "I can sense them. And they're waiting for us. If the attack comes from you, it will take them by surprise."

Tamlin nodded. For a moment, he went through the multitude of spells he had learned from both Haldur and Sagarum, selecting one that would work. As carefully as he could, he wove most of the magic together, leaving the last part of the spell unfinished.

As soon as he was ready, Tamlin nodded to the wizard, who threw open the gates of the palace. Crossing the threshold, he saw several guards look at him dismissively, and then return to their tasks, one of them stopping for a moment to shut the gate behind them. A wave of fear washed over Tamlin's mind; they had entered the lion's den, and there was now no turning back.

Sagarum picked the corridors carefully, leading Tamlin down a veritable maze. As they walked, a sudden cry of alarm was taken up. Tamlin's heart leapt into his throat. Had they been found so soon?

But the soldiers rushing past paid him no heed, instead racing towards the gate.

"The battle has reached here sooner than I thought," Sagarum mused. "Perhaps that will give us one more advantage."

"Do you think Jyhanna will find Feladon before we do?" Tamlin wondered.

Sagarum shook his head violently. "Don't use his name in here! It could call his attention to us prematurely. To answer your question: if Jyhanna does find him before us, she will die before she even realizes what has happened."

Sagarum opened a wooden door, the rusty hinges creaking as they moved. Before them lay a large staircase, the winding stairs leading high into one of the towers. The stairs were thin, however, and Tamlin was forced to follow behind Sagarum rather than walking beside him.

"Do you know why the wall is on our right as we ascend?" the wizard asked. "It is so that any enemy coming up cannot have enough room to draw a sword. Any soldier coming down, on the other hand, has plenty of room, since the wall is on his left."

"I did not know that," Tamlin said.

Sagarum turned, Tamlin nearly walking right into him. "You sound a bit too worried for my taste. Fear not; you will not have to fight Feladon. All you have to do is take care of the battle-magi, who are few in number, worn out by the campaigning, and not nearly as well trained as you are."

Tamlin gritted his teeth. "Let's get on with it."

Sagarum smiled, nodded, and spun around to begin climbing the stairs, taking them two at a time. For a moment, Tamlin had trouble keeping up with him. Finally, he met the wizard at the top.

"Be ready," Sagarum warned. "The battle-magi are on the other side of this door."

"I'll go first," Tamlin said.

Sagarum shook his head. "I have an additional ward that will protect me from their magic. Let me take the first spell they cast, and strike them before it is over."

Tamlin swallowed slowly, a cold sweat running down his back. With a nod, he prepared to weave the final part of his spell.

Sagarum thrust the door open, and as he did, there was a blinding flash of light. As the beginnings of Tamlin's vision began to clear, he loosed his spell, a fiery bolt striking the three wizards who stood before them, leaping from one to the other as they screamed in agony.

Sagarum blinked and regarded the charred corpses lying before him. "That was impressive. Where did you learn to control the spell like that?"

"One of Haldur's texts," Tamlin replied. "Where is

317

Feladon?"

"In there," Sagarum stated, motioning to a door at the end of the hall. "I can sense him now."

"I'm coming in with you," Tamlin declared, pushing down his fear as another urge came over him. For the first time in months, he again saw his first mentor's face as Feladon stripped him of his life.

"You don't have to..."

Tamlin nodded, the fear completely gone. "He killed Haldur, a man who loved me like his own son. I want to at least see vengeance, even if I do not get to kill him myself."

Sagarum looked at Tamlin, a new understanding entering his eyes, his gaze distant. "Very well. Come, then – let's end this journey."

With a great shout, he opened the door with a quick kick. "FELADON!" he bellowed.

The Archmagus gazed at the two intruders. Feladon sat at a table in a small room, torchlight providing the illumination the small window could not. On the smooth surface lay a map that Tamlin had never seen. "I had expected somebody else. Who *are* you two, and how have managed to come into the Powers of Succession?"

"I am the first Grand Magus," Sagarum declared. "I am giving you this opportunity to give me what is mine without a fight."

"You don't remember me?" Tamlin snarled, a rage beginning to creep up inside him. "You killed my master, drove me from my homeland, and you don't remember me?"

Feladon leaned forward. "You're Haldur's boy, from the forest! Now I remember you. You have grown. Do you wish to die the way your mentor did?"

"I'm here to watch him kill you," Tamlin said, gathering his power and preparing to weave a spell.

"Leave him out of it," Sagarum spat. "You have helped drive an entire nation to ruin, and imprisoned its leader."

Feladon grinned maliciously. "You have to be able to weave spells to kill me." Suddenly, his grin faded as Sagarum shrugged and raised his hands.

"I have learned a great deal in my lifetime," Sagarum stated. "Wards that will deflect all control magic, for example."

With a snarl of rage, Feladon launched himself across the room, hand extended. A bolt of fire shot out at Sagarum, only to be deflected out the window by a mere gesture. Sagarum and the Archmagus began to circle each other cautiously. Lightning struck the tower, showering both Tamlin and Sagarum with sparks. The ancient wizard only smiled, however.

"Scared?"

Then it was Sagarum's time to attack. With a broad wave, he sent several bolts of energy at Feladon, only to have the man grin as they bounced back at Sagarum. While Sagarum deflected them, Feladon launched another attack, driving the wizard into a corner. Still, Sagarum was able to fend him off, leaving the two circling once again.

"We seem to be evenly matched," Feladon declared. "But I will win, you know. You cannot defeat a Mindcaster with your spellweaving. I will take your powers of succession."

Tamlin suddenly felt an irresistible urge to step back out the door. It was almost as if some great event was about to happen; he could feel it wrapping itself around the room.

He saw Sagarum's eyes become sad. "Now I understand it," the wizard said. With a quick wave, he brought one of the lit torches on the wall flying to his hand. "Neither of us will get to keep them!" he snarled, leaping forward and gesturing.

"NO!" Feladon screamed, but it was too late. Sagarum barreled into him, driving the flame into both of their chests. There was an explosion of white fire, the shock wave flinging Tamlin to the side of the room. When he regained his senses, he saw Sagarum and Feladon trapped in an inferno, both of them burning like dry wood. Feladon bellowed in agony, his skin beginning to flake from pearly bones on his face.

"I reclaim what was mine!" Sagarum gritted, his skin only a bit less burnt. A glow pierced through the flame by Feladon's chest, and then the fire went out, the two wizards crumpling to the floor.

Tamlin rushed to Sagarum's side, barely able to choke back his tears. The old wizard was a charred ruin, all of the hair singed from his head, his clothes nothing more than rags and ash. He wanted to believe Sagarum would get better, but deep in his heart he knew it would not be.

"I had wondered why I could not see past this day," Sagarum breathed. Tamlin cradled the old man's head in his lap, tears beginning to flow down his eyes. "When the Oracle told me that my time had come, I should have asked him what the time was actually *for*."

"We'll get you to the healers," Tamlin sobbed.

Sagarum shook his head. "I'm sorry, my boy, but even I cannot survive something like this. I have no Dragon blood in me, as Delgar Dragonmage did. But, I had a feeling this might be, so I did prepare."

With a feeble grip, Sagarum brought Tamlin's hand to his chest. "All that is mine," the wizard declared, his voice fading even as he spoke, "I now give to you. Finish what we started."

Tamlin gasped as the Great Powers flowed through his arm, along with something else. Suddenly, he saw through Sagarum's eyes, as millennia of memories flooded his mind. The Western Lands as they once had been spread out before him, the face of a beautiful maiden bringing first joy and then great sorrow. He saw a betrayal in a dark room, a desperate escape, and then pathways through a great mist, where Daelyn and another man, a powerful figure with haunted eyes known as Delgar Dragonmage, waited. Himself and his companions, Jyhanna, Caelyn, and all the others flooded into his mind, their stories revealed by Hindsight, and Tamlin knew the great friendship that Sagarum had felt for all of them.

And then he was back in Feladon's casting room, looking into Sagarum's dead eyes. He was completely numb, unable to move, his mind still trying to comprehend the experience.

Although he was not certain how he knew, he was suddenly aware of Sagarum's wishes for his remains. With a mere thought, he set the body alight, the flames reducing it to ash within seconds. Then, he took the ashes and gathered them into his pouch.

The tears welled up in him again, and he fell to the floor, his chest wracked with sobs. Never again would he know Sagarum's fine wit, or the kind lessons he had received so often. How long he cried, he did not know, but even though his tears ran dry, his sorrow did not.

As he stood, Jyhanna and four soldiers burst into the room. She gazed at the burnt corpse lying on the floor, a look of agony on its visage.

"Was this Feladon?" she asked.

Tamlin nodded.

"Where is Sagarum?"

"He has passed beyond," Tamlin said mournfully. "The battle was too much for him."

"And you? You look different...more regal."

"Sagarum gave me all of his powers and memories," Tamlin sniffed, standing and bringing himself to his full height. "I will finish what he began, and bring this war to an end."

Part V:
Shifts in Power

Chapter I — New Beginnings

Jyhanna paced the throne room like an angry lioness, impatient at having to wait even longer. She had been in Laketown for two weeks – long enough for the most of the snow to melt and birds to fill the air with joyous song, and for an army that had been campaigning in Bandre to return and mingle with her own troops. The company she had come to know so well stood by the walls, joined by Abbot Artus, who had spent much of his time examining one of the intricate tapestries that flowed from the ceiling, and Gallant, who stood quietly in a corner.

"He'll arrive when he arrives," she heard Caelyn say. "He's been ill for some time."

As she spun on her heel for what had to have been the thousandth time, she saw Tamlin, now garbed in the red robes of an Archmagus, lean over and ask Caelyn, "What does King Caelgar look like, anyway? I've never seen him."

"When I was there, the healers were seeing to him,"

the monk replied. "He looked gaunt to the point of starvation, and very tired. I do not think Feladon was kind to him in that dungeon."

"We should have left weeks ago," Jyhanna complained. "For all we know, our best chance at killing the other two successors has passed already."

She glanced at Brodin and Telena, both of whom were standing together, holding one another as though at any moment they might vanish. Although she did not share their anxiety, she did understand it. This was their opportunity to get some land and settle down, to have a plot granted to them by no less than a king. In their place, she would have been nervous too.

A herald stepped into the room, horn in hand. With a deep breath, he blew a single clarion note. "All rise for his Royal Majesty, King Caelgar," he bellowed, and then stepped aside.

Jyhanna bowed her head as the old man passed her. Caelyn had been correct; the dungeon had not been kind to Caelgar. Throughout her life, she had heard stories about the robust king, a man who could drink most men under a table, and then fight as well as a hundred warriors in single combat. The figure that hobbled before her, supporting himself on a pine staff, might have once been such a man.

But he wasn't anymore. Wrinkles lined his face, and his eyes were sunken and haunted. His weak frame was almost a skeleton, and his limbs shook as he moved. With a grunt, the king climbed onto his throne.

"I must apologize for my appearance," Caelgar stated. "I fear that I am not myself, although the healers tell me I will recover in time."

Jyhanna dropped to one knee, motioning for the others to do the same. Once they had done so, the king waved for her to rise.

"Please, do not kneel to me," he wheezed. "From what

I have been told, I owe you all my life and my kingdom. It is I who am indebted to you."

"There were two others without whom we could not be here, Your Highness," Tamlin said. "Their names were Conadar and Sagarum. They were both killed trying to end this madness."

"I see," King Caelgar said. "Give their descriptions to the steward. I will see to it that a statue is raised to each man in the city square."

"Your Majesty," Abbot Artus cut in, stepping forward. "Please forgive my intrusion, but I was wondering what had happened to you. Until just before the siege, we had heard nothing of your condition, nor had we received any reply to our messengers."

The king nodded. "That is a fair enough request. It all started around a year ago, when Feladon proved to me that he had power and wisdom that would befit a chancellor. So, happy to have such a man at my side, I gave him a position of power, and delegated some of my authority to him.

"For a very long time, he proved his worth. The people adored him, the commanders of my army liked him, and every decision he made in my name while I watched was a good one. So, I came to trust him, and gave him more duties and responsibilities. This allowed me to finally pursue some of the arts and learning that I had never had time for. For a couple of months, I lived in bliss, knowing that my people were in excellent hands.

"It was only when the war came, five months ago, that I learned I had become a figurehead. It was then I discovered that sometimes you cannot reclaim the power you have given away. When I instructed Feladon to make peace, rather than plunging the kingdom into war, he merely laughed at me. I called the guards, but the ones who came were loyal to Feladon rather than myself, and

327

they imprisoned me in my own dungeon. He would not leave me alone, however."

Caelgar took a ragged breath, and for a moment Jyhanna thought the old man would break down into tears. Instead, he composed himself and kept talking.

"Sometimes he would come to torment me, asking me for secrets that were mine alone, and wracking my body with pain until I answered him. Other times he would gloat, telling me that all my subjects thought that I was free and hale; after all, they had been taking their orders for months through him rather than I. How were they to know the difference?

"Around three months ago, he told me that he no longer had a use for me, that his invasion of Bandre was proceeding according to plan and that I would be allowed to see his victory, and nothing more. That's when they stopped feeding me, and started only giving me a bit of foul-tasting water to drink every day. I think he cast a spell on me as well, for I grew weak far more quickly than I thought I would."

"I detect no magic touching you, Your Highness," she heard Tamlin say. "That does not mean, however, that you were not enchanted. He could also have been drugging the water you drank. I know of several poisons that cause the body to waste away."

The king blinked. "You speak with experience far beyond your years, young man."

Tamlin nodded. "I am Tamlin, heir to Sagarum, the first Grand Magus, and proper inheritor of that title. I hold the memories of an immortal. In a way, I am far older than my years."

"Will you tell me, then, why the world has been plunged into darkness?" King Caelgar asked, his gaunt frame leaning forward. "I would know why my chief advisor imprisoned me in my own castle."

328

As King Caelgar, Jyhanna, and the others listened, Tamlin told them of the original betrayal that stole seven of the Great Powers, and the battles for Succession. He then related his own part of the story, and what he had learned from Conadar and Sagarum.

Finally, when he had finished, King Caelgar leaned back in his chair, a thoughtful expression on his face. "This is all about warring wizards, then?"

Tamlin nodded. "That is an overly simple way of putting it, Your Highness, but yes."

"And there are only two left."

"Correct."

"And where are they?"

Tamlin took a deep breath. "From my scrying, I believe they can both be found in Toregien; they are invading that country, and they had planned to come north. However, now that the others are all dead, they will be coming after us. I am sorry for having put your kingdom in greater danger, Your Highness."

"So long as any of these wizards live, my kingdom is in grave peril," Caelgar said, turning to face Jyhanna. "You must be Princess Jyhanna. You have grown since I last saw you, haven't you?"

Jyhanna blinked. She tried to remember when she might have met this man before, but nothing came to mind. "When did you last see me, your majesty?"

"You were very young at the time," Caelgar stated. "I can understand if you don't remember. I think you were a little girl, playing soldier with your brother. Your father and I were very close friends, until about fifteen years ago. Then we grew apart, as people often do. I am glad you were able to help avenge his death; he was a good man."

"If it is possible, I would like to re-provision my army," Jyhanna said. "We have to march south to finish what we have started, and we are low on supplies."

"You will have far more than that," King Caelgar declared, rising from his chair to lean on his staff. "You have led the army that liberated my person and my people. For that, you have my eternal gratitude. What is left of my army, all the men I can spare, are yours. I would come with you myself, were I not so feeble thanks to that thrice-damned Feladon. And, any boon you wish will be immediately granted."

Jyhanna glanced over at Brodin and Telena, who were now looking at her with a mixture of expectation and pure terror in their eyes. Turning back to Caelgar, she bowed. "There are, in our band, two who have traveled far from a distant land, driven out by pagan customs that would have seen at least one of them slain. Their names are Brodin and Telena, and they are lawfully married under the eyes of the Eternal One. I have protected them since I found them, and I promised them that they would be able to settle down in peace, with some good land to till. I would have them settle in Fenegar."

Caelgar nodded. "Consider it done. It will take some time, however; what you have asked is not a simple matter."

"I don't understand," Brodin blurted. "Why can't you just give us some land?" A moment later, he sheepishly added, "Your Highness."

The king smiled kindly. "If I owned most of the land in my kingdom, I would give you a plot in an instant. However, the farmland is not owned by me, but by my Earls. Some of them have died, and many of them have lost peasants or had fields sewn with salt. Before any such grant can be made, a reckoning must take place, so that we may know where we can settle you."

"Your Majesty," Abbot Artus cut in. "When Southmarch was destroyed, the fields were burned, but not rendered sterile. Additionally, many who had labored on

330

our fields were slain. I would be more than happy to take this couple onto our lands, and even give them a plot of their own, so that their children may have something to inherit."

"Then the matter is settled," King Caelgar declared, gazing at the two young lovers. "You and your wife may settle on the lands of the Abbey of Southmarch."

Artus nodded and turned to face Brodin and Telena. "It will still be some time, for the Abbey must be rebuilt, and those remaining from Southmarch have pledged ourselves to serve Jyhanna's army in this campaign. If there is a safe place that you can both wait for us..."

"I fear there is none," Caelyn stated. "The walls of Laketown are broken, and the fighting has destroyed much of the city. Should another attack come here, this place would easily fall. And, there are no villages along the way that are any better off. It would probably be best for them to remain with us."

Jyhanna frowned. She hated to admit it, but the monk had a point. When the entire world was at war, there was no safe place to hide. At least if they were with her, protected by her men, she could know that they stood some chance of remaining safe.

"Very well," she said. "They will remain in the company of the brethren while we march. Speaking of which, Your Majesty, how long will your men need to join our own."

"No more than a matter of days, I assure you," King Caelgar replied. "They will be ready to march by the end of the week."

Jyhanna nodded, a sense of finality settling over her. "Then we set out for Toregien in three days. And may the Eternal One have mercy on our enemies."

331

Chapter II — The Road to Toregien

Jyhanna's army, now eight thousand strong and flying the flags of Toregien, Fenegar, and the Order of the Eternal One, marched towards the southern border. In the three weeks that they had pressed onward, spring had arrived in force. Birds twittered on the trees, and what woodlands remained standing blossomed with new life.

If only the land wasn't so completely empty, Caelyn might have been happy. Once again, he found himself heading to war, guided by others rather than moving by his own volition. He had become another kind of refugee, a camp follower of sorts, dependent on the luck of the army to see him through. Regardless of the pressing need of the campaign, it still felt like ashes in his mouth.

The land was deserted, at least by human hands. Fields around empty villages went unplowed. Crumbling ruins marked one small hamlet, while another had been burnt to the ground. Artus had ordered the monks to stop and catch up with the army later at one village, where the dead lay unburied on the ground. As they ministered to the fallen, Caelyn realized why such a thing had occurred.

Plague. Each corpse had the markings of a pox, the now-limp pustules, the jaundiced skin. Instead of burying them, the monks had been forced to cast them on a bonfire, to prevent the disease from spreading. The endless hunger, the devastation of the war, it had all helped cause the onset of plague. Fenegar would be lucky if half its population survived.

Brodin and Telena had taken it well, helping out where they could, thick scarves around their faces to mask out the putrid stench of decaying flesh. They were now officially a part of the monastic section of the army, and Abbot Artus kept them at his side at all times for their protection. But no matter what, he could not protect them from the horrific sights of the jaundiced corpses littering the ground.

Caelyn felt a tear come to his eye whenever he thought about it. The last rites and cremations had taken less than a day, but he knew that it was only the beginning. Those who had fled from the war were now in hungry and overcrowded towns, where the plague could spread like wildfire. It would be generations before the kingdom would recover, and years before the misery ended.

It was only later, around the campfire with his companions of old, that he mentioned what was on his mind.

"We've come too late," Caelyn said. "Whatever we do, it is too late."

Jyhanna blinked. "From Tamlin's scryings, our enemies haven't even come close to reaching the capital of Toregien yet. We stand a very good chance of stopping them before they can do any more serious harm."

Caelyn shook his head. "It is not what the other two Successors will do that is the problem. You've heard about the plague."

Jyhanna nodded. "It was very bad news."

"It will soon be like that everywhere," Caelyn said. "And then, since there aren't enough people to tend the fields, there will be starvation and even more illness. Most of the cities where the refugees have fled will become graveyards."

"How can you be certain of this?" Jyhanna demanded. Caelyn noted that her face had paled.

"I've seen it before," Caelyn replied sadly. "The same thing happened after the Kaegar Wars. The aftermath of the war killed more people than the war itself. It was one of the reasons that the Great Convention was drafted."

"Not all wars are like that," Jyhanna said, but her voice lacked conviction.

"Most wars are supposed to be battles between armies on distant battlefields," Caelyn stated. "The Great Convention tried to codify that, as though war was something that could be governed like a game. And some small wars could be – little spats between two kingdoms over a tiny piece of land.

"But a great war, like this one, cannot be governed by rules. Look at how quickly the Great Convention was ignored when it suited the Successors. When people fight over something important, they do not care who gets hurt; only that they win."

"There won't ever be a war like this again," Tamlin promised, leaning forward on the fallen log where he sat. "I will see to it personally."

"Can you change the nature of mankind?" Caelyn asked. "I remember, shortly after the Kaegar Wars and their aftermath, a visitor coming to the abbey. He talked about the conflict as something so terrible that it would be 'the war to end all wars.' But look around you - we now fight in a conflict just as terrible, and possibly even more so." Caelyn shrugged. "I guess the visitor was wrong."

"I cannot believe that the human race is such a fallen creature," Abbot Artus protested. "Look at our art, our literature, our chronicles."

"I think that is what redeems us," Caelyn mused. "I once heard, far back in my childhood, that mankind is a young, childish race. It is only now that I understand it. We have a need for violence that few other peoples share. Our epics and romances are filled with it. Perhaps it is our ability and longing to seek out beauty that will finally allow us to mature as a race."

Artus pointed to Brodin and Telena, who had fallen asleep in each other's arms, still sitting by the fire. They leaned against a flowering oak, snoring softly. "I think that is a message for all of us. We have a long march tomorrow."

Caelyn nodded. But when they had all gone to their various lodgings, Abbot Artus and Jyhanna carrying Brodin and Telena to their tent, all he could think about was plague-ridden bodies, from only a few days ago, and from thirty years past.

The conversation from the previous night had left Jyhanna disturbed. She had always thought of battle as a necessary evil, but something that could, and should, be held in tight control. But, no matter what arguments she tried to think up, she could not contend against Caelyn's cold reasoning.

We are a child-race.

Deep in her heart, she knew the monk was right. The Great Convention had been ignored in this war, and it would happen in the next great war, assuming there ever was one. She could only pray that there wouldn't be; the devastation from this conflict was sometimes too much for her to handle.

She shook her head, bringing herself back to the present. She was riding beside Gallant and the dour-faced commander of the army of Fenegar, a man named Guthwulf who had spent some of his time complaining that he was once again forced to be far from his wife and child, and another part of his time leering at Jyhanna. She forgave him for that, so long as he did not actually try to touch her. She had seen what long campaigns could do to men who had been away from their families for too long, how it could turn into something savage. She remembered once, during a border war with Tarese, having to hang three soldiers because they had gang raped a woman. All of them had been married, two of them had children, and none of them had seen their families in more than three years. All things considered, Guthwulf was handling the separation fairly well, and he had been able to briefly spend time with his family while they were in Laketown.

At least the weather was pleasant. The sun had risen high in the sky, and the world was green and vibrant. As they passed another abandoned village, the fields growing wild, she found herself sobered, but they passed the place soon enough, and she was left with her riding companions and the springtime. By midday, she was actually in a good mood, the depressing conversation of the previous evening forgotten.

"Something is up ahead," she heard Tamlin call. Turning in her saddle, she saw the wizard, his crimson robes fluttering in the breeze, coming up behind her.

"What is it, Lord Archmagus?" Guthwulf asked.

Tamlin winced. "Please don't call me that. I only wear this robe because I couldn't find anything in Feladon's closet that was a better color."

Guthwulf blinked. "What would you have me call you?"

"'Tamlin' is fine," the wizard said. "There is

something magical ahead. Something from one of the Successors, I am certain of it."

"Call up my personal guard," Jyhanna ordered. Gallant bowed and raced back to relay the order. "Do you know what it is?"

Tamlin shook his head. "I'm sorry, but I don't. There is a cloak of shadows around it that prevents my scrying from seeing it."

There was a rush of horses, and Jyhanna found herself surrounded by her personal cadre of knights. Ever since the battle of Southmarch, they had followed her with fanatical loyalty. She smiled; they were a mixed group, some from Tarese, others from Fenegar, but most from Toregien. It was truly wonderful when people put their differences aside to fight a common foe.

"Just ahead," Tamlin said, pointing up the road. "There, in that copse of trees."

Jyhanna called a halt. Behind her, she could hear the commands being relayed along the length of the army. "Can we go around it?"

"That would involve redirecting the entire army," Guthwulf warned. "It could take days with a force of this size."

She saw Tamlin shake his head. "It is too late anyway," he said. "Look!"

Even as she turned, she saw one of the trees literally uproot itself. Crawling along on its now exposed roots, the tree approached them, shaking the leaves off its branches to expose sharp points. Behind it, two others stirred, pulling themselves from the ground.

Tamlin raised his hand, a bolt of fire leaping from his palm. The fire impacted on the first tree, setting it ablaze. Still it came, approaching with an even gait.

"Attack with axes and swords!" Jyhanna ordered, the hickory aroma of burning wood filling her nostrils.

"Not lances?" Gallant inquired, drawing his blade.

Jyhanna shook her head. "It's a tree, not a man. Chop it down."

With a great battle-cry, her knights rushed at the oncoming foliage. With a quick movement, the first tree speared one of them, the sharp branch thrusting right through his mail-coat. Another knight chopped at the limb, bringing it to the ground with the injured man still impaled. Sap ran from the wound.

Beside her, Tamlin cast spell after spell at the other trees, setting them afire, or bringing lightning from the sky to crash down upon them. The magic didn't even slow them down. Still they approached, silent and menacing. When she glanced at the young wizard, she found a grim determination in his eyes.

Her men were having little luck; the first tree had managed to kill three of them already on its razor branches, and while they had taken many of its limbs, it showed no sign of stopping. Behind it, the other two were striding forward, smouldering from Tamlin's magical attack. Jyhanna's heart leapt in her chest. There could be no mistake: they were coming after her.

"Aha!" Tamlin cried. "I've got it!" Turning in her saddle, she saw him raise his hand, all the while glaring at the attacking foliage. The trees shuddered, their branches falling to the earth as they rotted right before her eyes. Diseased sap ran from their trunks, and they fell to the ground, dissolving into a mess of sawdust.

Jyhanna blinked. "What did you do?"

"It was an old trick Sagarum once used," Tamlin explained, his voice faltering at the end. "I'm sorry...his death still pains me."

Jyhanna brought her mount back a few steps so that she could pat Tamlin on the shoulder. "We all mourn for him, Tamlin."

338

"Will we see more of this along the road to Toregien?" Guthwulf wondered.

"I do not know," Tamlin replied. "Whichever of the Successors left this trap here for us might have counted on it killing the leaders of this army, and left the rest of the way clear. On the other hand, there may yet be other ambushes to contend with."

"What does your Farsight tell you?" Jyhanna asked.

"I am still adapting to these powers," Tamlin admitted. "I can only see the future in glimpses. I've seen myself in a dark room, and on a road filled with mist; I can only assume that it is the Great Road. I have also seen flashes of combat, although I did not know any of the faces or colors. I wish I could be more helpful."

"We'll all just have to keep a close watch out, then," Jyhanna sighed. "Thank you for trying, though."

"I only wish I could do more, Jyhanna," Tamlin said. "If you'll excuse me, I'm going to see how Caelyn and the others are faring."

As the wizard rode off, Guthwulf gazed after him. "Not one for titles, that Archmagus," he observed.

"On the paths we have traveled," Jyhanna said, "titles mean very little."

With that, she turned in silence back to the road to Toregien.

Chapter III — Transitions

Once again, her world had changed.

Telena sat by the fire, looking at her companions. They had camped on the border of Toregien, and would begin their march into the country tomorrow. Tamlin and Jyhanna were discussing some tactical matter, while Caelyn and Abbot Artus merely rested by the fire. She snuggled up to Brodin, seeking his warmth.

When they had begun, they were alone, two against the world. And then they had met Jyhanna, followed by Caelyn, Tamlin, and Sagarum. She had never imagined traveling with such a group, but found that after a while she could not imagine her life without them. Throughout the wilderness of the Shroud Mountains and the Old Forest, she had always felt that she would be fine, if for no other reason than her companions were with her.

And now, things had changed once again. Instead of a small group, she marched as part of an army. Sagarum's jovial presence was gone, replaced by the sage countenance of Abbot Artus. For what seemed the thousandth time, she forced back a tear – she missed Sagarum. Somehow, the old man had always been able to make her smile, even in the direst circumstances.

But he had died defending all of them, or so she had been told upon entering Laketown. That night, she had wept until her eyes were dry and bloodshot, her tears mingling with her husband's. Never again would she be able to grin at one of his wry observations, or marvel as he revealed yet another unexpected facet of himself. The place where Sagarum had sat by the fire while they had first marched through Fenegar seemed strangely empty, a hole that not even the kind and gentle Abbot Artus could fill. Sometimes Caelyn would say something characteristically dour, and she would blink at the silence that followed, expecting a witty retort that would never come. Although Caelyn and Jyhanna hid their sorrow well, she could see it in both their eyes; they missed the wizard as much as she did.

Jyhanna's voice tore her from her thoughts. "It seems strange to be so close. For all we know, there is just one more battle and the war is over."

Tamlin chuckled. "I've been living on the road for so long that I can't remember what it's like to actually stay in one place. I can only imagine what I'll do once this is finished."

"You'll have your work cut out for you," Caelyn stated. "After this, the Order of Archmagi will be in pieces. And you will be the new Grand Magus."

Tamlin shrugged. "I honestly don't think that is a bad thing. It is their complacency that has caused this in the first place. Perhaps they need life to be interesting for a while. If nothing else, it will make them remember who they truly are."

Telena winced. This was not the first time the

conversation had turned to this subject. If only they would talk about something that didn't have to do with the war. Especially when she had her own joy that she had just learned about.

"Do you think we should tell them now?" Brodin whispered.

"Tell us what?" Caelyn asked. Telena frowned. Every now and then she forgot that the monk had exceptional hearing, even if he didn't show it very often.

She shrugged. They'd find out soon enough, especially now that the morning sickness was beginning to set in. "I'm pregnant. I'm going to be a mother."

Even Caelyn's face lit up at the announcement. For a moment, she was bombarded by congratulations and good wishes. Abbot Artus promised a grand celebration once the Abbey was rebuilt, and Tamlin wondered who she'd chosen to be the godfather, whatever that was.

Telena found her mind wandering once again. A year ago, she had been a simple village girl, pining for Brodin's hand, and imagining what a life would be like with him. Now, she was a wife, shortly to be a farmer again, once the war was over, and soon to be a mother. There had been so many changes over the last year that she'd had trouble keeping up.

"It looks as though I have one more reason for ending this war soon," she heard Jyhanna exclaim. "I want your child to be born in a peaceful land!"

The words sounded odd to Telena. Before she had fled her homeland, she did not know that there could be something other than peace. Now, she had been witness to the horrors of war for so long that she could not longer imagine the world without them.

Tamlin wove the magic around the tent, carefully checking

his work in case some scrying spell found a weak link. Finally, the ward was to his satisfaction, and he nodded at Jyhanna and the others.

The early morning sunlight seeped through the cracks of the canvas, adding extra illumination to the small space. Tamlin gazed at Jyhanna, Gallant, and Guthwulf, all of whom were pouring over a map of Toregien.

"We'll be passing by Couer by midday," Guthwulf stated. "Should we be expecting an attack?"

Tamlin shook his head. "From my scrying, I have seen no other armies to the north. There is an ongoing battle to the southeast, which appears to involve a great deal of magic and...something else." He frowned, looking for the words to describe what he had seen last night while he had stared into Sagarum's blue stone.

"What's the problem?" Jyhanna inquired, misinterpreting his expression. "Are we being watched."

"No," Tamlin replied. "I'm just looking for the words to explain what I've found. It's a kind of oily darkness that obscures my vision. It isn't a ward, but something else. I really don't know what it is."

"Are you up to fighting it?" Guthwulf asked.

Tamlin shrugged. "I would have to understand what it is before I could answer that."

"From what I recall, the army is from the Haneric Empire," Gallant stated, pointing at a large country located at the bottom of the map.

"That will present a problem," Jyhanna mused.

Guthwulf blinked. "I've never dealt with the Haneric Empire. Surely they are like most of the other nations?"

"Far from it," Jyhanna said. "When the Arcalien Empire fell, the last surviving bastion of Arcalien civilization rested where the Haneric Empire is now. After a while they changed, and became something far from what Arcalus had represented. Now their court is known

343

for scheming, manipulation, casual cruelty, and from what I've heard, is a very dangerous place to be. Accidentally insult somebody, and they'll burn your eyes out. The fact that they think they are the most civilized people in the world doesn't help matters.

"Their military, however, like the Arcalien army, is one of the best trained forces in the Western Lands. They don't have a great number of horses, so they rely on infantry and archers in their battles. Their soldiers are all equipped with a short sword, shield, and a long spear. They are also fully armored."

Gallant cursed. "The spears will make a direct cavalry charge useless."

Jyhanna nodded. "Exactly. Furthermore, it is unlikely they will break in the heat of combat. We'll have to rely on shield wall tactics, and fight a defensive battle. If we can flank them, we can perhaps use the chivalry to our advantage, but otherwise we may as well not have them."

"What is the size of their army, Arch...er...Tamlin?" Guthwulf asked. Tamlin held back a smile at the man's discomfort. It really was amusing watching the man trying to grapple with seeing his betters as human beings, rather than some mystical aristocracy.

"Right now, larger than ours by a third," Tamlin replied. "However, by the time we get there, it will probably be comparable in size to our own; they are running into heavy resistence."

"Suppose we go to Regien, and let them come to us," Gallant suggested. "It has very high walls."

"Regien?" Tamlin wondered.

"The capital," Jyhanna stated, and then shook her head. "No. They can get reinforcements at any time, whereas we cannot be certain of any such support. If we allow ourselves to become the defenders in a siege, they'll simply surround us and wait until we starve, or whittle us down through skirmishes. We need to be able to advance, retreat, and regroup, no matter what the outcome."

"Speaking of Regien and Couer," Guthwulf began, "can we expect support as we enter the country? Or will we have to fight our way in?"

"With Gesanus and Lewys dead, and my brother Fillippe in exile, there is no government to speak of," Jyhanna replied. "Knowing the barons, they will be waiting to see what happens before they declare for anybody; for all they know, there will be a civil war between my brother and I once this great war is settled. So long as we do not appear hostile towards them, we should not be attacked. On the other hand, we can not expect any help, either."

"Will you claim for the crown?" Gallant asked.

Jyhanna shook her head. "I have never wished to rule, and that has not changed. I have always been more comfortable leading armies and traveling than I have been at court. Fillippe will take the throne, once he has been found."

"We should send messengers, though," Gallant suggested. "Some of the barons might support us."

"That is a worthy idea," Jyhanna said. "See to it, and have the heralds dispatched as soon as we reach the border."

Tamlin stood to the side, letting his mind wander as Jyhanna began to give orders for the day's march. It would be his second visit to Toregien, but this time he would be at the head of an army. He held back a smile; when he had last come this way he had been a frightened boy, leaping at shadows. Now he was something different, a creature of power on a mission of deadly earnest. At least he was no longer afraid; he just prayed he was up to the task ahead.

The army crossed the border at midday, just as Jyhanna had predicted. They marched across one of the bridges near Couer, careful to break their step, although Jyhanna had never been sure if they did it because it prevented the bridge from collapsing, or some sort of older custom. When they sent a messenger into the town itself, they found it abandoned, and several of the buildings burnt.

Jyhanna shook her head. She had known that the war would have touched her homeland, but she had always held back some hope. Now there was nothing but harsh reality, and she knew that no matter how far she traveled into Toregien, she would see destruction, plague, and death.

That night, they stopped around four leagues into the countryside, near a village that still had some residents. Jyhanna went in herself to reassure them that they would not be harmed, but she found herself addressing an empty square; shadows flickered between the buildings, however, so she knew that she had been heard.

As they marched the next day, she reviewed the events of the previous night. Of course they were afraid; she had come at the head of an army flying at least two alien banners. For all they knew, it was another invasion, or a civil war.

At least Gesanus hadn't been as cruel to her people as he had to Fenegar. As they marched past some fields, she saw villagers scramble out of the way, no doubt to avoid being conscripted. But at least they were there, plowing their fields and trying to continue their lives, even in the face of such horrific events. Perhaps there really was hope.

As she rode, she enjoyed the sunlight on her face, and the warmth of the new season. Spring had dawned, as it usually did in Toregien, with warmth and bright colors. Flowers bloomed by the road, covering the rolling fields, freed from their sleep during the icy winter. That night, for the first time she could remember, she did not need a heavy blanket to fend away the cold.

The sight of the fresh blossoms surrounding the camp in the dewy morning brought a tear to her eye. For so long, Jyhanna had lived in a grim world without beauty. For a brief moment, as she stood there in her tunic and trousers, she was transported away from the war, and into the joys of her childhood.

But then she heard the clarion call of revelry, and reality re-asserted itself. She returned to her tent, where her mail armor waited, and girded herself in case of any ambushes on the road.

Yet, during that day, and even the next, no attacks came. The countryside became even more vibrant and alive, and Jyhanna began to wonder if they hadn't come to the wrong country. There were no signs of those tree creatures that had come for her in Fenegar, or ambushes on the road. For all she could tell, the path was clear all the way to Regien.

Although no assaults came while they traveled, Jyhanna did not allow herself or her army to become overconfident. Every night, pickets were posted, and messengers sent out to whatever nearby barons could be reached. Invariably the messengers returned with a reply that offered moral support, but little else until the problem of Lewys' succession was properly dealt with.

Over the fire, Jyhanna griped about their lack of support. "A handful of knights!" she fumed one night. "Just one handful of knights to hold in reserve. I can't even get that!"

Caelyn had raised an eyebrow impassively, and then replied, "Why should they help you? They have yet to be touched by the invasion, or feel any of the devastation. You'll need to come up with something truly convincing, or they won't budge an inch."

347

But no matter what arguments Jyhanna tried, she always got the same messages back, even when she made it perfectly clear that the throne would go to her brother. She found herself gritting her teeth as she rode, thinking violent thoughts towards the barons in the north of Toregien.

And then, on the seventh day after they had crossed the border, a chill wind erupted from the south. Jyhanna found herself wrapping her cloak around her, and then reaching for something heavier, her teeth chattering.

"Is Toregien usually like this in the spring?" Guthwulf asked, reigning his horse up beside her.

Jyhanna shook her head. "Never."

When she looked at Tamlin, though, a shiver went down her spine. The wizard had paled, as though something had well and truly frightened him.

"What is it?" she said.

"The darkness," he replied, shuddering. "It's arrived."

Chapter IV — Sunderings

The chill turned to snow as they marched, forcing them to stop and take out the winter clothes they had stored only a couple of weeks ago. Despite the cold, Tamlin found himself sweating; as soon as the darkness had overtaken them, he had cast a ward of protection over the entire army, in case some magical attack came and took them unawares. While maintaining the enchantment wasn't exhausting, it was still enough of an effort to be tiring.

He turned as Jyhanna trotted up behind him. "Can you cast a spell to protect us?"

"Already have," he replied. He gestured around him. "But snow isn't magic, even if it may be unnatural."

The sight of his breath in the air distracted him for a moment. It lingered, a fine mist suspended before his face, lasting far longer than it had even in the coldest parts of the Shroud Mountains.

Something was definitely wrong. He could feel it in

his bones. He glanced to the south to see a large, dark collection of clouds rapidly approaching. In the shadows they cast, he noticed flickering lightning, obscured by what appeared to be a fine mist. Despite the calm day and lack of wind, it looked as though they might only have a few moments before it hit.

"A storm is coming," he said. "Best have everybody pitch what tents they can."

Roaring thunder filled the air, startling them both. Jyhanna kicked her horse into a gallop. He only hoped that there would be enough time to get ready.

"I've never seen a storm like that," he heard Caelyn say.

Tamlin startled. He hadn't heard the monk approach, hadn't even known he had left the rest of his brethren. The stealth that the man was capable of was frightening.

He brushed off some snow that had fallen on his nose, choking back a sneeze. "I've never seen anything like that either."

"Do you have any knowledge of it from Sagarum's memories?" Caelyn inquired. Tamlin felt a sudden pain in his heart as his mentor's name was mentioned. He forced it down and drew his mind back to the present and the oncoming storm.

"Sagarum never saw anything like it," he stated.

"I have the feeling that the storm itself was summoned," Caelyn said. "Just a sense, that's all. I notice that I tend to be more aware of what is around me than others."

Tamlin nearly laughed at the understatement, wondering for a moment if Caelyn was actually joking. But when he glanced at the monk's face it was impassive and serene, only the eyes revealing the slightest vague emotion. Whether it was humor or sorrow, Tamlin couldn't tell.

He turned his attention to the storm; it was now close enough that he could not make out its edges. In the distance, deep under the clouds, he heard a howling wind, bellowing like a tormented demon. The sound sent a shiver down his spine.

But Caelyn was right; as Tamlin tried to see into it with his spellsight, he was able to make out a singular purpose, although he could not determine what that or its origin might be.

Tamlin girded himself, wrapping his cloak as tightly around him as he could. Cold fear ran in his veins; he knew how to protect himself and the army against most magical attacks, but this was an assault of a sort he had never dreamed. All he could do was endure it and hope that no harm was done.

And then, so suddenly that he didn't have a chance to put up a proper ward, the storm was upon them all.

Caelyn put his hand up to cover his face, the snow and hail whipping around so hard that it stung wherever it struck. Even with his heightened awareness, he was barely able to see his hand in front of his face, much less where Tamlin had been standing a moment ago.

"Tamlin!" he called, staggering forward against the howling wind. It was all he could do to not fall back and seek shelter; he knew that at least some of the tents had been raised. All he needed to do was find them. But, the boy that he still had an obligation to protect was out there, somewhere, possibly suffering in the storm.

"TAMLIN!" he bellowed, projecting his voice as much as possible. Immediately after speaking, however, there was a blast of lightning, casting the entire scene in a tableau of aimless running men before plunging them into darkness with deafening thunder. In the brief light, he saw

351

a flash of red, but as he had turned to look, the darkness descended.

"I'm here," he heard Tamlin scream, the voice soft against the roaring storm. Slowly, every step a struggle as more of the biting hail and snow struck him, he made his way forward. He stretched out his hand, finally coming into contact with a silken robe.

"Tamlin? Is that you?" Caelyn shouted.

"Yes!" came the reply. The monk drew close, finally seeing Tamlin's face, scarred and bleeding from the hail. With a start, Caelyn realized that there was a stinging on his own flesh, and when he wiped his hand across his brow, it came away crimson with blood.

"I can't cast any wards!" Tamlin cried. "Something's blocking me!"

With the maelstrom around them, the howling noise and stinging hail, Caelyn was surprised that the boy could even think, much less realize that something was preventing him from weaving spells. The monk was only barely able to keep his own thoughts straight in his head, to keep his concentration in the roaring storm.

"We need to find shelter!" Caelyn bellowed. "I think I saw something this way! Follow me!"

Taking Tamlin's hand, he began to make his way through the storm. His awareness of what was around began to return, his senses slowly adapting to the horrifying weather. He became aware of men huddled in small groups around him, trying to shelter themselves in their cloaks. He gripped the boy's hand tight in his own, taking comfort in the fact that Tamlin squeezed back. He felt four people moving behind him, no doubt seeking some refuge from the storm.

As Tamlin's hand was ripped from his own, he realized that the men behind him were moving too confidently, completely unhindered. The revelation came too late, however – he felt a crushing blow on the back of his head, and then all was darkness.

The storm passed as quickly as it came, blowing itself out as though it had no longer served its purpose and had been given leave to depart. Jyhanna raised her head, wiping blood from the stinging wounds on her brow. For a moment, as her vision slowly returned, her senses adapting to the sudden quiet and light, she feared the worst, that her army had been overcome in the storm.

But, all she saw was her own men, slowly recovering from the onslaught. A couple of the hastily erected tents still stood, and she saw the wreckage of at least ten of them blown against some trees to the side of the road.

Still staggering, Gallant came up beside her. When she turned to gaze at him, she winced at the blood running freely down his face, and wondered if she looked the same.

"Are you all right, my lady?" Gallant asked.

Jyhanna nodded. "As well as I can be, all things considered." She took out a rag from her belt, wiping it across her face. The fabric came away stained crimson. "Find Guthwulf, Abbot Artus, Brother Caelyn, Tamlin, Brodin, and Telena. Make sure they are safe, and bring Artus, Caelyn, and Tamlin to me." She grimaced. "And then clean yourself up. You're bleeding on your tabard."

"Thank you for your concern, my lady, but I am fine," Gallant stated. "My armor protected me from the worst of it, although my ears are still ringing from the hail hitting my helmet. By your leave, I will carry out your orders."

Jyhanna nodded, sending the man on her way. She began to walk down the length of the vanguard, taking note of the damage. While everybody was still reeling from the storm, bleeding from wounds taken from the hail,

353

there appeared to be no serious injuries. Whenever she passed close by somebody, she gave them a reassuring comment, talking about how not even the weather could stop them.

The chill still cut through her cloak, made worse by the light padded tunic worn beneath her mail; she'd have to wear gloves to remove her armor, it would probably be so cold by nightfall. Finally, she returned to her spot in the line to find Abbot Artus standing alone with Gallant, pensively wringing his hands.

"What has happened?" Jyhanna demanded.

"We can't find either Brother Caelyn or Tamlin," Gallant stated. "They are not anywhere in the vanguard, and runners are being sent to the rest of the army to find them."

Jyhanna's hopes fell. The army was spread out enough that there hadn't been time for either of the two to make it out of the vanguard unless they had horses, an impossibility in the storm. As it was, they would have to spend a day finding all of the mounts that had bolted.

"Keep looking," she instructed. "And have your men find their horses; we're going to need to send scouts out."

As Gallant raced off and Artus offered his prayers to find the two missing men, Jyhanna cursed. With Tamlin missing, they had been rendered blind; his scrying had provided her with more intelligence than her scouts ever could. And, to make matters worse, they now had no protection against any magical attacks.

She barely noticed Guthwulf striding up to her, and when he did, she cursed herself again for not paying attention. If he had been an assassin, she would be dead by now.

"What should we do?" he asked.

Jyhanna shrugged. "We have to take stock of what has happened. Make camp, and set a strong guard."

"As you wish, Your Highness," Guthwulf declared, turning and striding away to follow her orders.

By the end of the day, as she paced in her tent, maps carelessly strewn across the makeshift table, her fears were confirmed. Neither Tamlin nor Caelyn were anywhere to be found; the search had even gone for a two league radius outside the campsite. No matter how she looked at it, her companions were now sundered, and probably dead.

She could only pray that they would find their way back to the camp somehow, but it was an empty hope and she knew it. If they had only been separated, they would have returned by now.

Abbot Artus had been in a bit earlier, informing her that all of the monks were praying for the safety of the two lost companions, and that otherwise, the army was fine; only a few minor injuries from the storm. Gallant had arrived only moments after the monk had left, telling her that all of the horses had been found, and they could set out at dawn, if she so wished it.

But now she paced, alone with her thoughts. She was tempted to join Brodin and Telena at the fire, but could not bear to see their faces, to tell them that the two men they had journeyed with for so long were probably dead now. It would be too much of a loss.

They would have to set out at dawn, she realized. Even though the storm had taken so much away from them, she could still use it to her advantage. Whatever Successor had sent it would probably think that the loss of Caelyn and Tamlin was too devastating for her to press on; if she did continue her advance, she could take the wizard by surprise.

A small cough came from behind her, the quiet sound of somebody clearing their throat. She turned to face the intruder, her hand instinctually going to where her sword would rest on her hip. It only grasped empty air, however;

with a start, she realized that she had left the blade leaning against the map table.

When she saw the newcomers, her heart fell. There were ten of them, all wearing the crimson robes of an Archmagus, the one in front, an apparent leader, gripping her sword in his hands, the tip pointed towards the ground.

She drew herself up to her full height. It broke her heart to come so far, and then be stopped like this. There was now nothing she could do; if they were going to kill her, they could paralyze her before she even had a chance to move. However, the very least she could do was die with dignity.

She took a deep breath and prepared to meet the Eternal One.

Chapter V — Games with the Mad

Tamlin awoke in the dark to the sound of dripping water. The air was damp and chilly, and he wrapped his cloak around him to keep some measure of warmth in. Slowly, his eyes adjusted to the darkness.

Surveying what he found, his heart began to sink. He was in an underground prison of some sort, trapped in a cell with thick iron bars. There appeared to be no door whatsoever. Brother Caelyn sat in a corner, watching him.

"Do you know where we are?" Tamlin asked, his voice raspy. He swallowed hard; his throat was extremely dry, as though he had slept for a very long time.

Caelyn shrugged. "I woke up a few hours ago, I think. I can't be certain, however. Down here, I've found no way of measuring time. Nothing has changed since then."

Tamlin glanced around. What little light there was came from beneath the cracks of an elevated heavy wooden door, several feet away from the bars of their cell. Tamlin cautiously touched the bars, relieved to discover that they were nothing more than they seemed.

"Give me a moment, and I'll have us out of here," he declared, rubbing his hands as he prepared to weave a spell with his mindcasting.

"Be very careful," Caelyn advised. "We were kidnapped, and whoever took us select their targets with care. I do not doubt that they know you are a wizard, and have taken steps to prevent you from escaping."

"I'll be careful," Tamlin promised, mindcasting the spell. He blinked. Nothing had happened; the bars should have simply melted away. Taking a step back, he motioned with his hands, trying to weave the magical energies in the air around the bars. But every time he tried to grasp a thread, it slipped away.

"I can't weave spells," Tamlin said, sitting down in shock. "Nothing works."

Caelyn passed him a water bowl from the ground, and Tamlin accepted the drink. "There are more ways than magic to break out of a prison," the monk said. "We just need to determine the weaknesses of this place."

"That will be difficult without light," Tamlin muttered, wiping some water from his chin and putting down the bowl. He tried to push down some of the hopelessness. Wherever they were, he was certain that Jyhanna wouldn't know how to find them, assuming she even thought they were still alive.

Suddenly, the door creaked, and light flooded the dungeon, nearly blinding him. As he shielded his eyes, he saw a tall, gaunt man descend the stairs from the door. With a start, he sensed the power in the man, and realized that he was facing another Successor. The newcomer's face was hidden in shadow, but when he walked before them and turned, Tamlin saw that his visage was thin and unpleasant, his lips curled into a permanent sneer.

"How are you enjoying your accommodations?" the

man asked. "I trust that they aren't too unpleasant."

Tamlin saw Caelyn approach the bars and shrug. "I've been in worse."

"I apologize, friend monk," the newcomer said. "My men had to take you along with the boy. I assure you, I have no quarrel with you."

"The boy is under my protection," Caelyn stated. "If you wish him harm, then we do have a quarrel."

The man laughed, a thick, unpleasant sound. "I fear that it will be short lived. Once I have what I want, I will dispatch both of you."

"You could have killed us during the storm," Caelyn said. "Why didn't you?"

"Because Hargan asked me to gather intelligence for his own attack," the newcomer replied. "Very shortly, your pitiful little army will be destroyed by forces beyond either of your imaginations. But, my scrying has revealed more mysteries than facts."

"Who are you?" Tamlin asked, calling on his own Great Powers. His Truesight welled up in him, flooding him with a strange sense of knowledge. With a careful eye, he watched the man.

"Consider you are both going to die soon, I see no reason not to tell you," the newcomer said. "I am known as Malichus, and I am the last person you will ever see."

His heart breaking, Tamlin sensed that Malichus was telling the truth with both statements.

"I am going to ask you some questions," Malichus declared. "And you will answer them, or else you will suffer anguish the likes of which you have never felt."

"Quid pro quo," Caelyn said.

Malichus blinked. "What?"

"Quid pro quo," Caelyn repeated. "It is one of the ancient tongues. It means that we will give you answers only if you answer our own questions."

359

"You insolent fool!" Malichus stormed, insanity creeping into his eyes. "I could kill you with a gesture, if I wanted to!"

With a start, Tamlin sensed that the man was lying.

"Really," Caelyn said. "It doesn't matter. Neither of us will tell you anything unless we get something in return."

"I should set your bones on fire right now," Malichus gritted. "But I won't. Instead, I will leave you in the dark, to contemplate your fate. Perhaps in a few hours, or maybe even a few days, depending on what I choose, you'll be a bit more co-operative."

Tamlin watched with new interest as the wizard stormed out of the dungeon, slamming the door behind him and plunging them back into darkness.

He wasn't certain how much time passed before his vision adjusted again. He tried counting his heartbeats, but lost track after two hundred. When he could see again, he glanced over to where Caelyn sat. To his surprise, the monk smiled at him.

"It is as I thought," he said. "The wizard's magic is as useless here as your own."

Tamlin blinked and crossed over to sit by the wall. "What does that mean?"

"It means that so long as we are careful, we have the advantage," Caelyn said. "We were probably put here using a secret door, either on the roof or in the wall. Considering that there are no new bruises on my body from when I was unconscious, I would guess that it was in the wall. That being the case, all we have to do is find it, and we can free ourselves."

"What makes you think that we can open it from in here?" Tamlin wondered.

"I haven't seen or heard any guards," Caelyn stated. "Even through stone, I should be able to hear something. But, the only sounds have come from Malichus. I would guess that we are alone in here with him. So, he somehow had to get us in, and knowing dungeons, the door would have closed behind him. Therefore, he also needed a way to get out."

Tamlin pursed his lips. "Why wouldn't there be any guards? That makes no sense."

"I don't know," Caelyn replied. "That concerns me. However, it could be that this Malichus has things he wishes to hide, and is unwilling to allow any soldiers in here. We are playing games with the mad, and will have to step carefully."

"So, now what?" Tamlin wondered.

"Now I will search for the door," the monk replied quietly. "You should get some rest. You will need it to finish this Malichus off once we break out."

"Are we leaving as soon as you find it?"

Caelyn shook his head. "We have a great deal we need to learn from this wizard. So long as he thinks we are unwilling prisoners, we can get him to talk. Now rest, and try to look defiant when he comes back; we must make this as interesting for him as possible when he returns."

When sleep finally came, so did the nightmares. Again and again Tamlin saw the faces of the three men he had killed in Laketown, three wizards guilty of nothing more than guarding their employer. He tried to go back, apologize for what he had done, but instead saw horror streak across their faces as his spell took their lives.

Finally, he awoke, lying still on the spartan cot, a cold sweat on his chest, soaking through his robes. Slowly, his eyes adjusted to the dark, and Caelyn's form rose from a corner.

"Nightmares?" the monk asked.

Tamlin nodded. "Ever since Laketown."

"Sagarum, or the people you killed?"

"My victims," Tamlin said. "I keep thinking that I could have done it differently, that I could have left them alive."

"You probably couldn't afford to have taken the chance," Caelyn said. "No doubt that is little consolation, however. I'm sorry, but those sorts of nightmares will stay with you always. They will fade in time, but you'll never forget their faces. The fact that you can have these ill dreams, however, is a very good sign. It means that you still have your humanity."

"What about yourself?" Tamlin asked. "How do you handle it?"

"The lives I have taken recently, I do not dream about," Caelyn replied. "There is still too much of me that is Garwulf for that. But, I can remember each face, and I can atone for them. The lives I took in the Kaegar wars, I cannot remember those faces at all; I was too dead inside back then. I do not know if I will ever be redeemed for those."

"Surely your actions now..."

Caelyn shook his head. "Killing is still killing, even when it is necessary. It still taints the soul. And I do not know what is worse: to kill unnecessarily and remember, or to forget those you have slain in the past." He paused, and Tamlin wondered if he was composing himself in the dark, even though his facial expression could not be seen anyway. "I am guilty of both."

The door creaked, and Tamlin leapt to his feet, followed by Caelyn. Slowly, theatrically, Malichus descended the stairs, a staff of some sort in his hands. Tamlin tried to make out what it was, but the light was too bright, and his eyes had yet to adapt. Finally, the wizard stood before them, leveling the staff at him.

As Tamlin finished wincing, he realized what

Malichus held. A crossbow, bearing a long bolt with a wide, vicious head on its string. He took a deep breath, forcing down a wild terror.

"I heard you talking about escape," Malichus stated. "Don't think for one moment that it will work."

Tamlin's Truesight welled up inside him. *A lie.*

"You can't scry in here, can you?" Tamlin said, his voice unsteady. "No magic that requires a weave of energy works down here."

"Be careful, whelp," the wizard threatened, leering forward to stare at him, a malicious grin on his face. "All I have to do to slay you is pull the trigger."

True. Tamlin felt the beginnings of a cold sweat.

"Kill either of us, and you get no information," Caelyn declared, stepping forward. "Quid pro quo. Something for something."

Malichus snarled. "You are playing with fire. Do you really think you have any leverage here? If I want you dead, you will die, every part of you in agonizing pain!"

A lie.

"The monk is right," Tamlin said. "I will give you the information you seek, if you'll tell me what I want to know."

"The basement of my tower nullifies magic," Malichus snapped. "I can only weave spells from the upper levels. Even I don't know how it works; it's been here since before the Arcalien Empire. Now, who are you? I have never seen either of you before, and yet I can sense most of the Powers of Succession in you."

True.

Tamlin considered his answer carefully. He had to choose a reply that would keep Malichus interested, but not give away any truly vital information. He sorted through the facts of his time with Sagarum, working out what he wanted to share. Even before he had decided what he wanted to say, the wizard grinned.

"So, you knew the very first Grand Magus. How fascinating."

Tamlin leaned back, suddenly certain that the man before him had the power of Telepathy, and a knowledge of how to counter it flooded into him from Sagarum's memories. "Do you have any of the Great Powers other than the ability to read minds?"

"Certainly," Malichus boasted. "But I'm not telling you what!"

A lie. Tamlin resisted the urge to smile; they had managed to draw Malichus into the game, and he now knew exactly where the remaining Great Powers lay.

"What is the name of the woman who leads the army?" Malichus demanded, leaning forward.

Caelyn stepped up to the bars. "Her name is Wighilda. She's a princess of the north, and the daughter of Garwulf the Slayer. They say that she eats the flesh of her enemies."

Although Tamlin expected the man to recoil in horror, he merely laughed, delight in his eyes. "Then perhaps I'll ask Hargan to let me keep her when the battle is over! Surely we would be a match made in heaven!"

True. Tamlin stepped away from the bars, fighting down an urge to vomit. The man was insane.

"What are Hargan's plans?" Tamlin asked, swallowing hard.

"To destroy your army with the help of his allies, take your powers of succession, and rule the Western Lands as a regent in a part of a much greater kingdom, an empire stretching across entire worlds!" His voice had risen in elation as he spoke, and Tamlin felt another chill shudder down his spine. "Imagine seeing the dawning of a new age."

True.

"What allies?" Caelyn demanded, and for a moment Tamlin heard a hint of fear in the monk's voice.

Malichus waved his finger. "I get to ask my question first. Is it true that you are the only other successor left, besides Hargan and myself?"

Before Tamlin could come up with a good lie, Caelyn impatiently replied: "Yes. Now tell me who his allies are!"

Malichus grinned. "The forces of the Damned One. Isn't it wonderful?"

Chapter VI — New Allies

"We have to talk," the first Archmagus said, his hands resting softly on her blade. "I apologize for disarming you like this, but for obvious reasons we all fear for our safety."

It was all Jyhanna could do not to collapse in relief. Even if they were assassins, at least now she had some time to talk her way out of it, or call for help.

"May I have my sword back?" Jyhanna asked, hoping that her voice sounded steadier than she felt. She ran her eyes down his face and body, taking note of his physique. He was not a young man, his thin face framed by a bushy white beard and a tangled mane of hair reaching down to the nape of his neck. While the others had a menagerie of moustaches and beards, they too appeared to be elderly men. She could not tell what shape any of them were in, which was a problem; if things did go wrong, she only hoped that she could move faster than they could.

"Once you have heard us, and we have listened to

you," the wizard said.

"I take it that if I call for help, I will either die before they get here, or they won't even hear me," Jyhanna said.

The Archmagus nodded. "That would be correct. We have been very careful to ensure that we will be undisturbed."

"How long had you been standing there?" she asked.

"Since shortly after the tent had been pitched," the wizard replied. "The concern you showed for your comrades is what convinced us to wait until we could speak with you alone."

"You were invisible."

He shook his head. "We do not use invisibility for stealth; only those who are foolhardy do. One who approached an invisible Magus does not know to step around him, and can thus trip over him. Instead, we cloak ourselves in wards that make us appear inconsequential. It is a way of clouding the mind. Do not feel bad that you were fooled; only the strongest of wizards can see through it."

"May I at least know to whom I am speaking?" Jyhanna demanded, trying to call up some of her former stature. She could only hope that it worked; she still felt alone and vulnerable, surrounded by enemies.

"Absolutely!" the wizard said. "Please forgive my poor manners. I am Georgian of Toregien, and these are my fellow wizards, all members of a small college of Archmagi in Regien. We believed that apprentices would benefit from the wisdom of more than one teacher, so we would instruct students together, each of us teaching them those subjects we knew best. Gesanus had tried to conscript us into his army shortly before he invaded Fenegar, but we refused to follow him. To bring a world to war just for a minor matter of succession is..." he trailed off, shaking his head. "Horrifying. And that doesn't even do the matter justice.

"When we sent him our refusal, he began to hunt us down. Some he forced into the army, some he killed. The rest of us fled; he was simply too powerful for us. Since then, we have been fugitives in our own land, living off the earth and desperately avoiding using any magic, lest it alert him to our presence."

As he talked, she saw the fear in his eyes. She nodded. It was not surprising that the one time they decided to take a chance, they were paranoid – it wasn't that long ago that she and her company were in similar circumstances.

"Gesanus is dead," Jyhanna stated. "I led the battle where he died."

"We had surmised as much," Georgian said. "Your army is of great curiosity to us, and we have watched it for some time. You march in, attempting to raise support, flying not only the flags of Toregien and Fenegar, but also the standard of the Order of the Eternal One. You arrive with a Successor who is not one that any of us have ever seen before, and he has now disappeared, leaving you without any magic at all. It is a great puzzle, and we would know if you mean us harm, Princess Jyhanna, considering what has come."

Jyhanna blinked. "What do you mean? The darkness?"

The wizard nodded. "As good a word for it as any. It is something unholy, more powerful than anything we have ever seen. And, it comes heralding an invading army with no fewer than two successors. If it is not stopped, you may have saved this land from one tyrant, only to have it fall into the clutches of another."

"Where is this army?" Jyhanna demanded.

Georgian held up his hand. "Before I tell you any more, I would know if you intend us harm. Understand, we may be old, but we can still kill you in a heartbeat if there is any treachery."

"I mean you no harm, Archmagus Georgian," Jyhanna assured. "I swear it on the honor of my family, and in the name of the Eternal One. If you will allow me to call my second, I will have you and your people billeted, at least for the night. After that, you may come and go where you please."

Georgian waved his hand. "That is a good oath, and your line is a worthy one. I think I can trust you. The ward of silence is lifted."

Jyhanna nodded and called Gallant. The knight looked around in confusion when he entered the tent. "Find these men some places to sleep," she ordered. "Preferably beside Abbot Artus and his brethren. They have had a long journey, and will likely require some spiritual comfort."

She saw Georgian turn to his fellow wizards. "Go with the man, but keep your eyes peeled. We may be among friends, but we must still be cautious. I will join you shortly."

Gallant, a befuddled expression still on his face, led the wizards away, leaving Jyhanna alone with Georgian.

"May I please have my sword back?" she asked.

The wizard started, looking down absent-mindedly. "Oh dear," he said, handing it back to her, point still downwards. "I'm sorry about that. I'd forgotten I was holding it."

She found herself smiling as she sheathed the blade. She remembered having a tutor like Georgian; he had been absent-minded, but had also been one of the most helpful people she had ever met. For a moment, she wondered what had happened to the man, but that sentiment was quickly swept aside by more pressing matters.

"Will you help us?" Jyhanna asked.

"What do you mean?"

She sighed. The verbal sparring was something she had always hated at court; it wasn't that she didn't have the subtlety to do it well, but rather that she didn't see why one should dance around an issue when it could be openly addressed. "You didn't reveal yourselves for one night's protection, or just to kill a princess-in-exile. You know that we will not hurt you, and you also know that we are without magical protection right now. Very shortly, we will be marching to battle, against forces that most of us don't understand. Your aid could mean the difference between victory and defeat."

"My purpose," Georgian said, "was to determine your intentions, and if you constituted a further threat against us or this nation. We now understand that you are neither. We are teachers, not battle-magi. Our goal is the gathering of knowledge. We would rather have your safe conduct than appear beside you on a battlefield."

"Your fellow Archmagi have thrust this world into darkness," Jyhanna said. "They cannot be overcome by swords and spears. It will take magic to fight them. Tamlin, the wizard we had to help us, has disappeared, and is probably slain. Tomorrow we must march without him. Would you have those who you detest so much succeed because you would do nothing to stop them?"

Georgian frowned. "We are not responsible for them."

Jyhanna leaned forward, hands clasped together. She repressed the urge to smile – she had him on the defensive. "You are correct; you cannot control the actions of your fellows. However, when you do nothing to stop members of your own order when they step so far out of line, would you not say that you are as guilty as they? How is inaction that allows them to win any better than actively joining them?"

Georgian sighed, and for a moment it looked as though he had deflated slightly. "Your reasoning is sound. I cannot speak for my companions, but I will stay and offer what services I can. Please remember, though, that I am not a battle-magus, and that the taking of life is abhorrent to me."

"Will you talk to the others?"

The wizard nodded. "I will. May the Eternal One have mercy upon all of us."

The next morning, Jyhanna learned that seven of the wizards had agreed to join her. The other three disappeared into the night, probably headed towards one of the seaports, or so Georgian thought.

She paced the entire length of the camp, asking if there had been any sign of Tamlin or Caelyn. Regardless of who she asked, the answer always came back the same: they had not returned. She took a deep breath as she returned to her tent, finding Abbot Artus, Brodin, and Telena regarding her.

"Nothing," Artus said, reading her face.

Her heart sank as she nodded.

Abbot Artus frowned, and a tear ran down his cheek. "Then we will pray for their souls, and hope that they have both found peace."

"What does that mean?" Brodin demanded. "You don't think they're dead, do you? Surely we can wait a bit longer!"

"If we stay here even another few hours, we may lose the element of surprise," Jyhanna said, every word difficult to speak. "I don't think either of them would have wanted us to give up just because of the loss of two men."

"Then they're dead," Telena said, her eyes glassy.

"All things considered, I don't believe we can assume anything else," Jyhanna said, trying to keep her own voice from degenerating into sobs. She couldn't meet either Artus' or Telena's gaze, and looked away instead. As she turned and called Gallant over, she heard Telena begin to

371

weep.

"Tell the men to break camp," she ordered, using the duties ahead to push her grief down. "We march to Regien."

"Yes, my lady," Gallant replied, marching smartly away to relay the order.

As she walked towards her horse, gazing upon the army breaking down the tents and preparing to march, a deep bitterness settled upon her. Two more companions, friends who she had become closer to than her own family in the past six months, were gone, swept away by the conflict around her. If nothing else, she would see to it that there was vengeance.

Chapter VII — Escape

"I guess I'll kill you now," Malichus said, leveling the crossbow at Tamlin's chest. "I have everything I need to know. Thank you for entertaining me with your little game."

Quick as an arrow, Brother Caelyn stepped in front of him. Tamlin swallowed, trying to keep himself focused. No matter what he did, however, he couldn't keep his mind off the deadly bolt pointed at him, one that could probably go through both himself and the monk at close range.

"One more thing," Caelyn said. "Where are the guards?"

Malichus chortled. "Guards? Why would I need guards to deal with you two? No, they serve another purpose; their bodies allow me to speak to the dead. The dead have no conception of time, after all, and I've been talking to them for years, divining the future. Soon, you'll help me too." With that, he pulled the trigger.

Caelyn moved so fast that Tamlin could barely believe what he had seen. With a simple movement, he plucked the bolt from the air, letting it drop down at his side. Tamlin breathed a sigh of relief; he would have another few minutes of life, if nothing else.

Malichus appeared completely aghast. "How could you...?"

Caelyn leaned forward. "Thirty years ago, I was known as Garwulf the Slayer."

Tamlin saw the evil wizard pale and stagger out of the room. Even before his form had retreated up the stairs, Caelyn leapt to the wall, tapping something on the stone bricks. A clicking sounded from behind the hoary surface, and a door slid open beside the monk, revealing a dark hallway.

"Quickly!" Caelyn urged. "We won't have much time before he comes back!"

Swallowing and taking a deep breath, Tamlin dove into the passage. No matter what was in there, it couldn't possibly be worse than waiting for Malichus to kill and...use him. He heard Caelyn enter behind him, and the door slid shut, smothering them in darkness.

"When did you find this?" Tamlin hissed.

"While you were sleeping," the monk replied. "For somebody as aware of his environment as I am, it was a simple matter to find the hollows behind the stone."

Although he couldn't be certain, Tamlin almost thought he heard an inkling of pride in the monk's voice. "Do you know where this goes?"

Caelyn shook his head. "Can you use your Magesight here?"

Tamlin closed his eyes, trying to summon his powers and weave a spell around his sight. But, like so many other attempts, nothing happened. Finally, he looked at Caelyn and shook his head. "I'm sorry. I'm still hampered."

The monk nodded. "Then I'll lead. Take my hand."

He reached out, waving his arm around until he felt Caelyn's robe. Tamlin gritted his teeth. It was so dark that he couldn't see a thing; it honestly didn't matter if he had his eyes open or shut. He felt the warmth of Caelyn's skin as the monk's hand reached out to clasp his own.

"Forward, as quickly and quietly as possible," Caelyn said, beginning to stride forward, Tamlin only barely able to keep up. "Then you have to kill him, and we have to get out of here."

"Why the rush?" Tamlin wondered.

The monk led him around what must have been a corner, as he found himself turning to the right and striding up an incline. "If Hargan has allied himself with the Damned One, then matters are far more serious than you could possibly imagine. At least we have the advantage right now."

"Do you mean that you are going to become Garwulf?"

Caelyn led him into another right turn, the slope becoming steeper and the ramp giving way to stairs. With a start, Tamlin realized he could see the barest shadow of Caelyn's form ahead of him. His heart leapt; they were finally approaching a source of light.

"I will not become Garwulf the Slayer again," Caelyn declared, his strides becoming longer. "I fear that I shall never be able to atone for the blood already staining my hands, and I shall not add to it. However, the name I once held still has power, and I think I have managed to make Malichus afraid. That will make him more prone to mistakes, and likely to attack me rather than you. Kill him quickly, and do not give him time to strike back."

Tamlin felt a sudden surge of energy around him. "Wait!" he called. "I sense a ward ahead." With a brief application of power, he pushed a hole through the magical mesh. He smiled as he realized what he had just done; once again he could use his powers.

"It's safe now," Tamlin said, holding up his hand and bringing forth an orb of light. "I will lead the way from here."

"Very well," Caelyn said, stepping to the side. "Make haste. Malichus will have discovered our escape by now, and may be coming down the passage towards us, or waiting for us on the other side."

Tamlin cloaked himself with a powerful ward. "I'm ready for him." Then he strode forward.

The hallway twisted and turned, always leading up, causing Tamlin to wonder just how deep in the earth they had been. As he began to encounter torches on the walls, he extinguished his magical lantern.

Finally, he came to a wooden door, resting on rusty hinges. Although he did not sense Malichus nearby, he could feel the other wizard moving up towards them. He quickly used his magesight to scan for any wards, and pushed the few aside as brutally as possible. He would have preferred to examine the weave and unraveled them with elegance, but he had no time for finesse. Thrusting the door open, he and Caelyn emerged into what appeared to be a large octagonal casting room, high arched walls rising from a stained marble floor.

Tamlin swallowed hard. Crucified on four of the walls were newly slain bodies dressed in the livery of the Haneric Empire. Each had its throat gashed open, and demonic sigils scribed on the tabards with blood.

"I use this room to talk to them," he heard Malichus say. With a wave of his hand, Tamlin pushed aside the bolt of fire that had been cast at him. He turned, regarding the wizard as Malichus strode into the room, a mad glint in his eyes. "It used to be a guard-room, I think. I had all the weapons removed long ago, so you may as well not bother looking, Garwulf the Slayer.

"They tell me the future," Malichus said, leering at one of the bodies. "Sometimes it is the past, or the present. The land of the dead is timeless, so they see all. Sometimes I take my pleasure of the women I bring here, if there are any. It is amazing how long they will last before they rot."

Tamlin felt his gorge rise. "You really are mad."

"On the contrary," Malichus said, raising his hands and beginning to weave. "I see things as they truly are."

Tamlin nearly didn't see the spell coming. Malichus waved his hand, and lightning streaked across the room, striking at his back. It was all Tamlin could do to leap out of the way, the bolt missing him and crashing into the wall.

"You have good instincts," Malichus mused. "But you are inexperienced. I like that; I think it will be a worthy challenge."

Tamlin concentrated, setting the floor beneath the wizard afire. Malichus screamed and leapt away, trying to pound the flames away from his robe. While the wizard was distracted, Tamlin formed a spike from the energies of the air, and drove them into Malichus' chest. The evil Archmagus was thrown against the far wall by the force, and crumpled to the floor.

As Tamlin stepped forward, he felt Caelyn take hold of his shoulder. "Careful," the monk said. "I can hear him breathing."

A chuckle rose from Malichus' mangled form. "Do you really think that I would allow you to leave this place alive? Even if you kill me, you won't survive to enjoy your victory!"

Growling in anger, Tamlin slammed another blast of energy into Malichus' body, silencing the wizard forever. But even as smoke began to rise from the burnt corpse, he heard and felt movement around him. When he glanced around, he gasped in horror.

Slowly, methodically, the bodies were detaching themselves from the walls. In that moment, Tamlin feared that they were doomed; it didn't matter what punishment he managed to inflict on the corpses, they would keep coming. He searched through Sagarum's memories, trying desperately to come up with some way of killing the dead.

"In the name of the Eternal One, I banish thee!" he heard Caelyn declaring, to no avail. The corpses began to circle them, cutting off any avenues of escape. Tamlin had a horrible vision of them rending his flesh, unstoppable as a force of nature.

As quickly as he could, he cast his magesight, a sudden idea coming to him. They had to be animated by something. If only he could find out where the power was coming from, and cut it off, he might be able to stop them. He looked around, not bothering to examine the weave of the spells around him, but trying to find some common link between all the bodies, if there was one.

Then he saw it: high above him, in the arched dome of the ceiling, lay a gem embedded in the stone. As a cold, unyielding hand gripped his arm and began to tear into it, he sent a single, desperate blast of power hurtling toward the crystal.

With a shower of shards, the gem exploded. The bodies flopped to the floor, the malevolent gaze in their eyes gone. With a great effort, Tamlin pried the clawing fingers of the hand that held him away from his arm, grimacing in pain as they tore even more of his flesh. But then the corpse let go, and he threw it to the floor.

Spinning, he found Caelyn breathing heavily, cradling one of his hands, blood seeping through his fingers. "Are you alright?" he asked.

The monk nodded. "A scratch, nothing more. The

pressure will stop the bleeding. I would prefer to find a healer as quickly as possible, though, just in case."

"Agreed," Tamlin said, carefully stepping past one of the bodies to stand by Malichus' corpse. He placed his hand on the dead wizard's seared chest, calling the Great Power to him. As he felt the energy flowing through him, a new awareness complimenting his senses, he took stock of himself and his surroundings.

They appeared to be above ground, or at least close to it; some sunlight seeped in through a crack in the ceiling. It might take some time, but they would find their way out. His own garments, however, had become a tattered mess, both from the storm earlier and the attack of the animated dead. Caelyn's own habit had not fared much better.

"I wonder if Malichus has anything that would fit me," Tamlin wondered.

Caelyn shook his head. "I can feel the taint of everything here. If you wear something of this man, you will be corrupted by his evil. I am certain of it."

Tamlin shuddered, realizing that there was a strangely oppressive feeling surrounding him, something he had never felt on the open road, or anywhere else for that matter.

"Fine," Tamlin said. "Let's get out of here. Best to leave before we find another of Malichus' surprises waiting for us."

It took them almost an hour to make their way out of the labyrinth of corridors and hallways, finally emerging onto a pleasant meadow covered with melting snow. Behind them stood a large tower, a single spire reaching into the sky, silhouetted against the sun. The stonework on the outside was beginning to crumble, however, the slow work of the millennia wearing it down. For a moment, he wished he had some idea of which way was east and which was west, but without knowing what time it was, even

Caelyn was having difficulties getting his bearings.

"There's some high ground there," the monk said, pointing into the distance opposite the building. "Perhaps we might be able to see something from there."

Tamlin grunted an agreement and began to follow the monk. It didn't feel right, being completely lost, unable to know what direction he was facing, and possibly even trapped in enemy territory.

By the time they had reached the rise, Tamlin knew that they were heading southeast; the sun had lowered in the sky, rather than risen, meaning that the afternoon was drawing to a close. That bit of knowledge made him feel a bit better, at least. Looking down from the hill, the view took his breath away.

They must have been on a plateau of some sort to begin with, for the landscape was several hundred feet below them, the ground sloping gently down before it emptied out into a green land speckled with snow. To the north, Tamlin saw an army in the distance, flying several flags, including the standard of the Eternal One. Just before them, however, stood a small army, bearing the colors of Tarese. In the south, a mass of shapes crawled over the landscape, covered by a darkness that blocked Tamlin's magesight.

"This is it," Caelyn said. "I can feel it in my bones. The final battle of this war will be fought there, down in that plain."

"Do you know where we are?" Tamlin wondered.

The monk nodded. "We are around a week north of Regien. If we hurry, we can reach Jyhanna in time to warn her of the great peril that now threatens us all."

"Are things really that bad?" Tamlin asked.

Caelyn turned to him, and a chill went down Tamlin's spine as he saw the earnest look in the monk's gaze. "We are no longer fighting for peace in the Western Lands, but for the very survival of the world. The darkness of the Damned One has come, and I only pray that we are in time to stop it from consuming us all."

Chapter VIII — Reunion

Jyhanna rode at the head of the column, flanked by Gallant and Guthwulf. Behind her, the army followed, a bit ragged since the attack by the storm.

She had only learned after they had set out that while few people were seriously injured, many of the food supplies and arrows had been destroyed, apparently by saboteurs. During the snowstorm, a fire had raged amongst the wagons, burning the precious supplies to ashes. By the time the news reached her, it was too late, and they had to press on.

She pushed down a wave of fear just from the thought of it. Even with Georgian and his wizards close by, she still felt as though she was trying to stop powers far beyond her understanding. Just concentrating on the march helped, but when things were quiet, she couldn't help thinking about what lay ahead and how much had been lost.

If only Sagarum were here, she thought, smiling for a

moment as she recalled the Archmagus's quick wit. He had been like a puzzle box; there had always been some new facet of his personality that could appear without warning at any moment. The same with Caelyn, or Tamlin, on whom their hopes had all rested until the storm.

But now they could only pray that they would be able to kill the last two successors in battle. No doubt that would mean all the Great Powers would be lost, but considering the toll the Western Lands had already taken, it might be a blessing. Better that nobody would ever fight over them again.

The sounds of a galloping horse snapped her back to the present. She glanced ahead to see one of her scouts approach, the mount panting from the hard ride. Coming up beside him, a soldier saluted.

"What is it?" Gallant asked.

"An army," the scout reported. "Right in front of us, and on good ground."

"What colors are they flying?" Jyhanna demanded.

"Taresian, I think," the man replied. "They have perhaps two thousand men."

"Tarese doesn't exist anymore," she pointed out. "It was destroyed when Taree was razed."

"If they aren't from Tarese, then I don't know where they are from," the scout said. "I'm sorry, your highness."

Jyhanna shook her head. "It's not your fault. Go back and tell Captain Berran to form a perimeter around them. If that army makes any moves, I want to know about it."

He saluted. "Yes, your highness!" With that, he galloped off into the distance.

Jyhanna cursed. No matter what, they couldn't go around them. First she would have to determine if they were enemies, and if not, try to form an alliance. If they were foes, they would have to be destroyed before she could move on; the last thing she wanted was to be attacked from the rear in the middle of a battle.

But all she could do was wait. They were at least two hours away from this mysterious force, and she could not allow herself to ride ahead; that would separate her from the rest of the army and make her a target.

The hours felt like they were stretching into days. She led her soldiers across the landscape, the hoofs of her mount crunching as they crushed the occasional patch of wet snow. The sun became hidden by clouds, the shadowy forms threatening rain, snow, or something even worse. Her spirits began to sag, and she wished that she had been at the fire with Brodin, Telena and Artus the previous night.

She hadn't seen them since Caelyn and Tamlin had disappeared. Somehow, having lost so many friends in such a short time, she felt as though they would be a painful reminder. So she had locked herself away in her duties, making certain that her charges were guarded at all times, but otherwise trying not to think about them. It had been a week since she had sat by the fire in the company of friends, and she suddenly found herself missing them.

Finally, Jyhanna crested a hill, calling a halt as she saw the force assembled below. To the east lay a wide plateau, stretching up so high that she could not see what lay on the top. Below her to the south sat the mysterious army, flying the pennants of Tarese, just as the scout had reported. Around them, she could see her scouts, waiting just out of arrow range to ride back and report if anything happened.

A small group detached itself from the main force and began to approach, flying a white banner. One of her scouts rode before it, tracking its movements. Jyhanna sighed. She would commend the scout for his effort, but it was a wasted one; she could see everything that was happening.

With a salute, the scout arrived, breathing heavily from the hard ride. Beneath him, his horse snorted in exertion. "Five men approaching, all mounted," he reported. "One monk, one wizard, and three knights."

Jyhanna nodded. "Thank you. Get yourself something to drink."

"Do you think its a trick?" Guthwulf wondered.

She shrugged. "Anything is possible. Have Georgian cast a ward around us, just in case. If there is treachery, we will not make easy targets."

"Yes, your highness," the general said, saluting and riding to the back.

"What now?" Gallant asked.

"Now we wait," Jyhanna replied. "We have good ground here, and if they attack, we can use it. We let them come to us. If they are here in good faith, then we will treat them fairly. If they have come for other reasons..." she shrugged. "We'll make certain we kill them all."

As the oncoming riders approached, Jyhanna's heart leapt in her chest. For a moment, she thought her eyes deceived her, for everything she knew told her it wasn't possible. Yet, in the end, she could not deny it any longer.

Brother Caelyn and Tamlin rode at the head of the envoy.

"So there is only one Successor left?" Jyhanna asked, supping on some tea that the monk had been good enough to bring. She sat in her tent, the canvas awning now containing herself, Brother Caelyn, Tamlin, Abbot Artus, Georgian, and the three-man delegation from the Taresian army.

"It indeed good news," the leader of the Taresian forces stated. His name was Prince Wiglaf, current head of the Taresian royal house in exile. Wiglaf scratched his

385

beard, still half the downy hair of adolescence. Jyhanna felt for the boy; he had been thrust into adulthood with little or no warning, and had seen his home and family destroyed. At least, from what she had heard, he had kept his wits about him in the ensuing chaos.

Jyhanna gazed out the tent flap for a moment, glancing out over her encampment. The two armies had combined, and now the Taresian flag joined the standard of Fenegar, the Eternal One, and her own banner on the pole by her tent.

"This battle should be easy then," Abbot Artus said, wiping his brow. "It will be such a relief to have only light casualties."

"It won't be that simple," Brother Caelyn stated. Jyhanna startled in surprise at the monk's grim tone; he almost sounded as though he was declaring the end of the world. "This last Successor has allied himself with the Damned One."

Artus' face paled. "Then we will have to fight the damned? There are too few of us for that. To wage a spiritual battle is beyond our abilities right now."

"It is far worse than that," Caelyn said. "If Hargan brings a demonic army to help him, he will bring the Great War back to our world."

Artus blinked. "I don't understand."

Georgian shrugged. "I'm afraid I am completely lost. My research has never been in religion."

Caelyn took a deep breath. "Our order was once a military order, based out of barrack-like temples. That has been forgotten, and the knowledge we once held has been lost. I only learned of this from my childhood sojourn with the Dwarves, who have longer memories than men.

"Ours is only one world on the Great Road, a path that leads from world to world. Some of the people in this room already know of it, but others do not. Needless to say, there are many other worlds than our own, all with their own peoples and histories.

"Since the dawn of time, the Eternal One and the Damned One have warred with one another, sending armies of light and darkness to battle for the fates of entire worlds. For the sake of not involving too many innocents, both would only fight in one land at a time. When either side won, the battle would move to another world.

"Some ten thousand years ago, the battle was fought here, in the Western Lands. The Eternal One was victorious, and the fate of this land was decided. So, our peoples are free, not enslaved by vile monsters and demons in a shadow-realm.

"Should Hargan call upon a demonic army to help him, it would bring the Great War back to us. We would not be fighting men, or even magical creations, but the darkest creatures of the Damned One instead."

"He cannot be allowed to summon them, then," Tamlin declared. "We will have to win the battle as swiftly as possible."

Jyhanna cursed. "That rules out our battle-plan. We'll have to charge right into spears and pikes."

"The high ground does give us an advantage," Prince Wiglaf said. "Our knights can be used to flank them, and we can use the infantry to stop their pikemen."

Abbot Artus grimaced. "Either way, there will be many casualties."

Jyhanna felt a chill go down her spine. "How do we know that Hargan hasn't already summoned them?"

"We would all know if that had happened," Caelyn replied. "The battleground would be without sunlight, and there would be no rain or snow. The land beneath us would begin to die. There is still snow on the ground, and the sun can be seen above us.

"Aside from which, once he has summoned them, he

would have to handle them. It would be easier for Hargan to just wait for the battle, and then let them loose should things go badly."

"We'll need a new battle-plan," Jyhanna grumbled under her breath.

"Sooner than you think," Caelyn said. "Hargan has marched past Regien already. He is only a day away."

Caelyn sat by the fire, enjoying the companionship of his friends once again. After his brief sojourn in Malichus' tower, he had forgotten just how much he had missed watching Brodin and Telena hold one another, and hear Jyhanna and Artus discussing some minor point about what was to come.

"So it's almost over?" Brodin asked.

Jyhanna nodded. "It will be a difficult battle, but the Eternal One willing, there is only one left to fight."

"What will be so difficult about it?" Brodin wondered. "Isn't there just a single Successor left?"

Caelyn leaned forward. He had counseled Jyhanna and the others not to tell the two young lovers about the possibility of the legions of the Damned One; it was something they would be better off not knowing. He got ready to cut Jyhanna off if she began to tell them.

"He has a large army," she said. "And he might have lots of wizards. It will be a hard fight."

Beside her husband, he saw Telena shudder. "I'm so tired of seeing death. I feel like I'm being just swept along in all of this."

"That's what it is to be a refugee," Caelyn said. "Take heart, however – it should all be decided tomorrow."

He stood and moved away from the fire, staring out to the south. At the very edge of the horizon, shapes began to flicker. He swallowed. Hargan's army was arriving, and would be ready for battle by dawn.

Caelyn prayed one more time for everybody's souls. Somehow, he knew his prayers would be needed.

Chapter IX — Legions of Light and Shadow

Jyhanna swallowed as she gazed upon the enemy. The harsh sunlight glared down on her, causing her to sweat in her mail-coat despite the chill wind. Tamlin and Guthwulf stood beside her, the general nervously glancing towards the horses. It appeared that there would be a cavalry charge after all. She gripped her sword in its sheath, but the action brought no comfort.

Hargan's army lay assembled before her, waiting on the low ground. But while some soldiers remained, many had become strange monstrosities, scales sprouting from pale skin. The rest of the force was filled with walking trees and rocks.

"We'll have to soften them up with fire," Jyhanna stated. "What few of the fire-pots we have left."

"I'll take care of the automatons," Tamlin said beside her. "Hargan has used one of the Great Powers to create them, but I know how Sagarum used to disperse them. I've already instructed Georgian and his Archmagi on how to protect you from any of his spells."

"That just leaves the soldiers and the wizard," Guthwulf said, climbing into his saddle and taking his lance.

She looked back to see Brother Caelyn stepping up, looking upon the enemy with a measured gaze.

"Any sign of the Damned One's forces?" she asked.

Caelyn shook his head. "We'd know if they were here. If they do come, our only hope is to kill Hargan before too many come through the void, and then slaughter all of demons that came through. If so much as one escapes, it can call upon more."

"My Lady!" one of the lookouts called. "An emissary!"

Jyhanna looked down the field to see one man, garbed in black robes, riding across towards her lines. The man stopped in the middle of the field and crossed his arms.

"There is a Successor among you!" he shouted, his voice echoing across the field. "Let him come forth, that I might see him."

Tamlin stepped forward. "I am Tamlin, heir of Sagarum, the true Grand Magus. I know you are Hargan, born in the Haneric Empire, and slayer of the Arbiter. My Hindsight tells me this. I am offering you this chance to meet me in single combat, and settle this war without any further battles."

Hargan laughed cruelly, the very sound sending a chill down Jyhanna's spine. "Now why would I want to do that? Especially when my allies have been so good to me, gifting me with the powers of a god! I will allow you this moment to surrender your life, and I give my word that you and your fellows will not suffer...much."

She saw Tamlin straighten to his full height, and for a moment he appeared to be somebody else, Sagarum reborn on the battlefield. His crimson robes fluttered in the chill breeze, and he crossed his arms. "If you wish to be sent to the Damned One in the underworld, then so be it. When we meet, I will kill you."

Hargan leaned down, touching the ground and stepping back. The earth began to shake, a deep crevice breaking through at the Archmagus' feet. "I don't think so!" the wizard bellowed maniacally. "My allies have come!"

Dark smoke began to billow from the crack in the earth, rising straight into the sky. Above her, she saw the clouds begin to darken, lightning flashing between them, but never actually striking the ground. At her feet, the grass browned and died.

"By the Eternal One, NO!" Caelyn shouted. "He's brought the Great War here!"

She turned to Guthwulf, forcing down her fear with grim determination. "It's time." Mounting her horse, she took up her lance and rode to the head of her line.

"Soften them up with fire," she ordered, sending a messenger back to the archers and catapults. "Infantry advance right behind us. FOR THE WESTERN LANDS AND THE ETERNAL ONE!"

The shout echoed through her ranks, was taken up as a battle cry, deafening her. With a kick, she sent her mount into a gallop, leveling her lance. Around her she saw her knights forming up, Guthwulf and Gallant beside her, ready to strike the foe. Before her, Hargan rode casually back to his lines, as though the charging cavalry didn't exist.

Flaming arrows and firepots sped overhead, impacting into the enemy ranks. The foe let loose their own barrage, sending rocks and deadly shafts towards her men. From afar, she heard the screams of the wounded on both sides, as the ranged battle played out.

Her mount went down, sending her into a roll. Instinctively, she came up, sword drawn, to face a monster the likes of which she had never seen. Its flesh was mottled, as though it had been riddled with some disease, but the muscles underneath rippled with power. Giant claws flashed at her, and she was barely able to dodge out of the way. From the inhuman visage came a bestial growl.

Spinning, she struck with her blade, slicing through flesh to spill the bowels underneath. The creature went down, screaming, and with another blow, she took off its head, ichorous blood spraying onto her tabard and mail. As she glanced around, her heart skipped a beat. Her entire cavalry was dismounted, the steeds lying on the ground, gored by the demons that even now were bursting from the ground.

Training and instinct took over. She began to carve a path to the rest of her men, spinning and whirling to avoid the deadly claws and fangs. Alone, she knew she couldn't stand, but together there might be a chance. Something struck her shoulder, and she found herself falling to the ground. Looking up, she gasped as one of the creatures reared over her, claws striking down to take her life.

Even as she rolled out of the way, the monster groaned in pain. She glanced up to see Gallant standing over the creature's corpse, bloody sword in hand. "You looked like you needed a hand."

She nodded, trying to catch her breath and push down the sheer terror that seemed to be surrounding her. As she gained her feet, a dark mist began to form, spewing out of the distant crack to obscure the land around them.

Taking her place in the ranks, she found herself fighting in a shadow-land, unable to see what lay before and behind her. She could no longer even make out the malignant crevice in the ground, spewing evil vapors.

With a roar, a group of monsters attacked her line. She

struggled just to survive, one of her men being cut down for every two monsters that were slain. Of her infantry, there was no sign. It was almost as though they didn't exist.

The battle is lost, she realized. She gritted her teeth, a killing madness taking her. Even if she could not win, she would die like a shield-maiden, surrounded by the bodies of her slain enemies.

With a great battle cry, she plunged into the foe, ignoring the wounds as their claws tore into her, spreading death with every blow of her sword. One creature's head she sent flying, another she gutted with a sweeping stroke before turning to yet another enemy. Ducking to avoid its claws, she cut it down at the knees, severing its legs. The monster fell screaming, and she silenced it with a stroke of her blade.

The mist curled around her, so that she couldn't see her own knights anymore. Blood flowed from a dozen minor wounds on her arms and legs. It didn't matter, though; all she craved now was to come to a good end. Singing an ancient battle song, she charged farther into the enemy ranks, bringing death wherever she strode.

Caelyn watched the battle with rising horror. Unable to look away, he saw the creatures burst from the earth, bringing down the entire line of knights and cutting them off from the infantry. He saw Jyhanna fight her way back to her men, nearly dying in the process. And then the mist came.

It blanketed the field, obscuring his sight so that all he could see below were vague shapes, fighting and dying. Lightning and thunder roared above, but no rain fell.

The exchange of artillery had become a constant noise, something that he no longer even took note of. Most of the enemy stones overshot anyhow, as though the foe was no longer truly able to use its catapults.

"This has to end," he heard Tamlin say. Spinning, he saw the wizard mounting a horse and barking a couple of orders to Georgian, who stood nearby. "Keep his attention on the battle, and don't relent on any of your attacks on his lines! Keep them under fire, no matter what the cost!"

"Where are you going?" the old Archmagus demanded.

"To end this madness," Tamlin replied, and then rode off. As he began to skirt the side of the battlefield, he suddenly vanished. Caelyn blinked, looking for any signs of the young man. There was a shape moving off to the side, but he skipped over it – it wasn't anything important. Then the monk turned his attention back to the field.

The Damned One was winning; he could feel it in his soul. There were now more monstrous shapes in the mist than those he could assume to be people.

Something began to rise in him, the darkness of Garwulf the Slayer combined with something else, something intangible. He forced it down, shaking with rage. He knew that he should be joining his brethren in prayer, but he was also certain that prayers would not help against these enemies.

He had once heard that the Damned One could be banished on a world where the Eternal One had already triumphed, if only a true and virtuous soul would open himself up to the divine. But, looking over at where the monks prayed in their tents, he could see that it was coming to no avail; the mist began to curl up around his feet.

The thing inside overcame him. He found himself growling in despair. "No."

He began to step forward, into the mist. He heard Georgian ask him what he was doing, but he ignored the wizard. The mist surrounded him, clouding his senses.

"No," he said, louder this time.

Another bit of knowledge, long forgotten since his sojourn with the Dwarves, rose up inside him. *Only one who has known darkness can truly know the light.*

Something giant and monstrous passed beside him, but ignored him; apparently, middle-aged monks were not as important as soldiers. A madness began to take hold, a wish to kill every foe in sight, to send them back into the depths from which they came. With a start, he realized that it wasn't Garwulf the Slayer rising inside him, and that the battle-lust was coming from the mist itself.

"NO!" he bellowed, dropping to his knees. Then he began to pray.

"Oh Eternal One, father of all, hear my prayer," he cried, casting his eyes up to the heavens, pushing down the killing madness that threatened to overtake him. "I have seen darkness, have slain thousands more than I can remember. I am cursed beyond words, seeking atonement and redemption, and knowing that I can have neither.

"I have been Garwulf the Slayer, the greatest killer of my age. My soul is not pure. But I have seen darkness, and I cannot allow it to pass. You have once triumphed on this world, and I beg you to triumph again. Redeem my soul, and let me become pure. Let me be your avatar, and the savior of this world. I OPEN MYSELF TO YOU!"

In that moment, Caelyn's world became filled with blinding and soothing light.

Georgian would remember the sight for the rest of his life. After he had told the rest of the Archmagi with him to attack the enemy ranks without rest, he had turned to see the monk leaving, walking into the mist.

"Where are you going?" he asked. "Brother Caelyn,

that is no place for an unarmed man!"

But the monk ignored him, and disappeared into the fog. Some of the strange mist curled around his feet, and a strange urge began to rise inside him. With surprise, he realized that he actually wanted to wade into the fog and destroy all of his enemies there. He shook his head, ridding himself of that ridiculous thought. Why, he'd be killed in an instant, an unarmed wizard walking into a mist he couldn't see through that was filled with monsters.

And then sunlight broke through the clouds, a ray of blinding light striking down into the fog near Jyhanna's lines. A single, deafening word bellowed out over the battlefield.

"*ENOUGH!*"

To his surprise, he saw Brother Caelyn standing tall, in the center of the light. With even greater shock, he realized that the monk had become a creature of light himself. With a sweep of his hands, the brother cast aside the mist, the fog billowing back and dispersing to reveal the battlefield below.

The infantry had fared better than the cavalry, which was decimated and scattered throughout the field. He could see that Jyhanna was far ahead of the lines, her sword still swinging at her foes as they retreated in fear. The action paused as Jyhanna's men looked around, shocked at their surroundings and the sudden absence of fog.

Then the sunlight came, pushing through and annihilating the clouds overhead. As it touched the demonspawn on the field, they fell, shrieking, their bodies turning to white ash. The earth beneath them came to life, brown grass blossoming green.

And then Brother Caelyn, the creature of light, faded, becoming just a man again. The monk fell to his knees, and then to the ground. As Georgian rushed forward to see if he needed help, he was certain of one thing above all others.

The Eternal One himself had fought for them this day.

Chapter X — Endgame

Jyhanna shook her head as the mist cleared. The blood-lust drained out of her, and she found herself bathed in a warm light. Before her, the creatures she had been fighting began to flee, but were soon overtaken by the gentle light and crumbled to ashes.

She glanced around, taking stock. Her own armor and tabard were coated with black blood, and she bled from at least a dozen stinging wounds of her own. Barrages still flew overhead, but no arrows seemed to land on the battlefield. It was as though the world itself had halted around her.

Turning and sheathing her sword, she strode back towards her own lines, wondering how she had gotten so far out of the formation. Each time she tried to remember, the events seemed fuzzy, as though they had been a waking dream of some sort.

And then she saw the monk. Brother Caelyn stood on the battlefield behind the infantry, a figure of light. Then, the glow faded, and he crumpled, first to his knees, and then to the ground. One of the wizards, apparently Georgian, dashed from the hillside to tend to the monk, and she turned back to her own ranks, wondering what she had just seen.

Then it struck her. The Eternal One had driven away the army of the Damned One. She swallowed. Suddenly, compared to the warring of the gods themselves, the magic of Hargan didn't seem terribly intimidating.

She paced the line, looking up and down her knights and the infantry that had begun to arrive. Guthwulf approached her, his armor and tabard as bloody as hers.

"We need to press the attack," she declared, turning to him. "Right now, we have the advantage."

"Agreed," Guthwulf replied, nodding. "But we should wait for the rest of the infantry to form up."

"That sounds good," Jyhanna said. "Gallant!"

But the knight didn't answer her summons. Jyhanna blinked, suddenly fearing the worse. She turned, looking to the wounded. As she walked down the line of bodies her heart fell, and a tear ran down her cheek.

Gallant lay on the ground, his guts opened and intestines scattered around him. Somehow, he was still alive, his breath shallow, moaning in agony.

"Oh, by the Eternal One, Gallant," Jyhanna croaked, kneeling beside him and taking his hand.

"I fought well, I think," the knight gasped. "Tell my family that I love..." His voice trailed off, and his head fell back, his eyes closing for a final time.

"I'll let them know," Jyhanna vowed, weeping silently. "They'll know you were thinking about them right to the end." Even as she wept for her fallen comrade, she cursed the madness that had swept away two of her friends.

"The lines are ready," she heard Guthwulf say. "What are your orders?"

400

She straightened up and drew her blade. "We end this insanity now. Advance, and do not stop until you have taken the enemy position. I want Hargan's head on a pike by sundown."

With that, she strode to the head of the line, brandishing her sword in the bright sunlight. "This is the final battle!" she declared. "Fight hard, and the war is over by dusk!"

A great cheer rose up from the assembled army, and they began their advance. The strange creatures of wood and stone loomed before them, scorched by the artillery and the magical attacks from her own line. Jyhanna noted that they were far fewer in number than they had seemed at the beginning. Beside the creatures, the half-men shuffled nervously, pikes raised in shaking hands.

There was a pregnant pause as both armies regarded each other. For a moment, Jyhanna thought that time had stopped, for not a soul moved. Then her resolve hardened. Just one more charge, and then she could rest.

"FOR THE WESTERN LANDS!" she bellowed, her blood rising as the warcry was taken up by the army. Then, with a wave of her sword, she led them in the final rush forward.

Tamlin wasn't even noticed as he entered Hargan's camp. The ward had worked perfectly; not even the creatures in the mist had paid him any heed. He had stopped to watch the mist disperse, awed by the sight of what had to be the hand of the Eternal One literally touching the battlefield. And then he had ridden forward, past a half-man picket, the man's face covered with scales resembling a strange snake or fish. He had given the animated wood and rocks a wide berth; being creatures of magic, they might detect him and realize what he was.

He had to sidestep to avoid a magical lightning bolt that crashed down beside him. The attacks led by Georgian were still in full force, wreaking havoc in Hargan's ranks. He dismounted, leading his steed around a hovering cloud of poisonous gas. Still, there was no sign of the evil wizard.

He finally found Hargan on his knees behind a group of infantry, screaming curses into the sky. Somehow, the Archmagus hadn't noticed him, even though he had to be able to sense the Great Powers resting in Tamlin's body.

Gazing out, he saw Jyhanna's army approach and pause. They regarded Hargan's army for a moment, and then Jyhanna screamed a warcry, the words becoming deafening as the entire army took it up. With a great crash, the two ranks collided, the soldiers before Hargan rushing forward to meet their foes.

Tamlin smiled as he decided how to announce himself. With a wave, he dispersed not only his own ward, but the enchantment that had brought the wood and stone to life. The trees and rocks fell to the ground with a crash, some even crushing the soldiers fighting alongside them.

Hargan glared at him, rising to his feet. "Do you really think that this is enough to stop me?" he gloated.

Tamlin used his Mindcasting to weave a complicated ward around himself and began to circle the Archmagus cautiously. "You are cut off from the Damned One, and your army will soon be crushed. You have a great deal to answer for."

"Do you think you can finish me?" Hargan asked, smiling as he held up his hands to begin a weave.

Tamlin braced himself for the coming spell. "I think that one way or another, the war ends now."

Hargan didn't even move his hands, but a bolt of energy burst from his palms. The blast broke right though Tamlin's ward, scorching his side as he dove out of the way. He grunted in pain, casting another ward and beginning to circle. With a wave of his hand, he called a bolt of lightning from the sky, Hargan easily dispersing the energy to the ground around him.

"You have Mindcasting," the wizard gloated. "I don't care. I never needed it, once I gained my allies. And, I can see the weave of your spells even as you cast them. I will kill you slowly, I think."

Hargan sent another bolt of energy flying, but as Tamlin dodged, he let another loose. The magic ripped through Tamlin's gut like fire, causing him to fall to the ground, gripping his stomach as he tried to force down the searing pain, the agony doubling him over and taking his breath away.

Even through the pain, one of Sagarum's lessons suddenly sprang to mind. *"An Archmagus with the knowledge and strength could become a conduit for these forces, allowing them to pass through him without using any of his own power. But the balance is eternal. It cannot be broken. For something to become strong, something else must become weak."*

"Do you have any last words, young wizard?" Hargan asked, looming over him. Tamlin began to chuckle as the irony of what was about to happen settled in.

Hargan's face became a mask of bewilderment. "What are you laughing about?"

"You've lost," Tamlin hissed, preparing himself.

"My word," Hargan said, leaning down. "You've become as delusional as Malichus in your death throes. I will have to let you linger, I guess. This could amuse me for hours. Tell me, why have I lost?"

With a desperate grab, Tamlin took hold of Hargan's robes. "For something to become strong, something else must become weak." And then he began to channel energy, the warm power flowing from Hargan down his arm.

Hargan screamed, trying to break away, but his strength had faded. Tamlin gritted his teeth, first directing the wizard's life energy to heal his own wound, and then driving it into the earth. As he did, Hargan squirmed feebly in his grasp.

"You can't win!" Hargan screamed, his face becoming long and drawn, as though he was now an ancient man. "I have allies! I am invincible!"

With a groan, the wizard pitched over, his eyes vacant and staring. Tamlin stood up, frowning at the dark spot that had marked his robes from Hargan's attack. Then he looked at the wizard's form, blinking in surprise.

He had no idea it would have been that effective. Hargan's skin had become pale and desiccated, drawn so tight across his bones that he looked like a skeleton with nothing more than the barest flesh. Tamlin kneeled by the corpse, noticing something blue flickering through the wasted flesh.

"The war is over," he said, placing his hand on Hargan's chest. "I claim the last Great Power." With that, the blue glow flowed up his arm, filling him with energy.

Even as it did, Jyhanna's men broke through the line, the shield maiden herself leaping forward, surprise on her face as she discovered there was nobody left to fight.

She stepped over, regarding the body on the ground. "Was that Hargan?"

Tamlin nodded. "It is done."

He saw her sigh with relief. "Thank the Eternal One."

The very moment that Tamlin had claimed the last Great Power, every Archmagus in the Western Lands sensed that something had happened.

They came out from their hiding places, from their tents in the armies they had been conscripted to, and in their cottages far away from the conflict, looking out towards the horizon. Somehow, even though they did not know how, they knew that the battle for Succession was over. But there was a potency in the air, as though they were about to witness great events the like of which they had never anticipated.

The pull to the Isle of Magic was irresistible. No matter where they were, they bid farewell to their families and apprentices and began to travel. Within a month, for wizards are skilled in magic, almost all of them assembled, with a few more lagging behind by a day or two.

Chapter XI — Final Journeys

It was their last day together, and Caelyn knew it. He saw that Jyhanna and Artus had put their best faces on the matter, but the war was over, and everybody's tasks had ended. Well, at least one of them had.

He sat at the fire, enjoying the company of his companions for the final time. Artus sat beside him, and Georgian and Tamlin sat opposite. Brodin and Telena nestled together, watched over by Jyhanna and Guthwulf.

"Now what?" Brodin asked. "I know that we're all leaving, so let's actually talk about it, rather than avoiding it."

Caelyn chuckled. *From the mouths of children...*

"Guthwulf and I will be leading the contingent from Fenegar back north," Artus stated. "You will, of course, be coming with us. By now, the work on the new abbey should at least have been started, if I know anything about King Caelgar."

"Just so long as there isn't any more war," Telena

said. "I've seen too much of it, and if I see another drop of blood, I think I'll be sick."

"Actually, you will live the rest of your lives in peace," Tamlin said. "I can see it in your lifelines."

"To just be farmers," Telena breathed. "It's taken us long enough."

Caelyn found himself joining in the laughter, surprising even himself. Well, he reflected, redemption can do funny things to a man.

"Will you be joining us, good Brother Caelyn?" Artus asked. "Your company will be most welcome on the voyage home."

Caelyn shook his head. "I must continue my pilgrimage, Father Abbot."

"Surely you have found everything you seek?" Artus said, a puzzled frown spreading across his kind visage. "I know from my own pilgrimage that it is not the destination that matters, but the journey itself."

Caelyn took a deep breath, trying to put into words his revelation while the Eternal One's power had flowed through him. Finally, at a loss, he said: "I know that I must go on. At least I now know what I must find, and how I will find it. I have my redemption, but I must still atone for my actions."

"I see," Artus said. "Do you know how long you will be?"

Caelyn shrugged. "I will certainly be back by the end of summer. I do not have too far to go."

Brodin turned to Tamlin. "And what of you?"

The young wizard smiled. "I am now Grand Magus. I have some duties to fulfill on the Isle of Magic, and then...well, I have my own road to walk."

"I'll be going with him, as will the others in my company," Georgian said. "Now that the Succession has been decided, we must all gather."

"Make certain that something like this war never happens again," Jyhanna said. "It will take decades for the Western Lands to recover from this."

"I will," Tamlin vowed. "I swear it by the Eternal One, and the Great Road."

"Will you come with us?" Telena asked, gazing at Jyhanna.

The shield maiden shook her head. "You no longer need my protection, and have nothing to fear in the company of Abbot Artus' monks. But, I must go to Toregien with my men and restore order, until my brother can relieve me of the regency."

"And then?" Telena wondered.

Jyhanna shrugged. "I don't know. I have seen far too much bloodshed now, and I feel as though I have lost a part of myself. I think I understand how Caelyn felt in the Kaegar Wars. Once I have finished my duties, I think I will wander around and find myself."

Caelyn glanced at his companions, then raised his flagon of tea. "Until we meet again, my friends – may our farewells never be forever."

As the others joined him in the toast, Caelyn felt something wonderful. It wasn't happiness, but it was close enough.

The next morning, the army had already begun to disperse. Caelyn bid his goodbyes to his companions and to Abbot Artus, accepting the man's blessings. Then, he set out on his own path, once again a lone monk on a pilgrimage. This time, however, he knew exactly where he was going and what would happen.

It took Tamlin and Georgian five weeks to reach the Isle of Magic. The Toregien harbor of Lorrayne, a picturesque port on the Inner Sea, was still packed with Archmagi trying to get to the island, and finding a ship was difficult, especially for a large party. But, finally they arrived, and Tamlin took up his residence in the Grand Magus' quarters.

He wasn't quite certain how he knew where they were, but his instincts guided him down the hallowed halls of the Tower of Wizardry, to a chamber that he knew only he could unlock. The moment he placed his hand on the ancient wood, the door opened, revealing a Spartan room with a large window opening to the west. On the bed lay the deep blue robes of the Grand Magus, and some papers still littered the desk.

Tamlin sat on the bed, wondering what the previous occupant had been like. He almost thought he could sense the presence of the man's soul, along with all the other Grand Magi, lingering in the chamber.

A knock sounded on the door. "Come in!" Tamlin called.

"You really should close the door behind you," he heard Georgian state, shutting the door. "They still don't know you are the Grand Magus, and they may wonder why an apprentice is sitting on his bed."

"I'm surprised that nobody has challenged me yet," Tamlin said.

Georgian sat on the chair by the desk. "They all assume that only the Grand Magus would be in this area of the building. So, anybody who is here, they figure is here for a reason. I think there is a naivety there."

Tamlin chuckled. "Are they ready for me?"

Georgian nodded. "Do you know what you are going to do?"

"Yes," Tamlin said, straightening up. "Tell them I will be a moment."

"Absolutely, Grand Magus," Georgian said, opening the door and leaving. With a click, the door locked itself shut.

Tamlin cast off his ragged red robe and put on the blue robes of office. To his surprise, they were soft and comfortable, and fit him as though they had been made for him.

The previous Grand Magus had Foresight, Tamlin thought. *Did he see all of this?*

He shook his head; he had other business to attend to. Rising to his full height, he opened the door and strode from the room, heading for the courtyard.

They were all assembled when he had arrived, a sea of red robes. As he entered, he glanced around, finally finding Georgian standing towards the back. "All hail the new Grand Magus!" the wizard bellowed, startling the Archmagi in front of him.

One of the wizards looked at Tamlin in disbelief. "That boy? Surely you jest."

With a flicker of Hindsight, the wizard's entire past opened up to Tamlin. "I am the true Grand Magus, Yuric," he said, startling the wizard.

"How did you know my name?" Yuric demanded.

"Hindsight," Tamlin replied. "And, I know that your first master, Claydus, taught you that the unexpected can come at any time. Do you doubt his words now?"

"We need an explanation!" a voice called from the back. "How is this boy the Grand Magus? We have never seen him before!"

"Georgian will tell you all that you need to know," Tamlin replied. "However, know that I am Tamlin, once apprentice to Haldur, and true heir to Sagarum, the first Grand Magus. In me rests the eight Great Powers of Succession, and in me they will reside for the rest of time."

"There are only seven Powers of Succession," Yuric said.

410

"Only seven powers were stripped from Sagarum when the Order rebelled against him," Tamlin corrected. "The eighth, Immortality, was passed on to me when he was killed."

A grumbling erupted from the assembled wizards, and for a moment Tamlin wondered if there was going to be another revolt. Then Georgian's voice sounded from the back.

"Tamlin speaks the truth; I was there when Hargan was slain. This is the true Grand Magus."

The crowd settled down, and Tamlin began to pace in front of them, his robes fluttering in the wind. "My first act, by all rights, should be to dissolve the Order. The Eternal One knows that it has caused enough trouble."

The Archmagi began to grumble angrily, but Tamlin turned on them, rage in his eyes. "SILENCE!" he bellowed, mindcasting casting a ward around himself, in case some fearful wizard mounted an attack. The assembled group was startled into submission. "Have no doubt that I could kill all of you with a thought! So many of you heard the call to power, and in following it, you forsook the laws of Succession. Yet you have not walked the world as I have, seen the harm that was done. I have seen villages put to the torch, entire plains filled with the bodies of the slain after battle.

"And while many of you scrambled for the power that the Successors offered you, the rest of you hid, waiting for it all to pass. By your inaction, you are as guilty as the others for the death and destruction that followed. Believe me, if I was to disband the Order, the rest of the Western Lands would thank me for it. The Eternal One only knows how many decades it will be before a wizard can walk in safety among the people, you have caused so much death!"

Tamlin took a deep breath, noting with satisfaction the pale and shocked faces that regarded him. "However,

Georgian was able to convince me otherwise. He is correct – the knowledge held by our order should not be lost. So, the Order of Archmagi will continue, but not as it has been.

"I am appointing Georgian to be the Steward in my absence. It has become clear to me that the Great Powers cannot exist in this world anymore; they have caused too much havoc. So, I am leaving this world to walk my own path. I may return some day, in the distant future, but I do not intend to come back during your lifetimes.

"Understand, though, that I will be watching. Any Archmagus that co-opts any of the Western Lands will be put to death. The same fate will come to any wizard who attempts to overthrow the steward. If I am forced to return, the consequences will be dire for all of you.

"Georgian," Tamlin asked, "do you accept the mantle of steward?"

Georgian stepped forward. "I do, Grand Magus."

Tamlin nodded. "Lead them with wisdom. When the time has come, pass your mantle to another of your choosing. Make the Order again the seekers of knowledge they had once been."

"I will, Grand Magus," Georgian said.

With that, Tamlin swept out of the courtyard, returning to his room. For a moment, he sat on the bed, breathing deeply. Casting forward with his Foresight, he saw Georgian guiding the Order to glories they had never dreamed. He smiled. His last task was finished.

Tamlin looked back into Sagarum's memories, remembering how to walk on the Road of Legends. Then, clearing his mind, he stepped onto the Great Road.

He found himself in a shadow land, a milky mist curling at his feet. A figure stood before him, indistinct in the fog.

"I had wondered how long you would take," the shape

412

said, his lyrical voice familiar. "I have been waiting for you for days now."

With a smile, Tamlin placed the voice. "It is good to see you again, Daelyn."

The Tuatha de Danaan stepped closer. "I see it is all done. Please allow me to offer my condolences on the loss of Sagarum."

"You knew all along, didn't you?" Tamlin asked. "Everything that would happen to me, you knew it."

Daelyn nodded. "My people have always been able to read the Wyrd of those who are touched by it. I knew that Sagarum would die, and that his powers would pass to you. I also knew that your future would be entwined with my own."

Tamlin motioned at the mist around him. "So, now what? I take it that it is time for me to follow the Road somewhere?"

"Now, my young Grand Magus, it is time for you to learn," Daelyn replied. "You are immortal, but you were not born to it as Sagarum was. You must learn how to handle the endless life that has been granted to you. Usually I would take you to my people, where many of us would teach you, but that is not possible now. Instead, I will instruct you myself."

"Time to go, then?"

Daelyn nodded. "You are no longer of their world. Like me, you have become a creature of the Road itself. The Great Powers made you into that."

"What of my friends? Will I ever see them again?"

"They have their own paths to travel," Daelyn said, smiling. "I think you already know that their futures are bright."

"True."

"Come," Daelyn called, walking into the mist. "It is time for you too to walk your own path."

Taking a deep breath, Tamlin followed, walking off to meet his destiny.

It was an ancient shrine, a small stone building lying in the mountains on the eastern border of Tarese. Caelyn stood in front of it, sweating in the summer sun, taking stock.

His journey had been long and uneventful. He had given what spiritual aid he could to the refugees still on the road, but news of the war's end had spread quickly, and the countryside had begun the long process of rebuilding what had been lost. There had been very little he could do, except offer his prayers for the land's recovery to be quick and painless.

The mountains rose above the small building, dwarfing it in magnificence. The hoary pillars had been worn away by centuries of neglect, and Caelyn wondered how long the shrine had actually been forgotten.

He took a deep breath. It felt strange, being at the end of his journey. It had been the better part of a year, and he had seen and changed so much. When he had left, he had been hiding behind his discipline, trying to escape his past rather than confront it. Then, he had been redeemed by no less than the Eternal One himself. It was mind-boggling.

The part of him that was Garwulf moved uneasily, but Caelyn easily pushed it aside. It was almost as if his previous identity was afraid of the place. The monk smiled; if what he thought was true, Garwulf had good reason to be afraid.

For the second time, he read the inscription on the top of the arched doorway. During his time at Southmarch, he had been exposed to several ancient languages, and now the tongue of the Arcalien Empire was no mystery to him.

The Temple of Rebirth.

Caelyn took a deep breath and stepped through the

door. As he crossed the threshold, he glanced around the temple. Light poured in from a hole in the roof, and the ancient mosaic on the floor was faded with age. But he could sense a power still residing in the place, knew that it was still holy ground.

And then Garwulf the Slayer was gone. The darkness that had lingered inside him for so long slipped away like the wind, leaving a deep contentment. Tears began to flow down Caelyn's cheeks. Atonement was possible; he knew that now. It was simply a matter of time.

He fell to his knees and began to pray, thanking the Eternal One for his redemption and guidance. And then, free for the first time in thirty years, Brother Caelyn began the long journey home.

Epilogue — Legends and Legacies

The great stories are neverending, for they are intertwined in the tapestry of life itself. However, sometimes the roles of the participants end, and their legacies become legend.

Although the position of Grand Magus was held open until the dissolution of the Order of Archmagi, Tamlin never reclaimed his office, nor did he return to the Western Lands. Instead, he preferred to wander with Daelyn, not only learning the secrets of surviving immortality, but also aiding the Tuatha de Danaan in his search for his people. Tamlin's exploits with Daelyn on the Great Road became legendary, and it was said that he was eventually the equal, in both power and wisdom, of Delgar Dragonmage.

Once they had established themselves, Brodin and Telena were the staunchest supporters of the reconstructed Southmarch Abbey. They named their first son Caelyn and their daughter Jyhanna. While they were never touched by

Wyrd, their son was, and he returned to Beregar as a missionary, helping to finally destroy the cult of the Harvester. Their daughter married well, and some of her descendants became powerful members of the Order of Archmagi, many of whom would eventually be wanderers on the Road of Legends. Millennia later, the last of that line, Teragon, would play an instrumental role in the salvation of the Dwarven people.

But while their line became great, Brodin and Telena's role in history was finished. Brodin passed away peacefully at the age of seventy, surrounded by family and friends. Telena survived him by a year, but it is said that she finally died of a broken heart.

Princess Jyhanna wandered in the Western Lands for another decade, celebrated as a warrior as renowned as Garwulf the Slayer. Her fate is not known, but many sagas state that she crossed the Eastern Wastes, and left the west forever.

Brother Caelyn finished his now-famous *Chronicle of the Great Wars of Succession* five years after returning to the abbey. The legacy of Garwulf the Slayer haunted him for the rest of his days, but the spirit of Garwulf never troubled him again. Twelve years after his pilgrimage, Caelyn took ill and died. Both the secrets of the Dwarves and his early years as Garwulf he took with him to the grave. It is said that in his final moments, he looked up to the sky and spoke one word before the end.

"Atonement."

About the Author

Robert B. Marks wears many hats, only one of which is a Stetson – he is a writer, editor, researcher, publisher, independent historian, and teacher. He has degrees in Mediaeval Studies, English Literature, and War Studies. He is the author of *Diablo: Demonsbane*, *The EverQuest Companion*, *Garwulf's Corner*, *An Odyssey into Video Games and Pop Culture*, and co-author of *A Funny Thing Happened on the Way to the Agora*. In his spare time, he has done everything from make mead to historical swordfighting to rockhounding.

He lives in the area of Kingston, Ontario, with his wife and two children.

Ingram Content Group UK Ltd.
Milton Keynes UK
UKHW021417040723
424531UK00015B/697

9 781927 537459